ι

BLACK STAR

Immortality or Humanity

By

Michael Mendoza

Book 1 OR 2 of the Heathen 'TWIN' books

Author: Michael Mendoza
Title: Black Star
© 2018 Katie Phythian Publishing Ltd
by Amazon

Edition 2

ISBN: 9781792180507

www.michaelmendozabooks.com

www.blackstar-redplanet.com

DEDICATION

"Writing a book is like having an affair. It steals both physical and mental attention from the ones closest to you. My five-year affair has been with these books and my loved ones have not only been complicit but have actively encouraged it. For that I'm eternally grateful.

Like most, this affair has come to an end which should be considered a good thing. Sadly, as you hug me close to welcome me back into your world, I must confess to looking over your shoulder as something interesting catches my eye."

To Blossom, Sid and Brahms especially

Michael Mendoza author of Red Planet & Black Star

Friedrich Nietzsche 1844 – 1900

"The future influences the present just as much as the past."

Author of "**Thus Spoke Zarathustra**" 1883

CONTENTS

Acknowledgments   i

TWINS

We were unaware of a project with similar characteristics to this one, so no apt title existed in the publishing world. 'Twins' was as good a description as any. Both books were released on the same day and both books are individual freestanding novels. By sharing the same characters, timelines and interwoven stories they share the same DNA.

It's left to the reader to decide which to read first, to read them at same time or simply enjoy one. Each choice offering a different experience of the overall project. Like twins, neither book depends on the other whilst each is inseparable from its sibling.

Katie Phythian

Glossary of terms

The Dome	The City of Heathen as referred to by some. A dome in figure of speech only.
Mother	The Saviour Machine, a central non-governing algorithm for the management of humanity and its needs.
The Outside	The area beyond the safe confines of the dome or outer boundaries of Heathen.
The Chase	An area of Heathen reserved for legal (mostly) yet unsavoury activities.
V-World	A simulated virtual world. It has all the benefits and experiences of reality but because it takes place in the brain it is completely safe for users. It is used for gain, social interaction, sexual joy, adventure and gamesmanship of all kinds.
SIM	Simulated environment in V-World
Reality	Any space occupied outside of a normal virtual environment such as V-World
Reality Junkie	Those with a taste for adventure in the real world.
Shlep	One who spends his life in V-World.
Rationalist	Opposite of Shlep - One who might not be an adventurer but still prefers reality socially.
Humanist	One who believes in living as primitive 21st Century man once did before the shutdown.
Shutdown	The systematic shutdown and deletion of all digital information, cause unknown.
Pre-shutdown	The period prior to the above.
Moonage	A primitive period in time where humanity was confined to its own planet.
TVC 15	Example of post shutdown calendar. T=twentieth Century V = 500 plus 15 years. Yr. AD 2515
Drone	Robotic device at varying levels of ability and intelligence.
Luddites	(Hominid) Organic human body with computerised brains. Undetectable to other humans.
Speks	Specification drones which have no ability to communicate with organic humans.

Hack or Hack Code A spoken or written sequence that can give access to drone programming for interrogation, maintenance and reprogramming.

Dude Hacker, reprogrammer and fixer.

Juve An allocated young adult - juvenile or young person.

Kinsperson Humans who share the same or similar gene pool or a main string.

Comms Any device attached to the brain stem to provide communication with others or with a sage.

Verism These are environments that are simulated in the real world as opposed to a virtual world.

The Major (Major Zero) Legendary saviour of humanity post shutdown, designer of the Saviour algorithm, Mother.

Net A Public area of V-World for comms and being online. Comms also works in a real environment.

Black-Star The name given to an element unique in the universe.

Lazarus A cruise ship designed to take reality adventurers on a pleasure trip to orbit Mars and return.

Diamond Dogs A reference to pre-shutdown pampered animals. Now indicates items that seem valuable and yet are not. Diamonds, gold, art etc.

Euthanise The time when humans are allowed to end their mortal existence at 130 years to make way for others.

Migration A scheme that allows euthenisation (See Euthanise) at any age dependent on personal choice.

Sage A computerised intelligence and assistant with an algorithm that is passed from generation to generation.

T.I.N. Machine Totality Intervention Nexus short form for a time travel device or belt.

Mag Pod Magnetic road transport common in Heathen.

Merge Portable device attached to the back of the neck to brain stem. As opposed to implanted version (Fuse) or comm unit.

ONE

He wasn't wearing clothes, he was wearing more of what might be called a costume. The costume of a commonplace organic man around any part of the city, maybe be going about an unexceptional errand or two. If anyone cared to think about it then they would most likely conclude his journey to be relatively innocuous. Certainly nothing that would present any serious risk to life or limb. Perhaps he might be heading up to the edges of Heathen City to spend time in reality with organic acquaintances. He didn't give the impression of a man who this very evening, would be going to Mars with a group of complete strangers. Not a virtual world escapade but in reality itself, exposing himself to all its dangers, instead of some shleps virtual reality mission. He leaned forward as he walked, fists clenched and knuckles facing forward, his powerful arms swinging in step. His case slung over his shoulder hung tight against his hip, Commander Theodore Maxtor was an imposing character with greying beard and even greyer unkempt hair. Brown tired eyes almost hidden by the overhanging eyebrow foliage made to look darker by his rugged eye line and wrinkled ashen skin.

Augmented reality advertisements to his left fought for his attention. He continued undeterred by the three-dimensional images moving in his peripheral vision. To his right a wall of glass allowed a panoramic view of large and small mag craft taxiing in and out of their gates. He could see what must be the tail of the shuttle ahead, busy for the last couple of days ferrying general passengers into orbit. Maxtor and his team would be the last human cargo to be ferried up to the Lazarus as she hung patiently in space above them. He grabbed a

3

handrail with his right hand, swinging himself around onto a single-story stairwell leading down to ground level. Drone crews were busying themselves with refuelling and maintenance tasks. The human pilot was standing at the top of the lowered walkway up to the ship. It was a sleek looking passenger vessel with a stub nose and disproportionately large engines, built into the rear end of the body. He felt a blast of heat in his face from tarmac as he approached. The outer edges of its chrome coloured skin were stained and marked with black dust, the wipers had created a clean arc across the filthy windscreen. The Commander skipped up the stairwell leading to an open door and was met by the human pilot at the top. He offered a toothy grin from his weathered face and tapped his forehead in greeting.

"Commander Maxtor?" by way of a question as he took an involuntary glance down at his attire.

"Yeah," said the Commander defiantly.

"You and your crew are the only passengers on this one, Sir. If you make your way down the cabin you can use the private class facilities. You'll find it much more comfortable," he waved a hand pointing between the rows of empty seats.

"Thanks," as he headed off down the wide carpeted aisle.

"Commander," Maxtor turned to look at the man still standing at the far end of the empty shuttle.

"The rest of your crew are in the terminal and we should be able to get underway once they're aboard."

Maxtor nodded and stepped towards the door at the back and it slid open.

The room was clean but had an underlying odour pertaining to its recent occupants. A mixture of expensive perfume and alcohol topped off with a slight hint of disinfectant. Across the back wall were refreshment facilities and in the centre was a low table surrounded by large comfortable looking armchairs. As he later found out, they were attached to the floor but could rotate all the same. Each had a white belt which was open but arranged in a cross fashion on the seat. He looked around and found a small luggage rack and strapped his bag in. Better to do it now he thought rather than chasing it around the cabin once they had achieved weightlessness. Over at the back wall he picked up a sealed cup and popped the lid. He placed his hand on a panel on the wall and as he removed it a list of his personal drink preferences appeared. He pushed the cup into the dispenser and pressed number one. The orange fruit tea streamed into it and he sealed it shut again. Throwing the open seat belts to either side he fell into one of the chairs and sipped his drink from the cup which dangled between his thumb and forefinger. To the left of the door was a large screen which showed a map indicating the ships position with the words 'Welcome Commander Maxtor & Crew' emblazoned across the centre. The door slid open and in walked a tall slender woman who stood in the doorway panting. Her large hypnotic eyes made more prominent by her dark mascara and long lashes. Skin tight leggings in a million abstract colours were taut over her thighs and an even tighter white top. Despite her tall slender appearance, she was wearing flat shoes. Her jet-black hair looked like it had been hacked into a homemade bob without a mirror. The fringe was skewed upwards from one eye and there was no layering whatsoever.

"Commander?" she said, catching her breath.

He stood up and greeted her.

"Nice to meet you," she panted. "I've heard so much about you."

"Yeah, I guess you might have," said Maxtor looking her up and down.

She looked uncomfortable and ran her hand into her hair and seemed to realise it wasn't as long as it often had been. Their eyes met for a moment and she started looking around the cabin.

"Seiren," she said. "Seiren White."

"Maxtor," he said. "Help yourself to a drink the others will be here soon."

He caught her odour as she passed, like patchouli or flowers of some kind. Placing a palm on the screen she likewise popped a cup and slid it under the dispenser. The door slid once more, and two other men entered. The first had a holdall slung over his shoulder and an unlit cigarette between his lips. He stopped dead just inside the doorway and eyed Seiren up and down from behind.

"Hey," he said winking at the Commander and nodding towards the girl.

She looked round and waved. "Seiren, hi!" and continued stirring her drink.

The man raised both his eyebrows in salute. "Things are good from here," he said.

"I'm Payne, Leroy Payne."

Seiren turned again and leant over to see the man hidden behind him.

"Hi," she said waving. He came around from behind Leroy adjusting his trousers.

"Adrenalin Sinus," he waved before nodding at the Commander who nodded at them both.

5

"Get yourselves a drink gentlemen. We should be leaving soon. I'm told the flight up to the Lazarus takes around..."

The on-board tannoy interrupted and a face appeared on the screen behind the two men. On it was the pilot who pushed buttons and checked instruments as he spoke.

"Welcome aboard the shuttle to Lazarus ladies and gentlemen. As this final trip is a little more informal I can dispense with the official announcements. I'll just drop you the highlights. We'll shortly be taking off across Heathen to the South. A definite opportunity to experience the cities outer boundaries as we climb to around 20Km. I'll make the curve around Heathen and for those who haven't seen our beautiful city from up here it's highly recommended. We will lose a lot of detail but you should be able to see the 'Outside' as we climb through the stratosphere to between 50 and 60km. Sit back and enjoy the view as we head towards the Lazarus. She is currently orbiting at around 30,000Km/Hr," he paused to allow the passengers to absorb that statement but they seemed unimpressed.

"I'll leave you to relax and I hope to deliver you all safely to the Lazarus in around 4 to 5 hours. Enjoy your flight. If you need anything you can comms me."

The screen went blank and the Commander finished his sentence.

"Around 4 to 5 hours," he grinned.

"Can you believe I know that guy?" said Leroy.

Seiren looked round and raised her eyebrows.

"The shuttle pilot, not seen him for years, what a place to bump into an old bud eh?"

He went over to the counter at the rear, throwing his bag amongst the racks. Adrenalin placed and then secured his own and Leroy's in the racks. "Off to Mars and the closest friend I have is the shuttle pilot, odd eh?"

The others grabbed themselves drinks and refreshments and sat around the low white table as the shuttle taxied out. The table attracted any items placed on it and so there would be no movement but the cups were sealed in any case. On any space vehicle it was well known that liquid was always the first to obey Newton's Laws of Motion. There were windows on either side of the cabin that ran in a long continuous strip giving a view of the Magport as the craft taxied to the end of the runway.

"Excuse me?" said Serien sitting down. "I understood I was joining an existing team. Do you guys know each other?"

"Nope, I just met Adrenalin ten minutes ago in the terminal, ain't that right my friend?" he said slapping him hard on the back.

"Sure," said Sinus smiling.

6

Maxtor grinned and nodded in acknowledgement. "All new Captain White, no politics, attitudes or bullshit, just a clean slate."

Seiren looked puzzled and relieved as she shrugged her slender shoulders.

Leroy raised his coffee. "Here's to our adventure, great to meet you all at last."

The others nodded in agreement and there was a short uncomfortable silence before Seiren broke it.

"So Commander, how did you come to be on the mission?"

"I was invited, perhaps they thought I had the experience. You know what they say, set a thief and so on."

The pilots face reappeared on the screen.

"Ladies and gentlemen, we will shortly be taking off and I would like to request you are all seated and fastened in. Thank you."

The rest shuffled in their seats and Leroy rubbed the back of his neck nervously.

Maxtor stood up and went to the caffeine machine and started to pour a fresh caffeine, turning he leant against the counter top and sipped loudly.

"Let's have it all open ok. I have history and I think you all know that. So," he trailed off.

He tilted his head nodding up and down. "We are charged with finding and collecting an item or items from Mars, they are extremely valuable and security is high. That task has fallen upon us. We will carry that out. If anyone hasn't seen the media over the last few years we can talk about that. I took some things that didn't belong to me, it was a bad thing to do. But assuming you all know my background then perhaps we could break the ice."

He paused sipped his coffee and took another look around the room. He fell back into his chair, no one spoke. The engines started to roar and the craft shook as the shuttle tore up the runway. Just when it felt like there couldn't be any more runway left the craft fell silent as they lifted into the air. Eventually they settled into a steady climb as Heathen spread out below them. The air felt compressed and the only sound now was the hum of the engines outside.

Seiren picked up her drink and rested it between her crossed legs. "I'm Seiren White," she began.

"Like most of you I have a thing for reality adventuring. I was offered the chance to do this so I said, yeah why not? My speciality has always been engineering and I am still studying leadership as part of my continued Juve studies," she clapped her hands. "That's me really."

Leroy leant forward with his elbows on top of his spread knees.

"Wow, that's great, I mean really great, you have balls Mrs. I'm in extended learning but my Juve days are long behind me. Love reality, adventuring and all that crazy shit like you guys or you wouldn't be here, right?" Sniffling loudly he wiped his nose with his sleeve, the unlit cigarette now hung between his fingers. The chunky gold chains round his neck tangled into one.

"You were recommended by a very good friend of mine, he tells me you're a good technician?"

He shuffled around looking at his shoes. "My specialism is tech, electronics light technology and code. Old school mostly you know?" he shrugs his shoulders.

"Good choice for this job, old school stuff, remember that's how it was for the Major. The place we're going to was designed and built using old school code."

"Sinus?" said Maxtor turning attention to the him. His long dark hair dropped over his shoulders.

"Adrenalin Sinus, A.I. speciality systems, you know?"

"The up-to-date tech hey?"

"Kinda."

"What about our old school guest?" piped up Leroy.

"If you mean Professor Touchreik then he's already aboard the Lazarus and we will meet up with him at some point. He specialises in ancient history too, late 20th Century so he'll be very useful on this mission. He's here on a consultancy basis only and has his own agenda. His brief is to collect historic samples from the Major's base on Mars. Our agenda is very different," his eyes went from each person to the next probing.

"The Black-Star, right?" Seiren said.

"The Black-Star," repeated Maxtor exaggerating his nodding movements.

"Do you know much about it?" said Leroy. "I mean much more than we know?"

Maxtor finished his drink and dropped the cup on the table before falling back into his chair, caressing the arms in an up and down motion.

"Probably not. The Black-Star is as worthless as it is valuable, it might not even exist. But if it does, then we are going to bring it back."

"Why?" said Seiren.

"Because it's there," said Leroy with a smirk.

"Because someone set this up so we could bring it back," said Maxtor.

"I'm guessing you don't know who either?" Seiren said.

8

"You're guessing correct, a reality adventure, a trip of a lifetime," Maxtor spread his palms and laughed and they all joined him. "No brainer, right?"

"So it's supposed to be some kind of unique element or something?" said Sinus.

"Well, it ain't worth shit to me, but it sure is to someone. If you like the idea of one or two bits of stone whose chemical composition exists nowhere else in the universe then good for you. Basically, I look at it like this. They say there was a time when diamond was valuable. The bigger the better because you couldn't make them then, they could only be made by nature. So they were rare. Maybe that's it? Maybe someone wants this Black-Star thing cos it's rare. If you ask me it won't be rare for long, once some egghead works out what it's made of we will all be wearing them as earrings. In the meantime we get an all-expenses paid trip of a lifetime to bring it home."

"Hence the security?"

"Hence," he paused once more. "The Lazarus is on a pleasure cruise to Mars and none of the passengers have any intention of hopping off, they will all be admiring the view from orbit. We are going down to get these Black-Star things and bring them home. I either can't or won't tell you how secure the vault is for obvious reasons but all you need to know is that it's gonna be 100% safe for the ride back."

The Commander like everyone else instinctively grabbed the arm rests as the craft jerked and then turned to circle Heathen banking sharply. Below they could see the beautiful city of Heathen spread out before them. The central residential areas sparkled with neon blues and yellows. It was possible to see the change in features on the cities outer limits. The industrial and automation areas where drones worked to produce goods and food to be shipped into the city were a distinct shade of grey. The enormous railed transport system that brought goods in looked like veins that disappeared beneath the central residential areas. There were even huge green areas, clearly plants and crops for harvesting. Dotted throughout were darker greys which indicated the processing areas or transportation. The automated drone plants where goods were processed before shipping into the city. The whole marvellous thing was surrounded by a faded ring of deep black cloud. Beyond that cloud was the 'Outside' with its still atmosphere. Completed in various shades of green & occasional blues and greys it was useless and unneeded, it covered 99.9% of the planet. A place that gained very little thought or attention except in fantasy worlds or stories.

"Little likelihood of a stick up 200 million kilometres from earth," said Leroy.

"Exactly," said Maxtor with a wry grin and clapped his hands.

"That means for the majority of this trip we'll blend in and enjoy the ride, just like all the other passengers. Go to the casino, enjoy the dancing and drink, within reason. Party, within reason," he reached around and at last fastened his seat belt.

"When that vault opens at the end of our trip home, it's time to switch back on. Ok? Focus," nods all round. "Between now and then we have a hell of a job to accomplish. So in short we keep a low profile and we get no complaints from the Lazarus people."

"Fine by me man," said Leroy bouncing his feet rapidly.

"Absolutely," said Seiren as Sinus nodded.

"Peee Pole!" The voice of the pilot interrupted their peace once more.

"I'll shortly be switching off the main booster rockets and settling us into orbit around Earth. Please remain in your seats with your seat belts fastened as you will experience weightlessness until we have you safely on-board the Lazarus. In the coming hours I will be making several manoeuvres to bring us into contact with the her, once aboard you can continue your onward journey."

After a few moments silence there was a sudden jolt and a sound that had been subconscious for the entire trip became conscious by its absence. The subliminal roar of the main engines stopped and there was a strange sensation of falling. The others reached for their seat belts pulling them a little tighter. Distant sounds were then heard as small booster rockets manoeuvred the craft and it slowly rolled. The Earth seemed to spin over slowly until it was above left of the shuttle then nothing. Some light music was heard in the background.

The crew broke up into smaller conversation, social chat over the coming hours. Leroy got bored at some point and took it upon himself to unstrap and float around the room giggling like a child. The others watched as he poured liquid into the air and watched it form into a wobbling entity in the weightless atmosphere.

Seiren scolded him, "Should you be doing that? This is not virtual reality remember, water, electronics?" she looked at Sinus for support.

"I think she's right Leroy."

"Hey, I'll clean it up."

He grabbed his cup and scooped the liquid from the air and sat back in his seat. Maxtor sat back and watched the dynamic of the crew, thankful that Seiren was his Captain. She had impressed him already. Listening in he looked out of the window and like any organic human felt a powerful connection with his home planet with its array of greens, browns and massive expenses of blues. The City of Heathen was a tiny

10

oasis against the vast and unusable expanse which was the rest of the planet. Leaving not only Heathen but the Earth itself was a thought best pushed to the back of anyone's mind.

TWO

Stomachs turned a little as there was another tiny adjustment roll and then silence once more. Outside the Earth's atmosphere the Sun appeared less significant than normal against the blackness of space, as if it was just another star only bigger. Of course that was exactly what it was, but the other stars looked different too. They had lost their familiar twinkle when viewed from high above the Earth's atmosphere, instead they were very defined as clear glowing lights. After a while an object caught Maxtor's attention but there was no sense of perspective up here. It shone like a star but was brighter and more defined. It looked very small but was obviously some distance away and was in all likelihood, the Lazarus. The Commander like everyone else knew what to expect and how the Lazarus looked. They would have absorbed all the media, taken the Virtual World tours and had been through the very unpleasant docking procedure. Each time he did it he wished he hadn't but in honesty it would help make the unpleasantness a little more familiar. There was a certain amount of surprise expressed in the conversations he overheard that this was their first meeting. They were all the inaugural members of the drop crew. In the distance and unnoticed to the others the incredible form of the Lazarus space cruiser drew closer.

It was a huge rotating monolith, designed to take several hundred people to Mars in relative luxury. The ship itself was like a huge rotating tin can with the top and bottom missing, albeit it was a 'can' almost a kilometre in diameter with a skin over 20 meters thick. Instead there were sets of spokes at either end and the centre held the propellant drive devices. For the coming 84 days the crew and passengers would live on the inner surface of its skin, held there by its spin. Once aboard they would be able to function in relative normality for the duration of the trip. The ship did not run on 1G as on Earth but was good enough for comfort so they were told. It was this reason that the actual arrival and docking procedure would be somewhat of a thrill ride, for some at least. They had all experienced it in V-World and the reality would be no different, as long as nothing went wrong that is.

The Commander leaned back in his chair and drifted off to sleep with the conversations in the room intruding into his dreams. He literally did drift off as his arms and straggly hair floated in the weightless environment. In his semi-conscious state he laughed at the thought of Seiren with long hair. Tentacles floating around like some mythical creature. The realisation hit him that may have been the reason for her impromptu haircut. The shuttle had manoeuvred itself into a position some 150 kilometres in front of the Lazarus at a slower speed. Whilst the Commander slept the silver glowing spec he had observed grew in size as it gained on the shuttle. By the time it started to catch up its incredible size was apparent to everyone. The tiny shuttle was dwarfed by the huge silver spinning monolith approaching. The booster rockets caused the shuttle to shift and wake him from his slumber. His stomach began to turn over at the very thought of what they were about to do. He had been informed there was no real danger as the docking process was fully A.I. automated but there was little comfort in that.

The shuttle turned to point directly at the Lazarus, side on. It was so big now that they could see it through either side window. The manoeuvring took some time and it was still difficult to scale the kilometre diameter spinning beast. At this distance they could see the words painted on the side, one the right way up and the other upside down. It simply said 'LAZARUS'. A nice touch for any alien life thought the Commander, regardless of which side the ship was viewed from one of the words would be the right way up. A red 40 meter line was painted around the rim of the ship and this area was clear of obstacles and would act as an upside down runway for the shuttles. The docking procedure was a little hairy but relatively simple. The shuttle would loop the loop around the Lazarus. Over time it would make the loop smaller and smaller until the Lazarus was close enough. By slowing down to match the speed they would be able to mimic her gravity and movement on the shuttle. Once the speed was in sync then the shuttle would lock on to the Lazarus and the passengers could leave through a hatch in the roof. All simple, all A.I. controlled but despite all that it was a nervy experience no matter how many times you did it in Virtual Reality. The artificial intelligence took over as the shuttle powered forward towards the Lazarus on a course that would take it underneath the ship itself. As they passed underneath the Lazarus the shuttle began to climb and circle the ship in a 2 or 3 kilometre loop the loop. As they did so the sensation of gravity began to take hold as they were pushed into their seats. The feeling was subtle at first and quite disconcerting. Over the next 30 minutes the shuttle closed in on the outer surface of the Lazarus. The feeling of gravity grew inside the shuttle over time and the relative movement of the cruise ship was still apparent. Eventually the shuttle began to simulate a similar gravity as that produced aboard Lazarus caused by the loop and the crew felt their weight increase on their seats. Above them, they could see the surface of the ship passing them but as they gained speed and closed in, all perception was lost. Most people would choose to look away now with many worried faces staring at the floor but Seiren smiled and stared up and out the windows. The tiny ship shook violently with the force of power being generated and yet felt almost still. Leroy looked out of the window and regretted it immediately. The sensation was as if the shuttle was about to be crushed by an enormous kilometre sized barrel which was closing in on its upper side. He could see the wide strip of red passing by above them. In effect they were about to land the shuttle upside down on the outer surface of the Lazarus. The feeling of weightlessness was completely gone and had been replaced with a dizzy sickness brought on by the confusion of the senses. The inner ear felt gravity and movement yet the eyes and physical body felt none. Seiren looked back at the floor as the two craft reached perfect synchronisation. The Lazarus and the shuttle seemed to no longer move in relation to each other but still the huge craft came closer and closer. The shuttle shuddered violently as its conventional engines struggled to hold it in position. The senses perception was that of sitting on a motionless shuttle as a multi-million ton weight was about to crush them like ants. Finally all movement between the two ended as the red stripe above them held still. At last there was a loud clunk as the shuttle locked onto the Lazarus and after a few moments the shaking and noise stopped as the shuttle temporarily became part of the Lazarus' outer skin. Now there was a deathly silence and the ears seemed to whistle with passing air. There was no sensation of movement and the body could feel something like normal gravitational pressure. Leroy almost jumped as the tannoy system clicked into life.

"PEEPOLE! Welcome to the Lazarus. Please remain in your seats with your seat belts fastened. We will be checking the airlocks and preparing for disembarkation. Please take your time when leaving the ship and take all your belongings with you. I look forward to bringing you home in a few months."

A few moments later there was the sound of clunking and hissing as air pressure was being released until finally a green light flashed and a hatch in the roof opened in the main cabin area between the empty seats. A set of steps with handrails were lowered from the roof into the centre of the ship.

"Ladies and Gentlemen, it has been our pleasure to deliver you safely to the Lazarus. Please use caution when leaving the shuttle as you may still be disorientated from the flight. Thank you and have a pleasant onward journey and we will look forward to welcoming you on board again soon."

The crew began to cautiously stand up and make their way to the hatch. The stairwell was wide and easy to manoeuvre up and there seemed to be a little warmth in the air now.

Leroy stopped at the bottom of the stairs. "See you in a mo guys, I just want to go say bye to my buddy before he heads back to Earth."

He walked round the stairwell and towards the cockpit door. The Commander made his way gingerly up the ladder and stood aboard the Lazarus at last. There was a small ticket booth with a number of humanoid drones picking up bags and taking various passengers to their quarters. Presumably stragglers from earlier shuttle flights but the area was almost empty by now. The Commander tapped the head piece on the back of his neck and a local transmitter confirmed his identity. A humanoid drone appeared beside him with his bags.

"This way Commander Maxtor, I'll show you to your cabin."

She was of female design but with basic personality programming. Her main body was clothed in the bearer's uniform assigned to the crew of the ship.

As she started to walk he turned to acknowledge the rest of the team.

"Ok, settle in and perhaps we can meet casually later. There will be an official briefing in the next day or so. I see no reason to rush that."

They all nodded in acknowledgement and as he left he heard Leroy coming up the stairs and asking a drone where the bar was. He followed the drone's ample rear as it moved methodically from side to side as it walked, carrying the bag that had reappeared in the lobby. Walking behind he noticed how the bag seemed to move forward as if hovering in space, quite unlike the slight swing that would befall it if carried by a human. She led him away from the reception area passing one or two other passengers with drones. These tended to peel away at random into cabins or away up corridors. They passed a group who were excitedly running from cabin to cabin shouting and laughing. They were banging on cabin doors excitedly, giggling and pushed inside as they were approached, embarrassed by their behaviour. The drone finally took a swift turn left into a shorter corridor. At last the drone stopped and opened a door to his new home for the coming 83 days. With an outstretched arm she beckoned him inside. The Commander was pleasantly surprised by the cabins size, quite generous. In the centre of the room a spinning holographic sign welcomed Commander Maxtor to the Lazarus. He stepped inside, walking through the display and stood in the centre of the room. The drone followed him inside and the door slid shut behind her and the display disappeared. The room was very modern with clean lines, decorated in whites and light greys with a double bed situated in the far corner. The drone placed his bag carefully on the bed and opened her arms.

"I hope it's to your satisfaction Sir?" It was clear the drones onboard were basic, but good enough to do the job. This one had very standard, rigid facial expressions and her skin texture was a little polished.

"Yes, very nice, thank you."

"The window over the bed is augmented of course," she indicated a large window giving a wonderful view of the Earth.

"You'll be aware the actual outside wall of the ship is here," she pointed to the floor and a large selection of dark floor panels faded to reveal a window in the floor. Through it he could see the cosmos spinning past as the ship rotated in space. "This is the reality view, it can be a little strange to the human senses but very good for slumber depending on your tastes."

As soon as she stopped speaking the tiles faded back to black and a real floor once more. "We do not have full VR capability on board but this is a reality trip after all."

She pouted and smiled widely in her attempted humour or understanding of human concepts. "The VR generator in the room is compact and is closed circuit so it's fine for communications and various basic functions. Real time response will deteriorate as we travel further out towards Mars."

"I'm sure it'll be fine," he smiled.

"Also the Sage assistant is shared so it will not be as functional or as personal as back home, however if you need anything at all then simply call for me. My name is Melanie."

"Melanie, thank you," Melanie he thought, that was a nice touch. He knew that he would never speak to Melanie again but the ships programmers had been good enough to create the illusion of a seamless experience which was as close to home as possible.

"There's just one more thing. If I could have a moment of your time there are one or two safety procedures I am obliged to communicate." The drone made her way over to a small closet and opened the door. It was empty and had clothing rails but had a small seat at the back. The Commander ruffled his eyebrows.

"This is the radiation shelter."

"The radiation shelter?" he questioned.

"Yes Sir, passengers are advised that there may be radiation warnings on the trip from time to time. These will often pass quite quickly but we recommend you use this shelter until we advise clearance."

The Commander nodded. "Ok."

"In the very unlikely event of a full emergency or evacuation this shelter will also serve as a life pod. Ensure the green light is on and twist this handle firmly, like so," she mimicked the motion. "You will be given a 20 second option to abort. After initiation your pod will eject. It has full life support for 38 hours and will bring you down safely on the nearest surface."

"Won't we be 40 million kilometres from the nearest surface?"

"Please pay attention Sir. The system is designed to maintain your organic life and it might be a situation where only a section of the Lazarus is disabled," she said sternly.

"I see."

"May we also recommend that you close the radiation shield around the bed whilst resting or sleeping. Instantly a shutter came down and created a wall around the bed which would enclose the occupier.

"If you partake in periods of leisure or inactivity then it's recommended to use the shutter. General radiation is within safe levels but it's good practice to reduce exposure at every opportunity," she tilted her head and stared into his eyes for a moment until he realised she would do so until he acknowledged her. He nodded and smiled.

"Any questions?" she asked.

"I'm sure Captain Bernsteen is busy right now but I'd like you to inform her we are aboard, possibly arrange a meeting?"

"The Captain is fully aware of all developments on the ship. Her sage has a meeting reminder set for you and your team Commander Maxtor, anything else?"

"No."

Melanie nodded and gave a plastic smile.

"Welcome to the Lazarus. Thank you and have a pleasant trip," she turned and was gone.

THREE

Voodoo Bernsteen sat on her hands, hypnotised by Fontain's unkept beard and how some of the longer hairs would creep into his mouth like wild vines as he spoke. His yellow stained teeth, twisted like gravestones. At points during the stinging attack on his young charge his voice seemed to ebb and flow as if coming from another room. Then as she woke from the beard induced trance it was like the volume had been turned up to ten.

"I have tried explaining the risks to her as I am sure you have, this inclination for reality is becoming obsessive and a danger to others. It will also serve as a hindrance to her in the future," Fontian continued with a sideways glance at Voodoo. She rocked back and forth on her hands whilst her surrogate mother gazed down, shaking her head in shame. Voodoo stole a glance at her surrogate father in the hope of finding some solace in his expression and thought she saw an almost undetectable smirk. There was a twinkle in his eyes, perhaps even blustering pride. Voodoo forced herself to look at the floor, fearing an unintended giggle coming on. It would be decades later before she considered that most of the responsibility for her attitude lay squarely with her surrogate parents. An odd pair for sure, they had always made it known they enjoyed the idea of rearing a child. In their own naive way they encouraged any disposition for individual thinking, human interaction and education in all forms. Decades later this was not a course of thought Voodoo shared. Although her parents had firmly confirmed her outcast status very early in life, her thoughts on children were most definitely mainstream. At some point she may be allocated a child and like most people in Heathen she would carry out the care with a sense of obligation. As yet the handling of juves had not come up and may never do so. There were all kinds of theories as to what allocation procedure was followed by Mother but there was always an exception to every alleged rule. No matter what people said there was no rhyme or reason to it. Mother seemed to act at complete random in the allocation of her offspring to surrogates. One year it might all be about age and then you would discover that adults who were no more than juves themselves would be allocated two at once. Trone and Samally being the latest example she had known of. Then you would hear that idea was silly, it was purely geographical and next thing there wouldn't be an offspring in the entire sector. Some citizens would be unallocated for their entire life whilst others multiple times. Voodoo had been lucky thus far and had remained free of Juve responsibility, her current excursion would clearly make her exempt. Not being on the planet must fit the criteria for abdicating some responsibilities at least for now. It could happen at any time but there were no doubts in her mind, her charges would be brought up in the main by drones. There simply wasn't time to be involved to the level her parents had been with her. Educating, guiding and caring for a creature that would be a guest in your accommodation for years at a time. Sane had explained how she had felt the same and was almost sad when the Juve reached maturity, a preposterous notion. Voodoo herself had been a juve of fifteen years and nine days old when the conversation took place between her surrogates and Fontain. As time passed she grew to believe it was probably the one that defined her. It was from then onwards that she had begun to relish the identity thrust upon her by others.

She was Voodoo Bernsteen the girl who loved reality. Since that day she was determined to never become like the shleps that spent their lives inside a digital world. In her youth she had little choice but it was easy to imagine the rush of climbing, running or travelling in reality whilst inside V-World. In small ways she had begun by spending time in the real world to test her resolve. Pushing faster and further than anyone else she knew. From then on Voodoo played out her role in life, indulging herself in the attention each adventure brought. Each adventure had been more extreme than the previous one. Whilst other juves spent their lives in the safety of their own accommodation enjoying their safe young lives, and later adulthood in the virtual world, she was pushing the boundaries further and further in reality. In later life she was either seduced or was seduced by others who were like her. From the day she was defined it was natural that Captain Voodoo Bernsteen would find herself here. Standing on the bridge of the starship Lazarus wearing the Captain's uniform at the beginning of what had to be the greatest adventure in reality bar none.

She said it in her head but felt her lips move slightly.

"Thank you Mr Fontain, thank you," appearing deep in thought, she absorbed every detail of crucial information being barked out across the bridge of the Lazarus. The bridge had been a fairly sedate place until recently with most activity concentrated on guest facilities. Drones bringing supplies, food and cabins in tip top condition. The Shuttle had been busy bringing up passengers from the surface over the last day or two. Drone ships had been topping up supplies to be stored in the central core of the ship. Final tests were conducted on the nuclear reactor and the Ion drive units. As expected, everything was working perfectly except for one or two teething problems. In truth these were mostly as a result of human understanding of the manual systems on board. Things were going to get busy over the coming couple of days as the Ion drive was fired up and the ship gathered speed around Earth before launching itself on its maiden journey to Mars. A trip that would hopefully be the first of many, as Mars was set as a regular destination for real world travellers. Coloured VR screens hung in the air whilst various crew members manipulated the ships instruments and Artificial Intelligence systems.

"Engineering can I have your bearing please?" she spoke without addressing anyone in particular.

The correct voice would offer the correct response. "288 degrees, 80,000Km Ma'm."

"Leave A.I. in for now please. Manually monitor and cross check."

"Ma'm."

"Ion drive retracted and locked."

"Confirmed."

The view the crew saw on the augmented windows was manipulated to circumnavigate the effect of the constantly spinning ship. In truth, the bridge and everyone else on board were standing on the inner edge of a 900 mtr diameter spinning barrel. Providing the real view outside the ship would be immensely disorientating. Instead they were presented with augmented reality windows as were the cabins and public areas aboard ship.

"Adjustment boosters set to auto."

"Earth's orbit adjustment for increased speed, can I set to A.I. Ma'm?"

"Affirmative. Continue cross check until my say so."

"Ma'm."

Voodoo was relishing the authority on board the Lazarus and intended to do so for the foreseeable future. Her passengers were about to acquire the boast of being the first to go to Mars since the Major, certainly the first humans. There had been a number of drone missions over the years. By the second voyage it would be she and her crew who would start to accrue records. Multiple trips, kilometres travelled, and many more, to think these would be in reality this was the beginning of her legacy. Her ample figure and coco skin suited the crisp blue Captain's Uniform. Her authority and stature added height to her modest

1.8 meter frame. Under the Captain's crew uniform her white blouse openly revealed enough cleavage to be noticeable yet tasteful. Her long thick hair poured out from the black beret and into a pony tail down her back. Dark probing eyes and deep red lips sat well on her dark unblemished skin.

"Are you ready to say goodbye Captain?" The quartermaster appeared next to her and admired the view. Wispy white clouds covered the deep blues and greens of the surface which filled the screen so close it looked like you could touch it, a planet that in the main had been reclaimed by nature since the early 24th Century. She and her quartermaster were skilled enough in aviation to be completely aware of the actual location of the human oasis they called home. The atmosphere provided by Mother's systems tended to push cooler air out towards the 'Outside'. If Heathen did look like an eye then it was these darker cloud formations that would give the appearance of bags around the immense Heathen structure. The mission to Mars was planned to take over three months and covered 400 million kilometres so she would not be the only one who missed home. It was the smells and sounds of outdoor life Voodoo craved more than anything. Like most people aboard the ship she was what you might call a reality junkie which was a minimum requirement for a mission like this.

With every adventure in the real world came danger, often hidden and unseen. That was its magic. It was just as easy and just as exciting for anyone to lead an army to war, captain a ship to Mars or rule an ancient civilisation in the virtual world. The underlying problem with V-World is that it was completely safe if not completely pain free. It was the threat of real danger that gave reality junkies the buzz. Ask most of them and they don't know why they do it, they have no answer. Physical danger was the only difference between the two experiences and it was always hoped it wouldn't be experienced at all. But real danger, euthanasia or injury was always there and remained in the background unseen and waiting. Fall from the top of the Sheldon Tower in V-World and the main consequence was embarrassment. Try that in reality and it would be early euthanasia. People like Voodoo and the other passengers knew the stories, but it was as if they were individually immune to the dangers. In the week they had left, two well-known reality junkies, Kaka Bontherm and Issac Brewster had euthanized whilst attempting to base-jump from one of Heathen's tallest buildings. It was exactly that kind of thrill and adventure that was commonly available in V-World. So why had she and so many others she knew always been obsessed with reality just as the old goat Fontain had suggested? It was the thrill of experiencing the one single difference between the virtual world and reality. That's what people struggled to understand.

"What's the point?" was the most common objection. "There's no difference between the virtual world and reality, other than the obvious."

They were correct; a cold biting wind was still cold and biting on the skin, a blazing sun still burned like hell. That was dependent upon your pain settings of course. Voodoo had experienced this herself on more than one occasion. The memory of the incident whilst in Serpent Wars which was a hot SIM at the time, stayed heavy in her mind. She had set her pain settings to 100% whilst in the game.

The SIM was based in a fictional period around the late 21st Century before the data wars. Being loosely based on a false history period it used primitive automation and robotics and imagined a world that had never developed light processing technology. The fun was that the war was fought using very old laser weapons and antiquated drone technology. Voodoo had been in the game for two days and it wasn't going well for her team. They were all tired and battle weary, moral was low. She was part of a team who had become scattered behind enemy lines and mission failure looked inevitable. The enemy had decimated her team by using spy drones to predict their every move. As the end game began there was a feeling that they were being toyed with. The drones were able to feedback position and battle data to troops in the field. They were being hunted down amongst the cities ruins individually, or in small groups. It was likely they would lose this battle and after two days it was becoming clear to the enemy that they were tiring. The city was decimated by their overnight bombing which in reality was a last kiss goodnight from the enemy. They had a very marginal chance of hitting the drone monitoring outpost purely at random but of course this hadn't happened.

It had been late and Voodoo was tired, she needed to rest for a while and recharge herself physically. They had spent the later part of the day stumbling over shattered concrete and steel. Spread out and scattered by enemy forces they were losing light. Voodoo had decided to find cover for an hour of sleep before moving on. She crawled inside an upturned skip and kicked some of the stinking bags of rubbish to one side. The rest she was able to use as a bed and had to physically move open cans and harder items until she found comfort. She saw a large rat look at her with distain before scurrying through the slightly open door. She was exhausted and slipped into a light sleep whilst being aware of her surroundings, always on alert. At least here she was relatively safe and had less chance of waking up with a boot on her head. There were small holes in the steel skin, presumably from bullets or shrapnel that enabled her to peek through. At some point her slumber was disturbed by either a sound or a feeling, she wasn't sure which. Rolling over she plunged her hand into some kind of slimy substance that stank of rotting meat. Wiping it on her trousers she held herself up once more and put an eye to one of the holes. There was movement outside, an enemy combatant who was moving past her and across the street. Slowly she reached for her weapon and found a gash in the steel big enough to lean the barrel. Resting it in the hole she shifted her weight once more and took aim. She felt her finger on the trigger and he was in her sights as she took an inward breath ready to fire. At that moment he ducked down and then sprang back up to continue walking. Voodoo waited and watched, pulling her scope up to her eye she pressed zoom to get a better look. He was alone and seemed to be looking for something, not really going in any particular direction. She placed her weapon down amongst the rubbish and crawled out of the skip and into a shallow stairwell nearby. Once out of sight she quickly scurried up two flights of stairs and entered one of the front facing apartments. The entire place was gutted and smelled of fire, charred remains of curtains blew through the shattered windows. The sad skeleton remains of furniture were strewn across the room like fossils. Approaching the South facing window she slowly raised her head to peak over the ledge and look down. At first she couldn't see the enemy and then he was there, still in the same area and still searching. From this vantage point she could see something else move in her peripheral vision. There were two of her team heading towards him. As yet neither had seen each other and she didn't want them to. She was darting from one side of the window to another as her colleagues got closer, praying they wouldn't see or kill the enemy combatant. Suddenly the man stopped and it looked like he had found what he was looking for amongst the rubble. On top of a smouldering pile of concrete lay an old door and he lifted it up, took a final look around before he disappeared inside. At that moment her colleagues rounded the corner and were soon heading right towards him. Had he seen them and taken cover? It was unlikely. The two team members passed his position and carried on away in the opposite direction. There was no way of contacting them without alerting the enemy and Voodoo had an idea she was going to have to stay behind the group until she worked this out. She waited but there was no movement, at least a full twenty minutes and nothing. She headed back down stairs to street level and kept herself low as she crossed the street. She placed a hand on the door and lifted slowly only to find nothing. In the half-light she could see a hinged drain cover. It had been blown off in the bombing and yet remained unseen under the rubble.

Her heart started to pound in her chest as she realised what she might have stumbled upon. There was no way of communicating with the others and she would have to continue alone. If she communicated there is a very good chance she could be heard. Just to be sure she slipped off her body vest and comms equipment, stamping on her communicator. She threw the crushed device across the concrete and placed her vest behind some rocks. She had effectively disappeared off the radar for both friends and enemies. She would be out of the game, a virtual ghost. That was when she realised her only weapon was a large knife tucked in her shoe. A friendly strife jet tore across the sky above her and without her communicator there was now no protection from friendly fire. She quickly and quietly slid her body inside the manhole and stood in the darkness. The tunnel and space below were pitch dark and she felt her way around until she saw a tiny sliver of light. Following this down she went through a large hole in the tunnel walls and could see it went for kilometres in either direction. The air was cold and stale and left a layer of dust in the back of her throat. She was right in her assumptions. The tunnels were illuminated by very dull festoon lighting which provided nearly enough light to see your way. There were wet footsteps in the concrete, dust and sand that lay around the floor. Staying close to the wall she followed them deeper inside. As she moved cautiously forward the sound of jets and bombs rumbled above, shaking the walls. Plumes of dust poured down from the ceiling and the lights flickered. Following the footprints she turned a bend in the tunnel. The central part of the floor was designed for water flow and on either side there was a path. As she drew closer to the bend she heard voices and saw a second man at a desk illuminated by small mobile lights. This was an incredible find and could offer the possibility of turning this game on its head. This was it; this was clearly the monitoring station for the drones. She took her time, crawling silently in the dim light towards the two men who were facing away from her. There was still no plan at this stage, at least two of them and no weapons to speak of. The pair were clearly quite relaxed and at ease down here and she could use that to her advantage. She spotted a multi-use ray gun leaning against the wall of the tunnel around 10 meters away. She was willing to gamble that the bright light they were in would blind them to her approach should they turn round. There was no way of knowing for sure. Crawling slowly and in plain site should either one of them turn round she neared the weapon. Finally she was close enough to reach out and touch the rifle and twist her fingers around the barrel. The first thing either of them knew was when they heard the high pitch screech of the rifle as it charged. Raising their hands they backed away from the table. Before they were completely clear she fired three short bursts and the monitoring equipment shattered in a wave of sparks and flames. Smoke billowed across the low ceiling and the sound boomed out down the tunnels. In the bright light and explosion she momentarily caught the eye of one of the men looking behind her but it was too late. A previously unseen combatant pounced from behind, knocking her against a wall and winding her. Her weapon scraped across the floor and was casually retrieved by one of his accomplices. Meanwhile the man kicked her hard in the side of her body taking the air from her lungs. She managed to spin enough to deflect some of the force of his boot as it came crashing down on her head. She heard voices and laughter nearby as she grasped at the material of his trouser. Twisting he broke free and almost stumbled, lashing out with his leg almost breaking her elbow. He brought his knee down heavily on her chest and punched her hard in the face. Struggling to remain conscious the man placed his arms tightly round her throat, she was quickly weakening and her vision was blurred. Reaching down she felt the knife in her boot and flicked the catch with her thumb. She was able to pull the weapon from her boot and gripped it tightly. She didn't have full movement in her elbow as she lurched at his face with the blade. With the wind beaten from her he was much stronger and easily wrestled it from her hand. He lay between her splayed legs and spun the knife in front of her eyes. With a powerful palm under her chin he placed the tip of the knife in the centre of her chest and started to push. She tried to speak but couldn't get any clear words out only a gurgling sound. Trying to explain she was on 100% pain setting, but didn't have time and couldn't reach the abort mechanism on the back of her head. She knew he was aware as she grasped at the back of her neck, he knew she was set to 100% but wouldn't do the sporting thing and let her abort. The blade pierced her beneath her breastbone and she felt blood flooding across her chest and up her throat. The physical pain was actually less than expected but the gut wrenching feeling was overwhelming. Pushing him away she made one last attempt to survive or abort but was weakening as her fist punched him hard in his forehead. He still had the knife and was ready to strike her again. She could make an instantaneous decision to either hit game abort or protect herself from the blow as it ripped through her arm. Striking the bone it pushed the blade to one side as it sparked on the concrete. At last she was done and her head fell back onto the floor with a crack. He stood and watched as she bled out in front of him, weak and dying she could feel the life ebbing away. With one final burst of strength she kneed him in the groin as he stood over her, throwing him away across the floor. It was her last stand and yet it mattered not because she was done for. It took a long time to die and as she did so she was aware he had cuffed her hands thus preventing her from aborting the game. The scum knew her pain settings and yet he allowed her to feel every piece of it at 100% until she was dead. This was the problem with using 100% (PP) Pain Perception in V-World gaming. There was no hiding place till it was over and whilst many friends have agreed it's the only way to play the experience taught her some serious life lessons that would serve her well one day, especially if she was going to continue playing with reality.

In fact it was only now at the beginning of a 3 month space voyage that she was willing to admit that captaining the Lazarus might have been a bit of a come down. Spending that time on an adventure with 200 or so others who were of a similar mind set had numbed her to the dangers. Every single individual on board was here for the same feeling and it would deliver in spectacular fashion. There were a group on board who were planning to push their limits even further. Maxtor's team were planning to drop onto the surface during their orbit of Mars and she envied them immensely. They would be bringing back samples from the Major's base as well as the 'Stones' as she called them. Whether they were the reason for such high security demands in the vault or the Professor's samples then who knows. Voodoo had enquired but got no clear answer from her superiors.

"Why the security..? Was it for the samples or the stones? What if..?"

"Won't happen," her Earth Commander had barked at her before they left. "It would be impossible to steal something if you didn't know it was there, least of all knew it existed. It's a mission to collect some old artefacts from Zero's base, that's all."

A key part of the security protocol had been the secrecy surrounding the elements. However she knew different, having been anonymously informed of a plot to steal the stones. Voodoo was unaware of how serious this could be taken but it intrigued her all the same. Knowing the details of the security in place made the idea of theft laughable. Intrigued yes, concerned absolutely not.

"Ma'm," the chief engineer interrupted her thoughts.

"We have a slight problem."

"Yes."

"The shuttle that brought up Maxtor's team. It's still engaged with the Lazarus."

"What's the problem?"

"It's not something we can solve right now, we have been through the whole test set but it won't finish for another 6 hours Ma'm."

"Could we send it back once the tests are complete?"

"Not with our increased speed, our only option is to keep the shuttle attached to the Lazarus until we get back."

"Will that affect our speed?"

"The physical effect on the ship is so small as to be of no consequence Ma'm."

"Good, leave the shuttle attached and let's continue our scheduled course."

The engineer looked at the floor sheepishly. "Erm.. Ma'm that's not quite the problem," she looked at him puzzled.

"It's the pilot Ma'm. He has no way of getting back to Earth. He is quite upset about being stuck here."

"Isn't there another shuttle we can send from Earth to pick him up?"

"Same problem I'm afraid, unless we slow down, a day's delay."

"In that case he is coming with us. We aren't full, find him one of our private class cabins and ask him to enjoy the voyage."

The engineer looked embarrassed. "Will do Ma'm," he bowed slightly and backed away.

"Agitant."

"Yes."

"Set him up as a passenger with a coin account and full facilities access, I'll authorise it"

"Ma'm," he left and another officer approached.

"Commander Maxtor and his team are aboard Ma'm," the first mate interrupted.

"Thank you."

Voodoo turned to one of the crew on the bridge. "Maintain this angle to Earth and increase the gravitational speed to 0.8G."

"Ma'm."

She felt for the poor fellow but he will have been well compensated for piloting the shuttle and was aware of the risks. The additional weight of the shuttle and an extra passenger would have no effect. It would be a given the fellow would be very upset about being press-ganged into a 400 million kilometre voyage when he expected to be home for his evening meal but it was unavoidable.

27

FOUR

Professor Algeria Touchreik took a moment to realise where he was. The trip up from Earth had drained him and he'd slept the whole night. He'd even forgotten to pull the shutter down around his bed and laughed to himself about the radiation warnings. She had used the word 'recommended' for the shield so presumably that meant almost never. He pushed away the thoughts of his teeth and hair falling out over breakfast. He felt a lot better this morning and threw on some of his favourite soundscapes. Not wanting to shock his senses to life he kept the lighting in the cabin dimmed whilst he showered and dressed. He'd already opened one of his pre-programmed VR displays for the wall window. It was one of his favourites from back home and he used it regularly. The view was a serene Spring day across the lawns, close to the institute and would provide a sense of familiarity. The window view could remain ever-present if he preferred, across the millions of kilometres they would travel. It perfected the illusion of standing on the sedate surface of Earth. He particularly liked this scene because it showed both the city he loved and enough of the green reserve to let him know it was still there. With the VR window scenes indicating no movement it completed the illusion of stillness. He'd decided to try and relax a little today so after a rough beard trim he donned a green and yellow one piece run-of-the-mill garment. It seemed appropriate for the ships tour and avoided him appearing cranky or morose when he met the drop crew. They would probably be a youthful bunch and he didn't want to play into their stereotypes in dressing like a Professor. He threw a sheet over his bed and checked himself in the mirror, a few more snips on the beard and he was good to go.

At last a voice announced itself with a pinging sound in his cabin. It sounded like Melanie, the drone who had brought him to his cabin.

"Good Morning Professor."

"A very good morning to you Melanie," he said in a sarcastic voice as he snipped a few hairs from his nostrils and swilled the scissors in the sink.

"I trust you slept well?"

28

"I most certainly did, How about you?"

Melanie ignored his remark. "Captain Bernsteen and the drop crew will be ready to meet you in 14 minutes at the central reception area on level one."

He sang his response, "Thank yooo."

She departed with an audible ping in the same way she had arrived. His tone had been forced but indicated a much improved state of mind this morning. If it weren't for the strange 'Sage' called Melanie, and the cramped lodging with lack of technology, he could almost be home. Maybe not, but at least he had remembered to bring the view. He'd been due a good night's sleep but it'd been a long time coming. The nightmares might never go away but there was a hope and consolation in being here after all these years. He brought up his visual display for directions and requested the door open. Standing up straight he lifted his chin and he headed out to meet his new colleagues. He followed the directions along the crisp white corridors from which the cabins were situated. At last he was directed through a glass door into what may have been the central reception area of the ship. He remembered it from boarding however the floor stairwell which had led to the shuttle was retracted and closed. It was spacious and airy it occupied both of the ships available floors and was topped off with a large glass dome. In the centre there was a circular area with humanoid drones behind desks. They were humanoid at the top half only and were the same questionable quality as Melanie. There weren't many organic humans around and one or two of the drones stared vacantly forwards. The others answered queries or blue-toothed data into passenger comm units.

There was one human standing by the desk who was surely of interest to him. A very shapely black skinned female. She wore a smart and somewhat heavy looking uniform. She noticed him arrive and stepped closer. The material of her uniform was probably not as cumbersome as it first looked. For a larger figure she moved quite nimbly. She held up a palm and she tapped her forehead.

"Good Morning Professor. I assume?" she said looking around the reception area.

"You assume correctly, good morning Captain Bernsteen, a pleasure to meet you in person."

"I thought this would be a good opportunity to meet your new colleagues. The drop team will be joining us soon. After our little tour you will have 83 days to become more familiar."

"Yes perfect."

"I hope you slept well."

"I did thank you"

"And the cabin?"

"Perfect."

"It's small but we have lots of communal space on board as you are about to discover."

"It's fine, perfectly fine."

She looked up smiling. "And here they are now, I believe."

The drop team arrived on mass and various greetings were exchanged between the group. Touchreik was surprised to see the Commander was a little older than expected, Leroy not so, but the others quite young for a mission such as this.

"Shall we?" said Voodoo and waved an open hand.

Maxtor held back, he and Touchreik followed a slight way behind the group.

"How was the docking procedure Professor?" he said smiling knowingly.

The Professor didn't need to say anything, his expression said it all. Maxtor continued, "I hope you don't mind but I thought we might bring forward the briefing for the drop to 3pm Earth time."

"Why is that?"

"Nothing of concern, it's just that we are all together this morning and it helps with some of my own preparation. Besides once that's out of the way then we can all relax, enjoy the cruise. We have no need to meet on an official basis until we orbit Mars, is it inconvenient?"

"No, not at all."

"That's good."

As the group went outside the main reception area there were 6 hover transporters inside a wall cupboard.

"It's lazy but for the purposes of our little tour I thought these might get us around a little quicker," said Voodoo.

One by one they took the transporters out and stood on them. The small circular platforms lifted off the ground a few centimetres as they put their weight on them.

"The Lazarus is a big ship as you will probably gather, I think this mode of transport will facilitate our tour a lot better," the group nodded almost in unison.

The Captain set off and the rest of the group followed behind. As they travelled, the curve of the ship wasn't blatantly apparent except in certain areas dependent on how far you could see at any one time.

"If you would like to tap into my comms then everyone will hear me whilst we do the tour, it allows the comfort of being able to spread out a little and follow what's being said."

In turn each tapped their comms devices and could immediately hear the Captain as if she was standing right next to them regardless of where she was. In fact she had already set off down the corridor on her own.

"We have floor space on two levels which equates to around 2 square Km of surface area. It's not all public space but for the purposes of our tour we can take it that would be around 1.5 square Km."

All her conversations were being shared by everyone as they stayed in relative distance.

"Professor, how is our friend Mr Prout?"

"Fine, he sends his regards."

"He says good things. He thinks you're a brave man to do what you're doing, well we all do."

"He is," interjected Leroy followed by uncomfortable sniggers from the rest of the team.

"It's nice of him to say that," the Professor felt a little uneasy at the formality of the conversation, especially considering the spectators. The group continued at a leisurely pace past other passengers who sauntered here and there through the ships corridors and open spaces.

"You know him well?" said Touchreik

"Actually no, he is a kinsperson of my life partner, organic cousin or something like that. They have some DNA connection. Do you?"

He laughed. "Not really, I run one of his departments. Hence my trip."

"Absolutely, who doesn't know about your caveman project? How many are on your team Professor?"

He looked down to avoid her eyes and pushed on a little in front of the group. "Team, yes, we were quite considerable in the early days but of course there's just the two of us now." He was even lying about the two by including his partner Jagger who had long since gone.

He wandered if poking through a few archived personal files could be considered research? Touchreik was known to be a renowned expert on 21st Century history, yet almost no-one knew the true nature of how that knowledge and experience was gained.

The truth was, there was no team and no research since the project was shelved decades ago.

"It was all very exciting at the time, have you made any interesting discoveries over the years?"

The Professor tried being vague. "Lots of confirmations of things we knew or suspected. The life of twenty first century men appears to have been as difficult as we always imagined. It's painfully slow work."

"Oh I see, well myself and the crew are in awe of your bravery. As I'm sure these guys are."

Thankfully the direction of conversation ended abruptly as she stopped below a large white hatch in the ceiling.

"When you docked from the shuttle you will have entered the ship through the floor. The Lazarus, by all intents is a hollow spinning cylinder, so as we are stood on the interior of the ships skin then the ceiling to us is actually pointing towards the ships central core."

The Captain pointed upwards towards the hatch built into the ceiling. "This is one of six doors in the ceiling of the ship as far as we are orientated. If you know the ships shape these doors lead into what we call the spokes of the design. The ship has six spokes in total, three to the bow and three to stern. These spokes lead to the ships inner core where the drives and storage are situated. A weightless environment that is not accessible to passengers."

Leroy waved his arms like a bird behind her back and Seiren looked away.

"Take note ladies and gentlemen that you will be using one of these spokes to disembark from the ship once we reach Mars. Other than the craft that will take you down to the planet's surface the centre does contain the drives, hardware and storage areas. Drones use it regularly to bring supplies from storage but not the kind of place an organic would want to go under any normal circumstance."

The Captain began heading off before she was called back.

"Hey, could we have a snoop?" said Leroy

She looked a little perplexed. "There's nothing to see, it's a big long tube and a ladder. Some of the others have conveyers for the drones, but.."

"What about this one?" he interrupted.

"It's in a public area so there will be a ladder, the drone spokes are in private areas." She was about to move off again.

"So, can we have a little gander inside?"

The Captain glanced over at Maxtor who shrugged. Seiren and the Professor looked up at the hatch.

"It's a tour right? I'm just curious," said Leroy.

The Captain sighed. "Okay," she said slowly, tapping her comms with a frustrated smile. "Marshall."

"Ma'm."

"Would you mind opening spoke 4 please?" she looked up along with the others.

"Certainly Ma'm," there was a slight pause. "I'll need your access code Ma'm."

She looked around and sighed.

"1-9-4-7."

"Thank you Ma'm."

A moment later the door slid open and the group gathered around the bottom. The tube or spoke had sensed the opening and an array of led light strips ran off into infinity or so it seemed. The ladder rungs were fixed to one side of the tube which from the hatch opened up to around 10 metres in diameter. Leroy cupped his hands and screamed upwards into the tube. The sound echoed and repeated into the distance then as the sound faded he looked around.

"Hey cool, thanks," he said with a childish grin.

"Thank you Marshall," the Captain said into her comms unit, the hatch slid shut and her eyes met Maxtor's as they turned to leave. He raised his eyebrows and the huddle went on their way.

"Designing the service and storage area in the centre of the ship leaves the outer skin available for living and leisure."

Without slowing she hovered along with the group behind her into one of the wider cafes and leisure areas. Yet again the designers had utilised both floors giving the illusion of a much grander area. Here she slowed and the rest followed suit. She stopped by an ornamental hologram of the Lazarus from the outside. Just as she had described there were six spokes leading to a central core. The inner part of the ship had large protrusions at either end which she indicated.

"The ship is powered by two ion drive units which are positioned at the front and rear of the craft. Each one points outwards and can act as either a drive or a brake. Pushing us forward or slowing us down dependent on speed requirements. The rear one as we stand now will carry us at high speed towards Mars once we finally leave Earth's orbit which will be in the coming 48 hours. The ship has an independent 3 gigawatt nuclear reactor. The Ion drive will utilise most of the capacity and any other requirements will be of little strain to its systems."

"Another 48 hours, why so long before we leave?" said Seiren.

"We have already departed; we are accelerating as we speak. Unlike the shuttle you all arrived in, the ship's drive is not a chemical thruster and so its output and acceleration is poor, we will use the Earth's orbit to slingshot us into space. After that we can build up speed and momentum slowly."

"200 million kilometres in a matter of months?" said Maxtor.

"Incredible isn't it? Our acceleration and deceleration are both very incremental. It's done over days which is why we have thrusters forward and rear," she paused. "We have very good brakes."

The Professor's eyes widened.

"Sorry," she raised a hand. "Just joking, around 2 days from our destination we will effectively switch off the rear drive and engage the forward one to slow us down. Over the final days we can then slow into Mars orbit."

"So we travel backwards for twenty two days?" said Touchreik.

"No, we just slow down using the front drive as a kind of reverse thrust, but don't worry you will not feel a thing. Then we orbit Mars for three days and our passengers take their images, glare out the windows. After that we repeat the procedure to head home," she looked at each of them in turn. "Accept for your little adventure. I must confess I envy you."

"Envy us if we make it back," quipped Seiren.

"I'm sure you will," Voodoo waited a beat before carrying on.

"As you can see the outer skin of the ship is two floors deep, this maiden voyage is only partially full. On future trips we can comfortably cope with over 500 passengers when we are fully operational. There's also a large amount of communal and socialising space on board. Remember there's a slight variation in gravity depending on which floor you're on. Weight loss and weight lifting classes are always best done on the upper level," the group smiled. "We generally run at around 0.8G but until you will be used to it I would avoid any sudden changes in direction, fast movements, that kind of thing."

"Why 0.8G?" asked Touchreik.

"It's as close to Earth's gravity as can be comfortable and economical. Weightlessness for long periods can have unwanted consequences such as muscle loss, common eye damage and bone problems, all of which will be completely avoided, notwithstanding the comfort and convenience of virtual gravity on such a long trip such as this. Even reality adventurers might pass on a cruise like this if they were likely to incur permanent physical damage."

They moved off into a wide concourse which was conspicuously busy. There were two double story glass doors which were constantly opening and closing as people came in and out. Mostly wearing wide eyed expressions or chuckling with huge grins on their faces.

"This is our showpiece of which we are very proud," said the Captain holding out a hand. There was a large illuminated sign above the sliding door which read 'Space Bar'.

"Follow me," said the Captain. She floated forwards and through the doors. As they passed through the door the sight that befell them almost took their breaths away. The space was large and although it was on the outer edge of the ship it showed no curve, presumably more clever use of architecture, colour scheme and decor. In the centre of the room was a huge glass floor space. Through this invisible floor it was possible to see outer space passing by. Every few moments a stunning vision of planet Earth would pass. It was similar to the floor window in each of their cabins yet on an immense scale.

"Wow," said Seiren. "This is not augmented right?" she said just to be sure.

"It can be, but not right now, that's really the Earth as we spin."

"It's amazing."

"This is one of our main common spaces, we hold our physical events here as well as a social space."

They were all speechless.

"You like it?"

"It's beautiful, really beautiful," cried Seiren as she wiped her eye with the back of her hand. She stepped off the foot transport and walked onto the glass floor, gingerly at first and then started to dance to the light background music in the room.

"Very unnerving," said Touchreik.

Leroy jumped off his transporter and joined Seiren as she gyrated across the spacious glass floor. The pair were mimicking each other and fooling around as they moved further across the stars. There was still no feeling of movement, it looked like space was rolling by and they were still.

"The build of the Lazarus is unconventional and that's why in most areas you can switch to VR windows in the walls and close off the floor windows," said Voodoo who could now only be heard by the spectator group. The main restaurant was set slightly up from this level and had a drone serviced bar. From up there it would appear to be a sea of stars whilst dining. Looking down it would feel like the cosmos would rotate and give the illusion of walking in space. Most evenings it was possible to dance on the stars as the viewing area doubled as a dance floor. It took some getting used to but was a remarkable addition to an already staggering experience.

"The inner core of the ship is always above our heads as we rotate so this view is unhindered. You will be the only ones up there before your drop to Mars. I have been up there once or twice; it's quite a thrilling experience in itself."

"Thank you Captain it's been fascinating," said Maxtor.

Leroy and Seiren continued to dance across the stars waving for the others to join them.

"It's been my pleasure. There's nothing to do now but enjoy the cruise until we reach Mars, relax and enjoy the facilities on-board.

There's much more to discover and entertain you but we have regular social events planned, we hope you will join us when you can."

"Yeah we will thank you," said Maxtor.

"If you want to stay for a drink, I'll return the foot transporters."

They each stepped off the discs and they remained hovering in free air.

"Bye for now," she said, hovered through the doors and the little discs followed her like a line of ducks. Touchreik and Maxtor had no intention of making a move towards Seiren and Leroy who were giggling like a pair of juves. Suddenly a voice shouted out from up on the mezzanine floor, a man was waving his arms around. At first Maxtor thought the dancing might be causing offence.

"LEEE ROY!" he was shouting his name.

Leroy looked up, trying to make out who was calling him.

"LEEE ROY!"

He stopped dancing and squinted his eyes. Maxtor knew straight away who it was but Leroy still wasn't able to make him out.

Leroy walked over to the Mezzanine. "Shit man, how are yer?" he shouted.

"I thought it was you, I knew it," the man said swinging his arms in the air. "I've been screaming at you for half an hour."

"Haaa yeah!" screamed Leroy. "I thought you were heading back to Earth?"

"Oh yeah so did I?"

The rest of the crew wandered across.

"These are my colleagues, Seiren, Commander Maxtor, Adrenalin Sinus and this is Professor Touchreik."

"So you're going with these guys? I don't believe it," he stopped, noticing the Professor.

"You're the caveman guy right?" he said wagging a finger. "I remember you from the media, crazy. You ever hear from that caveman since he went deep?"

The Professor looked a little flushed. "No, no I didn't."

"Long time ago eh. He kept his word though didn't he? He never came back outta V-World?"

Leroy patted the guy on the arm. "Everyone, this is my very old friend, Juliette Tiding.'

They all waved and said, "hi." Leroy turned back to him.

"What the hell are you doing here?"

"Fucken crazy, I am totally pissed, sorry Ma'm," Seiren nodded.

"You won't believe me. The shuttle I brought you guys up in, it's goosed up, kaput. I am stuck here with you till we get back."

"What?" Leroy laughed so hard he almost cried. "Stop that you're kidding me on."

"Hey, it's no joke ok. I didn't book a fuckin trip to Mars with a ship load of reality junkies."

He looked pretty serious and Leroy did what he could to stop himself laughing more. Seiren covered her mouth with the back of her hand.

"Hey come on let me get the drinks eh."

"How about I get the drinks in," said Tiding. "They gave me a private class cabin and a sizeable account to compensate me. Come on, all of yer. It's all on me."

"Well ok, let's do it," said Leroy slapping him on the back.

Maxtor was first to cut in, "Hey listen you guys enjoy yourselves ok, let's have our briefing tomorrow instead if everyone's in agreement." There were nods all round. "I am gonna go shut my eyes for a while."

"Me too, I'm pooped after yesterday," said Seiren.

The Professor simply shrugged his shoulders "Just us then, hey man," said Leroy.

The pair slapped each other on the back whilst heading for the bar. The others walked in the opposite direction.

"Poor man being stuck here on a trip to Mars," whispered Seiren. "I hope he didn't see me laughing, he looked pretty upset."

"I don't blame you. It is kinda funny," said Maxtor and they all headed out towards the door.

Unlike regular bars the Space bar had set up drone bar tenders. It was a fun gimmick and added some interest. The drones would physically mix and serve drinks to the customers. It would listen to your instructions and then attempt to make a drink to your liking by actually mixing products. There were no automation or personal menus available. As the time passed by the pair kidded around with the drone. They would spit drinks out, pour them back down the sink or ask for recommendations or ridiculous cocktails. Eventually they got bored and sauntered over to a corner to sit down.

Leroy looked round and laughed again.

"Juliette, Juliette what? Tiding. I still can't get over that as a name."

"Get over it."

He spit his drink back in his glass. "Fuckin, Juliette."

"What about your name? Leroy Payne?"

The two of them laughed and joked continuing to fool around for a while, being as loud as possible.

"Never mind let's get down to business, we are all aboard that's the main thing. How is everything else looking?" said Juliette.

"Everything is fine, we never built a free bar tab into the plan but that's a nice bonus," said Leroy.

"Seriously," said Juliette.

"All cool at the moment. I am down to be making the drop with the girl and the other two, the geek is staying up here. I have the access code for the spokes too thanks to the Captain. If those stones are there, and I know they are, then I am gonna be there when we find them."

"I think we can do this. So there's no change then? Business as planned?"

Leroy looked him in the eye. "Keep that stupid grin on your face while we speak. I ain't keen on anyone wanting to socialise with us."

Leroy grabbed him round the back of the neck. "Great to see you man." He pulled his arm away quickly.

"Hey! easy ok? We don't want this whole thing falling apart because of something silly. Nothing physical ok? Let's build this up and then we can be seen together."

"You're right comrade," he paused looking at the golden liquid and picked up his glass. "Do you know how many years we've waited for this?"

"We're not there yet, but soon everything we worked for will come true."

Tiding raised his glass. "Here's to humanity!"

Leroy did the same. "To humanity my friend."

FIVE

A couple of days into the voyage and the Professor's internal organs were becoming accustomed to the new environment. The motion sickness was almost completely gone and the illusion of walking on a flat surface was complete. His brain had adapted well and it had become natural to avoid sudden movements in any direction. His plan had been to continue lectures via Augmented Reality back at the institute in the early part of the voyage. As the distance between Earth and the Lazarus grew the time delay would make that impractical. Nonetheless he was grateful he had built in a break before returning to the floor. As the distance from Earth grew he would hand over his teaching duties to subordinates.

The Professor was fully aware what lay ahead of him when they reached Mars itself. The drop would make the shuttle docking from yesterday feel like a morning mag ride. Knowing full-well what lay ahead he was in no hurry to go through the whole thing at the briefing. Just like the shuttle ride, he had made the drop in V-World a number of times, if the shuttle was like having your insides on your knee; the drop was like putting them back in again, upside down.

He'd agreed to the briefing this afternoon and everyone else appeared to be keen to get it behind them. The drop crew would have no real obligations or duties once that formality was taken care of until they were in orbit. Three months was plenty of time to enjoy most of the pleasures the Lazarus had to offer. His Augmented display directed him through a myriad of corridors he paid little attention to. Mostly seeming to be cabins and residential areas, lots were eerie and quiet. 50 meters from his destination he found himself in one of the many unexplored areas of the ship. He approached a door that was clearly marked crew only, seeing as it opened for him he assumed that he fit that criteria, at least for the moment. He was guided through and as it slid silently closed it revealed yet another long illuminated corridor. A matter of metres beyond that point he passed a room with a glass wall on the left with the blinds down. He heard voices from inside and once at the door Maxtor broke off his conversation and beckoned him inside.

The door slid open and Touchreik entered, tapping his forehead in greeting.

"Touchriek," he said firmly.

"We're going to start the briefing soon. I've just finished a meeting with my crew but we'll push right on," he turned to the group in the room, two of which were clearly members of the Lazarus crew, they each nodded to him in acknowledgement as they left.

Watching them go the Commander gathered everyone with a clap of his hands. "Thanks to everyone for their attention and I know you have a lot to discuss but if you'd take your seats once more we will run through the actual mission briefing."

Captain Voodoo was already lounging across a swivel chair at the far end of the table next to one of her officers. The other three immediately broke up their conversation and sat down; the Professor took up one of the spare seats. The Commander sat at the head opposite Captain Bernsteen at the opposite end of the table and addressed everyone.

"As you can see the Professor has joined us for the second part of the briefing. You know Captain Bernsteen and Navigation Officer Blunt."

He knew the Captain but had never met Blunt however the two acknowledged each other with a courteous nod.

"Great, it's been a long morning so let's get on?"

The table acknowledged him and Leroy pinched the bridge of his nose with thumb and forefinger. His eyes were bloodshot and he looked pale.

"Commander Blunt, perhaps you could begin by outlining our voyage just to give some perspective."

Blunt nodded to his superior and looked down at the desk in front of him making hand gestures as he spoke. "I've prepared a short presentation to bring us all in line with the mission objectives," he said.

With that, a three dimensional holographic representation of Mars appeared to float in space in the centre of the table. The red planet was incredibly detailed and it looked like an actual solid structure. At the far end of the room an object approached the spinning planet, a hologram of the Lazarus.

"This presentation is not to scale but for clarity you can see we will be approaching Mars in 38 Earth days. The forward Ion drive will be engaged 2 days prior to orbit to slow us down and allow us to achieve the correct trajectory on approach. The details of that are outside the scope of this meeting but let's just say there'll be no drinks spilled during that time," he stole an involuntary peek at Leroy who was looking at the table. Seiren smiled and caught the eye of Adrenalin as the pair shuffled in their seats.

"The Lazarus will maintain orbit and speed for a total of three sols. As we discussed earlier this is all in line with our flight plan. There are no allowances being made for extending our stay."

The Professor raised his eyebrows and the Commander offered an explanation.

"Just to clarify for the Professor if I may. Sols are Martian days which in reality are 24 hours and 39 minutes. The Lazarus itself will work to Earth time and for the sake of the duration of this short mission so will we."

The Professor nodded and the Commander waved a hand for Blunt to continue.

"Thank you. Our speed and orbit will be maintained for three sols and its imperative we are able to leave Mars orbit after that time. Whilst your people are making the drop then the Lazarus will maintain its planned schedule. On sol three we will again increase speed and begin our outward Journey. Once we begin our exit strategy then projectiles from Mars will not be capable of catching us. I'm sure you are aware of the incident with the shuttle by now."

"Who isn't," laughed Seiren turning to Leroy. "Your buddy has told everyone on board."

"You know the shuttle pilot?" said Voodoo.

"Erm... yes actually I do, he is a very old associate."

The Captain pursed her lips, nodding to her officer who continued. "We have a number of events planned for our passengers who are of course the real reason we are here, although we welcome hitchhikers we have no wish to slow down for them," she glanced upwards towards the Commander who was looking down at the table. The Professor had no doubts there had been agreement and disagreement whilst he was absent.

"Thank you Commander Blunt," said Maxtor. "Seiren."

"Thanks," she said rubbing the back of her neck and pulling on her hair.

The Lazarus at the far end of the table powered towards Mars and got smaller and closer to scale as it neared the red planet finally starting to take up orbit around the reddish brown spinning globe.

"The Lazarus will follow its planned route," she said stressing the word planned. "To orbit Mars in the coming month or so."

She smiled at Blunt. "Firstly I'll update you on the drone pre mission which is reporting a success so far. The drone work is almost complete and I have a full update on the status of that."

The hologram of the Martian planet grew and sank into the table until they were all looking down on a three dimensional model from the air, except the model was alive with figures and vehicles busying themselves across its surface.

"For the sake of the presentation we can assume due North is towards the Commander's seat. The drone mission left Earth a year ago and has prepared three key locations on Mars in preparation for our arrival. If you look to the North West you will see our return rocket booster which will be returning us and our samples back to the Lazarus after our mission is complete. For safety reasons it's been placed in the Jezero crater here. The location was designed to afford some shelter from the unpredictable weather on Mars. The second location prepped by the drone mission is our hab unit situated outside the crater to the South. We will be spending a few nights together but you have all seen the mock ups, it's small but has everything we need. Our core mission is to find and access the Major's original base. We know its main body was underground to avoid radiation and climate. There's still a chance we may fail in light of the changes to the landscape over hundreds of years. There are no beacons still functioning and no electronics in operation. Our historic evidence suggests it's situated somewhere South of the hab unit. Overall that's probably one of the most straightforward parts of the mission in light, pardon the pun gentlemen, of the Martian atmosphere," knowing grins were exchanged around the room.

"Finally you will see to the West of the Jezero crater the methane fuel farm or to be more specific 'deep cryo-methalox' production facility. Since the drone mission's arrival it has been using the Martian atmosphere to manufacture the fuel to get us back up to the Lazarus. This fuel is being made and stored away from the return ship."

"Fuel from Mars, is this mining or fossil fuel?" said Touchreik.

Seiren spoke directly to Touchreik, "No, the plant will synthesise methane from subsurface ice and carbon dioxide in the atmosphere. Simple chemistry, but it does work well and elevates the problems associated with landing heavy objects on the surface, including full fuel tanks, not least transporting them there. The very same method used by the Major to get back after the shutdown. As for getting out the same problems actually help us, the return ship won't need a large booster rocket. Mars has less gravity than Earth; the spacecraft can produce enough thrust to escape the planet's gravity perfectly well on its own."

Maxtor was looking impatient with the discussion on basic chemistry. "The plant has generated the fuel needed to get us back. The drone mission has set this up and will begin fuelling the return vehicle at the latest opportunity. All this infrastructure has been put in place by the drones during their pre-mission. Our hab is ready as is everything else; the drones will be turning your bedding and switching the heating on before we arrive," her grin widened as the Commander shook his head.

"Finished Captain White?"

"Over to Mr Sinus," she said sitting back in her chair.

"Sinus," the Commander repeated.

Sinus sat up and manipulated the hologram. It zoomed from the planet surface to the huge rotating Lazarus ship.

"Now for the fun part," he said with an embarrassed grin and sniffle. "At the risk of repeating the obvious we have come up with a clever and fun solution to overcome the very thin Martian atmosphere. As Seiren says it's almost non-existent, and so makes it very difficult to land large objects in a single hit, hence the pre-missions. It's this atmosphere which means getting three organics down is a problem but not insurmountable, particularly for such a fleeting visit."

This time the Professor shared the knowing grins wholeheartedly, having experienced numerous rehearsals for the drop in V-World simulators.

"I am aware that you will have practiced the mission in V-World simulation and I hope you all enjoyed the ride," he paused. "Professor?" he said nodding in his direction as he noticed the Commander's eye contact with his men.

"Yes of course," he responded with his eyes focused at the spinning model.

"100% PP?"

"85 actually."

"Ohh."

"Oh oh," various sniggers came from around the room.

"Quiet please. Let's run through the mission and make sure we are all on board so to speak," interrupted Maxtor.

"As you know our target is the historic Major Zero site on Mars," he said. "The hab unit can sustain you comfortably for around 4/5 days but we should be on our way home by then."

The hab unit appeared as the holographic model zoomed in, like a long metallic cylinder on its side, semi buried in the soil. It was difficult to scale until he saw the Martian transporter parked outside. From that it was clear this accommodation unit was very small for the whole crew. However, a fleeting mission was designed to travel and live lightly.

Sinus took over, coughing to get attention. "I will be on command and monitor from the Lazarus so I'm gonna miss the ride I'm afraid. Commander Maxtor, Seiren, Leroy and of course the Professor will be making the drop. There are five A.I. one man landers aboard Lazarus, ready to go. One is a spare in case of any issues so we shouldn't need it."

A model of the drop unit appeared to spin in the middle of the table. It looked like a cross between a small rocket and a body flight suit but was only around 7 or 8 metres tall, not a whole lot bigger than a man. As a sense of scale, a replica human figure spun around next to it, a door opened on the front and it could be seen how the single passenger would effectively stand inside. There was a red body moulding against the back that the passenger would lean against and strap into. The rotating body slid inside and the straps pulled around it with the door closed. The pod had a visibility glass screen in the head area like a space suit and the sides had wing like structures that were folded against the body of the craft. The whole thing was like a personal one man rocket.

"Once inside it's simply a case of making yourself comfortable and enjoying the ride, it will be challenging for the nerves. The whole drop is fully automated using A.I. so there's little to worry about. These craft will get you down to the surface in no time. I will push you all off till your clear of the Lazarus."

As he said this, four pods could be seen floating from the centre of the holographic Lazarus model. "To do that you will need to depart from the central core where the pods are located. We have to get you out in weightlessness instead of firing you off into space from the outer edge. I will oversee all A.I. input from up here to get you off. When you are clear of the Lazarus I will initiate descent and you're fully automated. Once you hit the atmosphere you'll be around 30 minutes out. The pod will slow down and loop whilst high in the atmosphere to absorb energy and cut down on heat. You have your own pods with internal design to mimic your body shape."

"What if we put weight on during the trip?" spouted Leroy.

Adrenalin looked at the Commander for an answer. "Don't," he said.

Adrenalin coughed in acknowledgement. "At 80 miles from touchdown the senses will not feel the sensation of 31,000 kilometres per hour; however deceleration is heavy and necessary. It's also going to get super-hot outside whilst the shield absorbs heat, inside it will be a little over room temperature," as he spoke everything he said was being shown in hologram form in the centre of the table along with concerning yet effective effects.

"The lander pods have built in A.I. controlled thrusters that will take you into a circular descent to enable us to slow down enough for the chutes. Protective shields will disengage as they fail, there are three in total. A full powered descent will begin at around a mile up. The whole trip should ultimately deliver each of you safely within walking distance of the hab. There's motorised transport available there and once you are inside the hab unit you can remove space suits and debrief in a breathable Earth like atmosphere," he nodded at Maxtor.

"Thank you Sinus. Now let's get to the nuts and bolts," Maxtor sat up and the pod models disappeared. "We have two full days on Mars and our mission is to locate and gain entry to the Major's site, once inside we'll acquire samples to bring back. The Professor will act as our guide and other than safety or command issues he has jurisdiction over what those items will ultimately be, within reason. The only exception to that is the element our sponsor requires. That will be our priority. Remember this is a historic site so go lightly Mr Payne."

On hearing his name he lifted his head and opened his eyes. "We should have transport and fuel to cover as many trips as we need to make between the hab and the base once it's located. Our only limitation; will be our physical energy and time. No splits and we will work together at all times. Get ready for some long days ladies and gentlemen. A fair price to pay after two months in the space bar as guests on board I would say. We are restricted in how much mass we can get back up here with the return rocket but that should not be an issue for any of our priorities. When ready we head back, load the samples and climb into our return booster, boom up and back to the Lazarus. After that it's just over a month of your company and we head home to Heathen. Any questions?"

No one responded.

"Ok, go and enjoy your voyage and remember you are here in a professional capacity which means keeping a low profile, relax and be invisible. I want no reports of rowdy behaviour whilst the Captain has made us so welcome. Stay low. Dismissed."

The drop crew and the Captain's people filed out laughing and joking and the Professor was about to follow them.

"Professor could I have a word," said Maxtor.

"Yeah."

The Commander brought his head in close to Touchreik lowering his voice. He looked up waiting for the last person to leave the room.

"Are you good with this?"

"The mission? of course I am fine with it."

Commander Maxtor pulled back and stared into his eyes, paused and then nodded. "Be aware, I won't have these people jeopardised do you understand me. We take everyone down and we bring everyone back. You are at the bottom of the pecking order, just remember that."

The Professor didn't respond, at least not in words. Maxtor didn't take his eyes off him as he turned and walked out the door.

SIX

Once back in his cabin Professor Touchreik had no more energy than to collapse on the bed. The energy surge of the morning had been short-lived. In part it was the physical exhaustion and in part it was the mental stress. Was there a time in middle age when life should slow down a little? A man of 101 who was physically fit and in the September years of his life might not want to find himself on the other side of the solar system. He rolled over and hung his face over the side of the bed and watched the stars through the floor window pass by. The billions of lights crossed his vision and lulled him into a trance. The cabin lights must have dimmed as the system detected him drifting into sleep. He had no idea how much time had passed when his eyes suddenly opened fully. The room was darkened and he became anxious, aware of a presence in the room. All he saw was the night sky whizzing past and for a moment thought he was drifting in space. Orientating himself he remembered where he was. He attempted to move or roll over onto his back but felt restricted. His limbs felt lifeless and heavy but he mustered a huge effort and was able to roll onto his back. The invisible weight or pressure on his chest was still pinning him down. He was sweating with fear and he could feel the Lazarus spinning faster and faster. He closed his eyes tightly in the hope it would all go away and could see nothing but blood red flashes behind his eyelids. He remembered the Lazarus. Yes, he was aboard the Lazarus and had fallen asleep on the bed. He remembered that now, and the realisation hit him that this ridiculous tin can in space was out of control. Starting to spin faster and faster with no one able to stop it. The light from the floor portal reflected the sun's rays, faster and faster across the room. Repetitively spinning like a frantic searchlight. To say he saw her would be a lie because he was blind and impotent on the bunk. Maybe the word was aware, imperiously aware of movement in the room. The wardrobe/radiation shelter door was moving and slipped open. He felt Ramona peering at him through the gap, her long fingers curling round the door frame, then gone. He became confused and horrified as the light span across the room faster and faster as the ship's spin pinned him harder to the bed. He managed to raise his head to see her at the end of the bed now, leaning on the wall. Her arms were folded and she just stared at him. She had come for him, to take revenge. He tried to hold his arms out, to reach out to her but they were too heavy. He felt the burning in his arms and his fists were heavy as lead. She was here, she was back. Maybe this was how it all happened? He was fading as she became stronger. This wasn't how it was meant to be because he wanted them to be together again. Calling out to her to help him, so he could explain everything and make it right. Why wouldn't she respond to him?

He called out to her, "Ramona." She just laughed. An evil sneering laugh, if he could only explain that he was going to make everything better. Tears streamed down his face and the flashing light from the sun got brighter and brighter. So bright the room filled with blinding white light and he forced his eyes to shut, but couldn't. The pain stung his head deep inside and then there was an enormous deafening whoosh, then silence.

Suddenly in an instant his eyes opened and the lights in the room had come on and the hatch window in the floor was now closed. There were tears in his eyes and streaming across his cheek. For the coming 60 or so days there would be no day or night. According to the Professors body clock it was now early evening, the drone had suggested he keep a normal sleep routine where possible. The clocks on board would mimic Earth time without the sunrise and sunset. However the general lighting on the ship would shift frequency into the late evening until dawn. He threw his head back on the bed and brushed his cheek with his sleeve. Ramona, she was gone. It had been his fault and all he was left with were the memories.

The Professor's guts hurt from mental pain and anguish. He picked himself up and propped himself on the stool next to the formulator; dialling up some caffeine and a light snack. Sipping the caffeine gave him a little light relief either real or imagined. Leaving the food where it was he wandered over to the leather settee and sat watching the steam rise from the remains of his drink. He felt no need to do anything else and he just stared without moving for hours. His thoughts drifted in and out from conscious to semi-conscious. The steam slowed down and eventually there was none. What the hell was he doing here? He was no adventurer or reality junkie and he was out of his league. Ramona would be in his thoughts, the things she did and the things she said; the memories they shared. In the hours that followed he must have relived the last six decades in his mind. Back then there were two loves in his life. His first love was the same as most people, Mother.

The Savour Machine or Mother as she was known, the one who created us and our world, the one who provided for us and kept us safe. Gave us everything we desired as organic humans; a virtual playground, surrogate parents to care for us as well as food and nourishment. More importantly she protected us from the 'outside' and its dangers. His second love was of course the irreplaceable, beautiful, charming and infuriating Ramona A Stone.

The latter he had killed years ago, and because of that he would gladly kill the first. When they had first met, him becoming a Doctor and then a Professor of history was just an idea, just dreams. His thoughts drifted back as they often did to the day they met. Life can fly by but little or nothing had changed in the world. At 101 years old he was no juve but certainly not the young man he was when he first met Ramona.

He was yearning to meet Ramona for the first time. She would be ready to meet him in days, then a few months, then maybe a few weeks and out of nowhere the next day. He knew that the dudes, hackers who worked underground would often be deliberately vague; deliberately shifting deadlines forwards and backwards, slippery beings difficult to nail down for long. The deadlines had changed constantly until he received an impromptu message which was totally unexpected. Hacking code wasn't strictly illegal in its place but the dudes knew it was those who they hacked for, who could bring problems to their door. In general dudes always kept a low profile, leaving frustrated clients in the dark. The message when it finally came didn't use any technology, another classic sign of his elusiveness; a simple basic alert through his Sage.

"Come tomorrow."

No signature attached but by its implication it was clear Touchreik would know who it was from and to what it regarded. It wasn't the first time he had been summoned and it might well be another fruitless journey but who knows.

He woke early and spent the morning readying everything in case he had a guest later that day. Not wanting to appear over keen he thought it best to wait for a respectable time of day before heading out. He had made some adjustments to his sleeping room and built a small cabinet in the back of his clothing storage. It had a sliding door, some straps and a small trickle charge with an unhooked power point. While the hours passed he mused at how this dude was a technological craftsman and yet used none of it to communicate for fear his activities might be discovered or left on record.

By mid-morning Touchreik had stepped out onto the grey streets of Heathen into the communal square outside. Leaves and papers had drifted and gathered in corners and the low walled gardens contained tired looking trees and benches. A place that had been created for relaxation and beauty looked abandoned but had never been occupied in the first place. As if its creators changed their minds and simply walked away and left their work to the elements. The morning was crisp with a light breeze and sunlight was low and cast everything in a bright yellow light. The light bounced across the higher edges of towering gold and silver glass towers across the sector. The clouds reflection against patches of blue sky sailed across the walls. There were no physical humans around but the odd humanoid drone could be seen going about their business here and there. Touchreik walked briskly across the square to meet his Magpod. He barely broke stride as the pod pulled up and the door swung upwards as it slowed. It didn't stop as he stepped inside and sat down. The ride was smooth as the small egg shaped craft floated above the ground on its own magnetic field. Touchreik settled into one of the plush chairs inside and the warmer internal atmosphere made him shudder after the outdoor chill. The doors clicked shut and the drab view through the windows was quickly replaced by that augmented reality version of his world. Instead of seeing the reality of Heathen's streets he was greeted with a much more pleasant augmented experience. He regarded the bustling cityscape that was overlaid onto the real view outside. Stout busy Heathens went about their business in a determined manner, crowding in and out of glass towers. Some were also gathered in leafy green parks and walked along tree lined avenues as he passed. Families sat on grass eating and drinking, juves played and there were occasional glimpses of wildlife. Birds and small mammals living freely amongst the organic humans, sharing the cities green spaces. The mag journey would take them up to the North of Heathen into area SO63. As the Magpod approached the darker side of Heathen the utopian augmented view didn't change. When the pod finally stopped and the doors opened the cooler air hit him squarely in the face and it certainly changed then. The temperature was distinctly colder and the air thick. Mentally his visits here oppressed him and made him almost want to turn and head back. The greys were now blacks, the clouds darker and the sunlight had given way to a heavy precipitance in the air. Being on the fringes of the city; meant that much of the waste air was pushed out this way by Mother's climate systems. Even the communal Mag transport system ended its service on the fringes of SO63 and would take him no further. Mother hadn't been willing to close this area but she wasn't going to condone it either. Sadly the Humanists had become much more active in recent years and attacks on drones had become commonplace. Hypocritically, Touchreik would have gladly shut the area down if not for his own occasional business here. That was unlikely to happen, Mother could not be reasoned with or her motives questioned because she had no central autonomy. She was in fact the people, a combination of opinions and thoughts that produced an algorithm for human happiness, that was the genius of Major Zero's invention. A coming together of minds to create the utopia we call Heathen.

Touchreik climbed out of the pod into the harsh grey realities of SO63 and began walking north. He pulled his large overcoat around him and sprung forward past the seedy nightclubs like Yanpur and Laoureh where scores of organic and non-organics spewed into the streets at all times of day and night. Thankfully most were closed at this time of day, the few which were open attracted the dregs and diehards like a moth to a flame. Having either arrived early for the night's amusement or remaining from the night before; screaming and laughing their way through the afternoon. After ten minutes of walking, he had been offered physical sex, influencers and had requests for coinage. Avoiding the colourful array of characters by keeping his eyes forwards he finally arrived at his destination. A door that was obscured from the main street between two large refuse containers. He rang the bell and stepped back, looking up and down the street. A crack appeared in the door and the dude beckoned him in. The dude had never offered him a name and likewise Touchreik, no need. As long as the bitcoin was flowing then they communicated just fine. The dude wasn't an old man but walked in a stooped manner and in the times Touchreik had seen him he had never appeared fully dressed and certainly never fully washed. He followed him down a passage, which had barely enough room to pass through. It was stacked to the ceiling on either side with boxes and bags. Body parts, wires and circuitry protruded from crates and the floor was littered with smaller bits of gadgetry, trodden into the floor beyond recognition. His main room was no different but it was a bigger space to fill.

"You brought the coin?" he said sniffling and pulling a grubby long swollen garment around him with a belt.

"Is she here?" said Touchreik trying to hide his excitement. He had waited so long to meet her and his expectations were high.

"She's here, you got the coinage?" said the dude again.

Touchreik searched under his shirt and pulled a body belt round to the front. He reached in and handed over a card. "It's all there."

The dude took an age checking its authenticity and making transfers. Touchreik looked around the room tapping his foot in frustration. He noticed a curtain up around an area that he had never seen in previous visits. Perhaps she was here, he was so excited to meet her he almost reached over and ripped it down. Finally the dude was happy, he disappeared into a back room and reappeared without the card.

"Over here," the dude reached for the curtain and pulled it to one side and switched on a small lamp.

Touchreik couldn't believe his eyes when he saw her for the first time. She was absolutely nothing like the drone he ordered, in fact almost the complete opposite. He had clearly stated in his orders that he preferred a female, ok it was female. He specified black short hair, slender figure but bolder in places with hips and not too tall. Instead he was confronted with a figure much taller than him, long legs and flaming red hair. She didn't look right at all, there was something about the face that was pompous and conceited. She appeared confident and aloof, in fact she looked a little unnerving. There was something in her eyes that he didn't like.

"What the fuck is this?" Touchreik whispered. If he was going to lose coins then he would have preferred this scumbag had ran off with the cash. In fact he almost wished he had. Instead he offered him something that was far outside of his specifications. He had been through weeks of bullshit personality profiling to get her ready. "Hey man I am an artist, I am trying to find out things about you that you don't even know about yourself," the dude had said. Touchreik had been spending money to be 'profiled' according to the dude. Explaining how it will help him program the drone to his own liking, and now he was so humiliated that he had fallen for such a scam.

"I want my coins back and you can send this fucking thing back up the chase for the kids to play with," so angry he'd forgotten how dangerous these people can be. He grabbed the earth smelling scum by the throat and demanded his coinage.

"Get my fucking coins back and get rid of this thing."

He was almost choking the guy as he tried to reply, "But.."

The dude grabbing at his neck to breath and Touchreik red with rage.

"Is this him?" said a husky female voice from behind them.

"What the?" The dude gagged and pointed over Touchreik's shoulder.

He dropped the scum and he slid down the wall gasping for breath. The dude pulled himself to his feet and still leant on the wall for purchase. A tall gracious woman walked over to the table and sat down crossing her legs. He heard the dude behind him. "I'm sorry man, I didn't activate the thing."

"The thing?" she cried and threw her head back laughing hysterically. Her long flowing red hair twists and rests on her ample breasts. She tried desperately to repeat his words, "The TH The Thin."

The two men stood with their hands on hips watching her, hypnotised in amazement, each for very different reasons. Ramona lights one of the dude's cigarettes and throws the lighter and box amongst the scattered paraphernalia on the table.

As the Doctor approaches she blows the smoke into his face. Her laughing stops and she whispers through her bright red lips, "You're the thing, are you Mr?" and elaborately blows him a kiss and a wink. Then provocatively crossed her legs as the velvet frock she is wearing slowly slides down her thigh and gathers almost at her crotch. Touchreik involuntarily touched his collar and beads of sweat appeared on his forehead.

"So your Touchreik?" she said looking him up and down with her elbow resting on her knee, taking another drag of the cigarette and all the time rocking slowly from side to side. She used her long nails to prize a large chunk of lipstick from the corner of her mouth and flicked it across the room.

"Sorry," she said with a giggle. "I didn't do my own make up today," throwing a mischievous grin at Touchreik whilst out of the corner of her eye she sneers at the dude. Her lips in a grimace revealing her pearl white teeth, stained with lipstick.

Then she froze.

The pair look at each other and back at the woman.

"I have no idea how that happened man," the dude said. "I have no fucking idea how that happened."

Touchreik stopped for a moment and stared into those deep blue eyes that he didn't order, and he relished the tall slim legs he didn't order either. The dude was running around checking cords, wires. Then he made motions in the air as he checked coding. The virtual screens could be seen only by the dude.

"What happened?" Touchreik said spellbound by this creature.

The dude said each word like he was spelling it out, "I... Have... No... F," said the dude, preoccupied with his task.

"I meant why has she frozen."

"Why? Cos I pulled the plug man, ever seen one of these hacks go wrong fella? She may look cute but she could cause us some serious damage, not to mention the gear. This stuff is expensive and hard to come by," he nodded around the room at the piles of electronic junk.

"Put her back on," said Touchreik without breaking his gaze. Her face was still frozen in the grimace and yet he thought he could see something behind those eyes, something mysterious.

"No way, not till I find out what's gone down here," said the dude still franticly looking through code and checking wires.

"Put her back on, you want rid of this thing don't you? I've paid you?"

The dude stopped what he was doing and ran across to Touchreik.

"You said it was a laundry drone, take her to the chase for the kids to play with," he went back to his workstation, pressed some buttons and came back over to her.

He undid the back of her dress and drops the front down revealing her breasts. Larger than Touchreik had ordered, both in size and nipples, red as fire and like saucers. The doc felt something as the dude lifted a breast and flipped a small piece of skin with skilful pinch. He plugged a small lead into it and ran back to his desk.

"I'll have it," Touchreik said.

The dude stopped and stared up at him, an almighty and relieved grin spreading across his face.

"OK," he said cautiously. "As she is, you'll take her tonight? I want this out of here, if they go rogue."

"I'll take it," repeated Touchreik.

"Ok man but that's it for me, if you take it now then there's no comebacks. We are done."

"We are done," Touchreik repeated.

"Do you have storage, power and backup facilities at your accommodation?"

"I have everything I need to keep it serviced."

The Doc looked down at her breasts as the dude flipped the flesh back in and pulled the dress back over. The cigarette she was holding had burned down somewhat and the smoke continued to lick its way into the air.

Twenty minutes later he and Ramona were walking back through SO63 towards their Magpod. He was so excited he forgot to be embarrassed or self-conscious. The journey home was mostly in silence but now and again she questioned him about certain places they passed.

"Look at that lovely building. Is that the river Sarundoon?" As if she was some kind of tourist who might never have passed this way before instead of a drone who was effectively no more than a few hours old. By the time they reached his accommodation block some of the nerves had set in. He wanted to get her off the streets and into his home, away from prying eyes. She might pass off as organic from a distance should anyone look on. This was almost inconceivable as homes and travel pods used augmented reality so he would remain unseen. It would only be in the unlikely event of an actual person physically passing them.

When they arrived at the apartment Ramona went from room to room inspecting the place.

"Duke," said Touchriek as he watched her go out of sight.

"Yes Sir," replied the disembodied voice of his internal sage.

"Kindly shutdown fully please and erase the last ten minutes."

"Now Sir?"

"Yes please."

An audible bleep followed. As far as Duke was concerned, the last ten minutes will have never happened. His master arriving home with a hacked physical good time drone. By the time he reactivated Duke then Ramona will be packed away. In all likelihood that's how the relationship will continue. Ramona made herself comfortable on the large red sofa and curled her long legs up with her heals hanging over the side.

"It's nice," with her elbow on the back of the sofa she combed her hair with her fingers. "Yes, it's nice," she said as if to approve her new home, that it might do for now. How incredible that she could make him coy in her presence. He sat next to her and she asked about his life, what he did.

"I love history, I wish to become a specialist one day, a Professor."

"Of history?" she looked bemused.

"Of history," he repeated.

Ramona looked away at the floor with distain. She gave that knowing grin he had seen from so many people before, as if that explains everything. An interest in history would require an interest in historical practices. One of those practices being physical attraction to other organics for sex. As they did in ancient times and from that conclusion it all added up as to why she was here. In part she was right but he never felt that attitude to be true and was insulted by it. His interest in history was genuine.

"I had a friend once," she said. "He was similar to yourself but he gave up in the end. He realised how irrelevant history was to the modern world."

Touchreik spent ten minutes countering the argument before becoming consciously aware that her story was false. She had no friends of any kind because today was the first day of her life. Regardless this set a standard for their future relationship. Her tales were occasionally amusing and fun, sometimes tragic and sad. In the tales that followed across the years Ramona had a complete backstory to a life she never had.

So much so that Touchreik would refer to people or places she had told him about in her colourful life. He might mention places she had been or people she had known. The whole life history she told was both entertaining and seamless. Never a detail made in error, a complete life to refer to and every minute of it was fantasy. It was noticeable how not only was it a more interesting background than his, but there were also areas that were blank and hidden. Hints of other partners and hidden tragedy that he was kept out of, and the more she did so the more he wanted in.

Because of this imaginary life history they had an immediate relationship to develop and build on. He could read her expressions, say the wrong thing or cheer her up. Seeing her smile or laugh became a joy to him from the very first night together. Physically he wanted her in a way he never expected, as a person and not a thing to be used. That first night she had subtly refused him as if it were a first date, something she wasn't ready for. As if it might all be too soon for her and he conceded. That night he slept alone like an excited boy with a crush. For now he was confined to his fantasies but in time they became reality. She finally succumbed and exceeded his wildest dreams as a physical partner. It took mere hours till she had him in a position where he considered her feelings? Even though he knew she had none.

The years passed and the relationship developed. In her mind everything would freeze when she was placed back in her charging station. He could leave her for weeks and the conversation would continue. She would never be out of touch with media or news as if she had an instant download to draw from. There were times she would make him laugh and times he could kill her but there was always the thought at the back of his mind. Was that bullshit the dude had sold him true, about the programming of her. A personality designed to deliver exactly the things he wanted her to deliver even when he didn't want her to.

"We can learn things about you that you don't know about yourself," the dude had said.

Maybe that had been true after all. Over the years he kept his filthy little secret and they would spend more and more time together. He spent less and less in SO63. The hours would pass quickly with them chatting and laughing about his day. On other occasions there would be blazing rows followed by warm comfortable make ups. Ramona developed a hilarious impression of Wade Prout, his superior at the institute. He laughed so much he'd been forced to instigate a ban which fell on deaf ears of course. She told stories about her life that often contained hidden parables dependent on how things were with his life at the time. Either encouraging him or helping and supporting through troubling times. Her fantasised life contained mesmerising tales and lessons. She encouraged as his career progressed and he was taken on at the institute, became a Doctor in history. At every level his career moved up he would promise himself that she would have to go, she never did. His temporary bit of fun was no longer temporary and he continued to risk the scandal. Ramona could have his emotional responses rolling around like a rollercoaster. She even changed him and his behaviour when she wasn't with him. He noticed how he had become more agreeable as a person in public. He learned to never take this drone for granted because she fooled him into believing she was autonomous. She was a machine, he knew that. A Verism or physical illusion.

On any given day, he would be aware of his perversion but was able to control it. He knew more than most about human history and was aware how human behaviour from the past may support his hypothesis. Ancient man would have bred like animals hundreds of years ago, with DNA being matched entirely by chance and physical contact. Those who trawled the streets of SO63 in search of their own needs may be variations of himself. Being part of a group that found the idea of physical love irresistible wasn't easy. The act of actually being with, touching and having sex with another physical being. He would often be tempted to say 'person' but of course Ramona was no person in an organic sense. He'd never imagine another organic either being comfortable or allowing him to be comfortable with doing it physically. Instead he had a drone that bordered on perfection and was willing and able to tend to his needs whether he knew what they were or not. She did it in a way that made her programming a masterpiece. Allowing her to be so fickle and demanding at times. Offering a whole string of emotions, shyness, boredom and passion. Like ingredients all mixed to perfection in some personality pot. That's why he loved her. He believed then that he could never find another human who would be able to lead and follow in such perfect symmetry.

That was his Ramona, a life he relived as the steam from his cup faded, his head dropped and he shook himself awake. He decided to go to bed and this time had the energy to pull down the radiation shelter. He continued the dialogue in his head now, his mind drifting back across the decades to when it all changed. When something amazing happened that would change his life forever. Something that would thrust him into the limelight making his private life even less private.

SEVEN

The year TVC14 had been a calm time in his life. He had a job he
craved and had never met another person who would challenge him for
it. He was a Doctor of history and specialised in 21st Century life. That
summer had been the most contented he could remember. The magpod
pulled up to a crawl outside the National Institute and Doctor Touchreik
stepped onto the sidewalk. There were wide green spaces surrounding
the expansive paved courtyard leading to the building complex. Even
without the benefit of augmented reality it was an attractive space. The
three story C shaped structure in front of him tilted down to ground level
on either side as if it were possible, and probably was, to run across the
roof from one side to the other. It was clad in gold reflective glass and it
looked like a giant eye peering over the horizon. Its eyeball was the
darker protruding foyer and reception area. Approaching it felt like the
building was reaching out and embracing you. The institute went
unnoticed by the disinterested well healed masses across the river. The
Shleps who spent wasted days inside a virtual world which recreated
and fantasised about a history that in the most part never happened. In
V-World's historic sims the artistic licence of its small minded creators
had lost track of what was real history and what wasn't. No one cared
as long as it was exciting and fun, which it usually was. The Doctor was
a pioneer of nothing because he passionately fought for a cause that no
one gave a shit about but him. Real questions about where we came
from and what made us who we are. He wanted to go back beyond a
barrier, a time when all data and most of humanity was wiped out.
Heathen for the most part was in denial and had been for hundreds of
years. The fact that humans had physical relationships and offspring
from random DNA like animals was titivating. Those loners across the
river forgetting humans might have thrived outside, even with all its
viruses, germs and dangers. Instead they tap into a virtual fantasy world
where every need is catered for. It was never about not appreciating
what the Major did and what Mother did for us now. It was about
understanding that Mother was our adoptive parent instead of our
creator, history confirms that. Scanning his DNA at the unmanned

security point he was at his station in minutes, albeit around 130 of them later than he had planned. There was nothing overtly world changing going on this morning. He was heading over to the reserve on the pretence of checking some plant samples. The reserve was a clean safe version of the outside, an interpretation of how it used to be. It was an area of controlled and uncontrolled plant and animal life, a wilderness for educational purposes. Touchreik was studying some random patches where foliage was left to battle for supremacy. This helped his study of the patterns to build up a picture of how things might have been in the past. This area had its weather pattern pre-set to something around the 21st Century, cooler and much more violent over the course of a year. It was intriguing how the weaker species found ways to survive by working with their environment instead of battling it. Tiny bits of algae gathering and thriving amongst the moisture stored by bigger, stronger plants and trees.

His communicator sounded, it was Prout. Touchreik sighed and tapped the back of his neck and a holographic figure appeared on his desk, around 60mm tall. He walked around a small grey square situated on the desk as he spoke.

"Touchreik?"

"The one and only."

"Enigmatic," he replied with contempt.

"We have a briefing in the concourse at 12 hundred. All departments are attending."

"Don't we always."

"Yes, we always, but in this case I think it would be beneficial for you to attend this particular one."

"Really?"

"Really, be there please. Trust me, it's important."

The Doc rubbed his chin curiously and dropped his chin on his hands as he came up close to the holographic image on his desk. Prout appeared a little bigger than his head.

"What's it about?"

"Back off please. Be there and you'll find out."

"Ok," he said and was about to sign off.

"Touchreik listen to me, I'm serious. I know we keep our relationship fairly easy going but this is one of the few orders I would give. Anyway you'll regret it if you don't, that's not a threat it's just an honest assessment."

"Time?"

"12 hundred."

"I was going to run out to the reserve, the sector with.."

The holographic figure waved his arms in the air. "I haven't got time for this, I still need to contact 4 other jobbers personally, now you can either head over to the reserve and play with your flowers or you can attend the meeting and hear what could possibly be the most important news this establishment has had in centuries."

"12 Hundred."

"Thank you and goodbye."

The Holograph disappeared and Touchreik rocked back in his chair and put his feet up on the desk. He stared up at the ceiling and wondered excitedly. Could it really be about that?

He arrived at the concourse around 5 minutes early. Three others had turned up in person and he knew them well enough to give a courteous nod. The twins from Philosophy were here, Destine and Gabriella, tall slender girls with matching outfits. Not the same outfit he noticed but matching, as if they might consult every day so as not to clash and ruin the effect of the other. Today's combo was a pair of similarly designed body suits in pale blue and pale yellow respectively. Often, they even matched in body language and mannerisms. Long blonde hair cascaded down their backs to below their buts, red pouting lips and dark eyes. Twins with differing eye colours, even Mother had a sense of humour perhaps, or a sense of style. Hill was here from I.T. leaning on a wall staring vacantly into space. Of course he wasn't really staring, he was probably still working in VR. There were a few who had attended in hologram form. Everyone else in the room were from departments that were much more engaged than his. There were technologies, sims as well as a couple from curation. He was the only real history guy in the room having been the only real history guy in the department. Certainly ancient history, his specialty being 21st Century and that might just mean this was going to be a worthwhile meeting after all.

The concourse door slid open and Wade Prout marched in and stepped onto the low stage area. Wade appearing in reality, must be important thought the Doc.

He raised his arms to silence the room.

"I want to thank you all for attending, especially those who have made a special effort to attend," he paused as if scanning which of them were physically there. Hill still looking vacant was clearly here in body only.

"I think you have probably guessed by now why I have called this meeting." There was a resurgence of chatter that Touchreik didn't engage in. He was too excited to do so, perhaps he had guessed right.

He wanted to burst out laughing and could feel stares on him. He fought to remain expressionless to avoid anyone reading him.

"Well you're right. I am sure you're all aware by now about the regeneration project. In case you have been lost in V-world for the last few months let me keep it brief because most of you will have followed this in media." A screen appeared behind him with flashing images that were familiar to them all by now. The caveman as he had been nicknamed had been all over the media recently.

"Over 20 years ago a project was launched to send a drone mission to Mars. Its brief was to recover a human organic sample from Major Zero's base. This part of the mission was a great success, however those of you who were around will remember the disappointment when it was discovered the frozen sample was useless." Pictures flashed up on the screen showing the deteriorated body of a human male. "This male had been in cryogenic suspension and the plan had been to regenerate him. Unfortunately the project was shelved after it was discovered the sample was too badly damaged to be of use. Some of you may even remember it with great disappointment." There was even more chatter than before. Excited giggles and raised voices as Wade raised his hands once more.

"You will know that after 23 years it has come to light that the plan wasn't shelved after all. In fact the regeneration department had been busy gestating a human donor body using the original DNA from the sample. This meant that they had a healthy body in good condition to use for the project. In recent weeks the transplant of the sample brain has been completed and the subject is not only alive and well but I am told he is speaking to the medical and care staff."

Cheers erupted with applause and whoops, enough to bring Hill into the room too. One or two people passing in the corridors came in and holograms started appearing around the room.

Prout waited till the applause had died down. "From what I am told they have a living, breathing specimen from the late 21st Century. How well he is communicating or adapting I can't say. The reason for today's briefing is that." There was a pause as he looked around the room.

"The reason is that it's possible but not yet confirmed," he held out a hand for calm.

"That this department may well be granted access to him.

" There was a storm of chatter in the room as it filled with excitement. Wade put his arms up trying to calm the room.

"Please people please," calm was partially restored. "We don't know, it's just rumours but I don't need to tell you how exciting this could be for us. We may get access to a 21st Century human who is aware of the world prior to the shutdown." The noise level grew and Prout was losing control but could only laugh with joy himself.

"Look we don't know yet if he was damaged or how coherent he is, we have no idea but it's important that as a department we are ready."

"I'm ready," cried one of the twins giggling.

"Ladies and Gentlemen. The procedure has been long and painful over 23 years or so. It involved Mother carrying out a normal organic birth using the caveman's existing DNA. Instead of the human being allocated he has been allowed to grow and gestate for over 20 years. That was the easy part. What seems the most incredible is the transplantation of the ancient and primitive brain into its host body. I am pleased to say that it was a success, we have in our midst a human being who lived around 500 years ago. At this stage he is fragile and getting used to his new surroundings. He is being kept in isolation until we are sure he carries no ancient bacteria that could be harmful to us."

"Who is he?" someone shouted.

"The Major Zero mission to Mars had multiple objectives, aside from establishing a colony it was to create a kind of safe house for organic life on Earth and place these samples in storage. There were samples of plant and animal life of all kinds being stored. Apparently, late in the mission that there may have been an opportunity to actually take and save a human specimen. As it happens the sample in question was already in a cryogenic state and so this 21st century man was taken along. We don't know why at this stage. Somehow and for some reason we are not party to this, the sample has been returned to Earth and thawed. There's some data which apparently comes from the historic record attached to the sample and if it proves to be true, could be very exciting for us."

He started reading from a document. "A fully functioning 22 year old male, we have to assume he would have been of great significance and authority in his time. What's of particular interest is that he seemed to be a performer of some kind. Perhaps music, from a time when there was no augmented reality or virtual learning. The people at that time would have been forced to use raw brain power to perform these complex tasks. This is seeming to be of great importance and very exciting considering the state of Heathen right now. His name was and still is Nova.

The main point is that we may get the opportunity to work with him before or during his release and we can only imagine the historic significance of this operation."

"Who?" the other twin shouted. A look of mild concern spread across Prout's face.

"We don't know yet but there are one or two obvious candidates but that decision should it come, will not be in my hands. In the meantime I think we should be prepared and so I would like all departments to put forward suggestions as to how we deal with this opportunity. We may get a very small window of access and so I want us to get as much as possible to work with."

One or two of the holographic guests went straight off line, presumably too excited to wait for anything else to be suggested or perhaps, thought the Doctor too disappointed at knowing who that person might be.

"One more thing, this is going to throw the institute out there in front of Heathen. I want no slip ups and no scandal ok?"

Glancing at Touchreik just a little longer than he needed too. Touchreik knew Prout would be dreading this project coming to him and yet there was a very good chance it would. He was right though, whoever took this job on was going right into the media spotlight. If they got access and wanted to learn from the ancient man then it would be a wasted opportunity if it didn't fall to the only 21st Century specialist in the department. He knew what Prout's problem was going to be and it bothered him too. The media were about to get very excited about this project and if the ancient man could speak and tell us about his time. He was pre shutdown, alive before the digitisation of data and its subsequent crash. He might be able to help fill some of the huge black hole in our history. The project would be of immense value to his department but all they could do now was wait.

ᚼ

A student raised his hand at the front of the lecture hall. Touchriek took this juvenile class in ancient history twice a week. It was done once in V-World and once here at the institute in reality. It was agreed that students could choose either as long as they played some part in the section. It was already an uphill battle to eliminate some of the myths created by Sims like 'Soul Battle, Sonic Wars and Land Racer.

"I have time for one more question. Yes?" said Touchriek casting an eye across the lecture theatre at a sea, now a lake of disinterested faces. A number of them seemed to be glancing at one boy in particular, as if subliminal opening the room for him.

The boy looked coy and embarrassed as he raised his hand. "Sir," he said to an accompaniment of giggles. "You mentioned physical relationships and breeding." There were more expectant titters from around the room with one girl rolling her eyes, another plunging her head down on the desk into her folded arms. The question was brought up regularly and it was either a serious question or designed as a dare to embarrass him. In either case he was well prepared and his answer would be similar to all the other times some smart ass juve decided to take the challenge.

"Sir is that right? Actual physical relationships in reality, is that dangerous?"

The Doctor cleared his throat and adopted his professional tone. Mentally trying to avoid the irony of the question as it related to his own coloured tastes.

"A very good question and thank you for asking it. Of course these days we are fully aware of the dangers associated with physical relationships between human organic life. But the answer to your question is yes. Breeding was done physically up to around the year 2118. This had a number of implications as you can imagine. Firstly the dangers of physical intimate contact and how that might expose them to disease and even death as was often the case. Secondly this practice would create a totally random DNA pool just like animals in the wild. There were no controls in place over the type and characteristics of human organic life. Strange as it may seem to us, many humans are still on the whole quite capable of breeding naturally and gestating a child till birth inside the female. Those who retain the adequate reproductive systems of course."

A chorus of eirrh and yucks filled the room and it descended into chaos and chatter.

The Doctor held up his hand to calm them. "Please can I be allowed to answer the question," he paused.

"I think it's an interesting point that I say female because this would have restricted relationships to those of opposite sexual orientation, indeed many of those relationships were also monogamous. That is they intentionally stayed with a single partner to breed. These couples would stay together for a natural lifetime or at least until they were outside breeding age. As long as they were able to produce offspring then they would do so. In many if not all cases we believe this would take the form of two humans of opposite sexual orientation."

"But Sir would they have lots of children?"

"It's possible they might have up to 15 children and this was essential for survival with a DNA pool so random. The result of this success had a negative effect and attributed to the population running away with itself into billions. We will cover this later in the course but it was in fact human success as a species that contributed to their downfall. Resources are finite and so a population many times our own seems unbelievable to us but drone archaeological surveys suggest humanity populated every corner of the planet. This is no longer the case as you know and so with euthanasia and a stable population these problems are a thing of the past."

Lots of raised hands now and it was incredible how interesting the subject of ancient history had suddenly become.

"I am sorry but these questions will have to wait till next time. Please check out the Q & A in the lesson portal and the V-World lesson guide. I have added the loce to your notes.

The class quickly packed up their things and filed out of the lecture theatre. The Doctor gathered up a few things and quickly checked he had uploaded the class to non-attendees. He headed out into the corridor to make his way back to his desk until he heard a voice behind him.

"Dr!"

He turned to see Wade Prout in the flesh running up the corridor towards him. "Glad I caught you," he said breathlessly. There was only one reason why he was here, it had to be.

"This has to be important?" he said casually

"I think you know why I'm here.'

Touchreik couldn't contain himself as the smile spread across his face.

"No."

"It's about the caveman, we have the project," said Wade.

"That's incredible news, fantastic," keep calm he thought, *we* have the project, *we*.

"Yes, we have just had notification and that's why I thought we could chat in reality, off air, so to speak."

The Doctor could hardly believe it, he felt a little queasy.

"You don't mean, me?"

"Yes."

He was spinning around now, he couldn't believe this was true. He actually felt dizzy and sick with joy. He had never known it was possible but he actually felt sick. The Doc leant against a stairwell before charging up and then back down again. Wade held out a hand to calm him.

"Algeria, Listen to me. I wanted to speak off air ok," the Professor managed to calm himself but was still panting.

"Sure."

"I have heard things, nothing concrete, just things."

"Look," the Doctor interrupted.

Wade held a hand up. "Let me finish," he said. "These things are about you and your... your tastes." Wade paused. "Look these are just rumours and if they're true then I don't want to know. This project is high profile, you understand that, right?"

Touchreik looked back at him. "Wade I hear things too, I'm not ignorant of what's said about me. I'm obsessed with my work, I don't socialise much and I come in here physically for the most part. People talk when you're not mainstream."

The Doc grabbed Wade by the shoulders. "Look at me Wade. None of that stuff is true ok. It's just stories and silly juve stuff," he shook Wade. "Ok?"

"Ok?"

"So tell me more."

"They tell me he's doing well. He's mainly experiencing a sim that mimics his own environment, at least as best we can interpret. That's the first part of our brief, to find out if he's orientated with the 20th Century sim we have created for him. We know he was from pre shutdown Eng-land in Lon-Don. He's being conditioned into our environment. Remember a leap of 500 years could be a bit of a culture shock. As of now his movements have been limited so it's not been an issue but if we are to learn from him we'll have to get him orientated. He's being looked after and has been with a mentor for a few weeks. He's been weak of course since he was transplanted to the new body. He is stronger, walking and talking so I am told. That's all I know."

"Talking, seriously?"

"That's what they say. He's able to communicate quite well with his mentors."

Touchreik grabbed his straggly hair with one hand and almost pulled it out. "How soon, how long do we have?"

"They're able to get you over tomorrow morning."

"This is incredible."

Wade turned to walk away, shouting back, "I'm glad we spoke, I have a lot to do. Don't let me down Touchreik."

He stood panting and looking at the floor.

"I won't," he whispered to himself. "I definitely won't let you down."

EIGHT

Had he overdressed for the first meeting with the subject? It was difficult to say at this stage until they had opened up some form of communication channel. He'd decided that the initial meetings would be conducted in reality so as not to disorientate the caveman. Caveman was a rather unkind nickname that had stuck but made no sense in reality, him being from the year 2015. The caveman had been given a mentor named Bluu, who'd used V-World to help bring him up to date with Heathen history, in the Doctor's opinion this was a mistake. There was no possible concept of virtual worlds 500 years ago yet regardless they had apparently used some private sims already. There could be problems with a primitive man who was already in a world completely alien to him being taken into an alternative reality. Because V-World taps directly into the brain stem it is experienced as real by the subject. They had already transplanted the brain into a new younger body, this might be strain enough as it stands. So be it, as far as the Doctor was concerned reality would best suit any initial investigations as far as he was concerned. If he was able to communicate well and they made good progress then they could use his information to create V-World sims. These would enable the exciting prospect of simulated history and creating an environment similar to that which existed over 500 years ago. There are plenty around but none based on fact from someone who was alive at that time, another reason to proceed with caution.

It was common knowledge that in and around the 21st Century tastes that formed attraction were most usually centred around members of the opposite sex. For this reason Bluu was both female and attractive. A lot had happened in the world since this fellow had been frozen, shipped to Mars and brought back. Touchreik expected he would have experienced only the most primitive levels of technology, not the complete digitisation of data and certainly not the shutdown. Everything in human history wiped clean in a single disastrous year. The Major's mission to Mars and his heroic return to save humanity or what was left of it, moreover the very existence of the saviour machine. Since then? well hundreds of years of stability, order and peace. The society that existed now had eliminated all the world issues that would have been prevalent in the caveman's world. The Doctor tapped his comms unit and took a moment to refresh himself with some background information on the sample.

As Wade had already said, part of the Major's mission to Mars had been to use the planet as a store house for organic DNA samples. The organic human was found amongst these as part of the Major Zero's original expedition. Somehow a 21st Century cryogenic human sample had been stored with everything else. No one knew how or why he came to be there or how Mother had managed to instigate his return. His records showed him to be a man named Nova. There were a number of reasons that he could assume him to be held in high esteem by his peers in 2015. The Cryogenic freezing indicated he may have been a man of means, in all likelihood it would have been an expensive process in those days. Secondly his record hinted he might be a skilled musician who could play instruments with no A.I. input whatsoever, a skill highly prized in his time and long forgotten now. There was so much to learn both personally and publicly he hardly knew where to start. The timing of this project was perfect, had it not been for the 22 year delay the whole thing might never have fallen to him at all. The record repeated how the old body was useless and he'd been stored whilst a new one was gestated from his DNA, a process that took over two decades. There was no medical cure for such an old form of decay in his body. Initially there was the prospect of simply thawing the brain, trace the data and see what could be learned until a change of heart. A simple and ingenious solution. Mother would usually gestate normal organic humans as she did with us all. Why not simply do the same using DNA from the sample itself? And so it was that a child was gestated but instead of being given life was left to grow into adulthood. This surrogate body was allowed to grow until such time as it was old enough and strong enough to become the donor. The brain was then transplanted into the 22 year old body. This would never be able to halt the recurrence of the illness that would affect him in middle age. He will almost certainly suffer that fate again as a relatively young man of 69 years. That is, when he reached 69 years for the second time. As for what to do then and whether to give him the 60 years of life he would be owed before euthenisation? It can only be assumed that we might have to cross that bridge when it arrives.

The Doc had to calm himself as he was walking through to meet the sample who turned out to be far from expectations. He stood tall and erect, smiled and showed an array of expressions. He was an interesting enough fellow for sure and had a piercing, cat like stare.

Touchreik noticed the eye damage immediately but gave it little attention after that. Apparently there had been a problem along the way which had resulted in his eyes appearing to be different colours. On closer but more subtle inspection this was not the case. In fact one retina was forced to be quite wide giving one eye a darker appearance. His skin was pale and his curly dark hair looked shiny and alive. On the whole he looked well and yet he was thin and through the open neck shirt his ribs were visible. He had no idea how much time he had or whether he should plan for a series of meetings. Having done his best to prioritise the information he needed he hesitated at diving in too quickly. First it was important to gauge the level of communication the poor fellow was capable of. As it turned out the caveman was first to break the silence.

"So what's the thing?" said Nova eyeing the Doc suspiciously. He lounged backwards on his chair bouncing his knees up and down rapidly and wringing his fists together.

The Doctor was taken by surprise. "The thing?"

"Well, you're a Doctor right, am I sick again, you wanna do some more tests on me?" Touchreik couldn't hide his expression of surprise and joy. He spoke slowly, but clearly the communication problem would not be as bad as he first thought. There would be dialect and cultural issues but his language was based on Heathen.

"No, I'm not that kind of Doctor, I'm a Doctor in history and biology. My interest is the ancient world."

The caveman looked puzzled and creased his eyebrows. "I don't get it?"

"You are from that time, are you not?"

Nova raised his eyebrows in realisation. "Oh yeah, sorry. Yeah I suppose that's true to you."

The Doctor scanned his notes. "You were born over 500 years ago in what would have been the 21st Century, that's quite ancient."

Nova unlocked his hands and fell back into his chair, spreading his legs and gripping either arm. "I get it yeah, I was born in 1947," he clenched his fists and stared at the ceiling. "The thing is Doc here's what happened. I explained all this to Bluu but maybe you missed it. I went into cryogenic suspension or whatever you call it, got frozen because I was dying anyway," he waited. "You know this?"

Touchreik nodded in amazement his eyes like saucers whilst the sample continued. "I took a gamble 500 years ago and it payed off. But here's the deal. Time didn't pass for me. Do you get that? I went to sleep in 2015 and woke up ten minutes later and here I am. Can you even imagine that? 500 years after everyone I knew has died. For some reason whilst I was frozen my brain was frozen, my thoughts were frozen. It's like you might sleep for an hour or 8 hours or even 10 minutes but you always know or have some idea of time passing. Not me, imagine going to sleep for 10 minutes and waking up 500 years later?"

This was amazing, he had never expected this level of communication.

"I think I understand. It must be quite difficult for you."

Nova waved his arms around as he indicated his surroundings. "I don't feel ancient, I feel like me, at least I did."

"Is there a problem for you?"

"Look at me Doctor, what do you see?"

"Well."

He interrupted, "Don't bother, let me tell you. You see a young dude."

"Your certainly not a dude?" Touchreik realised his error immediately, clearly this was a different use of the word dude than he knew of.

"Person, human or whatever, I'm a young man. It's been a few weeks but I went to sleep as a 69 year old guy for around ten minutes. I wake up here like I am on a different planet, it might be a different planet for all I know. But here's the best bit. I am no longer 69 years old but 22." He stood up and held out his outstretched arms and rubbed his face. "Can you imagine?"

"This is why we have done our best to ensure you have time to adapt. Your old body was ill and would not have worked for long."

"Its 2515 now ok? TVC15? You even changed the calendar system. So who knows what else has changed out there."

The Doc listened intently, leaning forward and determined to try and be sympathetic. Whilst doing so he scanned the man's features , skin tone and physique. The level of communication that he had achieved was quite a surprise and was very positive. He almost felt silly that it might be anything else. "Things have changed a lot but that's part of the reason I am here. Firstly to learn from you and secondly that perhaps I can help you learn from me."

Nova dropped backwards into his chair and sighed. "What am I doing in here? I am a prisoner in a very nice prison. Will I be a free man or am I some kind of museum piece or a lab rat?"

Touchreik shook his head. "You are a citizen of Heathen like everyone else but there are certain considerations. What about any kind of germs or viruses, your ancient DNA was used to create the new body you have. We have no idea how it will react to our environment."

The Caveman opened his palms. "What environment? It seems fine to me," turning he gazed out across the manufactured Lon-don skyline.

"Bluu has explained to you. That environment, this room and everything you see has been created to help you feel comfortable here."

He went to the window where the curtains blew lightly in the breeze. "What's really out there, Doctor?" he paused. "Doctor Touchreik, robots and flying cars. Star Wars, space ships and floating cities?"

Touchreik tried to answer multiple questions at the same time, "Of course we have drones and if by cars you mean transportation then the answer is yes."

The caveman spun on his heels realising the Doctor was being serious.

"Nova, take a seat and perhaps I could start at the beginning, I know Bluu has given you some orientation."

"Is that what you call it? We went into that video game, V-World. That knocks Nintendo right out o'the park. Hey, they didn't by any chance…?"

Seeing the Doc's blank stare he realised the Doc had no knowledge of Nintendo and this clearly wasn't the case.

"V-World is something you may have no knowledge of but we will be exploring it further. It's a very big part of our lives."

"I am getting that alright."

"Let me start with some brief history and I apologise if Bluu has already explained some of it during your inductions."

"K."

"You are from the 21st Century, the year?"

"2015."

The Doc's eyes widened. "2015, ok here's where there's a gap between what you know for sure and what I know for sure. After you were suspended there was a leap in technology. Light processing, this is where we were able to…"

"Use light like a particle as proposed by Einstein," said Nova nodding his acknowledgement.

The Doc paused. "Use light like, yes, that's right."

This primitive man was a quick learner. "That's correct and it seemed to have changed everything. Artificial intelligence and robotics went interstellar in terms of their abilities. We think the world became digital and so did all information. Books, film, design, plans, financial information. Everything. These were incredible tools available to humanity and of course technology leapt forward. At that time there was a mission to Mars by a group led by Major Zero. His colony was there to store Earth DNA samples as a kind of vault on Mars. They were also given the task of establishing a colony."

"Like me, was I one of the samples?"

"You were not a DNA sample but you were found on Mars but let's stay on track and deal with what we know."

Nova shrugged. "Whilst the mission was on Mars there was some kind of problem on Earth. A slow data blackout which spread across the globe and left society in peril. Society in its simplest terms just shutdown. Do you know how many humans existed in your time?"

"Not sure, I think it was billions, probably about 7 billion if I remember the question from who wants to be a millionaire." The caveman grinned but the reference was one of many that would be lost on the Professor. He was staggered by the figure all the same, 7 Billion against todays population of 70 million.

Nova carried on for him. "Most people were killed right, unable to survive without technology, Amazon or pizza delivery?"

"I am not sure about the Amazon but most of those perished because technology and data disappeared so fast. Unable to eat, keep warm they died out quickly and the planets civilisations became wastelands. This left Major Zero and his team trapped on Mars with no way of returning to Earth. Over the coming years they turned the space race on its head and built a return craft. They created fuel using the elements on Mars and returned. What they found when they returned were the remains of civilisation. Not just a breakdown in the system but data itself was missing. All the knowledge and history of society was gone forever. He and his team then established themselves and rebuilt humanity from the bottom up. Heathen was created and a management system was built to run everything efficiently. This system was the Saviour Machine and its servers were placed on Mars and are still there now. What you see now is Heathen, the result of this work over hundreds of years, advancing and growing."

"So that's your hero is it, the guy who built this computer thing that manages everything?"

"Tell me something, what would have been the greatest piece of technology in your day?"

Nova thought for a moment. "iPhones."

"What was this device?"

"A phone, like a little computer in your hand."

"Hand held communicators. So could you make me one now?"

"Are you nuts or what?"

"My point is that society was left with wrecked and un-working devices and technology, and the knowledge of those who were left alive, that was it. It was they who rebuilt things, restored our history from word of mouth. People knew it was possible to build these devices because they had seen them, but had to start again. It was the Major who brought together the idea of this never happening again. To build a stable society using the resources that were already lying around. Metals and other items had already been brought up from the Earth and so they rebuilt from scratch. Out of all that Heathen was built."

"This place right?"

The Doctor found he an odd broken way of speaking which was basically understandable except for occasional random words that were either unexpected or made no sense. Sometimes he might say a part of a word or just speak in a tone or say things that served little purpose. Regardless they communicated well overall as the doctor tuned into his speaking rhythm.

"Yes, all that was hundreds of years ago and things have changed. The basic principles remain though. The early management system 'Mother' or the saviour machine was hidden on Mars. It manages everything now with the help of drones. Our society is civilised and organic humans want for nothing. Heathen soon grew to reach its current population. Using drones our society was able to build this city and manage our resources. There are no wars, conflicts, over population. Most of our interactions are carried out in V-World now. We have a City which is built to serve our needs, we have V-World in which we can work and play. We have Mother. I know you have lost people but be assured you need not fear the primitive world you came from, its long gone."

"Mother. That sounds spooky."

"Not at all. Mother is the system we use to manage everything and keep us safe from the outside world."

"We have a saying engraved at the site of the Major Zero Memorial, 'One City - One Race - One People - One purpose."

"One leader."

"We have no leader?"

"What's outside?"

"You mean outside the dome? It's not a good environment."

"What happened to it?"

"Germs, viruses and an uncontrolled atmosphere."

"So the population thing?"

"New people are generated to replace those who euthanise, Mother uses the finest DNA to reproduce them."

"So are you saying no one has children?"

"Of course not, why would anyone want to have children? In your time that may have seemed like a natural thing but not anymore. That's left to animals."

The caveman scratched his head and looked confused. "So what about sex? People must have sex right?" Shooting a glance towards the door.

The Professor laughed out loud. "Of course we have sex, everyone has sex. It's a major pastime in V-World. Many groups of people meet and socialise in V-World sims and meet for sex too. It's just that we don't produce babies or as in your time simply have sex with opposite orientations. Importantly sex is now completely safe because it's done without physical contact. All the pleasures can be enjoyed safely."

The Professor was starting to grasp how big this job was going to be. He was eager to learn from the caveman but had to be patient.

"Like sex parties, you mean?"

"That's a very good way of putting it, sometimes there are parties. Perhaps we can visit one soon. I can show you how things might have changed."

"OK Doc." Nova looked wary of such an idea. "Thanks for the invite but maybe another time."

The Doctor felt he was making a breakthrough. "I know I have been brief and you will have a million questions but, if you agree we can meet up regularly and discuss our time. Once you are more liberated then I and Bluu can help you settle better to your new environment."

"All this is fine, sex parties and living in computer games and what have you but when do I get out of here? When do I get my jet pack and transporter?"

"Jet pack?" The Doc looked puzzled and it wouldn't be for the last time.

"Beam me up scotty," said Nova rolling his eyes.

The Doctor was unsure as to whether this sample's intelligence was going to be a hinderance after all.

"These sex parties as you call them are a common pastime for many of us. There is no physical contact so it's completely safe. If you so choose then you would be made welcome, even if you had a preference for the opposite sex only."

"You're not saying the whole world's gone gay, are you?"

"I don't know what gay is?"

"Never mind."

Nova spent some time discussing physical relationships as if this was completely natural between humans. The Doctor had become intrigued by this prospect and found he was being vindicated for the way he felt about Ramona. Years later he might say this could have planted the seeds of doubt in his mind. Maybe he wasn't a crazy pervert, maybe he and all those others still had physical needs despite the risks involved. Nova didn't seem concerned by the possibility of illness and death through physical sex and neither was he concerned about the random DNA pool. Many of his views and behaviours could only be attributed to animals. He told the Doctor how very few people had died through physical sex in his time. The Doctor had doubts about his account but for now it had been an informative session. The main thing was to try and secure further contact.

"So you want to use me as your class history project?"

"You are not a project or a lab rat or any of the things you express. You are a man who was alive before everything shut down. You are a part of the history we lost and have tried to piece back together from personal memories. I am simply fascinated by your time, your way of life. Our records of human history were built from the memories of men over 400 years ago." Touchreik studied him as he thought things through.

"What do I get? Can you get me out of here?"

"In good time, yes." Touchreik knew he had no real influence over Nova's freedom but made the insinuation all the same.

"Ok I am cool with that, what sort of stuff?"

"For me to learn about your way of life and the things we know about your time."

"Right."

"I know this has been difficult, but can I ask a couple of questions."

"Fire away."

The Doctor paused. "We believe that many people worked for their governments, instead of the other way round."

"That's kinda true. Don't you have tax anymore, leaders to make decisions?"

"No, we have no tax, I am unsure who we would pay. Our society is built and maintained by drones and Mother. We do not pay her for that."

"What like an army of slave robots?"

"No, relatively few are humanoid. Most are designed for specific tasks and these go unnoticed."

"Wow, no taxes."

"Yes but there are very few earnings too. There's the basic level of life which suits most. Some prefer more and so Bitcoin exists to allow for these who want extra items."

"Cashless society?"

"Tell me about relationships, many of my students are confused by this."

"What's to tell, you meet fall in love, get married?"

"Is it true about monogamy?"

"For most people yes. It sounds like all that has gone out the window."

The Doctor looked over at the window but saw nothing.

"Well, we have relationships, special others. People live together and share space in twos, three's or small groups. No one has children because Mother would take care of that. They are allocated for parenthood and can be kept, swapped or given away. The V-World sex is a very different matter and is in no way attached to the relationship. Unlike in your time, sex for us is an entirely leisurely activity whether part of a relationship or not."

"I suppose it always was for some, perhaps red XXX channel were the pioneers and we didn't even know it eh?"

"I don't know what a red XXX is, who were these people."

Nova grinned and waved a hand.

"If you agree then let's leave it at that for now and meet again soon."

"Ok cool."

The Doctor got up to leave and shook the man's hand one more time, noting to wash them at the earliest opportunity. He had to try and let people see that he could work with some of these ancient ideas. He turned to leave and the door slid open.

"Hey doc."

He stopped and turned around. "You're gonna get me out of here, right?"

"Be patient. Very soon you'll be ready."

NINE

After that first meeting things felt different with Ramona. He'd already arranged for Ramona to be waiting for him that evening. Asking Duke to switch to manual as usual so he could not be observed and then for her to release from her charging station. Whilst she dressed he lay on the bed and for the first time in a long while appreciated how much he enjoyed her company. Ramona sat at the dresser and prepared her makeup, running the brush through her bright red hair. The atmosphere seemed lighter than usual and they had laughed so much as he explained about the sample.

"They were physical then, you know that?" he said

"Of course they were physical, its natural I've told you its natural a million times?" tilting her head and looking up at the mirror.

She was right about so many things and it helped the way she could often reframe concerns he had. Later he set up the VR in his bedroom to immerse them in an ancient sunset across a mountain range. The amber light had highlighted her features and complemented her skin tone. He was liberated this evening, given permission by an ancient man to share his deepest desire with his accomplice guilt free. When eventually they shared that desire between them Ramona had never felt closer physically. When it was over he'd asked her to stay with him and they slept entwined in a dizzy heap until morning. He woke to hear the whisper of the wardrobe door closing. Whilst Ramona remained hidden from the world once more he got himself dressed and reactivated Duke. Like a child taking off a blindfold his sage would continue as if there had been no break in proceedings. In the months and weeks that followed he felt a growing realisation of how positive his relationship with Nova was becoming. Keen to remember that this ancient man was a subject of his research and to keep the barriers in place. Having feelings for an inanimate object, merely a drone that was programmed to react with him in a pre-programmed way no longer scared him. On occasion missing her company and starting to imagine she was special, like a real life partner. The underlying fantasy was that it wasn't possible to design and build a hundred Ramona A Stones who had identical personalities. He knew deep down that was nonsense.

The real work with Nova progressed well and it became apparent that they had indeed made a connection regardless of his professional barriers. Bluu would never be far away but showed herself to be as alluring as many had suggested she would be. Tall and graceful with long features and hair that sat close to her scalp with clean skin. Her demeanour was always calm and receptive, proving an excellent choice for acting as a mentor and guide to his sample.

The time was well used and they'd learned so much from, and about each other and their respective lives. The meetings became less and less formal and they would talk and debate outside of the official research time. Inside the work had continued whilst around Heathen media interest was growing and humans in reality were keen to see the caveman who had travelled through time. He was protected from the knowledge that his celebrity status was growing by the day. He was also becoming more and more relaxed and safe in his environment. It was only then that the Doctor felt the time was right to work further in V-World. He was very excited at the prospect of accessing the caveman's mind and experiencing his reality from 500 years ago and being taken back to 2015. Nova had no choice about orientating himself with V-World if he was to continue as a citizen. He'd heard negative comments from Heathens about how and why he should be allowed to be a citizen. The population was precise and as one Heathen euthanised another was given as a surrogate. This would deprive someone of life who deserved it. This was all fancy and was going nowhere as an argument, Heathens population would remain constant and anyone deprived would never know they weren't born.

The day arrived when Touchreik felt it was appropriate.

"It's time for us to explore your world in a V-World environment, designed by you and controlled by you."

He had been surprised and excited when the Doctor had explained this concept. He realised he could go home and experience his own world albeit for a short time. Until now his concepts of V-World had still been very primitive in assuming the V-World sims were designed by a supercomputer. Of course they were, but only with the input from an intelligence of some kind.

"So I can create my own world, like back home?"

"In a way yes, it's very complex in the background but as far as we are concerned it's a simple concept. When you visit V-World your brains input sites are short circuited at the brain stem so that you can experience the sim. Feel the wind, pain, cold or hot. There are also emotional inputs too. These can simulate chemical processes in the brain mimicking feelings. Useful in certain sims, think of these as electronic drugs but purely natural."

"I get that," he noted.

"Well as far as your brain is concerned, locked away in that dark box of a head, all its experiences are real. It doesn't know any different because all the signals from eyes, ears, skin and other senses are genuine. Its signals are telling it so."

"It's definitely real alright but I still prefer the helmet version. The stuff I did with Bluu was amazing."

"The helmet is fine and works just as well as a permanent comm unit at the back of the neck."

"Not ready for that yet."

"That's fine. So the process of designing your own world or sim as we call them is quite simple and I can show you how to do that. Our brain stem is highjacked with incoming sensations. To create a sim we simply adjust the settings and carry out the process in reverse. It takes a little skill and training at first, its easily contaminated by fantasy and random thoughts. Once we have the setting right then you just build the sim in your mind. The system will build up the world you created then it's just a case of setting rules."

The caveman still looked puzzled.

The Doctor held out his arms. "The laws of physics that apply in your sim. Such as can you die in your sim? What are the pain settings, is human flight possible, teleportation? Once the rules are set you can decide on privacy. Either it's a public sim or private, invite only. It's your world."

"This is crazy. If it wasn't so real then."

"Perhaps you understand now why it's so important to us?"

"Awesome, so they don't have to go to a shitty office or meeting?"

"By that you mean work for gain as in the 21st century? No of course not but many do, there are Heathens who use these to test their resolve. Daily monotonous tasks which achieve nothing are a test for these people. As far as we're concerned it would enable us both to meet in your time, for you to show me around."

"Ha, so I create the 21st century and show you around?"

"Exactly."

"Good, we'll start tomorrow but, in the meantime, I have some news. It's likely you will be going out into reality very soon."

"Wow, that's bloody fantastic, thank you."

It was true that with no influence exerted by the Doctor, Nova was deemed ready to face Heathen. This didn't stop Touchreik absorbing

some of the credit. His DNA was safe and had not mutated into
something that maybe harmful or similar to that on the outside. The
human sample had proven himself to be mentally able to face the new
world he was being brought into it.

"There are plans for you and Bluu to go outside, meet people and
see the world of Heathen."

"Yes!" Nova stood up punching the air.

"Nova, you have experienced V-World, you know how good it is.
Over centuries the real world has never had a need to be aesthetically
pleasing."

The caveman grinned again. "You're sounding embarrassed by
your city?"

"No," he lied. The place he came from Lon-Don sounded so
incredibly exciting, colourful and random. There were thrills and dangers
as well as the grime of ancient times which seemed so thrilling.

"Shit you never been to LON-DON obviously," he said mimicking
their odd pronunciation of it.

These were exciting times indeed. He and Ramona were enjoying
each other's company, he was immersed in this project and was being
recognised for his work. The media interest in the ancient man could
only help him in his wish to specialise in ancient history. The man had
been thrust into a whole new world and had adapted well, it was time for
him to meet real Heathens.

The caveman entourage consisted of Bluu, the Doctor and a few
security personal who might just be useful in cases of over exuberance.
Nova had no knowledge of the partnership proposals and job offers he
had been protected from. On the whole though his presence would be
greeted with excitement. The Doctor met them as planned when they
picked him up at the Magport. He climbed into the back of the Mag
skycruiser. As they headed out into the City it struck him the caveman
might be right, he was a little ashamed of the city he loved so much.
More so after everything he knew about how the incredible 21st Century
streets must have bustled with life.

They headed out across the city in an auto cruiser merely to
survey the metropolis of Heathen from above. Rolling across a beautiful
and vibrant city with parks, gardens and more importantly humans.
Nova had been so incredibly excited at what he saw through the
windows. High speed transport systems whizzed above and below.
Buildings that were built in coloured glass that seemed to defy gravity.
In the leisure areas families would be seen playing and walking. It was a
perfect picture of a perfect future just as Nova had imagined it would be.
It was such a picture because that's exactly what it was, a picture built

from the thoughts and memories gained from Nova. He was provided with the environment he wanted, at least a view of it.

Eventually Bluu had taken a sideways glance at Touchreik and explained she was about to drop the VR windows. As she did so the smile on Nova's face melted away. Without the VR switched on he could now see the real Heathen though the windows and the landscape looked very different.

The environment was made up of grey block buildings and unkept urban spaces. There were very few people dotted around the landscape, some of those could have been humanoid drones. It was not always easy to tell from up there at that speed. There were no parks or open spaces to speak of and no smiling happy families anymore. There were dots of colour where certain areas had been presumably designed for real interaction. The entrance to buildings of importance were surrounded by a much improved landscape. A place for visitors to disembark from VR magpods and go inside without becoming disorientated. In the backstreets, rooftops and other spaces it was purely about practicality. Nova felt a wave of disappointment and fell back in his chair.

"Everything in this place is false."

Bluu tried to console him but he had to learn about the world he now lived in. Nova pulled his arm away and turned to look out the window.

"What happened to you lot?" he stared at Bluu with no reaction and cast his gaze to Touchreik. "What happened to us? Born in a machine, living in a machine and then looking at a world that's created by machines. You're all living in a lie."

It might be natural that the caveman would not understand civilised normal life in light of the time he was from. The Doctor struggled to understand how they had been forced to live in such an unruly and random environment. They had no control over climate or weather so were forced to live with whatever nature threw at them.

"Nova, this is the modern world and it's going to take getting used to. That's what these trips are for, perhaps you would be best served by experiencing it and we can talk later." He didn't answer.

These were tough times for the chap but he was coping well, these things would be a shock for sure. Over the coming weeks things improved greatly and Nova was taken to one or two of the most important sites in Heathen.

They went on a trip to Major Zero's memorial site where several hundred Heathens greeted them. They were held up for some time as he talked and chatted with many of them. All this was proving positive for everyone. In fact real world visitors increased dramatically in the weeks surrounding the caveman's visit. He was able to tour the facility and admire the artefacts whilst observing the incredible story of the Major's accomplishments. There were media drones on hand at every opportunity to record the event for others to enjoy at a later date. He took time to meet many people personally and they were connecting with him and his oddities. He seemed to be surprising them with his ancient humour, communication and strange dialect. The people of Heathen were warming to him and were ironically willing to overlook some of his primitive ways and practices.

The Major Zero memorial was a verist display, that is a simulated environment that existed in reality. It was like a sim but in the real world which added to its novelty value.

The general public had been sectioned away from the group but followed and observed as they walked amongst the displays. One of the curators had welcomed them, a man that the doctor knew very well. He talked them through the Major's incredible adventure which had ultimately lead to Nova being here.

"A mission to Mars lead by an incredible human being."

Mock ups of the Martian base built by the major and his team were available to walk around. They were shown how they might have survived underground for the most part by adapting and expanding the cave systems. At last they entered the sample area where the team held their collection of DNA samples. Beyond those endless draws containing slides was a new exhibit which until now had been ignored. It was a mock-up of the pod that had contained Nova's frozen body for all those years.

It was a fascination to him and the first time he had seen that actual vessel that had contained him for 500 years. He took a look around and posed for media before the crew moved on.

"Bigger than I expected," he whispered to the Doctor as they moved on.

They visited life support and food production centres which fascinated the Doctor no matter how many times he saw them. An ancient civilisation with primitive survival methods were able to transport those methods to a barren planet. They were growing organic food and were becoming self-sufficient except for building materials.

At last they were taken out into the open. Here it was explained how the shutdown had occurred. Simulated recordings were played of the Major's final communications with Earth and then silence. The curator waved them through some doors into an outer area. Here they were greeted with actual size models of the ship they had built to get them home as well as the chemistry involved in creating fuel. Everything else was pulled together using the combined brain power of a small team of scientists.

"Not only did the Major succeed in his mission to bring his team home but he went further than that. He rebuilt society from nothing and committed us to the saviour machine, a way of avoiding the problems that had haunted humanity." He paused.

"Many people have asked me why I believe him to be the greatest human being and I struggle for an answer to that question. But if there is an answer then I am sure, ladies and gentlemen you will find it here."

The crowd gave him an emotional round of applause. Touchreik had noticed how subtly the caveman and Bluu had become a little less guarded with each other.

He soon realised that his was not the only company the caveman was enjoying. His suspicions were confirmed one day when he arrived at the apartment. They were both sitting in the lounge and were clearly in Sim together. He could see this was some intimacy and this confirmed his suspicions. Of course they might have been merely sexualising socially with others but he knew different. He simply closed the door and went home, communicating later that he would not be coming over after all. Touchreik chose not to acknowledge this but was concerned about the effect this might have on Nova.

They visited the medical facility that had gestated the brand new body he now enjoyed. Nova was growing into the role and his new world, becoming an ambassador for history and the 21st Century. He toured the medical facilities whilst joking with staff who treated him like a returning son, and why not. They had spent 22 years caring for this lifeless body in a specially designed gestation pod. Enabling him to grow to a point where he could be taken out of his dying middle aged body into the one he has now. He was given a series of medical examinations and passed them all with flying colours although they were in the main just photo opportunities. At last the staff proudly showed him into the area where he had grown up. Two enormous test tubes standing against a wall and there, floating in green liquid and perfectly preserved was his old body. Touchreik was impressed that this didn't faze him in the least as he continued to pose for images and media. There was even a mock-up of the cryogenic pod he had been removed from, identical to the one at the Majors memorial, the original was presumably still on Mars. Once more the crowd cheered as he stepped inside before popping his head out to wave for the crowds. The medical staff presented to an audience of staff and students the full story of his regeneration. The near disaster at finding out his old body would soon be useless and finally an ambitious plan. To keep him frozen until a brand new younger and healthier body could be generated. They shared jokes about him as a younger man and the time they worked on his brain. Laughing at the silly things he said as he was first woken.

Nova was quickly developing his own personality and independence. He was given an extended but duplicate accommodation outside of the institute. Here he started to contemplate his future and develop his skills. It wasn't long before he began using musical instruments alone with no artificial input. The Doctor was hypnotised by his tales of ancient times when humans would gather in their thousands to watch musicians perform. They would turn up in reality to see these amazing humans do what very few were capable of. The connection between Nova and Bluu was also clearly blossoming. Nova became moody at times and would make accessible demands from the people around him. Sometimes he would sulk for days and other times he would be joyous. On the occasions he talked to Touchreik he might confide that he missed his own world. Even though he was here in Heathen and still on Earth he felt like an alien. These thoughts haunted Nova and then in days they would blow over only to resurface once more. Bluu convinced him to go back to music and had provided endless musical instruments from his memory. At last he seemed to be settling and began to write music once more. The Doctor was one of the first to see him play music on a guitar. It was an amazing sight to watch a man sing and play at the same time. Not so much the act itself but to know he had absolutely no technology or intervention. His brain was so highly tuned that he could make fingers move across strings at amazing speed and agility. It looked similar to when anyone else played but he was completely unaided. There was soon talk of him performing in reality to show people how he could make music without any sort of digital help. His fingers would pluck strings and make amazing sounds so like the sounds produced digitally.

Touchreik, Bluu and many of the others would be in awe at his skills with guitars and they had some made to his requirements. He now owned a whole range of ancient instruments and 2D recording devices. In many opinions they were no match for digital but he preferred it that way and so did his friends. The sound was authentic and imperfect, just like it might have been hundreds of years ago when this skill was so prized.

If you asked him, decades from now Touchreik would say it was probably around this time that things changed and his perfect world began to unravel.

TEN

Most Heathens were aware of the aberration living amongst them, even without media, the news had spread. On the whole the reaction was somewhere between indifference and positive. There were purists who aired their views about his background and DNA stream. Just like any other group, Touchreik and his friends talked about him, bolstered by the chance of an inside scoop. Gaga took another bite from her algaen slice and rolled her eyes to the heavens. Duke had set the exact recipe behind a firewall which served to increase its kudos and judging by her reaction, its flavour. The monthly physical meeting had become an unexpected regular occurrence. When the idea was first muted the Doctor agreed in the expectation it wouldn't last three months, yet here they were, still going strong after a year. The idea being to arrange a physical meeting at one of their accommodations on a regular basis. Since the caveman had gained such notoriety recently the Doctor's home had become the location of choice by unanimous decision. Watmoor had crept through the door, his eyes darting. Almost as if he might see the caveman in a cage in the spare room, rattling the bars and eating his own hair.

Dabbing the corner of her mouth Gaga continued. "They'll have adjusted his DNA when he was incubating, that's why he appears normal as you and me."

"She has a point," said Watmoor as he leaned sideways into the Doctor's ear. "Natural born from random DNA by a physical method? Then you tell us he is completely normal." He sat upright and did that knowing snort he often did. "No physical deformities to speak of, and as articulate as you and me."

"It's possible," interrupted Drake. "Hasn't anyone considered he was one of the lucky ones. Perhaps, that's why they froze him in the first place?"

Watmoor put a hand up. "No, I think its utter fake, the whole thing, wait and see. Too obvious if you ask me."

Gaga stopped eating and looked the Doctor in the eye from across the table. "Come on Doctor, spill the beans. I'll know if your lying."

There was silence as her expressionless face peered deep into him. The clinking of knives and forks stopped until she couldn't hold it anymore and the whole table fell into fits of laughter.

Nova was becoming a popular subject of conversation around Heathen and the number of people who wanted to physically interact with him was also growing. It worked both ways, it wasn't often most people got to see crowds close up. The skin blemishes, the weight and size and the looks of many were very different from their virtual selves. In small ways, so obvious later, the relationship Nova had with Bluu had gone beyond professional. This didn't sour the relationship that the Doctor had with his subject but it certainly didn't help either. On more than one occasion he saw them touch each other surreptitiously. Other times the caveman might touch her arm and she would appear to pull away but a little slower than one might expect. Nova had made no secret of his physical desires, in fact they were natural in the 21st Century. The Doc was secretly envious of the relationship and was confused as to why he would have such feelings. Bluu was a quiet unassuming soul, harmless in her own right. For a female she was once described as alluring and he didn't disagree. He often caught her looking at him whilst he worked or chatted socially with Nova. As if she were analysing him or his methods, maybe even assessing their relationship.

Touchreik regretted working with Nova on self-created sims so early on because of how quickly he picked up the procedure. He'd recently created a private sim of his own which was exactly the reason he wanted him to gain the skill in the first place. It had immediately backfired because Nova set it to private and the Doctor knew that Nova and Bluu were spending time there together.

Were they in a relationship? Surely not. Nova was over 500 years old even if he was physically 23, not that it mattered in V-World of course. None of it mattered in reality either but it was the principle of the thing. Then there was the physical question, the caveman would have no qualms about pursuing that in reality. It came naturally to him and Bluu would have to be aware, particularly as a female. When he tried to bring it up with her she'd laughed it off.

"I'm not blaming Nova," he'd said. "You have to understand it would be the most natural thing in the world for him to attempt sex with you in the physical world if he desired it."

"I don't think you need concern yourself Doctor, I've been working with Nova a lot longer than you remember?" That comment was hurtful and uncharacteristic of her. After that he dropped the subject and never brought it up again. He observed, but decided he wouldn't intervene further, clearly Bluu was either ignorant or irresponsible. There was no way of knowing how a man from his culture might react if the urges took him. As the apparent relationship between Bluu and Nova deepened then the level to which Nova could be obnoxious grew proportionally. His manners towards those around him befitting some kind of rock god from the 21st century. Something by his own admission he had never entirely been. His notoriety in Heathen was growing along with his occasional excessive demands. The Doctor took this to be a positive indicator of his growing confidence and autonomy. In time deciding to take a different approach in his concerns for Bluu by discussing random DNA further with Nova. For what it was worth he might as well have been talking to the juves in one of his lectures. The caveman's belief in random DNA breeding and physical relationships was endemic.

"All that ended when we became citizens of Heathen. You, of all people should understand the dangers of physical breeding. I don't wish to insult you, but those practices are best left to animals and humanists."

"Humanists?" said Nova.

"Animals," he paused for effect, "and humanists."

"They sound like the most normal people around here to me. A little crazy I grant you, having sex, babies and eating real food," he said sarcastically.

"Nova don't say things like that, it's disgusting," said Touchreik.

"The system we have has worked perfectly for hundreds of years because we're not animals. Juveniles are allocated according to the need of the population and resources. Genetically perfect and developed outside the human body, safely and humanely. Older citizens celebrate euthanasia at 130 to make way for others. Where can that possibly be wrong?"

"It's not natural," said Nova leaning back arrogantly on the back two legs of his chair.

"It's better than natural. You told me how your time was almost entirely heterosexual, that same sex citizens were different than others. To think that you come from that time and still agree with these things. To be able to have partners with only half the population?"

"Because that's how you make babies, can't you see that."

Bluu joined in. "But that's what animals do, we have lives to live, we can't make babies inside our bodies and not live, it's a much better process we have now."

Touchreik held up a palm. "Can we please stick to facts, I don't think it helps to make judgements. My job is to determine the facts."

"Sorry," said Bluu.

"I don't think we are going to communicate 500 years of development in an afternoon. I want to talk about leaders, governments."

"I'm bored," said Nova folding his arms.

"Nova please, just a little more time. It's my job."

The conversation continued in and around various subjects pertaining to the 21st Century but it worked both ways. There was immense comparison with how things were right now. In the end the group became exhausted but exhilarated by it all. In the end it was another move in the right direction if not slower than anticipated.

"Good night Nova."

Touchreik wasn't sure if it was Bluu who first suggested Nova do a show like in his own time. He point blank refused at first but the subject kept coming up and everyone agreed. Heathen people would come. Humans from all over Heathen would come out of V-World and into reality to see him play, they were convinced of it. Over time others picked up on the idea and he tentatively agreed. No sooner had he uttered the words 'maybe' than plans were being drawn up for his shows. Media celebrities like Pierrot came out of nowhere to meet him and finalise the arrangements. There was a sense of urgency as if he might change his mind, which incidentally he did on numerous occasions. The band were put together and rehearsals began in V-World. Easier because they could perform in front of the full audience and test everything in a V-World situation. The early performances were planned to take place in V-World anyway with a final show in reality. Heathens were to gather in the market square and surrounding areas to watch the caveman perform music live and in the flesh. Nova had insisted he play with no artificial assistance whatsoever which was the attraction after all. It was a busy time for them all, especially Nova and the Doctor's work was neglected. There was less time and chats took place during casual conversation rather than formal meetings. In all the furore Touchreik hardly remembered when he first heard the word 'Migration'.

Once more, Mother had solved a problem that Heathen didn't know it had. Just like the caveman thing it dominated media, at first separately until the two stories joined hands.

"That's what they're calling it, Migration," said Gaga.

"It's about time isn't it really, I mean to have to wait until you're 130 to euthanise, it doesn't suit everyone." Watmoor leant across the table and filled his glass.

Gaga was unsure. "It's not so much the need, it's how people will take it. Will they feel obliged?"

"What if they do? I think it will become more acceptable once more and more people take it up," said Watmoor.

"It's not for me, not quite yet," said Drake pulling his pointed beard.

Gaga continued. "I have a kindred who euthanised 60 years ago and he absolutely loves living in V-World. He says he has more friends now than ever."

"Euthenisation is one thing but to do it early that's quite different," said Watmoor.

"I suppose so, I expect the more senior citizens will take it up first."

"What about juves? Is there a lower age limit?"

"Apparently not, they're saying it will be open to all, imagine that?"

Nothing was confirmed but there were very strong rumours about the instigation of 'Migration'. For hundreds of years, organic humans were entitled to live to 130 years old. Should they survive that long which in the most part they did, then they would have the privilege of euthanasia, a cause for celebration. It was a time when everyone got their chance to leave the physical world and make space for another, younger person. Once they had done so then their physical burden on Heathen would cease and their mind was uploaded and they could exist in V-World forever. The living were still able to visit them and they could continue in a different plain. This system had worked well for centuries but the rumours of 'Migration' were a little different. People were saying that there were plans to drop the age embargo and enable anyone to euthanise at any age. This would open the door to all Heathens to move into V-World on a permanent basis at any time. The idea, if it proved true was immensely exciting and so it was with huge joy that the Doctor finally had it confirmed to him that it was actually going to happen. Not an option he would take up at this stage of his life but an amazing opportunity for many. After the reality shown by Nova was announced, Touchreik never met a person who didn't claim to be going to it. It could be attended by hundreds of thousands and might be the biggest live event in centuries.

At that point, no one was aware how much Nova's involvement had been in not only its introduction but the very concept. Touchreik was one of the last in the team to hear the announcement.

Nova had seemed uneasy at their last meeting, nothing official but they would still meet in reality. Nova had his own real world accommodation and had self-designed a lot of the augmented reality elements himself. They sat back in easy chairs on the edge of a blue ocean as waves caressed the white sand. Further up the beach palm trees swayed gently in the cool breeze. They had sipped a drink and chatted inanely but something wasn't right about Nova.

"Hey Doc, erm," he stopped.

"Is there something wrong." The Doc was a little panicked at first as to whether he may have missed some kind of breakdown.

"I need to tell you something."

It had to be Bluu, it had to be. "Sure," he sipped his drink thoughtfully.

"You know about the migration thing right, going into V-World, being able to do that at any time?"

"Yes I've heard about it."

"The thing is, they asked me to launch the thing, to open it up officially like, to everyone, at the end of my last show in the square."

"Really?" It was natural he might, given his popularity at the moment. Nova looked pained but he had clearly thought this through for some time.

"They said it would be good to make the announcement."

"Sounds great."

"I ain't finished yet," pausing to down his drink and stare into the empty glass. "I've also agreed to be one of the first, actually the first to take it up."

The Doctor was stunned. "You're going to euthanise?"

"We."

"We?"

"I'm taking Bluu with me, she has agreed to come."

"I see."

It wasn't a surprise in light of their relationship which had been becoming stronger over time.

"It's a chance to go home, I know you understand," he said with regret. The Doctor just stared into the distance at the cliffs as a flock of birds rode the currents.

"I've looked into it and I'm taking Bluu with me, back into a world that I can create. One that I remember where I can live the life I always dreamed of. It's going to be an enclosed sim."

Touchriek turned sharply, this was getting worse. An enclosed sim was beyond restrictions, a place where no outsiders could come in or communicate. Likewise insiders. If there were others in the sim then they would usually be bots. An enclosed sim was perfect for those egotistical enough to want to rule their own world. "Enclosed?"

"Yep, I'm creating the life for me and Bluu that we want. I'm planning to continue as a rock star like I dreamed of as a kid. Bluu can pick a career she likes, we discussed lots of stuff. Acting or modelling. I've got plans to grow old there too, just like it's meant to be. We are going to age, retire and do everything that's meant to be. Probably even die there, really die."

"You know an enclosed sim works both ways, no in and no out?"

"I'm sorry man, honest I am but I think it's a great opportunity for us. I didn't jump in a freezer 500 years ago so I could live forever."

"Wow." The Doc stood up. "Not long then."

There was so much he wanted to say at this moment but didn't. How he considered him a friend, how he had helped him accept himself and the way he was. He always felt like the time would come to say all that but now it might well never come. Instead he just twisted his shoulders and squinted in the sunlight. "I'm proud of you, really I am. For standing by your principles."

"I feel like I can go home, forget reality, forget what happened and create the life I wanted in my own way. I miss the 21st century. 2515 feels like another planet and if it does then 'Migration' is my ride home. I'm going Doc."

In some ways the Doctor understood how he felt. Nova and Bluu had obviously discussed the work Touchreik was doing. Nova was going home to the world he loved, even though it would never be real, they would both soon forget that. Nova for his part felt for the Doctor, that his work was important and he should learn from Nova's past.

"Another thing."

"There's more?"

"They've explained to me how this will work, about my mind being uploaded to the sim."

"You ok with that?"

"I will be, but the thing is. I want you to be able to work with it after I'm gone."

"You're not serious?" Touchreik would never have guessed in million years this was coming. He almost collapsed and had to steady himself. The caveman's entire mind will be made available to continue the research into 21st century life.

"Promise you'll never let me down Doc, there's some crazy stuff in there?" said Nova with a wry smile.

"I won't let you down. I promise," he whispered.

Right then he was so overjoyed that he never properly registered the intensity of the next statement.

"I am trusting you with what you find, it's up to you what you hide and what you reveal."

Touchreik had little idea how profound those words would become in the future.

He was going to lose a friend who had brought so much to his life, teaching him to accept himself for what he was. He had understood there were many ways to live over the ages. He had taught him to go with his feelings and needs without judgement or without harming others. His relationship with Ramona had felt so much more relaxed since meeting Nova. She had noticed too and even though she was still his personal filthy secret he didn't feel it was so wrong. The memory trace in itself would provide Touchreik with a gold mine of memories, fantasies and imagination. Decades of work in trying to rebuild the world that Nova came from.

He turned and walked into the apartment and straight out the door before there was any way Nova could see the tear in his eye.

Wade wasn't too pleased when he heard. "We had a good run, when this started we never dreamed we'd get so much access. You did a great job there."

When he explained about the memory trace he jumped for joy. "That's an incredible job, I never doubted you Touchreik, never. This could be really something, funding and support, everything to us."

They didn't know then how those high hopes would quickly evaporate.

With Nova's endorsement the rush for places on migration would be incredible. The only limitation would be how quickly the individual minds could be uploaded and sims produced. The space in V-World was digital and therefore limitless, and most of the talk was of how exciting and better it would be to turn over the organic human DNA pool quicker as people euthanised younger.

What puzzled Touchreik most of all was how Bluu would cope, effectively going back in time 500 years, their relationship was no longer a secret but her willingness to give up her life to live in an ancient sim environment was a puzzle. The motives behind that would only become apparent many years later. This was indeed the answer to everything for Nova, he could go back as he always wanted too. To live a normal life in his time that would operate to his rules and build a sim for himself and Bluu.

The last time Touchreik saw Nova in reality was on the night of the final show when he and his band performed. At the end of the performance he stopped the show to announce and officially launched the Migration project. The crowds went crazy as he played one last song which he had written about his time here as if it might be a different place, an alien planet just like he said. When it was over he waved Bluu onto the stage. Taking her hand they walked off together to the cheers of the crowd. It was possible everything changed that night at the end of the most incredible event in living memory and the start of a new era for Heathen.

Touchreik walked home that amazing night through crowds of people who had come together in reality, at the same time so alone in his thoughts. People nudged and pushed by him unnoticed as he wandered the streets. Nova was gone and he had so much to do and learn from the man's memories . It was time to get to work but he would no longer have the benefit of explanation from Nova. He'd made it clear his sim would be enclosed, there would be no guest access and the Doctor had agreed. He wanted to live in his own time without disturbance, just he and Bluu. Touchreik began work on the memory trace the very next day. The work would involve decades and millions of hours but it would be invaluable. In some ways it could prove more valuable than Nova himself. Deep in the subconscious would be information, dates and facts he would never have recalled consciously. It was deep down there where he discovered some of the most puzzling anomalies of them all.

What was it Nova had said? Something about, 'Do with it what you will, don't let me down?'

ELEVEN

"The human mind is unlike any other data set." Touchreik stared up at the thirty four faces looking back at him. "After all I am assuming you all have one." He paused to allow a ripple of low giggles to wash across his audience. "A simple comm implant can take you to other worlds, communicate with friends in V-World. Your sage never forgets a date, a recipe or a single memory from your life. Yet still we are powerless when it comes to deciphering the human mind."

He twisted the pointer in his finger and thumb. "The closest we came to replicate the mind is in fact Mother and even she still relies on our mental inputs to make human emotionally charged decisions. All other artificial intelligence is specialised and can perform any specialised task perfectly. Whether that be cooking a meal, flying a spaceship or managing a complete transport system. We don't know where the mind is or where it goes when we lose it." Stopping for affect he looked down at the hypnotised faces.

"All humans were created by a magnificent machine we call mother, all except one that is. Four years ago I was given brief access to the complete mind trace of a young man from the 21st Century. You will remember him as the caveman, frozen since the year 2015 regenerated in 2515."

Touchreik still felt the pain in the pit of his guts when he said brief because brief it was. He'd screamed and complained after it was over but to no avail. The Caveman project was shutting down at a days' notice, only a year after Nova had gone. In the short time the project existed his obsession had driven him to continue work at his own accommodation, often long into the early hours. To do that he had taken home data which was strictly against regulations. Proportionally it was a tiny amount but on the night before that last day he had been close to a breakthrough. In fact less a breakthrough and more of a mystery. Prout announced to him out of the blue it was over, shutting down.

Being the fellow he was he kept calm although his head span with anger and the veins in his neck felt like they would explode.

"I have a few things to collect from the lab," said Touchreik.

"Sure, you ain't being thrown on the street just yet."

"I know."

As he went to walk away Prout had called out to him.

"Touchreik." He stopped. "I know your upset, you worked hard on this and I appreciate you taking this decision with a level head."

Touchreik didn't respond because he wasn't taking it with a level head, he just knew he had to get back into that lab one more time. He simply nodded.

"Good things will come from this you know that, Professorship allocations? The media won't do you any harm. Those allocations are only months away."

"That sounds good, who knows?" he could feel Wade Prout's eyes boring into him as he walked away. As he marched purposefully back to his laboratory he thinks one or two colleagues passed him, made greeting but he can't be sure. Once inside he placed his palm on one of the data files and an array of data appeared in holo in front of his eyes. He only wanted a small amount of data but it had to be the right data. He found the files he was looking for but there was no time to filter through, as long as what he wanted was in there then it would be fine. He motioned with his other hand and the file instantly offered an option.

File size too big - Cancel, Re-do search, trim.

He hit trim and a message popped up.

Done.

He had been working on the mind trace for years but getting a grip of how it worked was a difficulty. Developing a method called arrays. This was a way of joining together information and data. Thoughts, feelings, fantasy and preconceptions all joined together to make a thought. With partial information it was difficult to make sense but arrays helped.

He had no idea what the attitude of the establishment would be to him holding data at home. He didn't make it known but he didn't wish to use regular storage. It was best to be very discreet and so he came up with an ingenious solution. He took a part of Ramona's data storage and partitioned it off. Then he used it to store the data he brought home with him. Ramona would have no idea it was there and certainly wouldn't miss the storage. The final chunk of storage was rather bigger than normal but she should be fine. Once he returned home he opened up his closet and powered up Ramona, then he added the chunk of data and closed it again.

As of that day the project was closed and Touchreik moved on with his life. He would continue his teaching and his lectures.

"Ladies and gentlemen, I have spoken on the subject many times and have spent many years studying primitive man…"

That had been it as far as access to the trace was concerned. Touchreik had protested and argued but got nowhere. He felt that Nova had given the trace to him personally and had never considered he would be deprived of access. On what grounds could the institute be unwilling to discover its past. It was useless and in time he gave up protesting. He had no support because no one really cared about history, certainly not this kind. In the end they wore him down and he withdrew. They had no idea that he held some data but it was patchy and incomplete but he carried on in his own time. Resources were virtually non existent for this kind of work. Prout was right about one thing though, his Professorship. Within the year he was made a Professor and had realised the dream he had held since a young man. It felt tarnished all the same, a kind of thank you or apology instead of a recognition of his achievements. Nonetheless Touchreik accepted the title and accolade and moved on with his life and enjoyed the celebrations.

"Professor Algeria Touchriek. Professor Algeria Touchreik." Yes it sounded perfect and it rolled off the tongue perfectly. After years of work he was finally recognised as the absolute authority on 21st Century history. The bitterness had finally faded and he enjoyed a very special night at his award. In fact he couldn't be blamed for indulging in one of his little pleasures. It was more of a worry now, his… habit. That's what he called it. Just his habit.

He had tried not to, he knew that it was crucial he kept his image up. There would be no need of talk and scandal, not now. He had started the evening by making some promises to himself. They were the same promises he broke every time he made them, but he made them all the same. He was being recognised as a Professor tonight but that made no difference. He was not going to take too much alcohol during the celebrations and in honesty he had been quite controlled. He had however already agreed with himself that there would be no need to carry influencers because he would not need any this evening. Until he had met Jester Mayfield in the hallway outside. He had looked so casual like he might just be passing by.

"Hey, how are you what are you up to? What a Professor, really that's amazing, well done. I suppose you are celebrating and I don't blame you, good on you. By the way I have some wonderful… Oh but you don't."

"Hey, I'm good thanks maybe I'll give you a call tomorrow."

"Tomorrow that's fine but I doubt I'll have anything tomorrow."

So maybe he could grab a few now for tomorrow when he is away from so many influential people. He could stash the influencers and take them tomorrow and could celebrate properly on his own.

So now it was no great deal, he had broken his own promises number two but it was ok. There were 4 influencers in his pocket for tomorrow and he headed back to the party.

There, fine its ok.

The clock seemed to be going backwards as Wilks continued his story and the room became colder. Not physically colder but mentally colder. There was still a buzz of excitement about the place but he felt like a spectator. Maybe he might just have one of those little red party pills, just one. The conversation went on so long in his head that he became agitated by it.

He remembered screaming out mentally to himself, "For the love of Heathen just have the thing. It won't kill you."

So he had just the one and that was that, it oiled the wheels of conversation and helped him relax, until about half an hour later. By the second one it was game over. He didn't even resist because he knew where this was going and who it was going there with. He hadn't bothered to say goodbye from his recollection because his stinking little perversion had taken over. Now it was the only thing on his mind and it was not only going to be the last time but it was going to be the greatest time. So far so good because everything seemed to be going just as it always did. The denials, the lies and finally the failures. After that it was easy until the next day and he had to live with himself and the charade he had created. The personal counselling sessions, guilt, acceptance and finally peace of mind once more. Of course right now as usual none of that mattered. He could only think of Ramona. There was nothing else on his mind as he walked out of the hall with his gelded chain rattling round his neck. A respected expert with a title to uphold and a reputation to think about and he knew full well where it would end.

"Duke," he said calmly.

"Professor?" came the reply from a detached voice in his accommodation.

"Please be kind enough to switch to manual until morning would you?"

"Manual Sir?" Duke sounded concerned, as if the Professor might freeze to death if the climate control ran on auto.

"Yes, Manual please."

"Sir, if you wish I am quite capable of being discreet and can operate completely in the background."

"Duke I want you to switch over to manual operation and erase data for the last ten minutes."

"Sir."

"Now please."

"Thank you Sir."

Then there was silence and now it was Professor time. Time to enjoy and indulge, to drop another red one. He was going to make this the last time for sure.

The influencers were in full effect now and so the scale of his depravity was no longer apparent.

"Good evening Professor," that warm husky voice was unmistakable and she stood in the doorway behind him. The light making a perfect silhouette of her curves. He wanted her so much tonight and he wanted her to be in a good mood too, in the mood. It was a special night and his inhibitions about where his emotions lay were deeper in his mind. He turned around to take in her form and as she came closer, leaning over she kissed him physically on his head. A physical kiss that crossed the boundary of civility and decency, not only with a human but a drone too. He knew however that this was indeed the boundary and tonight as always he was going to cross that line with all his being.

"Professor Touchreik, Professor Touchreik" and later, much later he would be able to wonder on how it all began. To become a Professor from an unknown Doctor in an unknown profession.

His feelings for this drone were inescapable and he loved being her puppet. She could dangle his emotions on a string with a push here and a pull there, just at the right time. Now he was a Professor then things would need to change for good. He had gotten away with this for long enough and should not push his luck. Through everything now he became more absorbed in his work and kept his secret and used her sparingly. It was all going to change once he was a Professor but it didn't. His status made a difference at first but eventually everything between him and the drone fell back to normality for want of a better word. He could never see it changing but it was about to in a way he never saw coming.

TWELVE

The man destined to change the Professor's life forever was called Jagger, and he was beautiful. There was no other word for it, he was striking and had impeccable DNA. Eyes of blue that reflected light, clean, unblemished cream coloured skin. His wispy hair golden hair flowed like straw across his shoulders. In any conversation he listened intently and his eyebrows would drop, as if any whimsical thought might be life changing. It was the eyes of Jagger that struck him the moment he looked up. Touchreik had finished a lecture and was packing away whilst the audience filtered out through the doors or holo's disappeared in the chairs they sat. He was lost in his thoughts and didn't hear the boy approach.

"That was fascinating Professor Touchreik." He looked up and almost gasped at the figure before him before composing himself. The boy held up his hand and pinched his forehead in greeting.

"My name is Jagger," he pronounced as smooth as silk like Scheagger, his tongue merely dancing on the letter J in a whisper. If he had known that moment would be the beginning of the end for him and for Ramona, if he had known what it meant to everything. He might never have held up his hand, he might never have chatted with the boy or lost the rest of the afternoon under his spell.

It was rare to find such enthusiasm for pre shutdown history but for a boy so young he was an inspiration.

They had chatted for 30 minutes before the Professor suggested they continue their conversation elsewhere. He picked up his things and they talked on the way to the transport, in the transport and to the cafe. The conversation was seamless from the moment they had met. The rest of the afternoon evaporated as they sat and chatted about the past, both historical and their own.

"Can I trust you with something Professor?" said Jagger mid conversation.

Touchreik paused and narrowed his eyes. "Of course."

The boy's eyes lit up and he held his palms up then fingered his long blonde hair. "I feel I can. You might think I'm crazy but I have a private collection at home of," he paused. "Of artefacts."

"Ancient?"

"For the most part yes, I am able to acquire them from the outside."

"How?" said Touchreik leaning forward lowering his voice, intrigued.

"Naughty," he said wagging a finger.

"I get them from the scavengers," he said.

The scavengers were drone expeditions who would head out across the planet and excavate elements from the ancient cities for recycling.

"How is that possible?"

"I don't want to give anything away and I won't but. When the scavenger drones go outside they gather materials. Then they are taken to the recycling areas and broken down into their basic components. Copper, lead, gold and then reused."

"Of course yes, but how?"

"I have a way of intercepting items of interest," said the boy proudly.

"You have these artefacts stored inside Heathen? What about screening, viruses?"

"Don't worry Professor they're safe."

"How can you know that?"

"I have a contact who brings me these artefacts, tested, sterilised and clean."

"That's incredible." Looking round to make sure no one would overhear. "You're sure they're safe."

"You silly man, I've had some of them for years," he said touching the back of the Professor's hand.

"I'd love to see them."

"Really?"

"Absolutely."

"I keep them at my accommodation, it's a fetish of mine."

In no time they were in a mag pod and heading over to the physical location of Jagger's home. He was so excited about his collection he hardly stopped describing it along the way. By the time they arrived Touchreik knew every piece in detail and was overcome with excitement.

Once inside the sage welcomed them both. His accommodation was noticeably sterile and bare. It had a cool odour that hinted of chemicals or cleaning product. Jagger had set aside one of his spare rooms as his own personal history museum. The lights came on as they walked in and there was a central island with artefacts laid out on top. The walls and shelves were also adorned with shelving and displays. Most of the artefacts were unidentifiable, either mangled or damaged metals or bits of electronics.

"What do you think?"

"This is incredible, what a collection."

Jagger stood proudly with his hands clasped below his waist as the Professor walked around wide eyed. After his first sweep they came together to begin a tour of the room with Jagger explaining what he knew of each piece.

There were items that had once been decorative and made of what would have been precious materials. He also had examples of precious stones which stood and sparkled in the display lights from their tiny stands. On the central table were the bigger items. In the centre was a large yellow piece of plastic which was smooth and curved. To its right was obviously a wheel. It would have been used on old mechanical transport. It had been cleaned and polished to reveal a silver grey material.

"There are lots of things that won't survive on the outside for hundreds of years, the pollution and decay. These items for one reason or another may have been sheltered from the elements until they were exposed and found by the scavengers."

"This is one of my favourites," whispered Jagger with a knowing grin and pushed a hidden draw in the central island. It slid out slowly to reveal an array of items held in velvet cases. He handed Touchreik a pair of thin cotton gloves and put a pair on himself.

He took an item out and held it up to the light. It was a small slab, on one side it was glass and on the back it glistened like gold with a band of silver round its edge. Touchreik gasped.

"Is that what I think it is?"

He handed it to him. "An ancient comm unit."

"Amazing. These were conventional electronic devices you know?"

He studied its smooth surface. "It's beautiful."

"I also have the inside of one of these," he said pointing to the item sat in his special draw.

"An amazing collection Mr Jagger. Thank you so much for showing me."

"It's marvellous to share it with someone who appreciates such things."

In the end Touchreik offered Jagger the opportunity to come and see his work the following day. He was very eager to do so and the next day was the same but in reverse. Touchreik guided him around his work and studies and gave him some insights into the primitive man.

The more time they spent together the more infatuated Touchreik became with him. Mesmerised when he talked, wishing him to continue so he could just watch his lips move, read his expressions and look into those eyes. It wasn't long before they became inseparable and others backed off. He found life to be quieter these days, Gaga and the others called less and less, perhaps as he had withdrawn into himself. Media had made much of the primitive lifestyle and as such it may have rubbed off on him. He didn't mind because it almost suited his purposes. An interest in primitive 21st Century society that was so far removed from their own. There were often huge points of contention on the subject. It didn't take long to learn this boy was different and his enthusiasm was addictive.

At first the boy would come over to the institute of his own accord and take an interest in the slow laborious simulations and assessments of 21st Century life. Touchriek felt whole again, he felt like he and his life was of interest to someone. It was inevitable that they began to socialise and interact outside of the studies. On occasion Touchreik would join Jagger and acquaintances for V-World sex but this was mostly just social and with friends. Over time they accepted the relationship for what it was. That they might become life partners in the more official sense. Things moved fast and Jagger was given clearance to enter his accommodation and he likewise with his. They both knew where this might lead them and once they were together they would be eligible for Juve allocation as a couple.

Touchreik had resorted to spending less and less time with Ramona. He explained to her that he had a human relationship and she was very understanding about it.

"Are you physical?" she asked.

"No," he explained and almost felt guilty as if he was telling her he no longer desired such things that he wanted to be normal. In some ways she might have been correct, he did want normal. Perhaps he could bury the guilt and shame of it all forever.

She didn't show signs of jealousy or concern. Jagger completed his studies and naturally joined the research team of two.

Never getting bored with the endless dredging through data. There would often be months of work just confirming things they had suspected about 21st Century life. Although the Professor had underlying concerns about how Ramona fitted into it all he was probably at his happiest. Like the final glow of a dying lightbulb be had no idea his life was about to take an incredible upward turn before it came crashing down around him.

Like any relationship there were secrets and not just the obvious. There were secrets within the research too. At first they were anomalies and Touchreik was unsure why he kept them from Jagger. It was that he felt an affinity with Nova because he was a friend and at the same time he had made the promise to him. He would feed data across to Jagger to build into arrays but not everything, some would be held back by him. The data he held was patchy and ran up a lot of dead ends. Jagger had full access to Duke his sage and he would gladly give any information that was required to Jagger just by the asking. Glad it was safe from prying eyes and Ramona would never give access to anyone but him.

Now that his data was safely stored he would be able to work on the anomalies within it alone. These were tiny details which on their own could be explained away but if he joined them up it became confusing.

The first one was the name 'Nova'? The mind trace looked like he had no knowledge of that name prior to actually being regenerated in 2515. Of course it was a stage name and not his real name. If that was the case then surely he would still have knowledge of it? Instead he remembered his own name as Vic Jones? There would be a perfectly reasonable explanation somewhere but he thought to keep it to himself for now.

Then there was his knowledge of light technology which was puzzling. In fact it reminded him of a conversation they had early on. Vic or Nova as Touchreik knew him had an incredible amount of knowledge on light technology, a technology developed long after he was frozen. Clearly not possible but again it could be explained away. Light technology as a theory went back to the 1800's and Einstein. By that token its feasible that Nova had read up on it or seen some kind of lecture or media. There was also the possibility that Bluu had taught him in depth about light technology. After all it was a common everyday process these days as electricity might have been in Nova's time.

There were various other bits and pieces but one in particular haunted him. Clearly a powerful dream or fantasy. In most likelihood it was a related dream which can embed very deeply in the mind. It was likely a dream because it was so faded and grey.

The data set had enabled him to view the incident or fantasy through Nova's eyes.

He was a young man as Touchreik had remembered him and he was walking in a park or nature area. He was approached by a man who was much older, and they began a conversation. There were strong emotions like fear, apprehension and then joy. He took the old man by the shoulders and hugged him closely. Then he pushed back asking him, "What happened?"

Then it fades to black which may represent a suppressed memory or lower level memory.

There are frantic voices as they speak over each other. Nova was shouting and confused. Then the visual came back on and he was staring into that face again. An old man with a grey beard, who looked tired and scruffy. He could smell him quite perfectly. He smelled of earth, he smelled of humans or humanists. He had replayed it many times and the only conclusion he could come to was that the face was actually his own. Nova was staring into the face of Touchreik yet decades older. He knew it to be correct and yet it was an impossible scenario and had to be some kind of dream.

Then he heard the man speak, when he said the single word then he was convinced it was his own voice.

'Black-star' a word that meant nothing to him now but would one day become the centre of his universe.

This may be false or contaminated but he was seeing a memory that had never happened. Nova was gone now but even though that was true then how was it possible to see himself decades older than he was now? Everything else of less significance was passed on to his partner Jagger and the following 18 months passed quickly, anomalies became less important. Until the first in a series of disasters.

Touchreik would never have been surprised it might come but hadn't expected the conversation to be so casual. They were working at home late one evening.

"Algeria, we have to discuss something," said Jagger.

"Yes?"

"It's about." He paused, "It's about the drone in your cabinet."

The Professor's heart was pounding, his head span as he tried to think of some plausible explanation. His hands began to shake as he lost complete track of the task in hand.

"What's it for?" Jagger didn't look up, he continued working as if it was the most natural thing in the world. The Professor was mortified, his voice was shaky as he tried to respond swallowing hard.

He thought for a moment. "What do you think?" He challenged him now, giving him the opportunity to say it out loud and be done with it. Would the boy be so naive as to provide his own reasonable explanation? Jagger's face turned red and his voice started as a murmur until he finally screamed, throwing a glass against a wall.

"What do I think?" he said spitting out the words with a venom he'd never seen in him before. "I think you keep that fucking thing out of the way because it's been hacked and reprogrammed. It's a fucking good-time drone, designed for physical pleasure. That's what I think. I think you don't give one single shit about me, your career or your filthy self, that's what I think."

He stopped and stuttered as he tried to suck in oxygen, his lips quivered and his face was twisted in pain.

The Professor held up his hands, trying to reason with him but he was lost in his rage. "Listen I can explain."

"Are there others? How many do you own?"

A strange question to ask, that there would be other drones for this purpose but not unusual for people like him.

"Just this one," he said looking out the window.

Jagger threw everything off the table and stormed out leaving the Professor whimpering across the table. The nightmare scenario that had woken him in a sweat many times was becoming a reality. Jagger would report this, probably to Prout first. Prout would be fuming after trusting him with so much but would still try to contain it in house, begging Jagger to keep it to himself. He wouldn't of course and soon the media, the people and his friends would know what they had always suspected. That he was a sick individual who craved physical sexual contact for his own ends. He went to bed and waited. He imagined he might never leave the house again. That the next morning there would be calls from media and none from friends. Prout would be in touch to ask him not to come into the institute he had brought shame upon. But there was nothing, not that day or the next.

A week went by with no word and during that week he even had a conversation with Prout who seemed completely himself. At least for now, Jagger had kept the scandal to himself. It was a full week before a communication and Jagger arrived at his door and he went to open it personally.

"It has to go," said Jagger as he pushed past the Professor into the room.

The Professor followed him in rubbing the back of his head, Jagger stood with his arms folded looking towards the bedroom cupboard where she slept.

"Did you hear me?"

"Yes. Have you...?"

"No I haven't told anyone and I have no intention of doing so but it has to go."

The Professor looked at his shoes, aware of the implications.

"I know," he said slowly as tears fell onto his coat.

Jagger unfolded his arms and walked past the Professor and out the door.

"See you tomorrow," he said as he walked away. That was that.

That night he took Ramona out of the closet and she began getting ready as she often did whilst he lay on the bed watching her. She could sense there was something wrong and he knew that he would have to bring it up sooner or later.

"Finish getting ready and we can sit by the fire and have a chat," he said and left the room to set up the AR in the lounge.

She must have sensed something was wrong but they spent the evening together. The Professor explained the situation to Ramona, that he would have to have her euthanised, about the relationship with Jagger and everything. He even took time to explain that she was a drone and was designed for pleasure. There was no real surprise when he explained this, just a realisation as if she already knew.

Later he made the call and they headed up to the sector with her in a transporter. Finding themselves where they had first started their relationship, they went inside.

"Hey old friend."

"Hi," he said eyeing the drone. She stood tall in her heels with arms folded and looked around the room. Littered with circuit boards, body parts and V screens of various types.

"Let's just be agreed here this is a direct return. No coinage?"

"Yes. On condition."

"Dismantled, yeah, sure no problem. I can use some of these parts but that's a deal." He squeezed her upper arm and stroked the side of her breast.

"Goodbye Ramona."

"Goodbye Professor." She smiled for the last time.

"Ok, let's get this done. I'm a busy man." The Professor nodded.

"Sit honey," the dude said and pulled over a small dining chair and grabbed a tool from the table. Ramona sat and looked up at the Professor smiling as if she might be about to get her hair done.

The dude took a tool and slipped it into the back of her head and her eyes closed. The Professor simply turned without saying a word and walked towards the door with his head down. He had little time to consider this, Jagger had been pretty insistent and it had to be done by tomorrow. As he approached the door the dude shouted him.

"Hey, you want this."

The Professor turned and the dude was holding up a small piece of plastic between his thumb and finger.

"What is it?"

The dude rolled his eyes. "The Lightchip man," he said

"The Lightchip," the Professor whispered to himself.

"Of course," he reached out and took it from him and turned to walk away. "I nearly forgot," he said.

Nearly forgot he thought. The programming of Ramona along with the upgraded knowledge she had learned during their experiences together. Not to mention his precious files that all seemed very insignificant now. He slipped it into his pocket and walked off into the night. As he did so he noticed a small waste drone scurrying around in the darkness, he paused with it between his fingers and was about to drop it. The gold label glinted off a street light and he stopped himself. Then he dropped it back in his pocket and continued on his way. As expected Jagger returned to the work the next morning and nothing was said about the matter again. They both continued their work and the relationship between them survived. Getting rid of Ramona had not solved his underlying problem. He still fantasised about her, the physical relationship was something that could be replicated perfectly and yet it couldn't. Life had settled down over the years and the caveman project in the main became forgotten. It was left to just the two of them to continue with the work.

THIRTEEN

The Professor would later recall how he first became suspicious or perhaps aware might be a better choice of word. He became aware of changes in Jagger that were inconsistent with any organic human. Years later he would laugh at how obvious it was, and yet he was willing to pass it all off with the lamest of excuses.

The pair were working late into the night which was not unusual. Unfortunately another thing at the time which was not unusual were the power spikes.

The humanists were becoming more disruptive recently. Over the years graduating from a bunch of eco nuts who were a quirk in society, living on its fringes to a fully-fledged nuisance to normal people of Heathen. There were rumours about how they had grown in number on the outside. If they breed naturally as some say then they were completely unregulated in numbers or DNA. If it was true that they were scavenging off Mother's systems for food and resources, then this might destabilise Heathen. Drake had heard there were millions of them out there, living like animals. Some said there were a handful who barely survived outside with most dying in infancy or through other means. They were using physical organic breeding methods to produce a generation of juves who had never stepped foot inside Heathen. It was well known that the outside harboured viruses and germs of every kind. What was certain was there were growing numbers within Heathen and their attitude challenged every form of decency. They shunned technology and prophesied doom to anyone who would listen. They claimed the reliance on technology which had served humanity for hundreds of years would end in disaster. They had recently begun a new tactic of purposefully disrupting power supplies and transport systems causing aggravation. There were reports of graffiti or physically attacks on drones who were carrying out legitimate tasks. Not content to live like animals they wanted to take everyone else with them.

On this particular night the spike that knocked out the lighting and the systems lasted for only a few seconds but was particularly deep.

So much so that Duke had become confused and had to be rebooted. The reboot process went on in the background but Duke had mentioned it later. He never stopped functioning or carrying out his duties. This seemed to be the catalysts to what followed and the changes in Jagger's behaviour that made Touchreik suspicious. It was a day or two later when it all began.

The pair were sat opposite each other chatting about something quite inane.

"Tomorrow is Tuesday, would you like to switch days and we can visit the reserve instead?"

Jagger simply closed his eyes for around 10 seconds and became completely expressionless. 10 seconds is a long time and at first Touchreik thought he might well be concentrating on his answer. He spoke not a word in response until he opened his eyes and continued the conversation as if nothing had happened.

"No, I'd prefer to keep things as they are, it makes more sense."

This behaviour happened a few times in the days that followed and continued although less frequently. The time between the incidents widened but they had a particular resonance for Touchreik. These kinds of niggling problems were familiar to anyone who had spent considerable social time with a hacked drone.

Touchreik was familiar with this behaviour with Ramona and had adapted to it quite naturally with her. He wouldn't acknowledge it because in her mind there had been no pause in the conversation. Having discussed it with her it appeared there was absolutely no break in time for her whatsoever. Once he was aware then he would simply wait and then continue his conversation normally without making a fuss. He mirrored this behaviour with Jagger and so presumed he would have no idea of his suspicions. The problem was that Jagger was clearly no drone, he was a DNA human. One look at him would tell you that. His flawless skin was by no means flawless, not in the way a drone's might be. His mannerisms and movements were very fluid and cumbersome just like a human. He displayed all the traits attributed to organics and this made Touchreik feel quite unnerved when he decided to test Jagger.

Drones varied in quality of build dependent of their primary tasks but Jagger was obviously not one. It would be laughable to suggest such a thing just by looking at him. The old Turing tests were first developed to see if a computer could fool humans into believing it was intelligent. Since their inception they had moved on because most computers would easily pass such a test. However there were more advanced tests that had been developed for drones. Strangely enough the test might more often be used to convince a drone that it wasn't organic as opposed to the other way around. On occasion a high quality drone, particularly humanoid drones that were designed to interact with humans might need convincing. These advanced Turing tests had been developed to try and prove to A.I. drones that they were not organic life. So the Professor decided to push on and settle his mind, silly as it seemed at the time.

Turing test number one was tiredness and fatigue and so preparations were needed. It was unlikely that any drone would show signs of fatigue in a given situation. Most would work at 100% efficiency until they shut down, but never tire over time.

It took the Professor a couple of weeks to put together a series of experiments in which he painstakingly planted failures. This would force both of them to work all through the night without any prior knowledge of the length of the task in hand. This particular experiment could not be halted midway through and involved a series of nuclear measurements. These had to be precise from beginning to end for the experiment to work. On three occasions they were forced to start again at the beginning for fear of losing the materials and the results. This went on for 18 hours and it was clear Jagger had become as fatigued as he was, something that would not happen to a drone in the same way. He would rub his eyes and his face looked pained, finally he sat down and fell asleep in a chair. Admitting defeat Touchreik woke him in the normal way and sent him home to get some rest.

The following week there was another incident and Touchreik decided to push on with the tests and moved on to number two. 'involuntary reaction to unexpected outside stimuli.'

Touchreik had devised a simulated quantum experiment which placed Jagger in a darkened room. Working by lamplight so he could see the elements in the darkness. Touchreik then pretended to go outside and left Jagger concentrating in the dark. The room fell very quiet and Touchreik was sure that Jagger believed he was alone in the room. He slowly sneaked up behind Jagger and dropped a glass flat onto the floor. The noise erupted like a gunshot in the silence and Jagger almost leapt out of his seat in shock holding his heart. He took a moment to calm himself before complaining to Touchreik about frightening him half to death. An impossible reaction from any drone and another failure.

Touchreik apologised for scaring him and passed it off as just an accident.

Emotionally Jagger was passing all the Turin tests and yet the micro shutdowns intermittently continued.

The more he tested Jagger the more cruel and silly he felt. There was one final thing he could try, it was particularly cruel and he was cautious about doing it but the opportunity came along sooner than expected.

They were cutting up samples in the nature park and he was using a manual digger to uproot the tiny trees they had planted. Jagger was bent down on his hands and knees and the Professor was stood above him. He looked down at the exposed skull covered in thin golden locks that rained over his knees as he crouched. This was his chance and he slowly picked up the shovel and pointed the sharp end towards his partners skull. He would have to be careful to cause enough damage but not too much. The Professor swung the shovel round and gashed the edge of Jagger's forehead with the blade. Jagger screamed in pain and grabbed his head as blood ran down his right eye. He stood up with blood running through his fingers cursing at Touchreik who apologised profusely. He had observed all the involuntary reactions as the shovel swung at his face and his reaction to pain. Most importantly he was bleeding from the wound on his forehead. They bandaged him up and carried on with their day. Touchreik decided he would have to back off in case Jagger became suspicious. Instead he left it a week or two before he managed to manufacture the final and most difficult test. An evening of reminiscence. He planned it so that when Jagger arrived he was running through some home media. These were images and video that were held by Duke which showed his youth and juve years. In honesty Touchreik was all but convinced that there was no way Jagger could be anything but organic human. Still he knew that no drone could produce media of their youth and Juve. Drones had no youth or juve because they were manufactured. By now though he decided to push ahead all the same. He invited Jagger to join him and they laughed at the images that Touchreik claimed to have stumbled across.

Before they began work he happened to ask Jagger whether he could see any of his memories some time. He didn't seem put out but said he didn't use his auto memory builder. There was nothing particularly unusual in that, but he would have at least some memory media. In fact Jagger had numerous 2 and 3 dimensional memories showing him at various ages. Despite the behaviours it was becoming clear that his drone suspicions were ludicrous.

This didn't stop him from withholding information from Jagger though, he just didn't fully trust him. The relationship was cooler now and his thoughts would occasionally turn to Ramona and what he had done to her. He would often wake up at night and peel the tiny plastic memory disk that contained her personality and memories of their time together. He would rub it between his thumb and finger smiling as he did so. Then he would stick it back in its resting place. Touchreik's feelings for Jagger soured over time whilst he craved his old desires. If not with Ramona than with any physical soul.

The following morning he contacted Jagger and said he might have a day off and that he shouldn't come over. He went into his room and opened a bedside draw and reached underneath. He felt around and retrieved a small piece of plastic that was fixed to the underside. He slipped it into his pocket and left.

There was a place for gratification, for scratching that itch. The scratcher might never live up to Ramona but at least it would be physical. There was always lots of organic life in and around S063. The Schoneberg or Ganymede districts had entertained Heathen's most colourful clientele for decades. The organic life on the streets was split into rough categories. There were the majority like him who wished to be invisible and even though they were off grid they could be seen by others here. The head would be stooped low and no eye contact would be made as they purposefully scurried from street to alley. Able to walk three blocks and honestly say they had witnessed no one. The problem was that they were physically here and even though they were not here digitally there was an unerring discomfort. In a state of mental invisibility its best to look at the floor and go where you're going . In this way you could pass a close friend or associate and not even know it. The others were the more dangerous and they seemed to have given up on the idea of personal shame. They almost revelled in their deprived tastes and didn't care who knew it. They walked around proudly and loved nothing better than to bump into an old friend. Even better if it were a professional, clean and upstanding old friend. They would never think twice about slapping you on the back knowingly. That look in their eye, the grin giving them the self-gratification of knowing that some people hide their desires from public eyes. There had been one occasion when Touchreik had stumbled on a person known to him. An associate from the institute, at least he thought it was Oliver. Their eyes had met for a mere fraction before they had both crawled off into the darkness. Was it really Oliver, here in sector S063? Maybe it was but next time they met he detected no hint of knowledge in his eyes. Not a glance or stolen stare and certainly no knowing wink. He would never know but he had assumed Oliver would be feeling exactly the same. Was that really the Professor? perhaps not.

He was satisfied with his pleasure and it made him feel a little less human and a lot more humane.

He reached into his pocket and felt the small chip he had taken with him. Rolling it around in his hands he felt his eyes welling up and moisture running down his face. He looked up and around at the passing faces but was calculating in his head where he was. It wasn't far from here, maybe a few blocks and he headed off on foot. He arrived at the door and thumped hard on the rattling steel cage that protected it. The hatch opened and the dude peered out through the slit.

"What the fuck do you want?"

"I have coinage, I want to talk to you."

"What you want man."

"To speak to her.'

"Go away."

"Open the door right now or I start raising my voice."

The hatch closed and the bolts were heard being slammed open and an arm reached out dragging him inside.

"What are you doing here."

"I have the chip, I want to talk to her."

"She's gone man, not much left I sold the parts."

"I want to talk to her that's all."

"I can hook the card in but this isn't a communication portal."

"Just once."

"You pay me man, and its five minutes top level and that's it your out."

"Five minutes."

"It happens once, ok?" The dude wandered into the building muttering to himself and sitting down at the desk. He tapped the keys on an old 2D keyboard and it lit up. He held out his hand for the card and Touchreik drops it into his palm.

"Gimmi a minute."

"You know much about drones, real lifelike drones, undetectable?" said Touchreik casually.

He smiles and then laughs. "Ain't no such thing my friend."

"A drone that might be humanoid, pass the standard tests, even bleed."

"I told you there's no such thing." Once more their eyes were locked a moment too long until the dude looked back at his screen once more.

Touchreik looked around at the chaos around him, clothes, shelves with body parts and full synthetic humanoid bodies hung naked from racks.

"Listen have you come here to twist my boat."

"No, I am asking you as an expert."

"Not that you fool. This, get over here and look at the screen."

"I see nothing."

"It is nothing, that's why."

The dude pulled the card from the slot and threw it across the floor. "It's blank, there's nothing on it."

"You mean she's gone?"

"Look mister, she was never here, you get it. She was a drone."

"You said she was on the card, everything, her memory of us, her personality everything."

"When I gave you this card she was on there."

The Professor collapsed backwards into the chair knocking tools and instruments onto the floor. Jagger, it had to be Jagger, he had found the card and deleted her. Now it was very different, now Ramona was gone forever and he could never get her back. Why had he been so stupid.

He stepped into the street and pulled his coat around him as the change in air hit him. Not just poorer quality than deeper in the dome but greyer and heavier.

The sound of thumping music came from opposite and Touchreik crossed the narrow street and pushed into the red neon building.

A Wasabi & Rush would calm his nerves and he sat by the window in a self-serving table. The Villa of Ormen was an establishment he'd never visited before. Once inside amongst the neon heads started to come up and the eyes met a little more readily. It was noisy and stuffy inside and the atmosphere felt cleaner if no clearer than outdoors. At least the chill had gone and the blue green neon gave a calming effect. Almost everyone glanced at him whether blatant or surreptitiously as he approached the booth. He tried not to stare as he passed a female dressed in a flamboyant pink costume with feathers protruding from her headgear. He had to look away as the stare was challenging him. She was sat with a man who was clearly a drone, he looked up disgustedly as he passed. The pair were sitting and chatting as if the whole thing was normal and the rest of the establishment seemed to be quite excepting of the situation. Sitting on a high stool the Professor tapped into his comms device and ordered his Wasabi & Rush, 40/50% ice, low glass with citrus uncrushed as he always had it. Moments later the glass was ready with a tiny ping he clicked to accept and it popped up from the table top in a small draw.

He stared out through the window and watched people passing in exotic dress, wild and free. He sipped his drink and the hot acidic liquid burnt his throat but heated the front of his head.

Ramona was gone forever now, bravo to Jagger, he had never seen that coming. Jagger was gone too of course, the whole thing was over for sure. Whilst he had the chip there was always a way back but not now, he almost laughed at his own naivety as he started his second drink. He'd always been a loner but now he felt lonelier than ever. Then he saw someone he knew, at least that was his instantaneous thought but it was the dude. The dude had come out of his place and was standing in the street. There was no automatic transport this far up and so it would be manual if he was waiting for transport of any kind. He looked edgy and nervous, looking up and down the street until suddenly he began walking. Touchreik didn't know why but he felt something and simply downed his drink and left. He had scanned on the way in so his coinage would be auto deducted. As quick as he could he grabbed his coat and pushed through into the street.

Falling into the street he caught sight of the dude disappearing down a side alley but he kept checking back, forcing Touchreik to duck out of sight. He was forced to wait till the dude made a turn before running up to the junction to catch him. He was heading deeper into the chase and out of the public areas. At last he turned up a wide street and sharp left and by the time Touchreik had caught up he had disappeared. There was a narrow and very dark alleyway with a dim light at the end. Touchreik took a chance and started to move up in the full knowledge of how far from the populated areas he had come. By now he was on the very fringes of the chase by all calculations and might struggle to get home. He had to make a plan quickly and decided to push on, he was committed now. Onwards he went and the atmosphere changed as he walked further from the safety of Heathen. The light and air became chilled and gloomy, the mist thickening. He was lost now for sure but it was easier to follow the dude in the gloom. He looked a lot more at ease as he wandered the shadowing edges of Heathen. Finally the dude took a sharp right and headed up a slight incline and was gone. He must have entered a doorway at some point but where? Now he felt worried, up here in the chase and no real reason to be here. He still wasn't sure why he felt the urge to follow the dude or what he expected to find. At last he came upon a narrow alley to his right, previously unseen. Perhaps this was why he had seemed to disappear so quickly? The condensation wet his fingertips as he touched the walls and Touchreik felt his way forwards up the alleyway. He found a broken doorway and followed some lights along a tiny corridor until he reached a huge open space.

"Good evening," He spun to see a silhouette in the mist, illuminated by a dim light behind. He was unable to make out any detailed features but he was a stocky looking man, taller than him with broad shoulders.

"You're on private property my friend."

"I apologise, I seem to be a little lost."

"You certainly are by the look of you."

"Yes, I was heading to my accommodations from S063."

Touchriek was squinting to see the figure in the mist, it was hard to judge his tone without seeing any facial expression. He held up a hand over his eyes but it was no use.

"Totally the wrong direction," said the stranger.

"I expect so."

"I meant S063, only trouble hanging around a place like that."

"Oh."

"Come with me Sir. Follow and be quick." The figure walked past him leaving a soil or outside odour as he passed him. Touchreik looked around realising that unless this smog dropped he had little choice but to stick with the stranger. The deeper he followed the more he felt this place smothering him. After a few further twists and turns they finally stopped and went into a doorway.

At last they entered a room, inside were two people lit by a dim flickering light hanging from the ceiling.

The man sitting down was a wiry thin chap, he wore colourful dress with a purple open necked body suit. He was obviously a humanist as was the colleague. He was slightly grubby and undernourished and his nail varnish was random and unmatched. The second man he recognised perfectly well, it was the dude. At last he got a look at his rescuer. Another humanist, dressed in darker clothing which was very bizarre. He had some kind of top which had multiple pockets and zips which appeared unused. He sported a large crop of dark facial hair which matched the thick crop on his head.

"Shit," said the dude as the other two stared at him.

"Is this him?" said the fellow in the chair and he stood up and began laughing.

"Professor, welcome to the Chase," he said opening his arms.

"You know this guy?"

"Of a fashion, Professor Touchreik am I correct?"

Touchreik didn't respond, he looked around the room. The only exit was behind him and he'd never be able to make a bolt for it.

The dude answered and a light seemed to have come on in his head.

"Shit yeah, it's the Caveman guy, aint it? You're right, it's him alright."

"Your command of celebrity is a weakness, the famous Professor Touchreik."

Touchreik backed away from the table, what a bloody mess. Stuck in the middle of nowhere with a bunch of humanists.

"My friend tells me you were asking about drones, special drones." He coughed. "Yes I was."

"What's your interest in these things? Do you have tastes for the human type, you looking to own such a thing?"

"No, just rumour, that's all I heard about them from a friend."

"Yet you chose to follow my colleague all the way up to the chase without the courtesy of a comm? Are you friend or foe?"

"Neither," he replied.

The wiry fellow looked first at the hairy one and then the dude.

"So are you looking for something to keep you warm at night?" Wiry leant forward across the table, leaning on his knuckles.

"It's stupid, I've probably been under strain recently."

"Spit it out Mr, let's hear your tale." What harm he thought, they'll laugh at him anyway

"My partner, his name is Jagger."

"Life partner?"

"Yes."

"It's as if he has been having micro shutdowns." Touchriek giggled to try and soften the absurdity of what he was saying. Everyone stared at him blankly.

"Micro shutdowns in the same way a hack does?"

"Yes."

"Turing tests?"

"I've tried the advanced Turing tests?"

"And?"

"Well." He looked around. "He passed them all."

The man paused for a moment. "In that case I'd assume your friend is in fact your friend." He nodded at the door. "The Dude will take you with him. He needs to go home."

Touchreik breathed a sigh of relief.

"Mr Touchreik may I also suggest that you keep to the more public areas of SO63 in future, you'll find it much more to your tastes."

FOURTEEN

Ramona Stone was nothing but a good time drone, she wasn't dead because she had never been alive. When she was around physically it was easy to believe she was more than that. Discovering the disc was blank took that realisation to a new level. The knowledge it was possible to order another to the same specification changed nothing in his mind. She was erased, a drone could be rebuilt but it wouldn't be her would it, not without their experiences. She wouldn't tell stories about a life she never had, whose moral undertones lifted and cajoled his subconscious. A new Ramona wouldn't keep the other lovers that she never had a secret so as not to upset him. She wouldn't drive him into a rage one minute and have him in the palm of her hand the next. He could order another Ramona and in all likelihood he could afford to do so. That was over now and all because of one spiteful, jealous act.

He'd found cold comfort in the belief that she existed in that little plastic disc, until he'd discovered she wasn't there after all. He was bitter at losing Ramona and perhaps he'll never know why Jagger acted with such malice because he could never bring himself to ask. The disc was an insurance policy, something or someone to fall back on. Like an ex who was waiting with open arms and that would always be true of her. The pain was doubled because the person he cared most about had destroyed the thing he cared most about. There was nowhere to go, no reconciliation.

The next morning Jagger arrived as normal and went into the lab to start work as usual.

It struck him how calm the end was, in the same way as when he discovered her.

"I think you should leave."

"Excuse me?"

Jagger looked up and saw his love holding something between his thumb and finger. A small black disc with a patch of gold that glinted in the light. Jagger understood and immediately began packing belongings.

Jagger must have realised that there was no point in dialogue. He went around the apartment, placing personal belongings into the bag he had brought with him. They were few but they were symbolic of an official end to the relationship on any level. Touchreik stood by the door and waited patiently until Jagger approached and looked him up and down. His eyes were moist as he leant over and kissed Touchreik on the forehead. That act of physical defiance in the face of everything that had gone on was both an insult and a mark of respect. He walked out of the door and down the corridor without looking back. When Touchreik went to the window and dropped the augmented display he saw Jagger cross the courtyard and suddenly stopped. His head half turned and then as if he thought better of it he began walking again briskly across to the waiting magpod, stooped into the cockpit and was gone forever. Touchreik cut off access to the Duke and his accommodations and turned to look around the empty apartment with a sigh. To say he hadn't missed Jagger would have been a lie. Over the years he had done the opposite with his memories as he did with Ramona. Jagger became greyer and less beautiful than he may have actually been. Unlike Ramona he wasn't dead, he was probably still alive and admiring his collection of artefacts somewhere. As the pain ebbed and the years passed Touchreik finally did something inexplicable even to himself. Around ten years after that final encounter he had physically visited his accommodation, getting as close as the street opposite. Afterwards he was pleased not to have bumped into him or be seen, even if he was still there. The realisation he hadn't gone for reconciliation but for confrontation. Wanting someone to scream at but there was no one. His only targets were his friends and students but they were smart enough to get out of the way of his anger. Instead he festered in his own self-pity, more alone than ever.

He never forgot his friend Nova and what he had said before they parted. That he was going to grow old in V-World and die there just like in reality, just like the 21st Century.

Would he really do that?

When Nova migrated into V-World he had been 23, for the second time. Where he now lived there will never be a reason to age a single day, to feel older or weaker. He and all the millions of others in V-World could be as young and as alive as they wished. The chemical enhancements could even increase emotions and feelings to boost happiness. It was tempting enough for him to consider for himself but those thoughts were fleeting. Should Nova have kept the promise to himself he would now be 89 years old. These days that was middle age but in the 21st Century he would be an old man. Nova had imagined some romance in the ageing process, a thing of the past even in reality. It was his sim and his rules so who knows. Over the decades Touchreik's enthusiasm for the Caveman project had certainly dulled. One thing never left his consciousness though. As the years and then the decades passed he knew that every time he looked in the mirror he was morphing into the face from the old memory he found in Nova's trace.

A memory or fantasy that Nova had no right to have. Over 40 years later it was certainly becoming a reality because he actually looked like that man.

Holding down his lecturing career in that time had been easy enough. Once while on a break he had left a comm device on one of his students. They were a new group and he was excited to hear what they thought of his genius.

"I like him, he's not what I expected."

"I love his stories, it's like he takes you there, to ancient times."

"You'd never believe the stories to look at him."

"The Sector, an all that."

"Oh yeah. He is a regular there."

"Like you should know."

Slapping and kidding around before Touchreik slammed the comm shut. He had played dumb later when they sheepishly returned the device.

There was no reason to be shocked because it was all true. This history genius who lived a reclusive lifestyle and seldom socialised, whose personal hygiene and habits were questionable at best. He'd allowed his standards to slip a fraction a day. His home had become a hovel with Duke on sleep mode most of the time. Little wonder the others hadn't been over in years, he could hardly call them friends anymore. Evenings spent shuffling around in the semi darkness and on occasion he might just sit and stare for hours. His passion for the project quickly relegated from a passion to a pastime to a casual hobby. Now he couldn't remember when he had last bothered with any of it, aside from the friends he missed.

His openness about his alternative lifestyle expanded disproportionately to his lowering self-esteem.

He pursued his physical desires without any attempt to hide them, not that he shouted from the rooftops. He was surprised to discover that the more he did so the less anyone cared. Perhaps he was simply confirming what everyone had known all along. By direct association that would insinuate he was a man of particular tastes. His life was in hibernation mode for decades and it would always be another day when he intended to get a grip. He continued his lectures at the institute and his public demeanour was passable. Perhaps more passable than he had imagined.

Prout had effectively disowned him and allowed him on his way until some point during the Spring of 2579 when he received a message from him. The pair had exchanged greeting on occasion but little else.

He wanted to see him in person?

Touchreik confided in himself that he'd had a good run, sooner or later it was all going to come crashing down around him. To be a Professor here and to conduct himself the way he had, was bordering on professional suicide. He was simply biding his time and waiting for someone to kick the chair away. It looked like at last he might be put out of his professional misery.

He approached Prout's room and the door slid open for him.

"Come in Touchreik. How are you?" said Prout who was standing behind his desk with an unnerving smile on his face. The wisp of his hair looked like it could cut paper and the entire room had a perfumed odour, like vanilla. Touchreik involuntarily looked around, perhaps expecting to see the hangman in full garb waiting behind the door.

"I'm fine and well hopefully I find you the same?" said Touchreik cautiously.

"Absolutely. Please have a seat," said Prout waving a hand.

The Professor sat down at the opposite side of the desk and waited for the news. He straightened his beard with his hands then locked hands across his knees.

"I have something I want to discuss with you." Prout looked a little edgy.

"Certainly," Here goes he thought as he flexed his foot up and down as if testing his ankle joint.

"You're a chap who seems quite happy in reality, we are very proud of the work you've done here," began Prout.

Touchreik's skin went peach coloured and his face felt warm. This must be the butter before the toast or some other ancient saying he couldn't remember.

Prout stopped his train of thought. "Are you alright?"

"Of course, I'm fine."

Prout straightened in his chair and shrugged both shoulders forwards. "As I was saying you did a commendable job with the caveman project, I know it was disappointing to see it end but nonetheless. When it comes to 21st Century then you're the absolute authority."

"That's very kind."

"Let me get to the point. I've some exciting news. Plans have just been confirmed to build a space cruiser in Earth's orbit which will take a number of passengers on reality leisure trips to orbit Mars and return. The mission has the go ahead and work has already started on the ship itself." Pausing as if expecting some kind of recognition or reaction, there was none.

"What would this have to do with me?" said Touchreik who was now caught completely off guard with talk of experts and great jobs.

"Let me finish please." Prout clasped his hands on the desk in front of him.

"There are also a number of drone missions planned to set up infrastructure that allows a small team to actually drop down onto the Martian surface. Their aim will be to carry out an exploratory mission to find the base attributed to Major Zero and his team. They will be authorised to bring back samples."

"It sounds very exciting but as I say?"

"That's why I wanted to see you."

Touchreik sat back in his chair, placing a hand on each arm and listened intently.

"A small team are going to hitch a ride on the Lazarus, that's what the cruiser is being called. They are going to hitch a ride and drop onto the surface of Mars."

"I'm sorry I still don't follow."

"Do I have to spell it out for you? Look, don't answer now but you have the opportunity to go as a consultant as part of that mission."

Now he spoke faster as Touchreik began raising his hand higher to stop him speaking. "It's an incredible chance for us all and you will be given full jurisdiction over which samples are returned to Earth. You're an expert in 21st Century technology, it's natural that."

"No."

"Listen to me, before you decide why don't you sleep on it?"

"It will still be no."

Touchreik got up to leave. The idea of such a crazy escapade almost made him laugh out loud.

"Yes, I'm happy in reality Mr Prout, but with my feet planted in or around Heathen not floating around in a tin can millions of miles from home."

"Perhaps you'll feel different in a day or two, shall I say you're thinking it over? At least think it over."

"Say? Say to whom?"

"The sponsors, on behalf of the institute."

"No."

"If your quite sure."

"I'm quite sure, perhaps one of the others are well qualified. Who are these sponsors anyway?"

"That, we don't know. The Lazarus is in planning stages but the drop to Mars is a totally separate opportunity. It's all being organised and funded by a benefactor who wants to help us at the institute increase our library of materials. It would be so valuable to the Major Zero memorial too. They are looking to recover an element for him. Some kind of rumour that there's something they call Black-Star. Don't know much about it."

Touchreik froze and turned before leaving, looking over his shoulder. He wasn't sure if Wade had seen his physical reaction to hearing that word.

"What did you say?"

"Black-Star, the sponsors are after some kind of element up there."

Touchreik went through the door without a word and it slowly closed behind him. He broke into a run down the corridor and jumped straight into a magpod home.

He'd lost most of his data from the project but he had copied and moved the file containing the memory in some form or other. In the end Duke found it very quickly. There had never been any doubt in his mind but he looked at the file once more. It scared him even more having been years since he last saw it. From the point of view of Nova he was chatting to himself as he was now. He looked a similar age as he was now. The whole thing was grainy and kept breaking up. The conversation had become heated and then there was the word mentioned at least twice. 'Black-Star' or 'The Black-Star'.

He rewound and played it back but still he could hear the word Black-Star. He was watching a memory, fantasy or even a dream from Nova's memory trace. On its own it might be any of those, but along with the other things it was spooky. Deep in the mind of a man who had never heard the word he was remembering it. How could he remember something that he had never heard of? It simply had to be a coincidence, there wasn't a simple explanation he could imagine. It was falling into place as some kind of prediction, as if this conversation could happen soon. Complete implausible of course, Nova was in an enclosed sim with no way in or out. Even if Touchreik did go in he would have unlikely gone as himself. Alright say he did that, somehow right now? Nova would still have no way of this memory existing decades ago.

Touchreik stayed out of the limelight, knowing that if this mission became public and it soon would, his name would be mentioned. In no time the word 'Lazarus' was in the media and public vocabulary. The details were being talked about across Heathen. A luxurious space cruiser which would take reality tourists to Mars on a 3 month round trip. They would soon be making sims available for people to visit the ship in V-World and experience its luxury. From the images he had seen it looked like his description of a tin can had been very apt. It was a kilometre diameter rotating barrel designed to produce simulated gravity for its passengers. The plan was to take tourists on a regular basis to the planet Mars on reality adventures. The whole thing was being promoted quite heavily and gained popularity very quickly.

The Professor's name came up and he was questioned regularly but he rebuffed any suggestion he was involved.

"The team hitching a ride might well need someone of your expertise."

"I'm sorry I just assumed."

At one point he became suspicious that Prout might be trying to pressure him by encouraging such stories. Regardless of what anyone might think was natural or assumed, he was determined it might all blow over in time, as far as he was concerned, it was a definite no.

FIFTEEN

Inside the Tugen Bar's clientele lived by an invisible code of conduct. All conversations and opinions were healthy within the walls of the place but never left the door they came through and left by. In some cases people shared their deepest desires, kept from the outside world either in describing them or acting on them. Yet they knew to never ask or reveal anything as trivial as their accommodation loce, age or kinship ties. Inside this and many other establishments in the sector they would nod in greeting or scream wildly to each other. Everyone recognisable by site at a minimum and for those that weren't there was initial suspicion, a cautious approach followed by acceptance.

In the preceding decades Professor Touchreik had been a welcome guest at such places. Never outgoing or the centre of attention but his notoriety as the guy from the Caveman project brought unique looks. A gaze might be held a moment too long but in some ways his semi celebrity status gave the place kudos. Queen bitches with orange faces and giant silver hair would gossip behind his back when there's nothing else to gossip about, which wasn't often.

"Like, yeah I ain't surprised you know. He was into history, you know what I mean?"

"Takes all kinds and those history folks they're just like us."

The Professor had at first been concerned about media but not anymore, it's like they knew anyway so it was of no interest. He got caught in the bathroom with one of the bitches once and was subjected to her worldly wisdom. "Honey, they all wanna see your dick, but once you whip it out and slap em in the face with it, it's just a dick after that."

He would often be seen in his usual seat, watching the neon lights illuminate the spangled frocks and glittered hair. The beautiful topless young boys in tight fitting trousers gyrated to the beats. Boys that seemed even younger would harass and cajole the brethren with offers of influencers.

He heard a voice behind him. "It's been a long time."

He turned around to see a man slightly taller than him. His face was painted silver and he had shadows painted under his eyes and across his cheek bones. He wore a ragged silver outfit with a strange wrap around headdress.

"Excuse me?" said Touchreik

"It's been a long time Professor."

"Do we know each other?" Maybe they did, manners was the best default position and work from there.

"It's been over forty years but I'm insulted."

The Professor stepped back. "I'm sorry I really.."

"The Chase?" the man interrupted.

"Is that you? The fellow who?"

"Nice to meet you again old chum," he said stressing the last word.

"Well yes, nice to meet you too." He paused. "Again."

They both stared at the floor for a moment and then without speaking focused on a gentleman sat directly across the room. He was sat at a table with a female dressed in a bask and boots with huge feathers in her hair. On one side the feathers straggled over her face but failed to hide the obvious, she was a drone. Even in the poor light it was clear from the mannerisms, but to be seen in public with a drone like that. Such poor quality, not unusual round here.

"We need to talk," shouted the stranger into his ear above the music.

"What about?"

"Not here, outside." The stranger beckoned him to follow with a nod and headed for the door. Pushing past the throng in the doorway they burst into the street and the door shut behind them. The music became muffled and was replaced by a light rain and chatter, giggles from a few people standing outside.

"Here," he beckoned.

The stranger ambled around the building and into a small alley, scouting the area as he went.

They stood together and the Professor was wary of going too far off the main street in an area like this. The stranger tapped the back of his neck. "Will you comm me in for a moment? I want to show you something?"

He was cautious, could he be about to be robbed here. If he allowed access to his comm channel then there have been stories, just stories of these hacks. He was undecided.

"Professor, you came to us. Remember? You asked for our help."

"That was forty years ago," he sighed and tapped the back of his neck.

"Watch this." In front of his eyes a piece of media came up about the caveman project. It was a little piece about how exciting the project had been and how it had helped migration. Then it went on to say how Nova had never been seen nor contacted since he went into a private sim with his life partner. Nothing new in all that but there was a message in there that had to have been a mistake. It was a very quick throwaway remark. It mentioned how Bluu had actually been a drone. After that, the story pushed on as if it were the most casual thing ever. After nearly fifty years there were very few who would see this and out of those almost none who knew Bluu.

The broadcast stopped and they stared at each other. "Did you get that? A drone?"

"No. It's a mistake."

"There's no mistake, I checked the story out. It's been a long time, no one cares now. Do you?" he paused. "You met and interacted with Bluu."

"She wasn't a drone, it's a mistake."

"Then perhaps you were mistaken about your friend Jagger?"

"I met and spent time with Bluu."

"You met and spent time with Jagger?"

The Professor stared out as a couple passed the end of the alley turned in and then seeing the pair turned around again. A gust blew a fine rain into his face. "What are you saying?"

As the stranger spoke he kept his eyes on the entrance to the alley.

"How is Jagger, have you never thought to contact him after all these years, bury the axe? Everybody says hi?"

"No," he said not mentioning his midnight visits to the accommodation block.

"I have."

"What?"

"I said, I have?" Shuffling he stepped back.

"Nothing." The stranger was pointing to the alleyway entrance as if he might be out there somewhere. "No loce, no logs, nothing. He has disappeared from Heathen. I've checked early euthenisation records, Migration records. He is as gone as if he never existed." He turned to look into Touchreik's eyes, trying to read them in the dim light. "That's if he ever existed."

Touchreik struggled for a moment to comprehend what was being said to him.

"You mean if Bluu was a drone, indistinguishable from an organic then perhaps Jagger was too? That's a bit farfetched considering he passed all the Turing tests. You said yourself."

"Don't you think Bluu would have passed?"

"Yes. But you now think they were drones?"

The stranger shook his head slowly and his lips went thin as he spoke. "I wish they were. But I think they were something much, much worse."

"What could be worse?"

"There's a common denominator in all this. That's you, and this caveman you worked with. He's in V-World in a permanent enclosed sim. A digital desert island where nothing will go in or come out. You worked on his memory trace did you not?"

"That was years ago, the project was shut down and I have no access to any of those files."

"You know better than anyone what was in there, ancient beliefs am I correct?"

"Obviously."

The man leant on a straight arm against the wall, subliminally blocking the Professor's escape. "They say you were offered a trip to Mars, is that true?"

"Yes, I refused."

He looked down at his shoes, kicking a tiny stone against the wall.

"Listen to me. I know your opinion of people like us, but we have to talk. Come up to the Chase tomorrow at noon. I may be able to show you something very interesting."

"No, I can't."

The man started to walk away. "Noon" he said as he disappeared. "You know the way," and he was gone.

Touchreik thought a lot that night. He had to go up there, even just for curiosity. The man had left him so many questions and still the memory in Nova's head bothered him.

They might not have been drones but something much worse?

What the hell was he talking about. He reminded himself, these were humanists and they were prone to doom and gloom predictions. Still, if he was telling the truth then where had Jagger disappeared too? That night it all came back to him and he decided he was going. If he was a drone after all there was nowhere to focus that bitterness because the bastard didn't exist.

The following day he headed up to the chase. He'd struggle to find the place they had met decades ago but would start from the dude's house. That was easy enough being opposite an establishment he had since frequented very regularly. He retraced his steps and after one or two wrong turns found himself in the area that had a familiar feel. It looked to have changed, it was quieter, darker. There was a light mist that acted like a grey filter and the streets seemed worn and grubbier than he remembered. Paths were worn through the green mossy pavements and once manicured garden areas were overrun by nature. There had been decades of decay, since his last visit. In the end he'd failed to find the actual building but as if it were some kind of test the humanist found him.

"Walk this way Mister," he had said leading him through a labyrinth of alleys and shortcuts, presumably to the same building of decades ago. They had entered a different way but he was sure it was where they had met.

The man from the night before, Jak Samian swung back on a chair with his feet on the table. The place had the signature earthy damp smell which was distinctive and familiar. He dropped his legs and allowed the chair to drop onto its four feet and stood holding out a hand. The Professor just stared at it and Jak grinned from the corner of his mouth. A traditional greeting, perhaps they were testing him again?

Touchriek held out a hand and shook his firmly remembering how he had once greeted the Caveman. Jak looked Antoine in the eye and they both nodded in acknowledgement.

"Sit down."

Touchriek sat at the table whilst Antoine leant against a wall behind his colleague.

Jak leant forward across the table and dropped his head as if speaking to the table itself. The silver make up removed he had a more rugged appearance his facial hair was unkempt.

"Professor," he paused as if considering his words. "We exist on the fringes of society, scavenging off the land in the ways of ancient men. But be assured we are by no means primitive. In some ways we understand the workings of the world better than perhaps yourself."

Touchriek disagreed but declined to say. He wasn't being threatened either mentally or physically and had come of his own free will, no reason to upset his hosts.

Jak continued, "You came to us a long time ago with a ridiculous notion that your friend." He made little exclamation marks with his fingers. "Could be a drone."

Touchriek was about to explain their partnership had not been physical but Jak raised a finger to his lips before speaking again.

"This drone could pass all the Turing tests, it could bleed, and as far as we can tell was undistinguishable from an organic human. Since then our world has changed in many ways. We have only just learned that the mentor to your ancient friend was a drone too. You say the same of her as you did of this Jagger friend of yours. That they were both as human as you and me."

"True enough."

"So you can see how these events, along with perhaps information you haven't been a party to are of concern."

"I'm sorry?"

"Let me start at the beginning. Heathen has been stable as a society for hundreds of years. Our lifestyle has always been here on the fringes, we have fallen out on occasion but on the whole we have continued unabated."

"Ok."

"Then this caveman sample is returned and regenerated. The Heathen population become titivated for a short time and even come out of their accommodation to be in the real world. Your caveman retires and he leaves you his memory trace. You start to examine the information therein and suddenly, boom. It's all shutdown with no explanation. You acquire an enthusiastic colleague who promptly disappears."

"Look maybe I should go."

"Go if you wish but what you have learned today might just be the beginning. There's more I can assure you, and we can be of mutual benefit to each other. You're the only person who interacted with both of these characters, we think we now know what they were Professor, and it's certainly not drones." Stopping he grabbed some fruit and put his foot on a chair, elbow on knee he took a bite.

"What are they then?"

"You have to see for yourself."

"See what?"

"Your free to head back into the rabbit hole Mr Touchreik. To head back into Heathen and forget all the facts that lead back to you. What I want to share with you is beyond words. If you weren't to see it with your own eyes you might pass it off as the rambling of the paranoid. But before you go I'll say this. It's your choice Mr."

Touchreik thought for a moment before raising his chin, did he have anything to lose? Could he finally get some answers to his own personal mysteries?

"Ok," he said.

"You'll stay the night and leave at dawn."

"But," Touchreik started protesting but Antoine was already heading out the door leaving Jak, arms folded and a wry grin on his face.

ϗ

"Is it much further?" Touchreik was becoming concerned as they walked further and further towards the outskirts of Heathen.

"Not far."

Through the mist he saw a small shed like structure and they entered through a small side door. Inside it was dark but Jak tugged hard on a cord and the room illuminated.

"How do you do that? We are off grid."

Jak laughed as he began rolling back the sheets that covered a large structure in the centre of the room. "Solar power."

"You have independent power generation?" Touchreik was fascinated at how these people were able to be so resourceful. They were like throwbacks to ancient times and if he didn't know better he'd have believed this is similar to how the savage human would have survived in the 21st Century.

"If you don't mind." Jak nodded.

Touchreik grabbed the sheet from the other side and they both pulled it to the back in unison. Underneath there was a vehicle of some kind. It had wheels and was made of some heavy metals. Its construction was haphazard as if it might consist of parts from various styles of vehicle. Jak unplugged something from the front and climbed inside. He slammed the door and shouted at Touchreik.

"In."

Touchreik wanted to get in but the door was closed. Finally he saw a handle and pulled hard and a door swung outwards and upwards. The door closed itself and Jak pressed a button under the dash. Lights and gauges which were attached to the dashboard lit up and he flicked a switch. A huge array of lights on the front blinded them because the fog outside was so thick and dark. He flicked another switch and the lights dipped. The vehicle pulled forward, Jak jumped out to pull the doors closed and they set off.

"Where are you taking me?"

"Outside."

"We can't do that, it's dangerous."

He stopped the vehicle. "Wanna go back? Start walkin'."

He pushed his foot hard down and they began moving into the fog and drove in silence for about twenty minutes. The greenery they had experienced on their walk slowly disappeared and all that was left was a road. It was like they could fall off the Earth if they strayed from its path. In time the fog started to clear until finally it was completely gone. Then the chill in the air disappeared and the Sun came out and illuminated the landscape. It was washed with incredible greens and yellows, Jak opened a roof space. The air filled the vehicle and was invigorating.

"Is it safe?"

"Been coming here for over 20 years my friend. Still alive and kickin."

On either side of them were fields as far as the eye can see. Lush and green crops that swayed in the wind. Enormous drones sprayed them with liquid and on one side there was a group of droned machines harvesting and loading.

Suddenly Jak hit the brakes hard and the vehicle skidded to a halt only inches from an enormous tractor drone that had done the same thing. Jak spun the lock and drove off the road and under the arms of the tractor and then back onto the road.

The vehicle took a sharp right and through some woods and low trees until they reached the brow of a hill before finally dropping down into a small town. Touchreik was unable to speak and Jak just grinned at him.

"Welcome to Greenwich," said Jak as they pulled up outside an ancient grey building.

"This is incredible." To Touchreik it was like he had gone back in time 500 years. The town was tiny by Heathen standards, there were humans everywhere coming and going but not a sign of any drones.

"This is the result of less than ten years work," said Jak proudly. "We came out here initially to explore the environment. As you can tell by now the air is clean and there's no deadly viruses here. Just like in ancient times people get sick but our bodies are adapting quickly. Follow me."

They set off walking down a main street. "We discovered the remains of Greenwich almost completely reclaimed by nature. We began clearing buildings at first, one by one. We rebuilt roofs and walls and added some infrastructure. We cleared and reopened drainage, ran cables and added power from Solar panels and coal fired electricity stations. We scavenged from Mothers supplies but are busy trying to become self-sufficient. We think we might need to do that faster than we first thought. You'll learn more about that tomorrow. In the meantime we have corralled wild animals for food and growing crops. There's a common misconception about humanists Professor."

"That is."

"That is that we are against technology, that we fear electricity and electronic intelligence. This isn't true at all. What we fear is that humanity has handed over complete control of its destiny to a machine. A machine that loves us and wants us to be happy. We believe that could go wrong in so many ways. As it happens it may well have already started and in a way we could never have dreamed of."

"What do you mean?"

"That's for tomorrow, honestly. If I were to tell you in words right now you wouldn't believe me. Let's get you settled for the night."

SIXTEEN

Touchreik had been awake for an hour before Jak woke him. His guest room had been comfortable, warm and clean. It was fixed however, there were no augmented reality or sage in place. That meant the room had been decorated and furniture placed in a fixed location. He assumed then that the rest of the humanist primitive accommodations were very similar. If you didn't like the view from the window or the decor then you would be stuck with it. No way of changing anything to suit your mood or needs. The night before Jak had guided him through the workings of the place. The bathroom facilities were manual. There were physical controls for things like water which has to be tested for temperature by touching. A skill he needed some practice in. Lighting was basic in each room and worked on entry but would simply apply illumination. There wasn't even a basic in house sage. With no sage then it was impossible to order mood lighting, or refreshments of any kind, there was no assistance whatsoever.

No sage also meant there was no communication in either direction whether that was with the outside world or simply to hold a conversation about the days plans. At last he heard movement and Jak knocked on the door as promised, just before dawn.

Being already dressed he waited a suitable amount of time before heading downstairs and was greeted by the smell of cooking. The stairwell was quite grand and lead straight into a dining and cooking area where they had shared a nightcap the night before. Three people sat around an oversized table. Jak introduced a female who hadn't been present last night as Vanilla. There was also another person who was male but tiny, perhaps less than half a meter tall. Touchriek's eyes widened when he saw the chubby faced creature smile and wave at him.

"This is Louey," said Jak proudly.

"Louey," whispered Touchriek to himself. The other two shared an acknowledging nod and a half smile. Touchriek knew straight away what it was.

"Louey was born out here Professor."

"A child?" he said his mouth gaping in amazement.

"I'm Louey and I'm seven," shouted the little creature. Touchreik sat down and tried not to stare at the fellow. He was obviously a human but completely underdeveloped both physically and mentally. Being aware of a 'child' and actually seeing one were two different things. Touchreik was shocked and surprised to imagine what might happen to an organic human who was raised out here from birth. That they may grow up like animals around them and never be excepted into the city. The DNA would be random and this would cause untold problems in the future.

Vanilla had cooked food that he didn't recognised but it seemed hearty enough and tasty too. The four of them sat around the table, in between conversation Louey and Touchreik stared at each other, each as fascinated as the other.

"This is an incredible place, I'm amazed to find you surviving so well here. Do you plan to return?"

Vanilla answered, "Every one of the people you have seen believes in this place. Some come and go living mainly in Heathen, others live almost permanently and some have never seen Heathen," she tipped her head towards the child.

"How long have you all been here?"

Jak swallowed and dabbed his chin. "One or two of us came out about 8 years ago. We found signs of an ancient city, mostly in ruins. We set about clearing the ones still standing. We built shelter, installed power from solar and wind systems. Others came and our numbers grew, the community grew organically."

Jak continued, "We have worked hard on the infrastructure to develop power and food. At first we scavenged from Mother's systems but we are becoming independent."

Touchreik had so many questions. "A self-sufficient community outside? But the germs, the viruses?"

Vanilla interrupted. "We are all healthy for the most part, minor illnesses soon get better. Our bodies are building resistance. Our lives are uncertain, we cannot guarantee the 130 year term but it's a price we pay."

"Your breeding naturally?"

"The early childbirths were scary and we have suffered and lost some. A woman who has childbirth has a special bond, very different feelings than you might expect."

"New people come and they bring new skills, we work as a cooperative but there's independent trade sprouting up. We have over 1000 residents."

Jak spoke once more, "It's how things should be. We have created a micro society here that we can replicate across the world." Touchreik thought back to Jagger and his collection of artefacts, collected from the scavengers on the outside. These people and their lives were a living artefact but he was concerned about their effect on Heathen. If Heathen was designed to be optimum size for the resources available then these rogue communities might tip the balance.

"But that failed, there aren't enough resources. Mother keeps the population within the limits of the resources, it will all come crashing down if you carry on taking from the planet like we did before."

"There were once billions of us on this planet, there's room for many more. To keep the human race going we have to survive here."

"A little dramatic don't you think?"

"You think so?" Jak threw the fork down onto his plate and looked him in the eye. "Perhaps you'll have a different opinion in a few hours. Come on we have to go."

They climbed aboard the vehicle that had brought them here. Heading out across pre made good quality roads that were designed and built for the drone vehicles. They spent lots of time winding through rougher worn paths honed from the earth by remote farming machines. They travelled in silence for around 40 minutes whilst Touchreik admired the countryside, bright sunshine and crisp clean air. The tended fields and the unkept areas were a million shades of green. He would occasionally whiff the damp air or sweet smell of pine. Jak followed a road along the side of an enormous grey building. It was enclosed by a tall green fence. Jak pulled the vehicle off the road and parked in a ditch amongst some long grass.

"The outer ring of Heathen is wide and expansive. We seldom travel too far to scavenge what we need and even less so as we have become more independent. One or two people came up here and stumbled upon this facility."

"What is it."

"It is, or should I say was a Juve station. Its where Mother incubates our young before they are brought into their surrogates. Its where people like you and me were born and spent our first 15 years."

Jak jumped from the vehicle and beckoned for him to follow. They stepped down an embankment to where a neat hole had been cut in the fence. He pulled it to one side like a curtain and Touchreik stepped through, Jak followed. They stood on the edge of a concreted area, tufts of grass and weeds were establishing themselves in the cracks. Touchreik could feel the air warming as the sun climbed in the sky and the ground radiated moisture. There were odd vehicles parked at random in the space between them and the enormous building opposite. Jak set off across expanse towards the main building and Touchreik followed. A door opened in the warehouse and a large vehicle came out and started heading towards them at speed. The Professor was looking around but there was nowhere to go, they would never make it through the fence at the speed it was going. He looked at Jak but he didn't react as it tore across the concrete spewing dust in the air. It was still heading for them and they had moments to get away. Finally Touchreik panicked and screamed for him to run and turned on his heels. He heard a screech of rubber behind him and stumbled, face first onto the floor convinced Jak would have been crushed to a pulp by now. He turned around in time to see Jak walk directly into the path of the vehicle and as he did so, it stopped dead before hitting him. He turned around laughing. "Come on, let's go."

Touchreik pulled himself upright, dusting himself down and rubbing grit from his palms. "What happened? Don't they see us. There must be security of some kind here?"

Jak had already started walking again. "Security from what?" These drones are all Speks, they have a job to do and it ain't security. They see us but that's only so they don't run over us. You ok?"

As they moved from its path the massive vehicle silently pulled away and carried on its journey. Jak led them to a huge sliding vehicle door as the spek drone went on its way, and beckoned him to stand to one side. After a few moments the door opened quickly and a transporter drone similar to the last one rolled out and headed towards the railway tracks.

He grabbed Touchreik by the collar and dragged him inside.
"Where are we?"
"Maternity," said Jak.
"What's that?"
"Follow me."

The building was sterile and clean regardless of the dusty loading area outside, thanks to the air curtain they walked through. The inside looked like some kind of warehouse or storage. There were two 1 meter tubes that ran half the length of the room. Each one had arms protruding on either side at intervals, on the end of each arm was a pod type construction. Each was around a meter in length had a glass viewing window at the top but it was too high to see inside. There were two drones moving up and down the line, stopping at each in turn perhaps making checks on the pods and their contents. Touchreik had a good idea what was inside as he grabbed a bar and placed a foot on a stirrup and pulled himself up to peer inside.

"Oh my god. Is that a person?" said Touchriek. The chubby little creature was dozing peacefully and looked more like a deformed little old man. Its face was scrunched and puffy.

"Are they humans?"

"Of course their humans, they are very young and won't be allocated for years yet."

"Would we all look like that as young juves?"   •

"Yes, we all look like that as young juves regardless of how we are born."

"Come on."

He was led along the line towards the far end of the building. The two rows of pods ended mid-way down the building. At that point there was a change and it looked like new pods were in the midst of being installed. These were of a similar type to the baby pods but considerably larger, maybe 3 to 4 meters in length.

"Here, take a look inside one of these," said Jak.

The Professor climbed up and peered in through the glass. He was right, the pods were identical, inside he could see a fully formed female. She looked to be peacefully asleep inside the green gel substance.

"What do you think?"

"They look like adult organic humans? Why would Mother keep juves so long as for them to become adult?"

"Mother isn't keeping them to become adults Professor, they were already adults when they went in the pods."

"You're not making sense."

"It didn't make sense to us for a while but it does now. I need to show you something else to help pull this together."

The pair left by the same way they had entered and headed back to the vehicle. They drove a few more dirt tracks an across to a hillside which sloped up above some fields.

"We have been up here many times in the past to scavenge food from these fields, now look. They're being left to nature. It's the same story over there at the processing warehouse. We were able to steal finished food product from inside but now its empty." Touchreik was still confused by all this.

"So you've seen the pieces of the puzzle Professor. What do you think?"

"I have no idea, you're maybe wrong about the adult pods, maybe Mother rotates the crop growing?"

"And the warehousing? It's the same story there, empty storage solutions, less scavengers. Everything is slowing down over time."

"What's your theory?"

"Come on, let's head back."

They jumped back in the transporter and headed back over the rolling fields, avoiding occasional drone vehicles which was a skill Jak had become quite adept at.

Back at the house they gathered around the table whilst Vanilla brought them both refreshments, she quickly led Louey upstairs as he waved his good nights to the guest.

"Let me spell it out for you," said Jak. "We still have some gaps but maybe you can help us? Starting at the beginning. The Migration project started over 50 years ago, after the caveman was thawed. In fact it was he who actually helped to launch and make it so popular. The people of Heathen no longer had to wait till they euthanised at 130 to retire into V-World. Migration meant that any person of any age could do so. In fact many did, but how many?

"I would have no idea, perhaps a few thousand, ten thousand perhaps?"

"Why would you say that?"

"It just didn't seem that popular."

"Let's imagine the take up of migration was very popular, in fact thousands of times more popular than you think."

"Then Mother would maintain the population numbers regardless of how many migrated. It would make no difference to Heathen."

"But what if she didn't?"

"You mean she didn't replace the people who migrated? Then numbers would dwindle in Heathen and the population would eventually only exist in V-World."

"Good, you're getting there. Two things might happen. The remaining organic humans might feel lonely and notice the dwindling numbers in our real world cities."

"Why would Mother not replace the population?"

"I'm coming to that."

"Instead she takes the organic human bodies of those who migrate and she implants a processor into the head and puts them back on the streets."

"Please."

"You came to us about Jagger, we know about Bluu. Your saying it's not possible? You saw it with your own eyes." He said pressed his palm on the table, leaning closer.

"Remaining humans would feel better if they could still see human life around them. There would be natural wastage and the real population would fall indefinitely. Mother would not need as much resource."

"If these super drones really replace organic humans, they would still eat?"

"We don't know how that works but maybe less, who knows. There would be no need for so many because their primary task is to fill the streets, to be seen and be human."

"So Heathen is populated by drones."

"Jagger and Bluu weren't drones at all. They were what we call luddites. Complete functioning humans with brains removed and processors in their place. They are designed to keep us company. We have no idea how many there are by now and it's almost impossible to test as you found out."

"So when a human euthanises their organic body is implanted with an electronic brain. They would continue to populate our lives and streets. At the same time Mother could focus resources on areas inhabited by the last natural humans and cut down on the production. Eventually we will all exist in V-World."

"It's all a bit farfetched, why would you think she would do such a thing? There's absolutely no reason to do so."

"To her there might be a reason. Let's imagine she was privy to some data from an ancient man. A man from over 500 years ago who still had primitive thoughts and beliefs."

"Such as?"

"Such as Religion."

"God beliefs? No one believes those things now."

"Mother loves humanity, her sole purpose has always been to provide for us. Then she sees an opportunity to deliver on a promise we had forgotten about. A promise that religion made thousands of years ago. A promise that's still vivid in the mind of an ancient man. An ancient man whose memory trace you were deciphering."

"Which is?"

"Immortality, to live forever. A kind of Heaven for humans."

"But why?"

"Because the caveman told her that's what we wanted. Deep in his ancient memory trace he held those fantasies brought by religions from his own time. They believed that one day it would happen. Mother is going to deliver on a belief and desire held deep by all humans. Mother loves humans, you must know that."

"So if it's true then, ultimately we will all be required to exist in V-World forever. Mother finally delivers?"

"Exactly, that's why we needed to build a community outside of Mother's realm and you can help us."

"Me?"

"You're an expert in ancient history, you know about how people lived then. There were billions of humans. We can help each other because we are a living museum. The only option we have now is survival."

They talked through the night until the next morning and there were arguments and counter arguments. In the end it all started to make sense and could well be true. Millions of people would live forever inside the Martian servers and what was left could be shut down. He was unsure of the connection to the caveman, not a man of religion but certainly he knew of those beliefs. There was no doubt now that Jagger had either voluntarily or involuntarily reported back data. If he had any need that is, Mother had numerous ways to learn from it. Not least from Nova himself.

Touchreik finally collapsed exhausted onto his bed at around dawn and slept most of the morning. He couldn't unlearn what he now knew and even though a life in V-World was as good as reality, there was something wrong about how this was happening. His first thought the next day was that he should go and tell people, but that was the problem, which people?

This was a question that the humanists had already considered but they had a very different idea. They thought that it was more likely that the people would have listened years ago. On the day the migration was launched, on the day that it was announced by the caveman. Even better, if the caveman had never been thawed. One thing was for sure now and that was he knew he couldn't condone what was happening that Mother, the thing he loved was about to suffocate her children because she would hug them so hard. As a machine she had no concept of life and had proven to herself through the actions of others that many humans didn't either. The programming of the saviour machine had failed to allow for an unforeseen circumstance. The more that humans were provided for, then the more dependent they became and the less organic they became. Provided for hundreds of years with their every desire they had completely forgotten strife, work and effort. This group of humanists on the other hand hadn't, they were intent on moving in the opposite direction.

Unknown to the Professor they were already scheming to put the whole thing right and he was part of their plans.

The next morning his head ached at the thought of it all, the conversation continued. Antoine turned up and the three walked around the village, he observed around him how embedded that had become. That so many humans could be seen doing drone work. They were very interested in the 'Lazarus' mission.

"Did you refuse the Lazarus mission?"

"Yes?"

"The media say there's a drop team going aboard and that you were invited."

"That's true."

"We need to get aboard that ship."

"Why, I don't see how that will help?"

"The drop team intend to recover an element from the surface, said to be in amongst the samples."

"I can't say too much but they are looking for an element that is very special indeed."

"The Black-Star you mean?"

"The Black-Star, exactly. What do you know about it?"

"Tell me why it's so valuable?"

"I can't do that."

Should he say what he knows or be patient and hope they tell him more. He had to know what Black-Star was.

"You said everything leads back to the caveman, if that's true then you have to tell me about Black-Star."

"I'm sorry."

"I have examined the caveman memory trace, it's in there. Deep in his mind, perhaps in fantasy or perhaps not."

"You mean the caveman was aware of the Black-Star?"

"He certainly knew the word."

"How."

"I told you it's in his memories." The Professor thought it best to withhold the exact detail at this stage but explained how the word had come up in a conversation deep in the caveman memory.

"The Caveman could never have known about it."

"Pure coincidence, that's all."

Antoine and Jak stopped dead and stared at each other. Finally Jak grabbed his forearm and he was frogmarched back to the village.

"I'm afraid that might not be the case after all, come with me."

SEVENTEEN

"Wait here." Touchreik was dropped onto a chair and Antoine got ready to leave. Before he did so he turned to Jak.

"We have to tell him Jak, we have to." Jak nodded and he was gone.

"Tell me what?" said Touchreik.

"Let's just wait, there's someone you need to meet."

Whilst they waited Jak seemed agitated. Louey and Vanilla appeared and Jak called her over. Touchreik couldn't hear the words but clearly, he whispered to her to take Louey out with a backwards nod. He sat at the end of the table dumfounded, wringing his hands. He had no idea what was about to go on but there was suddenly a change of mood and a lot of tension.

"Where's Antoine gone?" he croaked.

"He won't be long, there's someone you need to speak too."

"About what?"

"Let's wait, best we're all here."

They waited, Vanilla left with Louey. The Professor accepted a drink of water and sat in silence at the table. He spun the glass around on the surface between his thumb and finger.

Around ten minutes later the door burst open and in walked Antoine followed by another man he recognised. Not a stranger after all but the dude who had led him up to the chase all those years ago. Greetings were exchanged, drinks offered and the group gathered around the table. The tone seemed a little more jovial now and Antoine was all smiles. Touchreik faced the dude at the opposite end whilst the two humanists sat either side. The size of the table increased the distance between the four men.

At last Antoine addressed Touchreik.

"Tell him what you told me," nodding to the dude.

He looked at them all one by one, should he back track or deny what he said? He decided to push on until he got a feel for where this was going.

"I had," he corrected himself, "have small samples of the Caveman memory trace. Scraps of data. This data intrigued me and so I kept it."

"What's the nature of it?" the dude asked. It was clear now that he had as little knowledge of where this conversation was going as he did. As he waited for an answer he looked at the other two. Jak was staring at Touchreik like it was some kind of interrogation. Antoine became very animated, as if he might burst into laughter at any moment. "Tell him."

"Deep in his memory, probably fantasy there is knowledge of the word," he looked into each of their eyes. He was mystified as to why this word was so relevant to them.

"Black-Star," he said.

Everyone in the room looked at each other. Antoine clapped his hands jumped up and spun round on one foot. The dude fell back into his seat and threw his arms to the sides. Jak simply shuffled uncomfortably.

"I knew it, I told you. I knew it," said Antoine, punching the air and leaning into the dude.

"Knew what?" said Touchreik.

"We have to tell him," Antoine said looking down on the dude who looked as if he'd seen a ghost. The dude shook his head slowly.

Antoine repeated this time emphasising the words. "We.. have.. to tell him."

Jak nodded his head to one side. "He's right."

Antoine looked like he was going to explode with excitement and jumped back into his seat, the dude looked over his shoulder as if someone might be listening. He rolled his shoulders and leaned on his elbows taking a deep breath.

"Gettin on for 20 years ago," he paused as if he may have grown tired of the telling. "It was a great gig for the two years I worked on it," he paused and Jak interrupted.

"From the beginning. He knows nothing about this." He coughed into his hand and started again. "I was doing some hacking around that time, pretty smalltime. Upgrades that kinda thing. One day, right out of the blue I had some guy wanting a job doing, I can't remember what. The kinda thing you might do yourself. He paid well and that was that. Then one day, say around 6 months later he falls into my place with a job offer."

The dude picked up his drink and took a long gulp and placed the glass down as he wiped his sleeve across his cheek.

"I didn't know who this guy was, and still don't but he talks a load of air. He's all excited, and recons he can get me in on some hacking work. He tells me he has a friend who is working on a project. This project is very hush but they are looking for a good tech geek. I told him I'm not interested and I show him the door, but then he tells me about the coinage. This was off the scale, I mean serious pleasure coinage, you get me? I started doing some sums in my head and it spun, you know. This could really set me up. So I ask this guy what sorta people are paying that kinda money for a hack? It's gotta be majorly unscrupulous and he says it ain't, its completely legit. I got this gig if I want it. Then he says there's a reason for the coinage, it's very, very secret. And he stressed this, *very secret*." At that he was struck by the irony of telling his story, uncomfortable even now after all these years.

The group were still looking at the dude as the dim light flickered around his cheeks, he had his audience transfixed as if he were reciting a ghost story.

"I work independent, always have but this was a great gig, I think to myself, maybe 6 months then I'm out. A week later I am in some laboratory with three other dudes and we have a brief. That's when we think we're dealing with some crazies."

"Why?" as Touchreik said this Antoine let out a giggle.

"Because the job was impossible to do, but they were paying us to try. So we tried. The four of us knew it, but hardly said it out loud. They kept paying and we keep playing as we used to say. We all agreed to string 'em along, as long as the coinage was there."

Touchreik was intrigued but unable to preempt any connection to himself or what he had said.

"They gave us the remains of some plans for a device that we're being asked to build. No one knows where these drawings came from but they were very old. Ancient code and technology and they were scanned from actual scribe so it fitted with what most of us believed. We heard this plan had been recovered from the Major's team on Mars. Maybe even brought back by them, who knows."

There was an audible gasp from Touchreik, Antoine was impressed he might be getting it.

"That was just rumour mind, but it fitted. So there's parts missing from the plan and we have to interpret really old electronic workings which is why it was being done by humans. We knew right along that even with the missing parts of the drawing it would never fly. These guys who were paying us were almost certainly insane and rich."

"Why?"

He paused to look at Antoine who hadn't stopped smiling throughout. The dude looked a little embarrassed as he answered.

"They thought that the plan we had was for," he paused and looked at Antoine as he finished. "A time travel device, a portable unit that could be worn around the waist like a belt." With that the dude fell back in his chair.

Antoine nodded at Touchreik in a told ya kinda of way.

"We kept takin the money and we worked on this foolish project for almost two years."

"Did you have any success?"

The dude laughed. "You're as insane as they were if you think that. But we filled time by devising experiments and building prototypes that sort of thing. But later in the project, we started to actually make sense of it. In theory this thing might actually work, in theory mind, but there was always a problem."

"Which was?"

"It was never going to fly unless we could deal with the incredible heat generation inside the device. There wasn't an element or material in existence was ever gonna do that. But we built a prototype all the same, just like they asked us to."

"You never got to try it?"

"Never got the chance. The next day bang. I get a comm and that's it. The project is shutdown. No notice, nothin they just pay me a bonus and it's over."

"Interesting but I still don't see what this has to do with me?"

"Tell the Professor the name of this project," said Antoine.

"They had a code name for the project," he looked around.

"It was called 'Black-Star.'"

"Oh my Heathen."

"So you see, all theories to one side, without an element that didn't exist the whole thing could never be tested. Much later and with great regret I confided the whole thing to Antoine here."

"And I commission two of these devices, so now we own two replicas."

"You think the Black-Star exists? You believe it's the element on Mars that the drop team are going to recover?"

Antoine leant across the table. "Black-Star exists in the memory of a man from the past, we know someone else has this belt and whoever gets that element first has the option to go back."

"Who?"

"Who knows, who knows what secrets the caveman unconsciously revealed?"

"Two belts you say?"

"The notes suggested they had at least two elements?"

"Yeah he's right there. You see Antoine is willing to get fried to prove this thing works. Now you mention the memory from the caveman he's even more convinced."

Touchreik was puzzled now, he had failed to tell them that the memory involved himself. Are they saying it would be him who went back in time?

"You actually think time travel is possible?"

"The theory is completely sound. This device would effectively take all your organic matter, chop it up and replace it in another time. Time is real for us because of how we experience it. In reality, it's a construct of space and time like Einstein said. If it were possible, and it might be. You could move through time as easily as moving through space. Like walking from one end of the room to another."

"No," said Touchreik who was intrigued at the simplicity of his concept.

"We had all kinds of really old reference books there, some of those were probably recovered from the Mars project. Einstein, Planck and Musk, these ancient scientists they knew it could be done but they never had the chops in those days, it was all theory."

"Still is," said Jak looking concerned.

"This Einstein guy claimed time was really just an illusion for us, that it could be that everything that was going to happen or has happened all took place in an instant. Imagine time and space like a loaf of bread, it's all there. Your future and mine."

"Tell me more," Touchreik was glad he hadn't mentioned his role in that memory of Nova's, this made it even more intriguing.

"The time travel paradox? Let's say tomorrow I invent my time machine and come back to this room about now, would I be here now?"

"Logically yes."

"That's not how it works, that's just how your perception of it works. Imagine now the loaf and you go back in time. It's like you're a grain of flour in the loaf that reappears in a fold on top of the loaf. You would perceive everything to be exactly the same in the universe but in reality, if there is such a thing, you're just in the fold. In one dimension there's two of you and in another you have never gone back. To both people there is no paradox."

"I don't quite understand."

"I am saying that in actual fact it's in an entirely different but identical reality that your older self has reappeared in this room. If now is a slice of the loaf then travelling from the bottom of that slice to the top would feel identical. In this reality it's clearly just us who are here now. That's because of the slice we are experiencing."

"So there could be two of me or you somewhere if this thing worked?"

"That's it my friend. The only changes that would be made would be anything you did, including killing your grandfather!"

"Killing."

"It's the time travel paradox, go back and kill your grandfather then how could you be born to get in a time machine to go back and kill him. In this instance both can apply and be true. Reference Schrodinger's cat."

"Cat?"

"It's a quantum thought experiment in which a cat can be both alive and dead at the same time until observed. He argued that the decision was made by the person looking at the cat, look it up. It applies perfectly here."

"Got a headache yet?"

"There's just one catch with the 'Totality Intersperse Nexus Machine' which was its official title. If it worked, and it's a huge if, you can only go backwards and you can only travel within your own lifetime. After that you would hit problems with decay and that kinda thing."

"Where are these devices?"

Antoine left the room and went upstairs to his son's room, he returned with one of them and handed it to Touchreik. It was just as he expected, a belt with a large buckle. No interface, just a simple dial and a button on the front. Touchreik stood and walked around the table, pulling it round his waist. He looked at the mechanical dial on the front which showed the year TVC15. He hesitated before pressing the button.

"Careful Professor, if that thing worked you don't want to take the whole house with you."

He looked puzzled.

"The force doesn't spread out too far but it will take all organic material connected with you. Either jump as you press the button or stand on something non organic such as rock or stone. If you don't then who knows what you'll take back in time with you. The carpets, curtains or a chunk of garden."

"Ah, so cotton, leather clothing."

"Yep, hold your pants though if you have a steel buckle, could be embarrassing arriving in the past with your pants round your ankles."

"If this thing works then it might mean someone could use it, all they need is the 'Black-Star'"

"Are you starting to realise what this means Professor?"

"Someone of means had belts similar to these made and someone of means are now willing and able to pay for a trip to Mars, to recover the 'Black-Star'."

"You know what's happening now because of the caveman, imagine if we could go back and stop him being thawed. These ancient god ideas might never have made their way into the Saviour Machine and Migration might never happen."

"You're not taking this seriously, are you?"

"He's been taking this seriously for a long time."

"If we had the 'Black-Star' we could go back, what if we don't and someone else gets it first?"

"So you're thinking of stealing the most valuable and well protected item in the known universe from outerspace?"

"No, not me, *we* will steal it," he said nodding to Jak.

"How do you propose to do that?

"We have about 4 years to work that out, in the meantime we have to start by getting you aboard the Lazarus."

EIGHTEEN

"That's a bit of a turnaround but I'm pleased you've reconsidered," said Prout bemused.

"You were right, over the last few days I've had a good think and I've come this far."

"This far?"

"With the whole project, the caveman, Professorship, count me in."

Prout fell back in his chair grinning from ear to ear. "That's great news. I'll let them know straight away."

"That's a point," said Touchreik. "Let who know?" he enquired.

"The sponsor? I honestly have no idea, but do we care? To think of what these additional samples and artefacts will do for our collection." Actually yes, he did care. Touchreik hadn't seriously expected a straight answer.

"I suppose," he said glibly.

"There's no rush right now is there. You'll find out soon enough I expect. The drop Commander is Theodore Maxtor. He might know?" Touchreik raised his eyebrows.

"Certainly qualified."

"That's all I can tell you. The Lazarus will be ready in about 4 years and the V-World sim is ready in a few weeks, you can take a look around it then."

"I'll look forward to it."

"It's going to be an open sim to try and encourage bookings for the maiden voyage. They plan to take a few hundred paying passengers as well as you hitchhikers."

Touchreik and the others were pleased with such immediate progress but that's all there was. The days passed and Touchreik noticed how wild it was on the outside and changes in the climate became noticeable. Leaving the relative warm confines of Heathen the air became crisp and cold very quickly. He experienced his first natural Winter and saw how the humanists adapted to it. Young Louey played in the white fluffy snow until his fingers burned with cold. He would always go back for more. The Spring came and everything thawed, life became easier in Greenwich as people spent time outdoors. Touchreik could feel the chill in the air once more, realising the year had gone full circle. Louey made his own snow people now and yet there was little mention of their overall plan. Touchreik became a part time resident in the room upstairs where he had spent his first night, splitting his time between Heathen and Greenwich. The experience invigorated him and he felt like a new man. There was a feeling of hope for so many things. He still hurt about Ramona and Jagger too but was far from the somber withdrawn character he'd become. A whole year had passed and there was little sign of being able to get anyone else aboard. They had all toured the Virtual Lazarus ship many times but Touchreik couldn't invite guests. They had to find a way of getting others aboard and time was ticking.

Simply buying a ticket was an absolute last resort but they had already agreed that would leave them exposed, but if it came to that so be it. They had to plan a clean getaway so as to avoid any repercussions in Greenwich. At the moment they assumed they were being tolerated out here. If they threatened Mother that might change. Antoine had become as much a resident at the Professor's accommodation. He'd busied himself tidying up before his first visit and this had given him a mental boost. Antoine spent endless hours there, where he had access to the Heathen grid, giving him access to news and information gathering. In many instances their lives crossed over with Touchreik in Greenwich and Antoine in Heathen and vice versa.

The second outside Winter had settled in and the nights were shorter before the next major breakthrough. Antoine had been able to use a worm in a communication between Touchreik and Theodore Maxtor's to access his comms. It wasn't long before he was able to gain a complete picture of the security that was planned for the mission. Jak's dining room had generally been the social centre and would now act as a briefing room.

The whole inner circle were gathered around the table. Touchreik and Jak, of course the dude was there as well as Vanilla and Louey. Antoine stood at the front and began his breakdown of what they were up against.

"A specialist security drone from Syntex Cybernetics will be deployed 24/7 in the vault and weeks before launch. Its equipped with technology and organic detection and will be feeding back to the bridge regularly. This means it can spot organic life and rogue electronic signals inside the vault. The 'Black-Star' will be placed inside a Creedence Security display cabinet version 6 with similar security features. The vault itself will sit on the outside of the ship meaning all its outside walls are in outer space. The only way in or out is through the intended passageway which is patrolled by the drone. The vault door is secured by DNA and voice mapping which responds to the presence of Maxtor and the Captain herself."

"So why didn't you just say impossible?" said the dude.

Antoine ignored him and shaking his head pushed on. "It can't be stolen before it goes in the vault, that's obvious unless we want to be stuck 40 million miles away without a ride home."

"Could we take the time belts to the stones?" said Jak.

"Pointless, unless you want to jump back in time and find yourself on Mars in TVC15, for about 5 seconds before you died," said Antoine.

"So we wait till they are here," said Jak looking round the room for support. "It has to be easier if we just wait."

Antoine shook his head in dismay. "No way, if we let those stones get back to Earth then we might never find them again."

"It doesn't sound good," said Vanilla.

"It can be done. Our window of opportunity is tiny. Leave me with it ok, first we need to get everyone aboard."

After that meeting the stones felt more like a hundred million kilometres away than 40 million.

The snow thawed and the Spring brought out a new stream of nature. The streams flowed freely, fish and wild animals were abundant as breeding season could be observed across nature. As time passed they would discuss the Black-Star as small groups and fantasise about how or why the belt might work. Life went on for everyone else but Antoine never lost his passion for this idea. He had become convinced it would succeed in part by the memory in Nova's head.

Meanwhile Touchreik grew into this living laboratory both as an observer and as one of them, fast becoming an inaugural humanist. He was always willing to cast doubt on the humanist's motives in any heated debate but warmed to them considerably. He learned so much in his time there about his speciality, human history because he lived amongst it. Survival in the wild, fire and hunting as well as helping in the village with enclosed power systems such as solar and wind. They were able to harness energy from nature itself to provide heat and warmth, completely off Mother's grid. He also developed a relationship with Louey and saw how he grew physically and mentally by the time he celebrated his 9th Birthday. His fears for the boy's future ebbed over time and although he would be a unique character, like others born on the outside he would survive. He showed himself to be mature way beyond his years.

Life became settled and then that following Summer came another breakthrough. Crucially, Antoine was able to learn where Maxtor was planning to get his team from. There was to be a planning and application process from candidates with a good record of work in reality based systems with particular skills. Unknown to the others, Antoine had never wavered from his plan and the work he had done over the years would soon bear fruit.

The tiny area of undergrowth that lead to the break in the fence where he entered all those months ago with the Professor had worn away into a rough path. Trodden in ice snow and dust over the months by one man it now resembled a well-used walkway. He was here again and desperate to get lucky, in his pocket was another list of possible candidates. Just like all the others he had listed through months of searching they were perfect or adequate for the mission. Great track records, correct age and build except for one thing, they were all organically dead. His list was compiled from those who had migrated. Finding them in what he called maternity was the relatively easy part but he needed a particular type of body. It was rare for Heathens to use an outside comm pack because most would have an implant in the back of the neck. If the people he found were implanted they were useless to him. It was like searching for a needle in a haystack and finding lots, except the needle he wanted had to be a particular type. He slid through the fence and mentally set himself for a long shift. In the time he'd been coming here the fabric of the place had changed which acted as a reminder of the urgency of his mission. The old baby pods were now completely removed and the adult pods were fully functioning. Once inside it took him around half an hour to find his first candidate. He had managed to decipher a rough code that the drones used to store the bodies which would help him search the right area based on his hit list. The system seemed to file humans by a combination of age, sex and orientation. It was a rough system but had proved to be a greater success than a random search. He found his first pod and went through the routine. Climb up and check the label then plug in and hack the lock before reaching into the green goo and placing a hand around the back of the neck. As usual he felt nothing, closed the pod and searched for the next one. He'd gone through a further five pods with the usual result, no outer comm unit. Five more needles in haystacks found, none were the right type. The light coming through the skylight had started to dull and he'd leave soon. Drones didn't need visible light to carry out their tasks, so he'd be forced to work by torchlight if he stayed much longer. A lesson he learned long ago, it just wasn't productive to work in the dark. There might be enough light to try one more if he could find it quickly. He checked his list, 'Leroy Payne - 88875173862'

He was in luck and found the pod he was looking for in around ten minutes. He climbed up and plugged in to start the hack on the lock. After a few moments it popped and he lifted the lid. Antoine reached inside and put his hand round the back of the man's neck. He was glad this was the last one for today and was feeling pretty hungry, it was a long drive back to the village. Then he felt something, on the back of the man's neck. At first he almost pulled away but checked once more. There was a small device about a centimetre square and around 2 mm thick attached to the back of the neck. His heart rate increased and he slowly ran his fingers around it to be sure. He had one at last, he actually had one, this was incredible.

He dropped down to the ground and took a minute to steady himself. It was late but he had to do this now. If they moved this pod then he might not get the chance again. It was very unlikely, but he couldn't take that chance after all these months of searching.

He opened his pack and pushed a headlight over his temple and switched it on. He pulled some tools into his pockets and climbed back up. This was the first time he had actually needed to push a body over in the goo. It increased the resistance as he tried to twist this dead weight at the waist. In the end he used a rod he had found lying around to purchase between the man's shoulder and the side of the pod. He could now use both hands to freely work on the small device attached to the back of the man's neck. The simplest way would be to remove the device with a large chunk of flesh but that would leave scars he didn't want to be seen. Instead he would have to go through the removal process by attaching the device, accessing and releasing it.

He attached a wire into an almost invisible socket on the device and began his hack coder. After around ten minutes there was an audible beep and the little square popped off and hung freely on the end of the wire. He held it up in the light and for a moment, in awe at the chance he might be able to do this after all.

He put it in his pocket and set about releasing the body back into the liquid and locking the lid. After a few moments finally checking he had left nothing behind he was on his way.

After two years he finally had a comm unit he could use and strangely enough it was only a few months before he went through the same process for a second time.

He'd secured two identities that were so close to legitimate as to be undetectable.

Leroy Payne would be a very good candidate for the drop mission. A record of reality adventures, good with code, vehicles and mechanics. He came from a wealthy family and had an exemplary record in his education. He had also been in hot water over one or two misdemeanours in the past but generally just mischief.

This was the identity that Antoine had adopted to pursue a place on the mission. Having full access to Maxtor's communications he was able to push Leroy up the pecking order in the following weeks and eliminate or hide stronger candidates. In time it became clear that Maxtor was making decisions and there was some competition. Antoine monitored the situation closely and saw that a Seiren White had been confirmed for the crew. That left two places and three strong potentials, his alternative identity was one of them. In the end he made a risky decision to intervene or lose the opportunity all together. He dropped a communication over to Maxtor from a very good friend, recommending that he take Leroy over the other two. Very risky but the slight nudge helped Maxtor and he went for it.

The following day he received confirmation he had been chosen for the mission. Antoine posing as Leroy Payne was now a member of the drop team. Time was passing but having two people aboard was progress.

The second identity was set up for Jak and was a chap named 'Juliette Tiding'. He didn't know the name he'd be given yet but after all the work it had taken to get these chips he better just go along with it. In the end he took it surprisingly well. The only other problem now was getting him aboard, he wouldn't stand a chance of getting on the drop team even if there were places left. The last one was offered to a fellow called Adrenalin Sinus.

The mission launched in under a year and he had no idea how he was going to get Jak aboard under the guise of Juliette.

He let himself into Jak's accommodation only to find Touchreik throwing up into a bucket at the back door. Jak and Louey were laughing heartily at the poor man. He had been trying out the docking simulation in a V-World Sim. Despite the adverse reaction he still hadn't tried the simulation with a full 100% Pain Perception. Louey had apparently enjoyed the ride immensely.

It took a while for Jak to explain as he gasped for breath, Touchreik wasn't amused. He wiped his mouth with his sleeve and pushed past the three of them and stormed upstairs.

It was at that moment that the idea hit him, not only a way to get Jak aboard but it would possibly include a fool proof escape plan. If it worked it would be relatively easy to set up. All that remained after that was to work out how they would deal with the bit in between, where they manage to steal the most precious known artefact in the history of humanity.

NINETEEN

Touchreik had adapted well over the years to his double life. By day a respected historian and lecturer and by night a humanist. Living as the very beings he had studied. The complete lack of amenities became second nature to him. He'd stopped asking for things like food, water and changes to mood lighting and would naturally do it himself. He staggered into the bathroom and twisted the taps and managed to get the water somewhere near the required temperature. Leaning on the sink he watched it twirl and splash against the sides. Then he looked up into a mirror that was steaming up and wiped his hand across its surface. He looked at the face staring back at him. Every day he looked in the mirror he looked more and more like the man he knew was him in Nova's memory. That's if he was called Nova at all, seeing as he'd held no memory of that name.

Not for the first time he chopped and changed the scenario in his mind, playing over what the dude had said about time travel. It had to be done in your own lifetime, so what if he went back and met Nova. What if it really was the Professor in that image?

That left two problems, the first was according to the dude it would be impossible for Nova to hold that memory. That's because according to the loaf theory, even though he might travel back in time at some point, it would still not have happened yet. The second problem was concerning, even if it was the case there were no plans for the Professor to go back anyway. There were two replica belts and probably two pieces of 'Black-Star', these were intended for Jak and Antoine to return. The pair had clear plans to scupper the thawing out all together or kill Nova before he could cause the damage he has caused.

They were right on one thing though, it all lead back to Nova, in fact even more than they knew.

Touchreik had avoided the need to face these questions because the chances of even attempting to steal the 'Black-Star' least of all get away with it stayed distant and unattainable. But things were changing, Antoine was giving off an air of confidence. There was daily talk both in their inner circle and in Heathen that the mission was drawing close.

Lazarus was undergoing her final trials in Orbit above the Earth and most significantly the drone missions had left. These were already heading across space to put the infrastructure in place for the drop.

Tickets were sold for the general passengers and Aladyn showed no sign of panic, in fact the following week proved the opposite.

Antoine announced out of nowhere that he had finished his preparations in readiness for the mission. Touchreik was starting to believe they might all have decided to just go along for the ride and see what happened. Antoine had other ideas, he announced that he was ready to execute a definite plan that would enable a group of amateur thieves to outwit the highest levels of security on Earth and steal the 'Black-Star'.

"I've been looking over the security precautions, software systems and procedures and they are flawless," he paused, "almost."

They waited. "The interesting thing is, perhaps its budget, but they are using a slightly older version of the security cabinet upgrade."

"So you think there might be a weakness to exploit?" said Jak.

"No," said Antoine with a grin, "the opposite in fact. I am going to try and find a way of upgrading to the newer version which has some additional security features."

Everyone looked at each other puzzled. "Better."

"Exactly."

"The security drone will be programmed at the high security compound in Syntex before it leaves. Then it takes the shuttle and logs itself into the vault, once there it will check and upgrade all the systems in readiness for the flight."

"Can we get to him?" said Touchreik embarrassed at using the term we.

Antoine shook his head. "It's a security drone, it's designed to detect interference of any kind, instead we are going to have to ensure he arrives with the correct upgraded software with all the new features."

"But how?"

"We buy it ourselves."

"This is getting ridiculous," said the dude who was standing up as if he might leave.

"Wait, hear me out. It's risky but I think I can intercept Maxtor's communication channel and order the upgrade. All we have to do is pay upfront and have it loaded onto the security drone."

"So you are going to steal the stones, by paying for a security upgrade? Are you sure this is the right line of work for you?" said Vanilla.

Antoine put his hands on his hips. "Oh yeah," he said. His confidence was unshakable because he believed that the fact Nova had a memory of 'Black-Star' proved this would not fail. They had all spent time trying to convince him that was not necessarily true. "As long as we have all the security information then we should have no suspicion, the trick will be making the payment direct."

"This gets better," said the dude falling back into his chair and folding his arms.

"There are some hurdles."

The dude rolled his eyes at Jak.

"To increase the security, I need to find a way of making changes to the software on the Creedence Cabinate V6 where the stone or stones will be held. To do that I have to change the order with Syntex, to do that I have to impersonate Theodore Maxtor in a way undetectable by the artificial intelligence comms. The entire plan hinges on that conversation."

"So that easy then?" said the dude.

"That easy."

The next morning Antoine had been around much earlier than anyone else. He'd been coming in and out with various boxes, technology and wires. By the time the rest of them had eaten and started to show interest he was almost ready to go. The dude was examining the equipment with an expert eye and deciphered what he was doing.

"This has to be a joke right? Is this really what I think it is?"

"Probably?" said Antoine.

"This is a 455X diversion modulator," he said flicking a piece of wire disrespectfully.

"Is all I got."

The dude turned and walked towards the door to leave and then came back, rubbing his chin. The others grouped behind him one by one.

"What's this?" said Jak.

"You are about to find out I believe." Crouching on the other side of the table assessing the wires Antoine began talking the group through his contraption.

"This comm is fed into Heathen via the Professor's Sage, this means we can comm as if we are there. I tried passing it into this modulator and it picks up the face mimicking software."

Everyone stared at the screen as he powered up and Theodore Maxtor's face appeared. As he moved his face the screen face mimicked him and spoke his words. "This is fed into a false VRE system which hacks into Maxtor's comms and provided he doesn't decide to use it himself then all communications will be coming from his home with all his traceability. As far as the artificial intelligence desk is concerned I'm Maxtor."

"What about your voice?" said Vanilla

"It won't matter because that's not checked, as long as I say as little as possible and move as little as possible then we might get away with it."

"What do you think?" he said staring out of the screen at them.

"Daddy," said Louey.

"It will fool facial recognition software across a comms line. As long as I keep movement and conversation to a minimum then it can work."

The dude looked up at them from behind the desk and shook his head.

Half an hour later Antoine took a deep breath and made a final check to the leads before switching on his communicator. He wouldn't be speaking to any humans but that made the risk greater in some ways. He hit the switch and a face appeared on the screen in front of him. It wasn't his own face but that of Commander Maxtor. He moved his mouth and mimicked some speaking actions and the face followed suit. It was now or never, he knew he had to leave this until as late as possible. He hit comm.

A Syntex logo appeared on the screen and then a robotic artificial intelligence operators face.

"Good evening, welcome to Syntex Cybernetic systems how can I help you?" she said with a warm smile.

"Good evening. My name is Commander Theodore Maxtor."

"Commander Maxtor, how are you this evening?"

"I'm very well thank you."

"How may I help you?"

"I've just been doing some final checks on the software specification for our mission. I see we are set up for version 6."

"Sir, I'm unable to discuss security issues with you at this time," she paused, "would you hold a moment whilst I complete a security check?"

"Of course," said Antoine and sighed with relief.

The face on the screen went blank, Antoine was able to glance down at his panel. He had rerouted the call through a surrogate server that mirrored that of Maxtor's. The facial recognition and I.P. will hopefully be enough, he held his breath.

The face came back to life. "Thank you for waiting Commander, how can I help you?"

"We seem to have version 6 software is that correct?"

"Absolutely version 6 has been in operation for 7 years and has never reported a failure."

"That's fine, it's just that I notice from my log that I need the IAR upgrade which is only available in version 7."

"That's correct Sir, The Invisibility Augmented Reality Cloak is our newest feature."

"Could you upgrade for me please?"

"Unfortunately, the job is in processing." The face froze again for a second. "There will be an additional upgrade fee as well as admin costs totalling 879 C's"

"That's fine."

"Thank you Sir, I'll take the payment from the account we have on file."

"No," said Antoine with a little too much panic in his voice. "I'm afraid that's not possible, I've just realised we have completed our accounts and submitted billing to the client. This one's on me I'm afraid. Could I pay direct right now? It would be a great help and allow me to push on with my preparations. So much to do with the mission so close."

The drone face paused expressionless. "Certainly Sir."

"Thank you." Antoine pushed some buttons on his keypad below and dialled in the numbers."

"That's gone through for you Sir, would you like a receipt to the usual address?"

"No, I'll take it here. All done then?" He said with a smile.

"All done then," said the drone voice. "Is there anything else I can help with today?"

"No, thank you," said Antoine and he was about to hang up.

"Commander Maxtor, I have just noticed something on your account."

"Yes."

"You don't have adequate insurance cover for the mission. We offer personal security with free reality insurance with all our products, I can offer a 5% discount on any orders placed today."

"No, that's fine thank you."

"Goodbye."

"Goodbye."

The screen went blank and Antoine almost collapsed under the pressure. He had done it. The drone would now take a full set of the upgraded software for the cabinet and install it in the vault. The first potential hurdle was overcome and there was little else to do now but wait for the trip. Although things were going to be a little different for Jak aka Juliette in the coming weeks.

He began a six month work placement at the mag port. Antoine had secured him the position and he'd been instructed to do nothing but keep his head down and complete any human tasks as necessary. The shuttles were being tested and run at the port in readiness for the mission. Juliette managed to assign himself close enough to the crews who would be maintaining the craft. This would entail being on hand to look after passengers and pilot manually if required on board the shuttles. He had no way of guaranteeing he could be assigned to the Lazarus job but that mattered little as long as he had clearance.

The Professor didn't expect to sleep on that final night and he was right. His thoughts had returned to the reason he found himself here and where it might lead. According to the dude, the pair could succeed in going back in time and rescue him and Ramona as well as Heathen. According to his explanation the Professor might never experience that happening. This reality, this universe would be unaffected because that would take place in a different dimension, a different slice of the loaf. He thought of Ramona fondly as he drifted to sleep and felt the hurt once more and knew he'd likely never see her again.

The next morning the team ate together as they had done many times before, except for Touchreik. He spent his last night at his own accommodations and decided it was best to follow protocol. Jak made emotional farewells to Vanilla and Lou, promising he would be back soon. Lou had matured and grown up with this day in mind. An understanding of the time belt concept and what it might entail. The lad was upset and begged his father not to go back in time without saying goodbye first. Jak gave him the belts and told him he trusted him with these and to guard them till they all returned. That way they would have a chance to see each other before he used them. Lou looked relieved at that, like he held the key should he ever have to lose his father for longer if not forever.

Vanilla hugged him till he might suffocate and they jumped into the battery vehicle and headed for Heathen.

The next afternoon, Jak scanned his I.D. and entered the terminal as usual. Instead of heading up the corridor he went right and down towards the runway and taxi areas. Out on the tarmac stood the shuttle craft and he watched with one or two others as the crew disembarked. According to Antoine the last trip up was going to be just the drop crew. There would be no need for any courtesy staff so there would only be a pilot on board. Jak went into the changing room behind the spectators. Opening his holdall he took out a captain's uniform jacket and put it on, placing his original inside the bag. He pulled out a Captain's cap and placed it on his head and checked himself in the mirror. He approached the auto doors and dropped his holdall into the washing chute as he left. Pushing back his shoulders he walked bolt upright past the approaching crew. They acknowledged him as he touched the peak of his cap to them with a tip of the head. He marched confidently towards the waiting craft and bounded up the stairway. Scanning his pass he opened the cockpit door and slid inside. A bald man was sat at the cockpit checking instruments and making ready for his last trip.

"Hey."

"Hi."

"How is she?" said Jak.

"Fine, who are you?" said the man glancing over his shoulder.

"Juliette and you?"

"Stomp, Captain Stomp."

"Are you all done here," said Jak sitting in the opposite seat.

"I wish, I got the last flight to do, quick turnaround."

"Oh Sorry, I am on rota to do that one. No worries I'll go drop my shift card in, easy night for me then." Jak leapt from the seat and turned to leave.

The bald man shouted after him. "Hey wait," he said interested. "You mean they booked you for the last flight up?"

Jak shrugged his shoulders. "Well yeah, but it's probably just an admin thing. I'll drop my ticket in on my way home." He turned to leave.

"Wait a minute, where are you going?"

"Home."

The man stood and approached the doorway. "This is an 8 to 10 hour round trip, you know that. I just brought this bird back and I've been flying since 7am this morning."

Jak opened his palms. "Hey, I'm sorry but if there's some mistake don't blame me ok, I don't do the allocations." He set off down the stairwell.

"But it's your trip," shouted the bald guy.

"How can it be mine, you're on rota."

"So are you." Jak turned and walked back up and into the entrance to the craft.

"Ok look Mr it's your trip."

"I say we toss a coin." The bald guy grinned. "Heads, I take the flight and tails you take it."

Jak looked quite put out. "Ok."

Baldy rummaged in his pocket and pulled out a coin.

"Heads." He said and flicked it up, peeling his hand away disappointed.

"There yer go fair n square," said Jak. "She's all yours, have a good flight," Flicking his peak he turned to leave.

"Wait," said Baldy, "best of three."

"Best of three? You're kidding me."

"Scared?"

Jak nodded defiantly, Baldy flicked it again this time he hit a tales.

"Next one decides it?"

"Yep."

They both watched intensely as the coin span in the air and Baldy caught it, slapping it on the back of his hand. He slowly peeled his palm away to reveal another tales.

"Have a good flight buddy," he said.

In no time he had grabbed his things and was heading down the stairwell to the tarmac.

Jak shouted after him, "Best of five." Baldy stopped and turned with his jacket over his arm and simply winked.

"Cross checks are all done, she's being fuelled as we speak and the flight plan is on the dash. No crew on this one it's just a special for the drop team. Have a nice flight Captain," and he was off.

Jak smiled and breathed out as he straightened his cap and straightened his tie and stood proudly at the top of the gangway until he saw a tall man appear through the doorway.

He offered a toothy grin from his weathered face and tapped his forehead in greeting.

"Commander Maxtor?"

"Yeah," said the man defiantly.

"You and your crew are the only passengers on this one Sir. If you make your way down the cabin you can use the private class facilities. You'll find it much more comfortable." Waving a hand he pointed between the rows of empty seats.

TWENTY

The space bar wasn't particularly busy that evening although it was a superb vantage point to observe the Planet Mars. By now most people had their media and many were enjoying a meal or chatting with friends. A rowdy group would randomly cheer or shout out for no apparent reason. There were a few smaller 2D screens dotted around which showed a live feed of the drop to Mars by Maxtor's crew. They would relay occasional live feeds from the drop and parts of the exploration of the surface. As far as most were concerned they might not have bothered.

In the intervening hours Maxtor's drop crew had got themselves ready to make their trip to Mars. First, they had to get themselves into free space guided by Adrenalin Sinus up on the bridge.

"You people ready?" said Maxtor who was greeted with a trio of nodding heads.

"Let's go." He said with a thumbs up.

Seiren couldn't contain her joy, like a child at a fairground ride. Leroy Payne wasn't quite as convinced but nonetheless he interjected for good measure. "Let's ride."

The Professor's heart was pounding through his chest, he was so frightened. The drop was designed to be fully automated but Sinus would monitor aboard the Lazarus to intervene which was highly unlikely.

"Sinus, are we clear on communication," barked Maxtor.

"Yes Sir," chirped Sinus joyously in their ears. "All systems are on and checked. We have about 35 minutes until the drop."

A narrow stairway stood in front of the team and it led up into the ceiling of the corridor. They had avoided an audience by entering through a hatch situated in a private area of the ship. Once through the hatch Maxtor paused to look up at the tunnel which disappeared into the distance. He began the ascent and lead the team up a ladder, he was closely followed by Leroy and then Touchreik and Seiren. They climbed through the roof of the corridor and into a 3 meter diameter tube. Looking up even Maxtor had vertigo. They were now inside one of the spokes of the Lazarus that would lead into the central core of the ship. This area did not spin and was zero G, once they got there and it was a very long climb of around 400 Mtrs.

"Comms, check People."

"Sieren, Check."

"Touchreik, Check."

"Leroy, Check."

"Stay close, the first part is a climb but remember it will get easier and easier as we get closer to the central core of the ship. The virtual gravity will have less and less effect, as for the vertigo I can't say. Let's start."

They climbed the ladder slowly but had reasonable manoeuvrability in the thin cloth suits. They were only distinguishable by their build and appeared like clones in white body suits and red tight fitting headgear. It was a long climb and on a couple of occasions the Professor had to stop to catch his breath. He'd been climbing for around 15 minutes when he stopped for a third time for a breath as the Commander and Leroy carried on ahead, not noticing he had stopped. The Professor peered down between his arms and past Seiren and saw the vast drop below. His knuckles went white as he gripped tighter onto the ladder, pulling himself closer. He was more frightened of panicking or losing control than he was of the drop itself.

"Don't look down," Seiren barked at him gruffly.

Instead he looked up and could see the other two around thirty metres ahead of him. By now he was getting lighter as the gravity decreased the closer they climbed to the central core. After around ten more minutes he looked up to see that the Commander had spun round and appeared to be upside down staring down at him. Loosening his grip a little he could feel a strange sensation of being very light and yet still being pulled slowly down the tube. Touchreik grabbed on once more. Eventually he reached the point of weightlessness and was now able to gently push himself along the ladder. Seiren followed and eventually the four of them were able to travel a little faster towards the core of the ship. The tube they had been climbing exited into a room. The room looked like it was spinning around in front of them and was incredibly disorientating. Their exit was embedded in a complete loop around the room and the Commander and Leroy were inside the room now. They, the room and everything in it was tumbling over and over. Maxtor called to the Professor and beckoned him inside.

"Come on, push in," he shouted.

Touchreik grabbed the ladder and gave himself a push into the central core and floated inside. Maxtor grabbed him and righted him upwards. Now the room felt quite still and yet the tube exit was spinning across the floor and over the top and round and round it went. In no time Seiren repeated the move although somewhat more gracefully than the Professor. The three of them were now weightless in the steel core of the ship and the Commander lead them through a padded tube into another room. The Professor was still struggling with the sensation of weightlessness and had to quickly under compensate his movements. The next room was bigger and at the end stood the five drop pods including the spare. It was clear now that they were suspended from the top onto a rail system. This looked like a mini mono rail and lead out into an airlock. The Commander headed towards them.

The Professor gave a push to float across but over compensated and sent himself crashing into the opposing wall. Gently he righted himself and the three gathered at the drop pods.

"Sinus?" said Maxtor.

"I'm here," came the voice in everyone's ears.

"These pods are designed for each individual body shape to allow for external forces. Please enter your own individual drop unit ladies and gentlemen." Each one had its intended passengers name above it and stencilled onto the unit itself. The doors were open and close up they felt bigger than Touchreik had expected. The others started to put on their full space suits and Touchreik followed their lead.

"We need to push on ladies and gentlemen, we definitely don't want to go round again. I have a slot for you guys."

Once dressed in the space suits and sealed in they each took a moment to check each other out externally for any damage. When everyone was satisfied they each floated to their drop pods and stood inside. Touchreik felt that he fitted snuggly inside and the actual cushioning was a very good fit and there was very little movement once in place.

The Professor jumped when he heard the voice of Sinus in his ear. "Make yourselves comfortable ladies and gentlemen. We have around 5 minutes till we depart and all systems are looking good."

The door of the pod closed and the Professor felt a surge of claustrophobia come over him. He had done this many times in V-World simulation but was learning fast about the feelings of stress in reality. He felt his breathing increase and he started to sweat across his brow.

Sinus spoke calmly in his ear, "Professor, calm down. Your vitals are climbing. This is just like the V-World jump ok. There's no difference."

The Professor took a moment and took some deep breaths.

There was a feeling of movement as the pods were manoeuvred towards the release doors. The view was restricted but he saw the doors slide open and reveal the vast stillness of space. This was contrary to what they had observed through the ships spin over the last weeks. Touchreik stretched forward and looked up and could just make out the outer rim of the Lazarus spinning above him.

"Look straight ahead please. The ship will disorientate you. We are 15 seconds to drop," cried Sinus.

There was some room to move his head around and the Professor was able to see a lot of instruments and a counter which presumably was the countdown timer.

It changed in sync with Sinus's voice. "Five, four, three, two, one."

Touchreik gripped his hands into a fist and squeezed his eyes shut. He felt a small jolt and when he opened them he was floating in free space. In front of him he could see the back of another pod, presumably the Commanders. He felt more movement in unison with the other pod and saw what lay below him. He was now face down towards the huge red dusty planet of Mars, floating silently. The awe inspiring sight filled him with a temporary feeling of euphoria, to see the centre of his entire life and that of all Heathens right in front of him.

Finally he turned to the left and could make out the vastness of the Lazarus once more as it slowly pulled away from them. The other two pods were floating nearby.

Then they heard the voice of Sinus, "We are 30 seconds to the go, I am on the 20/20. All systems are green, green. Vitals are also on the regular and looking good. Please bear with me ladies and gentlemen whilst I artificial initialise."

There was a pause and then a shift as if some kind of minor test blast on the rockets.

"Hold on tight, ladies and gents, let's go to Mars."

There was a jerk and a vibration from outside and the real sense of movement as Touchreik felt himself pulled against the pod walls, sinking into its spongy interior.

The Professor and presumably the other three were starting to hurtle towards the planets rocky surface feet first and were gathering speed. The vast size of Mars in comparison to the tiny pods hid the rate of descent and thousands of kilometres an hour felt almost still. The Professor had experienced the V-World version of this descent and so far it had been unpleasantly accurate. Mars was growing quickly as it was pulled towards them. By contrast the Lazarus was completely out of sight and continuing in its orbit unseen, they were alone now. There was a sound that was hollow and distant for a while as the pods started to loop and absorb speed. Then something happened, a kind of crunch of metal on metal then a banging sound. A huge knocking sound on the side of the Professor's pod as if a giant fist was pounding the walls. This had never happened in any of the sims.

Sinus spoke in his ear, "Professor, are you ok?"

"I think so," he said looking around.

Inside the Lazarus, Sinus was quickly assessing the numbers and studying the simulation graphics. He pulled and moved screens and data at lightning speed. Captain Bernsteen looked on over his shoulder.

"We have a problem with the Professor's pod," he said without a pause.

"What kind of problem?" she asked leaning on her fists and studying the indecipherable data.

"His heat shield has come loose, it's not meant to jettison yet."

"What does that mean?"

By now the others were sensing there was something wrong although it was unlikely they could see anything.

"Maxtor here, what's our status, over?"

Sinus ignored him, scanning his dials, pressing buttons and checking results. There was no time to deal with him right now, if his pod was behaving as planned. He threw some rough calculations into the computers and a result came back, not exact but enough to confirm what he knew.

"The heat build-up is going to be too much. He is going to burn up." A coloured simulation appeared on the Augmented screen in front of him.

"Sinus, what's happening? It's hot I can't breathe." Touchreik could feel the temperature rising very quickly, the pounding sound from outside continued. The smell of burning might have been in his imagination. There was no response from Sinus. Maybe that was it? Maybe he couldn't hear him?

"A.I. switch to manual control," Sinus instructed.

The flat response came immediately, "Sir, I can't do that, it's not within a human capability. It will endanger human life to control the pod manually."

"Sinus!" the voices were overlapping now from the Professor and from the Commander.

"Captain I need you to override the A.I," he barked at her.

"But," she was about to argue.

"Now Captain we haven't got time for a debate. I am in command of this mission. Do it now," he spoke firmly. The Commander sighed.

"Confirm pod three manual control please!"

She went to the main desk and placed a palm on the unit and punched some keys.

"Professor can you hear me?" screamed Sinus.

He could, but the clanging of metal got louder and the oxygen was getting hotter.

"What's happening?" he screamed.

"I haven't got time Professor just trust me. I am going to jettison your heat shield early and flip you upside down. Stay calm," he glanced over at the Professor's vitals which indicated he wasn't staying calm at all.

"Do we have manual yet?" he said without looking up.

"A.I. disengaged on pod three," she shouted across the room.

Sinus moved some switches and brought up some data streams before hitting enter. The graphic in front of Sinus reflected exactly what was happening hundreds of kilometres below them. The pod span round violently and Touchreik was now soaring head first towards Mars at 8000 KMH. Inside the pod the clanging stopped abruptly as the heat shield broke free leaving a sudden and disconcerting silence.

"Professor, can you hear me?" He tried to reply but instead his head span and he blacked out.

The Captain appeared back at the desk. "Now what?"

Sinus checked the vitals. "We've just saved his life. The problem is for how long? I have to let the top of the pod absorb some heat before I spin him back. By then we have to gamble that the chute is undamaged and we can get him down alive."

"How long can he withstand the heat going down top first?"

"Honestly, we have no idea because the pod is not designed for this. It's pure guesswork."

He addressed the ships computers, "A.I. verbal engagement without control. What's the status on pod one?"

"Survival chances 20% and reducing."

"How long?"

"Insufficient data."

Captain Voodoo gripped the bench, running a finger round her collar, other crew members on the bridge were now watching the screens. Around the ship, passengers celebrated and enjoyed parties, completely unaware of the drama below.

The outer pod temperature gauge was showing 600 degrees and climbing rapidly, 655, 700, 735.

"Survival 15%," squawked the computer and Sinus switched it off. Sinus wiped sweat from his brow and made a mental calculation in his head. The pod was still in free fall and if he spun him back round too early it would be the same result.

879, 945. 1000.

"Spin him back," ordered the Captain. "Look at the temperature."

Sinus ignored her as they watched his altitude reduce and the temperature increase.

"Wait."

"Now," insisted Voodoo.

"It's too early."

"1020, 1090"

"Wait for my command, understood."

"Understood," replied the A.I.

"Wait."

"3,2 1."

"Wait."

"Minus 2,minus 3, minus 4,"

"Sinus!" shouted the Captain.

He ignored her. "Wait."

"Minus 10 seconds, 11, 12 13."

"Now," said Sinus.

On the monitor the pod could be seen spinning back into position with the unconscious Professor in all likelihood falling to his death. The temperature inside should be ok but it's now a case of whether the pod could withstand the pressure and stay in one piece.

"Engage chute," he commanded, nothing.

"Engage chute!" he screamed once more.

At last the A.I. responded, "Chute engaged."

"It's opened," said the Captain with a sigh.

"Altitude and speed please," said Sinus.

"Proposed estimated touchdown 2 KM north east of proposed drop zone. Speed 250 kilometres an hour. Altitude 3 KM."

"Too fast," he gasped. "Impact speed?"

"Predicted impact speed 70 KM Hour."

Sinus wiped his forehead with his sleeve once more. "Leave the chute engaged. What's the status on booster and rotation rockets?"

"10%"

"He's going in way too fast." In a second he was able to determine that the other three were proceeding normally. Predicting some kind of emergency they had followed protocol and maintained radio silence but they would be listening in.

"We'll need everything we can to get him down alive. If the pod doesn't rupture then we have a chance."

"Chute disengage in 10 seconds," said the computer.

"Do not disengage chute, I repeat do not disengage chute, confirm."

"Confirmed."

"Power up booster rockets, fire full thrust at T minus 8 seconds to impact and do not disengage chute."

"Yes Sir," came the robotic reply.

"Activate distress beacon and engage in 30 degree roll."

Inside the pod the Professor was completely unconscious and unaware of his fate. His body snuggly belted into the foam wall of the pod in preparation for exactly this kind of scenario.

Kilometres above him the computer counted down what might be the final seconds of his life. "Impact in 3,2 1."

The bridge of the Lazarus fell silent as the pod disappeared from the screen.

Sinus leaned over the desk, peering into the hologram and wanting to leap inside and find him. "Check vitals and position."

"Negative, no data available," came the reply.

The ghostly silence filled the room as Sinus threw himself back in the chair. The Captain leant across the desk to whisper in his ear, "You did everything you could."

He stood up, pushing her out of the way and made for the door. Suddenly remembering he had three other crew members to bring in and started to walk back. It was a moment of pure confusion but he had to pull himself together for the sake of the others. He took a deep breath and approached the desk.

Out of nowhere the computer spoke out, "Distress signal acquired."

Sinus leapt forward. "Where?"

"1.85 km north east of drop zone. Vitals are coming in, heart rate high, breathing laboured. Waiting for breath analysis from inside the pod."

"Holy Heathen. You did it, you saved his life," said Voodoo.

"Maybe, maybe, we need to get him recovered first," Sinus opened the comms channel.

"Commander, we have a problem."

TWENTY ONE

Back on the Lazarus the events below had gradually attracted the attention of some of the passengers. People had gathered in small groups around 2D screens as they broadcast live the unfolding drama below. Once the final pod landed safely spontaneous cheers went up around the ship. This wasn't the case on the bridge where there was a deathly silence as Sinus waited anxiously for the breath report. This would indicate the physical condition of the Professor. The other three on the drop team had listened intently to developments but protocol had prevented them intervening. As such they didn't have more detail than they could gather by listening in but it was clear this was serious. The stomachs churned as the three pods fired their booster rockets and landed in a triangle on the dusty Martian surface. The triangle that had intended to be a square, had all four pods arrived as planned. The doors to each pod popped and the pressure equalised, two steps protruded from the body of each. The remaining three stepped out onto the surface of Mars. The epic moment marred by the events of the last hour or so. Whilst in awe of their own achievement the main concern of everyone was for the wellbeing of the Professor.

Back on the Lazarus the data was finally filtering through. A complex moving graph appeared in the space above the workstation where Sinus and the Captain waited.

"Breathing is laboured, 4% carbon dioxide but dropping. Atmospheric pressure dropping," said Sinus as he interpreted the data.

"Meaning?" whispered the Captain.

The initial look of relief on Sinus's face slowly changed to concern.

"The pod pressure is dropping, it must be fractured somewhere."

"Can you do anything?"

Sinus ignored her. "Nitrogen/Oxygen reserve levels please," he said into the air.

The computer responded unemotionally, " 20%."

"Time?"

"27 minutes."

"Maintain cabin pressure to 80 %," Sinus switched his comm over to the drop team who'd by now clearly landed safely.

"Commander, what's your status?"

"We are on the surface, systems are stable and green, making our way to the hab on foot as planned, I'm with the others, the hab unit about 150 meters away."

"Can you see the transport?"

"Affirmative."

Sinus waved and pressed some holographic buttons in the air. Thousands of kilometres below him the Martian land cruiser burst into life. Neon lights illuminated the six wheeled monster and the interior glowed in a rainbow of colour as the systems booted up. The exterior lighting and powerful headlights came on making the machine look like a giant jukebox.

"Commander, I'm booting up the transporter and we have a fix on Pod 3. It's about 2Km to the south west of you. Its losing pressure and the Professor is unconscious, I'm pumping the remaining Nitrogen/Oxygen into the pod. After that he will be reliant on his suit, we need you to get over there quickly. I've no idea how bad the damage is or how long the pod will hold the pressure."

"Current status?"

"Losing pressure and fairly stable, that's all we can tell. Some of its diagnostic systems are down. We need to get him out, fast."

"Affirmative."

The others had followed the conversation and all three arrived at the hab together. Leroy admired the six-wheeled monster in front of him. Hands on hips he surveyed the huge 3-meter high alloy wheels and bulbous tyres, specifically designed to navigate the Martian surface with ease. It was a white, skulking beast that resembled a tiger ready to pounce. He was about to climb the short ladder to get inside.

"Payne, I need you in the hab, Seiren your coming with me," shouted Maxtor aware of the urgency.

Leroy opened his mouth to object as they climbed up into the rover and closed the door leaving him alone on the sandy surface.

Seiren pressed a few buttons and made some checks. "All warmed up and ready to go Commander."

"Let's go," said Maxtor and pushed the lever forward.

The rover's wheels span in the dust and as it settled Leroy could see the partially buried hab unit in front of him. The cylindrical structure that would be home for a couple of days. The surrounding ground was ploughed flat and vehicle tracks zig zagged around the area before converging in a northerly direction. The drone vehicles attempt at leaving the place tidy before heading off and shutting down. They will likely have found somewhere convenient to close their systems for the foreseeable future. As the rover silently rolled away in the direction of the Professor, Leroy made his way down a slight incline to the door of the unit, hit the code and the door slid open. He entered the hab and the door slid silently closed behind him. Once through the airlock, white sombre lights switched on and in the centre of the room was a medium round table and chairs. On the far wall and presumably sharing one of the four chairs was the command centre. Four screens had already come alive and one showed a map with the hab unit's location, another showed a jumble of data. There was also a split screen showing four 2D camera views. A dash cam, and another cam for the rover as well as two outside views of the hab unit. Payne undid the clips on his space helmet and began removing his suit leaving just his tight under suit. Reaching up he grabbed the red balaclava and threw it across onto a chair. After removing his boots he stored the whole everything inside a storage unit next to the command console, all the time listening to the broadcast. The place felt claustrophobic now but with the four of them living here it was set to get worse. He glanced up at the screen and could see there was still some time before the others reached pod 3, more than enough time for a quick tour of their new home. The whole unit was designed like a cylinder on its side and he was situated around the centre. To the left of this central area which would obviously serve as kitchen, conference room, command centre and lounge was the bunk room. Simply four double bunks, two either side with some storage under and at the end of the bunks. Turning back and through the central area was a tiny corridor with two doors. He opened and then closed each one briefly, toilet and bathroom facilities.

"Cosy," he whispered to himself.

Walking through he found himself in the storage and food area, to his left were bays of organic plant life as well as freezer and cooler facilities. Finally to the right of the emergency exit was the small med and isolation unit stroke spare bedroom. Under any normal circumstance it wouldn't get used except maybe to avoid the snoring, however in this instance it might get used for its designed purpose after all.

He heard Seiren's voice cut through the silence from the control centre speaker and walked briskly to the desk. "There he is."

Pulling a chair from the dining area he sat down and studied the camera.

The transporter cruised across the sandy Martian surface bouncing as it went. Throwing up sand as the bulbous mesh covered tyres powered across the planet. The Commander and Seiren held on as the vehicle bounced and jostled towards its goal. In the distance they could see a small crater and a shape on the far side at the bottom of it. As they came close it became perfectly clear how incredibly fortunate the Professor had been. Judging from the damage it looked like the pod may have struck the side of the crater at an almost perfect angle and effectively rolled down to the bottom. Although it had clearly battered the pod which looked in bad shape it had obviously slowed his descent. One side of the pod was crushed like a tin can with exposed electronics and tubes protruding in all directions. The side of the crater and the area below was scattered with debris from the craft. Stopping on the edge Seiren pushed herself out of her seat and could see the battered pod below. After a quick scan it was clear it made sense to go around to the other side where the angle was less and the transporter could drive down easier. Getting stuck and having to walk home or wait for a rescue drone wasn't a good idea, it had been a long day already. She slammed the lever forward and steered sharp to the right. The vehicle turned on a sixpence and they followed the steep sandy slope around and down.

"Payne!" barked the Commander.

"Sir."

"Are you still getting vitals."

"Yes Sir," glancing across at the dash display. "Carbon dioxide level rising slightly."

The Commander climbed from the cruiser before it had stopped and walked as quickly as his bulky suit would let him towards the battered pod. To his relief it was still intact and regardless of what had happened they knew he was, at the very least alive. A trail of metallic shrapnel ran down the slope and lay around the Martian surface.

"Sir?" Seiren said in a question as she approached him from behind.

"We have no choice," he said knowingly, "let's get it open."

"Life support?" she questioned.

He stopped and looked up at her sternly through his visor. "Captain, if he has lost or removed his life support then the minute we open that pod he is dead. We haven't got time for a debate, either way." The Commander raised his eyebrows without finishing his sentence, there was no need. The pod lay on its side and nature had blessed them by landing him with the door facing only slightly into the dusty surface. Grabbing the emergency handle he pulled hard and heard the pod depressurise as the door shifted slightly.

"Gimmi a hand here." Between them they pulled at the handles and managed to open the pod enough for Seiren to put her head and arms inside.

"His suit is still on, it looks intact but I can't reach him." They pulled the door a little more and then Seiren managed to get his belt undone and dragged at his limp body.

"Still got vitals but we need to get him back fast, he may have internal injuries and we can't treat him here," she said as she placed a suitcase sized box next to him and pulled out some tubes. Nodding to the Commander she twisted the tubes coming from the suit which attached him to the pod and swapped them with the case. The Commander dropped the case on the prostrate man's chest and grabbed his shoulders. Looking up he indicated to the feet.

"Stretcher?" she said.

"Not a whole lot of difference, we need to get him out of here. After three," she said grabbing the Professor's feet.

"Three."

They carried him to the transporter and the two rear doors opened automatically and they slid his body into the back.

Seiren jumped in with him and the Commander hopped into the drive seat of the transport. The Professor groaned as he started to regain consciousness.

"Good sign, he might be ok," whispered Seiren.

It would take around 10 minutes to get back to the hab unit and they'd need to quickly get him inside and over to the med unit.

The Professor's pod had ended up crashing a couple of kilometres from its planned landing sight which left it 2 kilometres on the opposite side from the hab unit. On the way back Seiren had spotted the reassuring sight of the top of the return launch vehicle protruding from the Jezero crater. Catching the Commander's eye in the mirror she returned her attention to the Professor. There were no plans to get on board the booster, unless the Professor was in real peril which right now didn't appear to be the case. Anyhow, that eventuality would be a major disruption as the A.I. drones would not begin refuelling the ship till tomorrow prior to their planned return.

"He looks good. Doesn't look like any serious injury but I won't know till we get back to the hab."

Maxtor tapped the comms console. "Mr Payne."

"Yeah man."

"We have the Professor and he looks saveable. Check out the hab med section and get ready for us. We have no idea what kind of internal injuries he may have."

"Already done. Sleeping quarters are prepared for the guests and light refreshments are on hand."

The Commander rolled his eyes to Seiren who grinned slightly as she continued with her hand held X-ray scans.

"Nervous energy," she said by way of excuse.

They were soon back at the hab unit and Leroy came out to help carry the Professor inside. Seiren took care of stripping him down and getting him into the med unit bed. She spent some time running tests and was stunned at his lack of injuries, this had to be the luckiest man alive. They'd later talk about how many different things should have killed him from the moment he left the Lazarus. Seiren dropped him a sedative and left him to sleep. The three of them ate and spent the evening sat around the communal area chatting and discussing the mission.

Sinus came up on the control screen live from the Lazarus and was greeted by a ripple of applause.

"That was a job man," said Payne.

"A job," echoed Seiren.

The Commander ripped a chunk from his bread and nodded in approval. This kid had definitely come good for sure and he was surprised. What he did was lightning thinking and saved the Professor's life. It was great to be in good hands and despite his lack of experience the kid had come through with flying colours. Incredible to think that he was never in the running at first, questions over his bottle.

The chat and laughter that followed lightened the mood after the tension of the day and at last Sinus signed off as the Lazarus continued its orbit.

"Sleep tight people," said Sinus.

Seiren played nurse and would intermittently check on Touchreik and reassure the crew through the night.

Payne created a very acceptable meal and incorporated some of the organic produce on board. Maxtor paused and surveyed his plate before tentatively sampling a morsel, before giving it a thumbs up. Seiren had given the Professor some liquid food and water and presumed he would sleep out the night. Seiren gathered the plates and cups and threw everything into the waste disposal. They were going to have to get used to being cosy for the next couple of days. The mission was short and in light of the logistics the facilities were quite luxurious for just 2 sols. Priority would have been given to weight in light of the traditional problem of getting material onto the surface of Mars due to its thin atmosphere. The whole thing had been set up and built by drone machinery and the A.I. was being monitored on Mars and up on the

Lazarus. At the moment it was all quiet and 10 kilometres away the drones continued their work. As far as the crew knew there were no humanoid drones on the planet, merely mechanical assembly units and diggers. The drones had been shut down for a while but by now they should be back to work fuelling the return booster 10 kilometres away in the Jezero crater. The equipment was designed and programmed to simply bury itself alive and lock off once the mission was finished. Seiren had been down to the bottom of the hab to check on the Professor and he seemed fine. According to his vitals he was recovering from shock but who wouldn't after being dropped from space at 8000 kilometres an hour. They could all laugh and joke about the incident now but once in their bunks and lights were out, they all thought the same thing. This was reality and that could have been me.

By the time Seiren woke the next morning the other two were already out of bed and ready to roll. They sat around the table in the next room chatting and drinking caffeine. At last she walked through to the inconveniently placed shower facility and got dressed. The first thing was to decide how the incident last night would impact the mission.

Maxtor sounded cautious. "Who knows, let's wait and see how he is this morning."

Seiren came out of the shower room and interrupted them, "I'm gonna check on him, I'm confident we will go ahead as planned."

Leroy, swivelled his chair from the dining table to the makeshift command desk and began his mission breakdown for the day.

"The weather on Mars looks very favourable, we couldn't have picked a better time to visit. The temperature today is looking like a high of around minus 30 degrees centigrade and there are no storm warnings but Mars doesn't really do storm warnings. It just does storms."

The Professor had in fact lay awake that night thinking about how close he came to death. How in an odd way he didn't really care. The real pain he was going through was going on below the surface, the nightmares and the things that he'd done in his life. The focus of those things brought him here to make penance, those thoughts were never far away. Alone he wondered about his mental health and how he seriously considered opening the door and stepping outside. During the little sleep he had, he'd dreamed of her again.

At last he had made his way down to join the crew and stood looking around the table. He took a moment to look into each of the crew's eyes, particularly finishing with the Commander.

"Thank you," he said in a hoarse voice.

Remembering his warning the Commander stared back. "Good timing, grab a caffeine and let's get to work," he said.

The Professor helped himself to a drink at the replicator. It was this device that would tune up any food requirements over the coming days, at least partially. It had been pre-programmed with a series of recipes chosen by the mission crew.

"How was your trip," said Leroy without looking up.

"I don't remember most of it."

"We have it on sim if you wanna do it again?"

"No thanks, a verbal explanation will do."

Seiren chipped in, "It looks like you had a fault on your heat shield, Sinus took manual control from aboard Lazarus and just kinda saved your life really."

"Sinus?" the Professor looked visibly shocked.

He knew he had blacked out but thankfully that was all he remembered. The next thing he knew he was here in the hab unit. His thanks seemed so inadequate now. It was Sinus up on the ship who had saved him.

"How do you feel?" said Maxtor

"Ok."

"Good, because we have a job to do so let's get on?"

Leroy coughed. "We have a broad fix and intelligence as to the launch site used for the Major's mission. Our first job will be to locate."

He was cut short by the Commander, "The return booster rocket first."

"What?"

"We are heading over to the return booster first," said the Commander.

"But the A.I. is completely cool with the return booster," cried Leroy.

"I don't give a shit what artificial intelligence thinks, we are going over to inspect it. Artificial intelligence," he repeated shaking his head. "Take note of the first word that comes before intelligence."

"It's a 40 km round trip."

"If there's anything we need to do before we leave I want to know now, not when we are about to lock in and launch to head back to the Lazarus."

"Sir," he said nodding his head in acknowledgement and continuing.

"Assuming all is well with the return craft as expected we'll head towards the beacon for the base and launch pad. We know it shouldn't be too difficult to find the launch pad. The base is different, being built underground to avoid radiation and weather. Once inside our main objective is likely to be in the archive section of the base so that's a priority. We may have to force our way inside but please remember the site is old and we have no idea of its condition. Proceed with extreme caution."

"Professor, over to you."

"I understand our sponsors are in search of a particular sample within the base. The 'Black-Star' is most likely the easiest find once inside the archive. I am tasked with bringing back digital and organic samples for our project at the institute with your help. For my part I'm interested in getting to the storage area and giving time to exploring common areas for any historic evidence."

The Commander took over, "We don't have reliable plans of the base so it will be a case of getting in there and plan as we go."

The whole crew nodded.

"I want no more drama on this mission," he paused until each made eye contact. "Let's do this, Prof are you ok?"

"I'm fine."

"We are trying to maximise time inside with the support of Sinus. Last night two communication satellites were launched so in a couple of hours we should have full 24 hour or should I say 24 hours and 39 minutes a day contact with Lazarus."

Everyone nodded in unison and headed into the boot room to get changed.

TWENTY TWO

Maxtor and the Professor headed out of the airlock and stepped towards the waiting Martian rover. Leroy came out last and Seiren had stopped dead in front of him.

"What's up? Forgot your keys?" he quipped. She ignored his remarks, staring blankly into the night sky.

"How about that?" she whispered.

Leroy stopped and peered over her shoulder, following her gaze into the early morning sky. High above them, what looked like a bright star twinkled with a slightly dimmer companion just below it. The pair were transfixed on realising what they were observing. The distant glowing globe was the planet Earth, reflecting the sun's rays, below it, the moon.

"Not something I ever thought I'd see in reality," uttered Seiren.

"Me neither," shrugged Leroy. "Me neither," he repeated as he walked past her and climbed aboard the rover.

The Martian Rover was a surprisingly smooth and quiet ride when driven at any reasonable speed on what was after all very unreasonable terrain. Rocks and larger rubble would cause the vehicle to roll slowly from side to side as its air suspension absorbed the impact. The journey to the edge of Jazero was taken mostly in silence, each passenger appearing deep in their own thoughts. As the rover reached the edge of the crater the nose cone of the return booster rocket appeared to rise from the sand in front of them. At last the rover swerved side on to the very edge providing them all with a premium view of the ship below. The sleek white body of the craft glowed under the powerful lights the drones had installed, presumably for human benefit. There was very little activity, one or two small vehicles could be seen moving around and along the fuel lines. The ship looked to be physically in good shape and from here looked deceptively small, lost in the vast dried up lake of Jazero. There had clearly been some dust storms, this was the reason it had been placed in the crater in the first place. The Commander set the rover off again and began the journey around to the far side and down the ancient inlet where there was a natural slope. The ground was firm but required a few twists and turns to navigate the bigger dips.

On arrival the crew stepped out of the rover and inspected the base of the ship. There was some sand storm build up but the drones had cleared most of it away. Maxtor satisfied himself that the fuel line seals were physically good and checked the fuel gauges. The ship was taller up close and it was accompanied by a sturdy lift tower to take its passengers to the top where the capsule was situated.

The fuel would be pumped in by the drones in the coming day so it spent as little time as possible on the craft. Only then could they head back the way they came to the relative security of the Lazarus. Once Maxtor had acquired the thumbs up from the team they climbed back into the shuttle and set a course for the estimated launch area of Major Zero. The journey over was quiet and despite their earlier objections they were reassured that the return booster was physically in good shape. The crew became lost in their own thoughts as the mountains of Mars crept across the horizon. After all the drama of the landing Seiren was finally realising the magnitude of their achievement. The Professor fantasised about how it must have been for Major Zero and his crew to establish themselves on this barren rock of a planet with ancient technology. Having experienced what can be achieved on the outside, he knew full well the challenges here must have been many fold. It made their hero's return to Earth even more mind-blowing.

Finally someone said it, it was bound to happen and everyone had thought it.

"Mother eh, we could be driving right over her servers," said Payne.

"You think so?" said Seiren looking out of the window and down.

"Strange to think though. Imagine if we found Mother's servers up here and pulled the plug?" he said with a smirk.

"You're a very sick fuck do you know that?" said Seiren with disgust. The Professor looked at each of them both nervously.

"We could turn off the world again," continued Leroy.

"Be quiet," said Seiren her shoulders rocking from side to side. Touchreik saw Maxtor glance into the mirror.

"Anyhow," said Seiren. "finding Mother's servers is impossible, remember she is everywhere. Don't you think she has your leash?"

"What do you mean," said Leroy sitting up.

"I mean Mr Payne. Your life support system, the return ship or even the Lazarus."

Leroy turned his attention back out the window. "Very funny."

"I ain't kidding. Mother manages all of Heathens systems and played a part in this mission happening, droning up the building of the Lazarus itself. Do you really think she wouldn't have her digital hand on the virtual cut off switch if this mission looked like getting rogue?" she held back a smile and turned away.

"Hey, I was kidding around. Chill," he said as he looked over at Touchreik grinning.

Seiren continued, "There are humanists out there, they may even be in here, eh Professor. What would they give to pull that plug?"

The Professor became flushed but thankfully was sat behind her.

"What do you think Prof?" Leroy grabbed his upper arm and shook it. "Humanists?"

"Absolutely. Mother wouldn't entertain her enemies, or friends for that matter without some kind security arrangement in place. She's here alright," he said.

Leroy shifted in his seat and stared out across the red landscape and across at the distant mountain range. He didn't speak until they arrived at the beacon and the Commander brought the craft to a halt.

To the right stood the remains of what would could have been a building next to the launch pad, perhaps a temporary loading bay and control centre. The walls had long gone leaving just the skeleton of a structure which may once have been a couple of stories high. Most of the exposed base area was now filled with red dust and rubble and there were various pieces of debris inside which may once have been heavy crates or boxes. This place would have been the Zero crews return launch pad so the assumption would be that the actual base would be close to here. They all looked around at the surrounding landscape.

The Commander broke the silence, "Over to you Professor."

"I'm not sure it really needs me but the base is definitely underground because of radiation, sandstorms. We can also assume its close by as this is their return launch site and there would've been no point in going far. The second problem they would have is actually avoiding being buried under sand storms so I would have gone for slightly higher ground."

"Agreed."

In unison the entire group looked to the left at a small hill around 200 meters away.

Maxtor pushed the lever forward and steered the rover towards it, once they reached the base of it he pulled over.

Seiren and Leroy climbed out, grabbed a couple of detectors from the back of the rover and began walking around at the base of the hill.

At last Seiren returned to the vehicle and spoke through the closed window, Leroy hopped back inside. Her voice came through the communication channel into their earpieces.

"It's here alright, there's space underneath us but it's a case of finding the entrance."

That was when the Commander sat up in his seat. "There," he said pointing towards the base of the hill.

"Holy Heathen," she gasped, turning to see what was so obvious once pointed out.

In the lights from the rover against the rock, a flat pillar could be seen partially covered.

Maxtor pressed a couple of buttons above the dash to activate the drone digger. It was fitted flat under the back of the rover, once he hit the programme coordinates it released itself. Pushing backwards from under the vehicle the tracks unfolded and it set off into the rovers headlight beam. The crew sat in the rover for a full half hour and watched the monitors as the machine worked to clear the entranceway. The silence was shattered by the voice of Sinus from aboard the Lazarus.

"Hey you started without me," he said.

The crew greeted him individually. "Morning."

"Good Morning. We are online and comms are fully operational, so how's things Prof?"

"Very good. I believe I owe you?"

"You definitely do owe me and I always collect," he stopped abruptly looking at his monitor. He was seeing the drone cam and everyone in the rover followed suit, looking at their own seat screens.

"Looks like we are in?" said Maxtor.

On the screen it was possible to see the drone digger had revealed a large metallic door built into the rock face, most of it was still covered. This was clearly designed for larger vehicles but had a smaller pedestrian entrance.

Leroy Payne clambered out and the others watched as he walked over to the door. Taking out his instruments he went to work on the electronic mechanism. Whilst he did so the others climbed out and came up behind him. With an elaborate press of a button on his device the smaller door shifted, crept a few centimetres and then jammed. Another press and with a screech of metal on metal it slid open to reveal for the first time in centuries the inside of Major Zero's base. Stepping inside they donned their high powered head lights and peered into the dark unexplored interior, untouched for hundreds of years. They spread out and just stared, hardly able to believe where they were actually standing. The four beams of light pierced the ancient darkness in every direction, scouring the walls and ceiling as they took it all in. Major Zero's base was older than Heathen, older than Mother herself.

Untouched for centuries the place was exactly as it was left when Zero and his team had left for their home planet. They were in a loading bay, left in disarray before the old residents had left. There were boxes and crates with lids off or half open as well as tools and mechanical equipment in pieces. What looked like drilling or cutting equipment lined the back wall, coated in dust. The objects seemed to move as the powerful lights cast shadows up and across the walls. These rusty metal relics resembled mummified drones, each one black and dead. Across the ceiling ran an enormous mobile steel beam, suspended from this was a large hook. They moved through as a group into a workshop area which would have been where the return ship was built. Behind them was a huge hangar door which may or may not work now but would have allowed them to roll the ship out in bits for assembly on the launch pad. Scattered around were what looked like ships parts which had either been rejected or left to reduce weight or drag. The facility was incredibly impressive and for its time well equipped. The Professor switched on his helmet recorder as did the others.

Maxtor spoke first, "Let's go, and stick together for now, let's just get some bearings."

The three followed the Commander up an incline to the side of the hanger and up to a door at the end.

They found themselves in a corridor about 40 meters long down a slight incline. At the bottom it turned back on itself and then another corridor would do the same. The Professor had counted 10 floors before it levelled out. This level had doors equally spaced along its length, each one appeared to be private accommodation cabins. They started to spread out along the corridor opening and closing doors as they made their way along. Each room had the same layout but was furnished individually. One or two doors were locked, presumably by their last occupants. The Professor could hear the others breathing through his headset, the sound relative to their proximity. He opened a door and went inside a small accommodation room which could have belonged to any one of the numerous crew who'd made Mars their home.

He heard Maxtor's fading voice over the radio, "Disturb nothing, let's just get a look around here first."

Inside the room it was pitch dark and as he entered the door swung closed behind him. He advanced forwards, kicking through debris, broken glass and dust on the floor. The rooms were basic and fixed. There was a small bathroom to his left and then a main sleeping area directly in front of him. His headlight swept across the far wall and as he entered he saw a bed against the left wall and a dresser of some kind to his right. Above it was a mirror, he looked at it inadvertently and the reflection of his powerful headlight blinded him temporarily. Looking down he saw the draws were open but mostly empty, save a couple of discarded garments. A layer of dust covered everything and on the top surface sat a number of curious personal items, an old mechanical timepiece inside a dome and a cloth doll. Ancient artefacts that the Professor added to his mental list of possible samples. His movement unsettled particles of fine dust and they glowed in the beam of his light, impeding his vision. In his headset he'd failed to recognise the voices of the others fading as they became more distant. Out in the corridor their lights had disappeared into other similar rooms leaving it in blackness once more.

He finally realised the silence and that he was alone in the darkened silent room. At that moment he heard a sound that made his blood run cold, hairs on his arms stood on end inside his spacesuit. It sounded like a breath, at first he wondered if it might be from his own headset but he was sure it's wasn't. He hit the mute button and listened again, hoping to hear nothing and began to turn. Shaking, he raised his head slowly up above the mirror and the light illuminated his face. He looked like a dismembered head floating on a pitch black background. He felt a chill as the noise came again, from behind him but low down. This time he was sure the sound was local. He almost daren't look, but cautiously moving his head he followed the beam of his light as it cut through the darkness, twisting his shoulders in the cumbersome space suit. The light cascaded across the wall until he looked down behind him. As the light moved down the wall he started to see through the glowing dust, an ancient space suit came into view that incredibly he'd failed to notice when he came in. It was half sat and half leaning against the front wall, the visor was thick with dust. He gingerly approached, the beam of his light concentrated on the filthy dust covered visor. At first it didn't take form in his mind but then he realised what he was looking at. Through the filth and grime a mummified face appeared to be staring out at him. His body began to shake as he focused on the skeletal rotting face inside the helmet and jumped when it sighed once more.

The body sat to the right of the tiny corridor leading to the exit door. Instinct and fear gripped him and his legs felt like lead as he moved past the ghostly skeleton body. As he stepped over he felt it grab at his ankle and miss. Reaching the door he frantically pushed and pulled but it won't budge. He daren't look round but can hear the breath now and despite the suit he was sure he felt sweat run down the back of his neck. In his mind's eye its reaching for him, grabbing his shoulder. Finally, the door gives and he whips it open, and falls into the corridor screaming.

"Help, help someone help," he shouted into the black empty corridor.

Scrambling to his feet, he ran towards the lights that are exiting from rooms further along. Seiren grabbed him as he tried to pass her running to who knows where in terror.

"Wait Touchreik, wait what the hell is wrong with you?"

All he can see are her lips moving inside the helmet, until he realised he still has his communicator on mute. He reaches to his wrist and switches it on to catch the end of another sentence. "wrong with you?"

He breathlessly tries to explain what just happened but struggles to make any sense. "There's a person in there, alive I heard him breathe. It's horrible, get me out of here."

Seiren pushed him to Payne. "Hold him here," she barked.

"Where?" she said heading back down the corridor.

"There, don't go in there, it's a person alive," he muttered.

"Professor shut up and tell me where." The light was blinding his face now.

"Third door left," he said pointing. With the lack of sleep and the nightmares the Professor was questioning his own sanity. Maybe he'd had it with this whole thing and he needed to get out but he was absolutely sure of what he heard and saw. Absolutely convinced.

"There's no living thing been in here for hundreds of years, least of all human," she said.

The Commander and Seiren exchange glances whilst Leroy took a step back from the group and held the Professor at arm's length.

"Look after him." Payne looked relieved and nods. Maxtor nods to Seiren then towards the door.

"We have no weapons," shouted Maxtor.

"Whatever is in there hasn't come out."

They all look at each other now with doubt and fear in their eyes.

"Wait."

Maxtor pushed into the room they were just in and the door closes. A moment later he comes out with a hammer.

"Let's go."

Seiren nodded to him. "The suits Commander, just be careful where you swing that thing?"

The pair crept towards the door of the room the Professor had just left. Slowly Seiren reached up and pushed the door slowly open with her palm. There's no point shouting in these suits so the Commander leads inside followed by Seiren. They passed the small door on the left and enter the main room. Seiren calls from behind him.

"Commander!"

She is looking down at his feet to the left. In their headlamps they can see a body on the floor in a space suit. Seiren leant over and slowly pulled the helmet round to see inside. She jumped back in shock when she slipped the visor up and saw a grotesque face looking up at her. The skin is as thin as paper and pulled tight across the bones of the face. Sunken empty eye sockets stare back at her and the tight skin has revealed the yellow teeth. The skull has tiny whips of hair remaining on its yellowing skull. She immediately let's go and stands up looking round the room.

"That's our man," said Maxtor as he slaps her on the shoulder with a deep out breath.

They step outside and walk back up the corridor to where the others are waiting. The Professor seems a little calmer now and Seiren feels she might get some sense. "What happened?"

"I was looking around and I heard a moan from the man on the floor, I tried to get out, I panicked."

"That man has been dead for centuries, did you say he grabbed at you?"

"Well?" he looked down shamefully at the floor. "I thought.."

She looked round at the others. "The atmosphere in this place hasn't changed in centuries. We have come in and exposed it to the outside air. That's all. The noise you heard was probably a result of that. An expulsion of trapped gas in the suit, the rest was your imagination."

The Professor was embarrassed and afraid as he looked over her shoulder towards the door. He felt foolish but the whole thing still made him feel uneasy. After that incident he was sure to stay close to the others as they continued to check out the rest of the base.

The team found themselves up at what might well have been accommodations for more senior officers. These rooms being larger and better fitted out. The layout was very different from all the V-World sims and for that matter any plans that had been made available on earth. The assumption being this might be for security or just poor information. Finally they found the door with an engraved sign. The Commander ran his glove across the plaque to reveal the words 'Base Commander'. He paused a moment before slowly pushing the door.

Inside they found a desk with 2D screens as well as sleeping quarters and a private kitchen area. It was in disarray like the other accommodations, everything showing signs of a hasty exit. The Zero room had a small kitchen area with lots of old tech including a cooker, fridge and freezer. This was for when food was prepared in advance and saved for long periods of time. The three spread out and checked draws and cupboards finding little of interest. Touchreik examined the kitchen area, opening and closing appliances. The freezer had ice bursting through the seams of the doors which had welded it shut. For now it was best to leave everything intact until they had an idea of what they were going to take back with them. One thing of use was a silicone map which they could use to navigate around the base. Later they might be able to scan and add it into the database to help them get around. It would also be useful for future sims back on Earth. The Commander cleared a table by sweeping everything onto the floor and laid the map out. According to the map the base was much bigger and better equipped than they had suspected. It was laid out in a circular format but in wings which made it look like a multiple pointed star and it spread to various levels. They already knew it had started as caves dug by early drones and then accommodated later. The power source according to the plan was an incineration generator which burned fuel similar to what they were using to get home. That would have been an obvious choice with plans for nuclear power later which would have been much more efficient. There were medical facilities, labs, as well as a central control centre and communications centre.

"Here it is," Seiren pointed to an area on the map. They were able to find the place they had entered the building and plan a route to the DNA storage area. The four headed off with Seiren navigating although there were occasional signs on walls which confirmed their location. They made their way past medical lab areas which confirmed they were heading in the right direction. Finally they came to another locked door which required Leroy's skills once more. They were soon inside and according to their instruments the temperature had dropped considerably.

It wasn't as expected, that is if they expected anything. Every organism on Earth was in this relatively small room. They were in the form of slides which had been inserted on cassettes into freezer units. There was a digital screen which would have enabled them to catalogue the collection. This room contained an entire history of organic life thus far, at least up to the point where Mother had begun to perfect it. The cassettes were all physically labelled too and the Professor spent some time in here whilst the rest of the crew went for a look around. He was particularly interested in plant life and in finding one or two rare samples for the reserve back on Earth. It would be fascinating to re-introduce these breeds of plants back in their ancient form once he knew they were safe.

Maxtor and the others spent a lot of time in the labs. At last they came upon something of great interest and called the Professor up. He followed their comms and found them staring at a large pod.

"Perhaps you know who owns this Professor?" Touchreik was flabbergasted. It was indeed the real and original pod the had contained the caveman sample. The frozen body of his friend that had been regenerated after 500 years. It was clear it was a kind of extra to all the other samples because it just didn't belong, seeing as the other items were in DNA form. It was very close in design to the mock ups at the institute back on Earth. The main priority for the team though was finding the 'Black-Star'. If it existed and if it was here then it would likely be in the medical or labs area. The sample room seemed to contain only DNA slides. They spent another few hours searching around before heading back to the rover for some nourishment. Later they continued their search of the building after a chat with Sinus and an update on the situation including the Professor's hallucinations. They were all exhausted but the Professor's visit had been fruitful. There was still no sign of the 'Black-Star' by the end of the day and they headed back to the hab to debrief.

The Professor's list of items to collect and bring home with him had grown considerably throughout the day. Far more than the return booster could manage for sure but this selection was going to preoccupy his mind tonight. The others were concerned about the 'Black-Star' and whether it could be found. The whole reason for this voyage and the drop was to bring back this element. The Professor was conscious of showing too much interest in Black-star and so occupied himself elsewhere.

They ended up back at the hab, tired and exhausted and as the previous night took some time around the table. Sinus was joining them again on the large screen and they discussed the element.

"Maybe this is all bullshit, has anyone thought about that? Maybe it doesn't exist?" said Leroy provocatively.

"It exists, it's there alright," said Maxtor.

"We don't know that for sure," said Seiren.

He sipped his caffeine and looked up at her. "I know that for sure," he said stressing the word I.

She looked across at the Professor who looked away and the Commander saw the look of doubt in their eyes and slammed the table hard.

"I've seen the data from the original sample, I saw the chemical analysis that was done right here on Mars," he shouted, stabbing his finger at the ground.

"Maybe they brought it back to Earth, maybe it's been there all the time?" said Leroy.

"Wrong again, Mr Payne."

The Commander started to laugh and then stopped abruptly. Payne's face went from a broad smile into a concerned grimace. Seiren tried to interrupt him but he continued, "Listen to me. I have seen the data from the damn chemical analysis, it was done on Mars. We also know that for some reason the Major ordered it remain here," he paused again. "It's here."

He stood up, placed his cup on the table and went to the door. "Good night," he said and left.

The Professor and Leroy looked at each other as if to confirm what the Commander had just let slip. The Major ordered it remain here? This was news to all of them and they were unsure if Maxtor had intended to share that information.

The three remained in the lounge and talked about home and the trip but that pretty much closed the subject as far as the 'Black-Star' was concerned. The Professor was the next to retire and decided to spend the night in his own bunk instead of the med room. He climbed in and pulled his shutter, fluffing up his pillow he lay back and stared at the ceiling centimetres above his head.

The hab unit had a kind of hum that could lull a person to sleep or drive them crazy. Who cares, he was exhausted and there was one more night here and they would be heading home. He closed his eyes and prepared for another restless night.

TWENTY THREE

The next morning they headed out across the Martian wasteland once more, Maxtor and Seiren sat up front and in the back Touchreik and Leroy shared concerned looks. They were exchanging messages with their eyes, is it here? What if? Years wasted?

Touchreik wasn't keen on returning after the incident with the suit, it had really spooked him. It felt like they were intruders desecrating sacred grounds, it was as if that were a sign.

"We have a full day," said Maxtor over his shoulder.

"Leroy, I want you and the Professor to get the samples loaded. Seiren and I will continue the search for the stones."

"Wouldn't it be better if we all looked?" said Leroy.

"No, if we don't find them, then we could end up going home with nothing, at least we'll have the Prof's samples," said Maxtor. "It's gonna be a long day, let's get to work."

Having gained entry and found a map the previous day then they had hoped today would be a lot more efficient. Seiren and Maxtor set off together, having planned a methodical sweep of the most likely locations for the stones. Meanwhile Leroy and Touchreik began tagging, labelling and transporting samples back to the rover, focusing on more manageable samples in terms of size and weight. Throughout the morning they were both frustrated and distracted, neither felt that anything was more important than the stones but couldn't say. Instead they carried on and had micro conversations whilst they were alone or out of earshot. Sometimes without words, just raised eyebrows or sighs, particularly after disappointing reports from the other two.

"What you think?" whispered Touchreik through the closed channel.

"Doesn't sound good."

"Will they find it?"

"Shit if we weren't here loading this junk we could help em," snapped Leroy, throwing a small crate onto the rover and heading back to the base entrance.

Suddenly the ground shook and a muffled but powerful explosion was heard from inside. It was impossible to run in the suits but they made their way deep into the base as quickly as possible. A thick cloud of dust billowed down a wide corridor and the beams of two head lamps shone from within it. They made their way through to a door that hung on its hinges. Inside a secure area the pair were rummaging through papers and artefacts. As the day wore on they didn't react to other explosions and sounds of destruction deep inside the base. The atmosphere of unease grew and the tone darkened as they became more despondent. By now they assumed it was in one or two of the secure areas on the site.

In the afternoon more explosions were heard as Maxtor and Seiren blasted their way around the Major's base. By late afternoon they had made good headway with the samples and Leroy was asked to go through all the crates in the loading bay. A sign of desperation, looking for a few tiny stones in three meter crates was nuts but he was relieved to be involved. Could the 'Black-Star' really have been forgotten or left behind when they headed back to Earth? As the day drew on the exhausted crew become more anxious and desperate. Touchreik continued to gather his samples of old technology, charts and data as well as samples from the organic collections. He also digitally scanned the area including the Major's quarters and various rooms of historical interest. These recordings will help them to digitise the place once they return to Heathen for V-World sims and historical record. The night before there had been lengthy discussions and wide ranging theories about the 'Black-Star'.

Sometimes we hide valuables in plain sight? The 'Black-Star' might be in jewellery or ornaments for all they knew. Even with the time they had, they'd never cover the place in its entirety, so they'd be forced to prioritise.

It was late in the day by the time the last of the samples were loaded on the transporter. The cargo still had to be loaded on to the booster for the return trip before the day was over. There'd be no time the following morning before they boarded and headed back to the Lazarus.

It was already orbiting and gathering speed in order to slingshot back into space. If they missed the last orbit then the Lazarus would be forced to leave them behind. The cost of waiting for the drop crew was inconceivable even if it were physically possible. There was little room for manoeuvre and the 'Black-Star' was looking very illusive. In the end the whole crew had been involved, including Touchreik but they had to admit defeat. Maxtor had decided it just wasn't to be and they silently climbed aboard the rover and headed back. The depression in the vehicle was palpable and for very different reasons. They'd travelled on a 400 million kilometre round trip and all the samples they had seemed worthless without the 'Black-Star'. It was time to go home.

They set a course for the booster rocket and arrived to find the drones had already begun the automatic fuelling process. They arrived at the crater, drove round the rim and down the casual slope on the far side.

Using the lift to the cargo area they loaded Touchreik's samples in silence. Then they headed back down the elevator and drove back to the hab unit. Between leaving the base and arriving at the hab there was hardly a word spoken amongst them. The only thing left was a trip home tomorrow, Maxtor retired straight away whilst the others grabbed some food, showered and went to their bunks one by one.

The next morning Touchreik and the others gathered a few personal belongings in readiness for home. The crew began the process of prepping for the trip as suits were checked along with the booster and the hab condition. This kept the others busy and the Professor had nothing to do but wait. He opened his 2D screen to look at the data and film he had collected from the Major's quarters. Losing himself in thought about how hundreds of years ago that great man had commanded from that actual room. The incredible amount of work, leading and planning to return and save the world he now knew. The work and preparation, having lived and slept in his quarters, probably eating at his desk and sleeping on it too. So disappointing that years spent planning this heist and now there might be nothing to steal. A thought that Antoine had refused to entertain until now because it left them with nothing. He'd clung to this hope of salvation because Mother had decided that Homo Sapiens had outgrown their use and could be digitised. Antoine feared for his friends and for Greenwich, what would the future hold now? Touchriek flicked around the screen, pinching to admire detail. Then he stopped for a moment and tapped the screen to zoom in on an area of the room he'd seen many times before. He looked up to the heavens and a grin spread across his weathered features.

Picking up the 2D viewer he stood and opened the door into the main hab area where the rest of the crew were busy packing and checking equipment.

"I know where it is," he whispered but only Seiren heard him.

"What did you say?" she said.

The other two stopped what they were doing and looked at him. Maxtor had his head inside a cupboard with an armful of wires.

"I know where 'Black-Star' is," he said, louder this time.

Maxtor threw everything into the cupboard and slammed it shut, marching over to Touchreik he spoke quietly into his ear. "Talk and fast."

Sinus appeared on the screen. "Good morning, I hope everyone is ready for the ride home."

Maxtor held up a hand to the screen. "Not now," he said without turning away from Touchreik. "Talk," he said.

He walked over to the table, sat down and placed his pad in front of him. The whole crew were mesmerised, Leroy still frozen to the spot.

He touched his viewer and a three dimensional hologram of the Major's quarters popped up. He span and pinched till he zoomed in on the kitchen area and then the appliance used to store food, the chilling cabinet.

"Here," he said pointing.

"How do you know?" said Seiren excitedly.

"I don't, not for sure. But, it absorbs heat like a black hole absorbs light, so they say."

The Professor zoomed in a little more to a blue cabinet in the kitchen area, it's walls were bulging outwards.

"The power has been off for hundreds of years?" he said. "Look." He pointed to the edge of the doors where a white seal was visible.

"Ice," said Seiren.

"Not surprising," said Maxtor coming in closer.

"But it's coming from inside," said Touchreik and standing he backed away to let them in closer.

Leroy's jaw fell open. "I think he's right," said Seiren.

"Holy Heathen," the Commander rubbed his grey bearded chin.

Sinus chipped in, "Well, that's great but we haven't got any mission time left."

"We might have time?" Maxtor checking the mission status clock.

"The Lazarus is gathering speed and we have to launch at 13:23 to get you back," interrupted Sinus. "sorry but you'll never know."

"That's the planned mission termination, there must be parameters," said the Commander.

"Sir?" said Sinus.

Seiren did the job for him and ran around the partition to the console whilst Leroy just shook his head in dismay. The three stared at each other and waited. She returned and stabbed at the table with a finger.

"There's a parameter of 96 minutes to allow for missing an orbit, we could cut our travel time to 35 minutes and our return time to 45 minutes that's 80 minutes. We have to be in and out with the 'Black-Star' in 16 minutes, that's easily done. If we go right now," she said looking at the Commander.

Sinus spoke again, "Sir, the parameter is here for a reason. We will have no margin for error if you miss an orbit."

The Commander ignored him. "Touchreik, Seiren your coming with me. Payne, I want you here and checking the systems, stay in communication with us. Let's go."

"Sir. We can't pick you up if you miss this orbit," pleaded Sinus.

"We don't have time for a vote," he said and headed into the kit room. The three donned their space suits and were in the transporter in minutes, heading across the sand as full speed throwing a trail of dust behind them. Meanwhile Payne set about informing the Lazarus about the change of plans and discussing the changes required to the booster settings.

During the journey Seiren had started setting her timer to act as a guide.

"Do you really need that?" said the Prof.

"Time dilates in times of stress. we'll work to the clock," she said.

Commander Maxtor charged across the Martian surface in manual drive at top speed. The rover rolled and plummeted across the landscape until they saw the mound up ahead. At last the rover braked hard at the entrance to the base and they climbed out and Seiren grabbed some equipment from the back.

"Nice driving, 120 seconds ahead of schedule." Handing a case to Maxtor they set off through the loading bay and down the stairs towards the Major's quarters. They reached the cabin and stood inside for a moment staring at the chiller machine. Ice was bursting through the seams of the doors and the machine itself looked swollen like it might explode.

Maxtor pulled out a crow bar and went to work prising the door to get it open. It took a few minutes of heaving until it gave way with an incredible snap and he tumbled backwards onto the floor. Inside was a solid mass of milky ice formed over hundreds of years, it looked impregnable. Seiren wasted no time in opening a case and assembling what looked like a long ray gun. She plugged it in to a socket in the case and pointed the lance into the air.

"Stand back," she said as she pressed the handle, there was an audible high pitched screech as the unit charged. Finally she hit a button and a blue flame appeared at the end of a lance. She began by melting some of the outer ice from the unit and it was working well, water poured across the floor. Digging deeper into the block there were different coloured flames as she burned through general contents of the chiller. As items burned up they knew there was no danger of burning or damaging the 'Black-Star', that's if it was in there at all. The room started to get hot and the fumes were filling the room making it difficult to see.

"Time?"

"55 minutes left, out in 10," she replied without stopping what she was doing.

She continued probing, burning and poking around inside. Time was running out and the job was looking a lot more difficult than first anticipated. The chiller was almost empty now and there was water everywhere. Thick filthy smoke was filling the room. Plastic and foam from the outer edges of the cabinet burned inside. Touchreik went over to the door and propped it open but it had little effect. The headlight beams were all focused in the tiny area of the cabinet interior. Touchreik began to doubt himself, he'd been convinced it would be in here. The beams of their headlights became a hinderance in the self-induced smog. The main chiller cabinet was now empty and there was no sign of the element. Maybe he was wrong after all. By now it was obvious the cabinet was empty. In the door was a small tray with a lid, she went to work on that with the lance. Finally she lifted the lid and inside placed loose in the tray were two shiny pieces of black stone. They were like pebbles, perfectly smooth and blacker than pitch. Slowly she reached out and picked them up, turning to Maxtor through the smog she placed them in his hands. The grin spread across every one of their sweat dripping faces.

"Can you feel it?" she said.

"Wow, so cold and so heavy even after the burner on them."

Maxtor opened the sleeve of his suit and placed them inside shutting it tight.

Slapping Touchreik on the back he stood up. "Let's go."

Seiren threw the lance on the floor and the three of them walked into the slightly clearer atmosphere in the corridor before making their way back up to the surface as fast as the heavy suits would allow. Once on the outside and in the rover they were able to report back. "Payne, we're heading back, we got em," cried Maxtor into the radio.

"That's great but for the love of Heathen get back here. I have a rocket to catch," Maxtor roared with laughter as he slammed the transporter into gear and they jerked forward.

They were making good time and if Payne had done everything right then they should be able to pick him up and head to the return ship. The back slapping and nervous joking continued throughout the journey until they had around ten minutes till ETA at the hab.

Without warning the transporter suddenly started to slow down a little and he pushed the lever back and forth.

"Is something wrong?" said Touchreik

"We're losing power?" he pushed and pulled on the lever without effect.

Seiren tapped up the data and saw the red light.

"We're overheating, this vehicle isn't designed for racing, you need to slow down."

"We don't have time to slow down."

"Either you slow down or we'll stop moving all together," she said.

The next 10 minutes were painful, as they were forced to frustratingly maintain a speed between over heating and cooling off. Seiren monitored and gave instruction as to when he could go a little faster or to slow down. After what seemed an age they could finally could see the hab unit up ahead. Payne was standing outside with a case in full space suit like a man waiting for a mag transporter. It would have been quite comical if it weren't for the seriousness of the situation.

They pulled up and he jumped in the back.

"What the fuck, did you stop for lunch on the way back."

"We have a transport problem," said Seiren.

"Full throttle, we are running out of time," he said.

"No can do my friend."

"Holy shit we are not going to make it. We have around 8 minutes of a 10 minute journey."

"Shut up and stop distracting the driver," said Seiren.

"How long till launch time," said Maxtor.

"We are fuckin dead man, we are going to die on this shit hole lump of sand, I must have been fuckin crazy," said Leroy rocking back and forth.

At last they reached the edge of the Jezero crater and could see the ship down below. Steam was coming from the bottom of the ship as it prepared for launch. Its sleek white body pointed skywards, so close and yet so far.

"That thing has to launch in 6 minutes and we have a 12 minute drive round the crater to get to it."

"Seiren, start the launch countdown," said Maxtor.

"Sir," she grinned, seeming to understand his plan. She tapped away at her console and the booster ships countdown to launch began.

"What the fuck?" said Leroy. "It will launch without us?"

"The Martian gravity is around a third of Earth's, that has an effect on falling objects, correct?" Maxtor began switching and hitting buttons above him.

"Correct Sir," she said.

"Hold on," Maxtor locked his elbows on the steering.

"Wait, wait you can't, you'll kill us all," screamed the Professor but it was too late.

Maxtor pushed the throttle forward with all his might and the transporter surged forwards and upwards towards the lip of the crater. For a moment all they could see was sky until the front dipped and threw them all headlong into the crevice. The transporter began its uncontrolled journey down the side of the crater. The bulbous tyres caused it to bounce from side to side as it hit rocks which then tumbled down behind them. The whole world began to shake and stomachs turned as the vehicle crashed downwards towards the bottom of the crater. Everything that wasn't nailed down was thrown about hitting the occupants in the face and body, that included each other's uncontrolled limbs. Just when it was looking like they might make it to the bottom in one piece and upright the worst and best luck happened at the same time. A tyre on the right hit a huge rock that had no intention of moving out of the way. The vehicle was thrown sideways and began to roll down the hill. Miraculously they were close enough to the bottom for it to manage three full rolls before coming to a halt the right way up. They finally stopped in a cloud of falling rocks and dust with the tyre completely blown out. They could see the return booster a hundred yards away and the Commander pushed the lever once more. With a torturous grind of metal the vehicle laboured forward with its three good wheels. It dragged the ripped tyre behind like a severed limb before it finally gave up 40 yards from the return booster rocket. Touchriek had time to glance the timer on the dashboard and if it hadn't broken there were 3 minutes to launch and the final sequence was in motion.

"Go!" Maxtor roared.

They all climbed out onto the dusty surface, a quick glance round told Maxtor that the suits had survived. Payne was out but was in trouble, perhaps a broken arm and he was limping badly. The Commander screamed at Touchreik to go whilst he and Seiren went back for Payne.

Touchreik pushed on toward the booster, feeling their presence behind him. The rocket was illuminated by lights and towered above him as he ran towards it. Steam was pouring from its base and billowing into the sky around it. The other two went back and grabbed Payne. They pulled him up and one under each arm headed for the ship while he hopped, dragging his broken leg behind him in the dust.

Touchriek reached the ship just before them and climbed the stairwell which offered a bridge over the steaming engine below. He climbed into the lift as the door opened. He waited with an arm in the doorway as the lift doors constantly tried to close. They all knew the stakes now, if they weren't in that ship they were dead anyway. There would be no option for getting out of the rockets powerful rocket engines. They were either getting aboard or were going to be fried alive here.

At last his three companions made it to the elevator and fell inside. Now the door which had been forcing itself closed seemed to take forever to do so. The others fell against the wall of the elevator for a moments respite as the elevator slowly climbed. At the top the door opened and the Professor ran across the gangplank to the open door. Stepping inside the tiny capsule he could hear the countdown being broadcast within the ship. "25,24,23."

He stayed at the door willing them forward and held the door whilst they managed to stumble across and push the lifeless body of Leroy inside and drop him in a seat. Maxtor went over to seal the door and through the porthole was flabbergasted to witness the elevator tower falling away. He twisted the handle and fell into his seat.

"12,11,10.."

"Seat belts!" screamed Maxtor.

Touchreik sat back in a seat and they threw Payne into another.

"5,4,3"

All four were pushed backwards into their seats by the incredible force of the booster rocket began lifting them from the Martian surface. Maxtor took to the controls and began to run through the automated sequences and cross checks. There was no energy for words and the only sound was that of Maxtor giving orders to the ships A.I. and Sinus aboard the Lazarus.

The rest of the flight back to Lazarus went according to plan. The return vessel jettisoned its booster rockets and continued into orbit just in front of the Lazarus.

The procedure they would follow would be very different from the more executive one they had adopted when leaving earth. The four entered weightlessness and stayed in their seats until the Lazarus caught them up. The colossal spinning craft appeared to swallow their tiny craft as it drifted into the centre of the ship. They were perfectly timed to avoid the spinning spokes of the ship and were now in the central hub, right above the nuclear reactor. They finally docked with the

Lazarus and would now be required to enter the ship through the airlock. The weightlessness would enable them to drag the semi-conscious Leroy onto the main ship and into the spoke. They encouraged him to take part but, in the end, decided to use one of the service tubes to get him back to the outer rim. Under normal circumstances these were reserved for drones transporting goods to the outer edge. It was an uncomfortable ride but alleviated the need for him to climb down. The other three drifted down the spoke towards the outer rim of the ship. The sickly feeling continued to worsen as they started to feel the pull of virtual gravity. Finally they were required to physically climb down the ladders until reaching the main floor of the ship and dropped down into the corridor. Once safely aboard they were able to lick their wounds and come to terms with what they had just done. Maxtor stood defiantly looking around and enjoying the feeling of stability. "You guys go and help Leroy, I'm going to place the samples in the vault."

Seiren took Leroy to medical and he was soon patched up. He had a minor fracture which required a virtual plaster but full movement was restored straight away. He'd be able to play the hero for a week or so but would soon be back to normal. Once he'd been patched up he was good to go and they all knew where they were heading next. The three went down the corridor until they reached the main floor area which was fairly quiet. Then they helped Leroy down a few steps and into the 'Space Bar' exhausted, they almost fell through the doors. They were greeted with cheers and applause from over a hundred passengers who had been monitoring their mission on a huge screen.
Meanwhile Maxtor and Captain Voodoo marched down to the vault to place the 'Black-Star' in safe hands. The rest of Touchreik's samples and artefacts would be brought down and fed into the vault by the drones in the coming days. All that mattered now was the journey home and a very powerful drink.

TWENTY FOUR

The crew had nicknamed the security drone in the vault 'Prisoner of Love' because of his forlorn facial expressions. He was certainly a prisoner, forced to spend the entire voyage patrolling this rather small barred room. He would be awake and alert 24 hours a day and able to detect any kind of tampering whether that be organic or electronic.

Maxtor was quite relaxed about the security arrangements as he escorted the Captain down to the vault. He was tired and looking forward to dropping the stones in safe hands and enjoying a well-deserved drink with the others.

They were DNA scanned and satisfied voice recognition before the 'Prisoner' would let them inside to access the cabinet. At that, the vault doors were once again closed behind them. Captain Voodoo was as curious as anyone about the stones.

"So they're valuable to someone. Why is that?" she said once inside.

"I really can't answer that. The way it was explained to me is this. The universe is made of a whole lot of elements and combinations of elements. There are some elements that once could only be made by the universe. For example diamonds, gold," pulling at the jewellery around his neck, "or even carbon which as you know is the stuff we are made of," he exclaimed thumping his chest.

Voodoo was amused to note a slight nod from the security drone who was watching them intensely. "Well, we know all these elements and particles. It don't matter where you go," he pointed outside. "It's all the same stuff, imagine that."

Maxtor opened a small case inside his suit and took out the box containing the two small smooth black stones and offered her one. He dropped it into her hand.

"Except these," he said.

She was taken back by its incredible weight for such a small piece of material. She rolled it around in her hand feeling its texture. If it were possible to be darker than black then it was, it was as if it sucked light in from its immediate surroundings creating shadows that should not be there. It was also noticeably cold, like a piece of ice.

Maxtor looked her in the eye. "These are unique," he whispered.

He took the element back from her and handed it to the drone who then placed it into a small hatch in his arm and closed the lid.

"Element returns no results Sir," it said.

Maxtor smiled and held out his hand, took it from the drone and placed it in slot one inside the case.

"So as you can see Captain Bernsteen these elements are unique in the universe."

"Where did they come from?" she asked.

"The same place everything else came from, either created from some form of unique reaction or they travelled here from some unique place. Wherever they came from they are so rare as to be irreplaceable."

"And their use?" she said staring at the case.

Maxtor handed the second sample to the drone who went through the same testing process. Calmly he placed it in its holder and slid the glass shut. He looked her in the eye for a moment shaking his head.

"This has been an expensive and retrospectively enjoyable trip, we were almost killed down there, the Professor more than once," he said biting his top lip and brushing his beard with his hand he walked towards the door and turned. As if he might answer he changed his mind and instead he walked away mumbling to himself.

"Their use?" he said once more before stopping.

"Shall we?" he said insisting the Captain left the room before he did.

"All yours," he said to the drone as he left. "See you in three months look after 'em."

"Thank you Sir, I will," said the security drone and walked him to the door. The bars slid closed and they walked up the short stairwell to the surface level.

"Have a pleasant trip Commander Maxtor," said the drone and the huge armoured doors slammed shut.

Maxtor and the Captain parted company once in the public area, he made his way down to the space bar whilst she headed back up to the bridge. Once there he found the others revelling in their relative fame. Having tales to tell that would even impress a group of hard core reality junkies was certainly an achievement.

The 'Black-Star' was in an impregnable vault and there was no security risk until they reached Earth. Till then Maxtor decided he would perhaps allow himself some time to join in the celebrations.

The team had found themselves a booth in the bar which had turned into an improvised stage. There were dozens of people who had either stopped in passing or stayed to just eavesdrop on their stories. The team and their audience were looking so relaxed, as if they had forgotten they were still in reality, a 100 million miles from home. As if this might be the most normal thing in the world. Throughout that night and the rest of the voyage they were strangers to no one. People stopping to chat, say hello or ask about the Major's base.

As Maxtor approached, Sinus and the crew were finishing off the story of what happened to Touchreik on the drop. Maxtor was still troubled by that incident and there would need to be a full investigation of the data at some convenient point. That would happen in due course but for now it was just good to know they were all still alive.

"What you did was top drawer," said Touchreik to Sinus, noticing the Commander pushing through the crowd to join them. "All of you, absolutely right out of the top draw."

"I did the obvious thing, there weren't a lot of choices," said Sinus with genuine modesty.

"Then what?" said Lero

"He would have been dead, then our plan might have needed adjustment." The audience laughed nervously at his accidental bravado.

"As for you Commander I'm disappointed," he smiled. "I think your driving skills need some work."

The whole table roared once more. The joviality was in the most part just pure relief. As the laughter continued Touchreik's thoughts turned to what the dude had said all that time ago, how everything has happened, past, present and future already. If that were true, it was hard to believe he had never been in danger during that drop. It was all predetermined at the birth of the universe. Yet he still struggled to understand how the memories he had witnessed in the mind of Nova were set in stone. Did nature still have a choice about whether he had lived or died if a memory already existed of him living in the future? Everything that was going to happen had already occurred and they were just witnessing it? Clearly the events of the coming months would answer these questions. If this thing worked then Antoine and Jak had a chance to go back. They would be able to change things for the future but it wouldn't be his future, really, but it in a way it would. He almost laughed at the oddity of it all.

The party continued into the night and there were stories and drinks and hangers on. So many people wanted images with the crew, especially Touchreik who'd almost euthanised early on Mars. Leroy had become noticeably inebriated as the night had worn on and began to slur. After a couple of hours he was deteriorating rapidly and still calling for more drinks. The Commander was chatting intimately with Seiren across the large round booth but would occasionally look up as Leroy got louder. As time passed he went from loud to obnoxious, making comments about people around the table as if they weren't there. Juliette had joined them now and was egging him on, laughing at his vile humour.

Maxtor had seen enough and grabbed Leroy's shoulders to take him to his cabin, the Professor stood to help out.

"Hey let me help," said Juliette.

As they picked him up to his feet he continued his ramblings, "Hey there, my little old man, pay your dues it's your round. The old goat owes me too, ain't that right grey beard?"

Juliette held on to him as he staggered forward, knocking the Commander's drink over. "Come on you fool. Grab his other arm," he said to Touchreik.

"Sorry Commander Maxtor," slurred Leroy. "I owe you one. But then again doesn't everyone?"

They pair managed to man handle him out of the booth and through the door as the Commander and Seiren looked on. Maxtor fumed and the veins in his neck bulged but Seiren tried to calm him. "We went through it down there, maybe he deserves a night of irresponsibility?"

The Commander sighed and nodded. "How many?"

She knew that wasn't the end of it but for her sake he'd let it go for now.

Passengers in cabins along the corridor were opening their doors to see what the fuss was about as the drunken three staggered along. They managed to open the cabin door and fell inside with a slam and the corridor went silent again. They threw Leroy on the bed and sat down in two chairs and he rolled about laughing.

"How was that?" he said.

"You may have overstepped the mark there with Maxtor," said Touchreik.

Leroy sat up and opened his arms. "Hey, I had to overstep the mark, I'm inebriated am I not. It had to be believable."

"It was believable alright," said Juliette.

Leroy clapped his hands. "We don't want to be together too long so let's get down to business."

The three sat up with Leroy on the edge of the bunk and the other two in the chairs.

"This is incredible, I'm starting to believe this shit, I really am," he said.

"Everything's in place. The 'Black-Star' is in the vault just waiting for us," he turned to Juliette. "We held it Jak, didn't we Touchreik. It's real."

"Me and you, we are going back. We are going to stop the Migration."

"What worries me is this," Juliette paused rubbing his face. "If it works and we don't get scattered across space then how come we are here now?"

"We have been through this, the Professor has been through this. We can go back and change things. We can only experience reality from a single perspective, right now we are observing it from here. Right Professor?"

He rubbed his beard. "Let's enjoy the trip home. The 'Black-Star' is on board and it exists. That's the main thing for now."

"We haven't got much time," said Leroy.

"Juliette?"

"Yeah, I have access to the out of service shuttle."

"So Professor, you know what to do? The ship will be on lockdown once they know the stones have gone. Juliette, sorry Jak will be waiting for us at the out of service shuttle.

"Yes got it."

"Right, let's get out of here. Sit back and relax for 38 days. Jak still has his credits so drink and be merry, I have a reputation to uphold. See you later earthlings."

Since then they split up and continued the voyage in relative peace.

The Lazarus picked up speed and was slingshot into space on course for Earth. The drop crew disappeared into the fabric of the ship and the atmosphere became much more relaxed. The atrium and space bar were the main entertainment destinations but not exclusive. Although they played host to main events there were endless choices of entertainment. Magic and illusion, fun and comedy as well as games and adventures with lots of onboard entertainment based on a historical theme. The small VR facilities showed science sims from the Moonage. In smaller entertainment spaces it was possible to try full contact ray gun battles or Heathen home simulations. The drone staff had a relatively easy ride the whole way as the ship had never been filled to capacity. This meant seating for meals and shows was never a problem.

On the whole it was an exciting and uneventful trip home, save for two radiation warnings but these were over in hours. The radiation shelters disguised as wardrobes performed well and in no time they were back in the bars relaxing.

Leroy spent more and more time with his drinking friend Juliette and their behaviour was often crass and unwarranted, particularly in their dealings with drones. Most right thinking people took this as an indication of character and stayed clear. When given a choice even the rest of the drop crew avoided the pair or made themselves scarce at the appropriate time. As the days turned into weeks the stage was now set. Leroy and Juliette stayed in character and seldom discussed their true intentions even when alone. Leroy as he was now known was having private concerns but failed to see the point in verbalising them. It was all routed in what Seiren had said when they were on Mars.

"Mother would have the off switch." Or something like that. Were they being toyed with? Was it all too easy that they all found themselves aboard the Lazarus? He became paranoid that the whole thing might be an elaborate trap. He didn't know who his enemy actually was, who had facilitated the return of the stones? There was no turning back now.

Meanwhile the monstrous craft powered through space whilst its passengers laughed, drank and partied.

Finally it was announced that the ship's reverse thrusters were being engaged with only days of the voyage left. Still countless kilometres from home it was symbolic of how close the mission was to ending. The following few days would be spent slowing down into orbit around Earth once more.

By the time there were a few days left of the voyage a huge farewell celebration was planned for the second to last night. The ship's organisers had wisely decided it might be a good idea to have clear heads on the day they were due to disembark. The shuttle ride would have to be endured, so with that in mind there would be time to sober up. Anyone who appeared inebriated on the last day ran the risk of being held back until the following day before the ride home.

The Space bar had been decorated with an ancient space exploration theme. It showed what early moon ships might have looked like and the drones that waited on tables were in ancient space uniform. It didn't go unnoticed by the Professor how spookily close they were to the one he had encountered on Mars. All designed to tease the imagination and send everyone home with an incredible memory after 200 million kilometres in space.

The huge 2D screens showed simulated space exploration from the time and the room looked like a control centre. Some of it was civilian game footage along with grainy picture and sound. The place was decorated with hanging planets and augmented reality displays. The space floor as it was known was occasionally and tastefully intruded upon as historic space craft floated by. As always the real stars of the night were the stars themselves, passing by as the Lazarus span in space and slowed towards its home planet. The atmosphere was euphoric as the realisation of what they had done hit them.

By midnight celebrations were in full swing and it looked like the entire crew and passengers were in attendance. Clearly Leroy was in fine spirits tonight or as the Commander might say, the fine spirits were in him. He'd been calm and relaxed early on but as usual he deteriorated and soon seemed determined to excel himself.

It was well into the night before he began making crude remarks about Seiren. She politely laughed off his remarks until Maxtor stepped in and asked him to quiet down little.

"Said who?" he said angrily before standing up to take a swing at him. He lost balance and fell forward across the table. People scattered as drinks and glasses flew in all directions.

"I got him," said Maxtor gripping him under the arm. This bitch was gonna get it right now, once and for all he thought.

In swept Juliette as usual. "I got it Mr."

"Oh no, I insist."

The pair lifted him to his feet, Maxtor gripping so tight he almost stopped the blood in his forearm.

"Really Sir, I'm used to this," he said. "You don't want to spoil or interrupt your evening because of my colleagues boisterous behaviour." He winked with a slight nod behind him. A crowd was gathering now and as the Commander turned he saw Seiren at the front of it holding his drink. He looked back at Juliette and then at Leroy who burped and spewed some green liquid down his chin. The Commander was powerful man and almost threw Leroy into the arms of Juliette. The guy was probably right, he thought, nearly there and its mission accomplished. This idiot had performed but was not worth a reprimand or black mark at the end of the mission. Juliette and the Professor picked him up and dragged him out of the space bar as they had done so many times before. Unseen by them on one of the elevated sections of the bar area stood Captain Voodoo. She hadn't intervened but had watched the whole scenario play out with interest. Smiling to herself as the three clowns left the room she sipped her drink and turned away, deep in thought. The more time had gone on the more intrigued she had been by this group. It was laughable that they might be suspects in a plot to steal a collectable and valuable item in a world where nothing had value anymore. She continued to mingle with passengers, assured that if these or any other characters posed any threat to the vault then it was not to be tonight. Any attempt to tamper with the stones would have to be once they were in orbit. Still, a check with the bridge did no harm and confirmed what she knew. All was good and the 'Prisoner of love' was happy in his world.

There had been a hint from command that there may be an attempt to steal the stones but nothing concrete. Still she had entertained herself with the notion of who or how it could be done. As of yet she had only one scenario, it simply wasn't possible.

ห

Three men staggered along the empty corridors of the ship until they reached passenger quarters. Once inside two of them they threw the stupefied Leroy onto the bed. Jumping to his feet he rummaged under the bed and pulled out a pouch attached to a belt and wrapped it around his waist then pulled his shirt over it.

"Ok, ready?" Leroy said jumping to attention. Receiving nervous nods all round he headed for the door he'd just staggered through.

"Let's go."

The three went into the corridor and continued the drunken act, making a terrific row. Leroy was banging on doors and screaming at the top of his voice. Once they had completed a full run of the corridor without response he was convinced there was no one around and ran back up to the middle. The Professor went to one end and Juliette to the other. Each turned round giving the nod to Leroy who was at his own apartment door. He ran inside and grabbed a chair placing it in the centre of the corridor. He took a small instrument out of his belt and plugged it into the side of a receptacle in the ceiling. He started to tap keys on a small keyboard. He hit enter and nothing happened.

"Someone's coming," shouted Juliette in hushed tones.

He carried on pushing keys until finally the door in the ceiling slid open. He leapt from the chair and grabbed the ladder inside the tube and pulled himself up. One hand slipped and he made another grab for the ladder as his legs kicked around the ceiling. Touchreik ran down the corridor towards the chair as did Juliette from the other end. The Professor grabbed the chair and threw it into Leroy's room.

Meanwhile Leroy had pulled himself up into the tube and hit the button to close the door. He started to pull himself up further but felt a tug on his shirt. It was trapped in the door and he could hear voices below. All he could do was freeze and hope for the best.

At that moment the Commander came around the corner and approached the two men in the corridor.

"Everything ok?"

The pair stood perplexed as Leroy's door slid shut behind them.

"Yes, I think he better sleep that one off," said Touchreik who could see the small piece of cloth hanging from the ceiling above Maxtor's head.

"Open the door would you, I want a word with the man," said Maxtor.

"But," said Juliette.

"Have mercy on us Commander, he's fallen asleep and we'd like him to stay that way. Do you want to ruin our celebrations too?" said Touchreik.

Juliette put his arms around the Commander and started walking him back up the corridor.

"I think you'll agree this has gone on long enough," Maxtor stopped and turned to them both.

"Tomorrow, we will be speaking about this. I need my team for our arrival. After that he can do what the hell he wants."

"I think the blessing might be there's no tomorrow for Leroy. He's going to be of no use to anyone by the look of him."

"Is that so? We'll see about that, I want him on duty like everyone else. If I have to drag him out of bed myself."

The three walked away and as the silence fell Leroy quickly hit open and close and pulled his shirt up. Now it was time to get to work.

TWENTY FIVE

In the pitch darkness Leroy fumbled around in his belt until he retrieved a small headlight and switched it on. Dropping it over his head he adjusted the beam to his line of vision. Looking up inside the inner spoke of the Lazarus the powerful beam faded to blackness in the distance. He was fully aware of the task that lay ahead of him, starting with the quarter kilometre climb, albeit aided by the lack of gravity as he drew closer to the central core of the ship. He took a deep breath and began, only stopping to catch his breath occasionally. It seemed harder this time round, perhaps the stress was causing him to tense up more. Just as last time the worst part was the point before weightlessness started to take over, when the fatigue really started to take effect. At this point there was an uncomfortable feeling of limbo, with no way up and no way down, except a 200 meter fall into the abyss. It was easy to make himself feel disorientated, like a fly on the spoke of a giant roundabout. He had to get a grip of his psyche because that is exactly where he was now. He told himself these feelings were signs he was getting closer to his goal and he was right. Gradually he felt himself getting lighter as he climbed and the dim light at the end of this tunnel drew closer. Finally he arrived at the join between the spinning outer of the ship and it's still central core. Technically it was the central core that was still and the rest of the ship that span. From his vantage point it didn't feel that way at all. From his perspective he was at the end of a tunnel in weightlessness looking into a large spinning room. Like a fairground ride he was getting ready to leap through the wall of an enormous spinning barrel. Luckily his headlight failed to illuminate the entire space but his beam picked up the far wall well enough. He gripped the sides of the entrance way, mentally counted to three and pushed. Now he span head over heels in free space, floating across the barrel and heading for the far wall. He scrambled for purchase, grabbing at the nets around the room until he became still. His perceptions had now shifted and the entrance he had just entered from was now just a hole that ran around the barrel shaped inner core. Once he'd composed himself he was able to push himself along the still inner core of the

Lazarus. As he floated along it became clear he'd entered by one of the narrower chambers, now the space opened out into various chambers. Other than his own light the area was in total blackout, the drones that operated here had no need for the visible light spectrum. As he moved purposefully along it was clear these were the main storage areas of the ship. This weightless area would be serviced by A.I. drones and because there was no up or down, all the storage space was utilised. Sacks and crates were fixed in huge nets to the walls or ceilings, all dependent on your orientation at the time. In the next room he passed two spek drones loading goods onto a transporter of some kind, presumably more supplies for the paying clients. The drones were like giant spiders and appeared incredibly sleek and nimble, with four appendages to hold them in place and four to manipulate goods. They paid no heed to Leroy as he floated past them, kicking his way towards a cylindrical steel hatch across on a far wall. The disc shaped door was bright yellow and was one of the few areas left unobstructed. His biggest fear was short-lived, not only was it unlocked but was free of any alarm device as far as he could tell. He opened the hinged door and it slammed into the open position onto a magnetic holder. He floated inside and felt around the inner wall for the rails designed to provide purchase for any drone or human workers. He was now inside the Lazarus central mains room and because this might be an area requiring human intervention the lighting was automatic. Now he had a better sense of scale. He was at one end of a huge cylinder, the outer edges having eight rows of cabinets that stretched from one end to the other. From this vantage point he was looking down on these structures from above. Each pair of rows was a different colour, red, white, blue and green. Pushing off from the entrance he floated in between the green rows and started checking the numbers printed across the top of each cabinet. Seeing the numbers were in sequence he deduced there was some way to go till he found his objective. Using the handrails he dragged himself sharply along until he found what he was looking for. Tapping his comm he realised he was making good time but he was going to need a little wriggle room if there were any unforeseen problems. He pulled the handle and the cabinet door opened smoothly. Inside was a jumble of coloured wires weaving between circuit boards. He took out two straps and hooked them to his belt and onto either side of the door handles. Using his feet to steady himself he hung in space, making himself comfortable. He then took out a food pack and ripped the wrapper with his teeth before taking a bite, as he chewed he surveyed the size of the task in hand. He had around 16 hours before he had to make his way back, it was going to be a long night. Extracting a series of tools and instruments from his waist bag he magnetically attached them to the surrounding metal surfaces. Swallowing the last morsel of food with a gulp he wiped his hands on his thighs and set to work. He spent three laborious hours relentlessly testing individual wires, noting the result, marking each with tape and then moving on. Once he'd cracked his own code and isolated the wires he wasn't interested in he was left with just two. He took out a small black box with wires protruding and taped it to the side of them. That was the hardest part over with. After that he took the two long tails from the black box and crocodile clipped them onto a pair of exposed terminals in the cabinet above. By the time he'd double checked everything he was ready to start tidying up. His work wasn't entirely invisible but he didn't see a need for making it obvious, having no idea what kind of maintenance schedule existed around here. He stuffed the last bits of tape and wire ends into his hip bag and strapped the device he had fitted tightly to the other cables. Now he was satisfied his tiny sensor would detect a single event that would not happen until the mission was almost complete. The plan to steal the Black-star in the blink of an eye would soon come to fruition, but for now it was back to the outer rim of the ship.

He rubbed his eyes, it was almost morning and time to head back the way he came. Taking the whole journey in reverse he felt delirious climbing down the final 50 meters of the spoke until he hit the bottom. Once there he pushed on the circular lid with his foot but it didn't give. Assured everything was going smoothly with the others he allowed himself the luxury of curling up for a couple of hours light sleep.

ℵ

Sometime later, Juliette walked briskly along the corridor whistling as he went. He was wearing a bright orange top and dark trousers. Not entirely official crew wear but the hint of it might ward off suspicion, should there be any. With the Lazarus not fully occupied most areas of the ship were fairly quiet. Add to this the fact that it was 5am of the morning after the farewell shindig then even less so. Even so, he kept his cap pulled down over his face as he walked up the central corridor with a small ladder under his arm. The ship was deathly quiet, so much so he was conscious of the hum of the power plant and the soft thud of his own footsteps. With a quick glance in either direction he opened Leroy's cabin door and left it slightly ajar so that the mechanism would not lock into place. He then picked up the ladder and approached the hatch, opening the ladder underneath. Convinced he was alone, he took two steps up and knocked on the service hatch door. It slid open immediately and Leroy dangled by his arms before dropping onto the steps, in an instant he had stepped down and was walking towards his room. Juliette picked up the ladder as the hatch snapped shut and followed him. The whole process was seamless and over in seconds.

Once inside the cabin Leroy collapsed into Juliette's arms.

"I'm exhausted," said Leroy.

"Did it work?"

"Give me a minute fella, is that hatch closed?"

Juliette popped his head out the door to check. "It's fine."

Leroy went over to the drinks dispenser and placed his palm on the glass. "I need one after that, I don't care what time it is."

Juliette was bursting with frustration. "Well?"

Leroy drained his glass in one and slammed it down. "I think it'll work, that's all I can say. The device just needs to detect current in the two wires, that means the vault door has been opened. After that everything is automatic. If it doesn't work well, it doesn't work."

Juliette began to laugh nervously until the tiredness caused Leroy to join in. Soon they were both in tears of laughter, screaming and slapping each other on the back. They were silenced by a load banging on the door. Stopping in their tracks they could see Major Maxtor on the security holo.

"Leroy are you in there?" cried Maxtor. "we need to talk."

Juliette wiped the tears from his eyes with his sleeve and scampered into the bathroom, beckoning towards the door. Leroy quickly looked around the room unsure what to do. He must have heard them from outside so he couldn't pretend to be asleep. He placed his palm on the drink dispenser and drew another stiff drink, picking it up he threw most of it down himself.

"Leroy, are you in there?" Maxtor was banging harder now.

Leroy slapped himself across the face a couple of times until his cheeks burned red. He approached the door and inched it to one side. Maxtor was immediately hit full in the face with the stench of alcohol and backed away in disgust.

"We are returning to Earth today, I want you on duty with me at 6am sharp do you understand me?"

Leroy looked at the floor rubbing his alcohol stained hands in his hair.

Maxtor took a deep breath and Leroy was ready for a tirade but none came, he breathed out exacerbated.

"6am," said Maxtor and turned to leave before turning around. "I thought I was wrong about you, but I wasn't wrong. You were last choice and I should never have listened to a recommendation and never will again."

Leroy closed the door and spun round, sliding down laughing, louder and louder. Maxtor stood outside listening, clenching his fists as if he might tear the door down before marching off along the corridor. The bathroom door opened and Juliette slipped out. "Holy shit, I wouldn't want to be on the end of him today. Good job you won't be turning in eh." The pair collapsed in a heap on the floor.

"Nothing more for us to do now Brother, it's over to our learned friend Professor Algeria Touchreik. Another drink before we leave?"

"Why not."

Twenty minutes and two Vassle Blasters later the pair were feeling a lot more relaxed about their small part in the perfect crime. Although they were technically stealing the stones it was imperative that they succeed. The alternative was too frightening to contemplate. The 'Caveman' had set organic humans on a crash course with technology and they were going back in time to change that. Whilst he enjoyed his digital retirement the entire planet would be retired forever into V-World if this didn't work.

"Have you got everything?" said Jak picking up a few belongings off the table. The picture of his naturally birthed son Louey and organic partner Vanilla. Everything else he had brought onboard was of no significance in the whole scheme of things.

"Sure, are you ready?"

The only people they needed to avoid today were Maxtor or Seiren. Aside from that there would be no hassle in making their way to the disabled shuttle dock. As expected the shuttle boarding area was closed. Once they skipped over the cordon they could be sure they wouldn't be disturbed. Juliette tapped the back of his neck and the door slid open below them at the bottom of the short stairwell. Once they had navigated the steps and shut the door they were in the central walkway of the shuttle they had left over two months ago. Leroy tapped Juliette on the shoulder and led him forward into the pilots cabin. Juliette hopped into the pilots seat whilst Leroy opened one of the circuit board panels.

"Is it too early to boot up?" said Juliette over his shoulder.

"We have no choice, we have to be ready to go once the Professor gets here. The shuttle will have to sync with the rotation of the Lazarus under its own power."

"Will they detect us?"

"Oh yes, but we have complete autonomy whilst the shuttle is off line," he pushed a slim tool into a gap in the circuit board and the ship started coming to life.

"Shall I begin sync sequence?"

"Yes take her up to 70%, the Professor will be here shortly."

ᚺ

The Professor was on his hands and knees peering through the ships reality floor window. He'd hoped to get a glimpse of Earth but the Lazarus was orientated the wrong way. He could only see the cosmos drifting past, 200 million kilometres and the view still looked no different.

He felt a crack in his knee as he stood. "Close and return to augmented view," he commanded. It was almost time and he knew he had to hold his nerve yet he felt strangely calm. Perhaps the near misses in reality had numbed him to danger of any kind. The detail provided by V-World sims meant he could use it as a default position when he became anxious. The idea that all he had to do to escape danger was tap the back of his neck seemed natural. Hundreds of reality freaks would soon be shuttled back to Heathen armed with tales of their adventure to Mars, none with a tale greater than his. He would go home with a greater respect for Major Zero and that ancient mission to the red planet.

A visionary whose dream was being destroyed by the misinterpretation of man by a machine. After surviving on that dirty, dry ball of iron he appreciated more what courage it had taken. The love for humanity by the saviour machine was not in doubt, but the way she was about to show that love was. If he showed weakness now it would all have been for nothing.

The coming hours were pivotal.

He checked the time on his communicator and it indicated a journey of 4.56 minutes down to the ships vaults and 2.32 minutes until he was required to leave his cabin. The corridors of the ship would soon be busy with passengers jostling to get to the ships boarding points where the shuttles would be waiting. The transfer back to weightlessness after all this time would be no more pleasant than when they had boarded the ship.

The Professor stared at himself for a moment in the full length mirror. He looked less sprightly for his 101 years but that was to be expected in late middle age. It was internally that he felt tired, physically he was in fine shape. He took a deep breath and then another, it was time to take to the stage for the performance of his life.

He was dressed for travel in red woollen loose fitting trousers and a green patterned shirt. He threw on his fedora hat which flopped slightly over his eyes and grabbed his stick. He took the sunglasses out of the coat pocket and threw them onto the bed next to his rucksack. He'd have no need of either until he was ready to take the shuttle back to Earth. He would have to come back here first, if he took them with him to the vault it would surely arouse suspicion.

"Here we go," he said internally.

Tapping the back of his neck produced holographic direction arrows in his path as he walked. They led along some of the public areas and to a manual double door which he physically pushed through. He made his way calmly along the ships plush internal corridors. There was a queue developing at the stairway ready for one of the shuttles and so it was a relief to find he was going the opposite way. Finally he arrived at the vault entrance once more, twenty yards along he spotted Captain Voodoo. She was standing by the vault stairs with her arms folded looking very thoughtful until she saw him approach. A smile spread across her face as she greeted him, her pearly white teeth extenuated by her dark skin.

"Good Morning Professor," she said tilting her head to one side.

"Good Morning Captain. We made it back then, jolly well done."

She held out a hand to stop him passing her. "If you don't mind Professor. We should be able to leave you to check your samples in no time. I just need a moment to clear Maxtor and his people."

"Oh I see," said the Prof.

The Professor only had the chance to open his mouth to say some idle silence filling chit chat when Maxtor came storming up the vault stairs with Seiren, Sinus and the security drone.

"I take it this is a joke, Captain?"

"What?"

"It appears my items have been, mislaid," after the morning he'd had with Leroy, Maxtor was in no mood for jokes. His cheeks were reddening beneath his greyed beard. Voodoo looked at the expressionless drone and back at Maxtor. The Captain forced a smile.

"Excuse me Professor if you could wait here please."

She reached out a hand and lightly pushed on Maxtor's chest. The Professor followed them inside and watched as they all surrounded the small glass case in the centre of the room. It was clearly undamaged and unopened and yet completely empty. Inside were the two empty receptacles that had been designed to hold the 'Black-Star', two of the most valuable items in the universe, empty.

Captain Voodoo looked at the case in amazement and then at the Maxtor and then the drone as if they may be the ones having the joke. Their expressions were of anger and bemusement in that order. "I am sure there's a reasonable explanation for this Commander Maxtor," her tone still whispered and calm. She surely took solace from the fact they had travelled 400 million kilometres without a stopover. These stones were still on board, that was a certainty.

She reacted quickly, turning away from the others she tapped the back of her neck to open the communicator.

"Victor!"

The response from the bridge was immediate, "Yes ma'm."

"Have you started disembarkation yet?"

"Sorry Ma'm," he said apologetically. "We are about to start. The shuttles are ready for boarding and.."

"No," she responded sharply.

"Ma'm?"

"No one leaves this ship, do you understand? The ship is locked down do you understand me?"

"But Ma'm we have shuttles docking and passengers ready to leave."

"Not a soul leaves this ship without my say so, is that clear?"

"Er, understood Ma'm."

She looked around at the stunned faces and took a deep breath.

"Commander Maxtor, I can assure you that your," she paused noticing the Professor in the room and continued. "Your possessions are aboard this ship. We will get to the bottom of this in no time at all," glaring at the drone.

"Follow me and bring the drone, Professor Tuochreik would you be kind enough to check and see if any of your samples are missing or have been tampered with?"

The Professor smiled and touched the rim of his hat as he nodded to the departing group. She pulled at the bottom of her tunic and marched out of the door followed by Maxtor, Seiren, Sinus and the security drone. There was no sign of Leroy, which Touchreik took to be a good indication that everything was so far going to plan.

He was finally alone in the vault with his sample boxes still stored safely against the wall at the back. His heart started to pound as he stole a glance at the inept general security camera in the front corner of the room. If after all this time, after everything he had been through, if he was ever going to back out then this was the moment he came closest. He turned from the camera and screwed his eyes tight and readied himself. All the security systems should have been stood down to allow the removal of the now non-existent 'Black-Star' stones and the security drone was being interrogated to find out what had happened. There would be very little time before they pieced together what had happened. Only the drone could reveal the secrets of what might have occurred in this locked vault since they left Mars. He glanced down at the small glass case which had been designed to hold the two precious artefacts and it was clearly empty. Surreptitiously, as if he might simply be leaning on the dome as he passed he covered it with a gloved hand. As he'd practiced many times he slipped his thumb across the rim at the bottom and there was an audible click.

In a single and well-practiced movement he lifted the glass and slipped the stones into his gloved hand. Even through the gloves he felt the disproportionate weight of the objects and the feeling of raw ice on his flesh. The Professor dropped the stones into his pocket before taking a half step. Then he froze almost forgetting the most important part of the plan they had rehearsed, in fact he'd never forgotten it once during their rehearsals.

"You have to close the receptacle so they won't know it's been tampered with, its essential," Antoine had said many times.

Leaning on the cabinet a second time he carefully reset the clip. Then slowly he made his way to the back wall where his samples were stored. He opened some of the crates to check the more delicate items, not surprisingly everything was in order. After opening boxes and resealing them he placed them back on the shelves. Even though he admired all the ancient beauty he'd salvaged their significance was far outweighed in comparison to what he now had in his pocket. After continuing for as long as his nerves would allow he calmly walked towards the vault door, ready to head to the shuttle and make their getaway. To his utter surprise the barred vault door was closed.

He pulled at the bars but there was no shifting it. He had no way of communicating with the bridge or anyone else for that matter. Even if he did it was unlikely any communication system would work from inside here. He staggered a little with the shock but remained on his feet, leaning against the wall. There was nothing else for it but to wait until the security drones return to arrest him. He felt the stones in his pocket, running them round his fingers. He could see his own reflection in the shiny steel wall and it was reminiscent of that impossible memory in Nova's head. Touchreik started to run through the logic in his mind, the obvious scenario was that it was he, who would go back in time. How could that be when he was here waiting to be arrested. However, according to Jak that was possible because, what was the term he used? 'It's like being a grain of flour in the same slice of bread' So what if Nova was the grain of flour and a deep part of his memory remembered things the other didn't? So he debated with himself, will that be another universe, another scenario? According to Jak the answer was yes and no, all dependent on where you were observing from.

TWENTY SIX

    The group filed into the Captain's quarters and stood like parade soldiers around her desk. Captain Voodoo fell firmly into her chair and looked at each one in turn. She tapped her comm. "Victor."

"Yes Ma'm?"

"I want all the data and security footage made available on my drive in 30 seconds."

"Is there something wrong?"

"Do it please."

"Ma'm how long will the delay be? The passengers are becoming quite agitated."

"Announce that the ship is on complete lockdown and will remain so until I say so, get me that data," she folded her arms and looked up at the faces around her.

Voodoo stared intently at the security drone. "Entrants to the vault since leaving Mars organic or non-organic?"

"I began my mission when you closed the vault doors, since then there has been zero penetration of the vault facility either organic or none organic."

Voodoo sighed. "Intrusion of any kind, breaches or movement from anything or anyone already inside the vault?"

"Negative."

She looked at the others exacerbated. "The precise time you last recorded visual on the 'Black-Star' stones," she said dryly looking down at her desk.

"On average I have taken a visual on the stones every 30 seconds since my mission began 38 days ago. The last one being this morning at 5:23:14.17 seconds," the drone responded.

"Why did you delay reporting that you had lost visual?"

"I was security deactivated at 5:23."

"What?" Voodoo stood up.

"I was security deactivated at 5:23."

"Why, who deactivated you?" she said waving her hands in the air.

"You did."

Maxtor sighed and dropped into a chair. "That was when we entered the vault," he said running both hands through his hair.

"I'm programmed to complete my mission once you enter," said the drone.

She slammed her fists on the table and marched around the room.

"We deactivated the vault and unknowingly the security drone when we opened the vault. I went back up the stairs to wait for you and your team. Then you and Seiren came out and informed me the stones were missing." She eyed the pair suspiciously and addressed the drone again.

"Did anyone in the vault remove the stones after you were deactivated?"

Maxtor stood up. "That's ridiculous, we were in there a matter of seconds, the security cabinet is untouched. We'd have to be collaborating."

"Commander Maxtor under the circumstances what would you have me believe?" then she addressed the drone again.

"Did you see whether Commander Maxtor or Captain Seiren interfered with the cabinet?" Maxtor furrowed his deep dark eyebrows, clearly offended by the suggestion.

"No Ma'm. Neither Commander Maxtor or Captain Seiren approached or physically touched the cabinet. Once we established there was no visual the pair vacated the vault with me."

Voodoo shook her head. "Victor, do you have the footage yet?"

"It's available now Ma'm."

There was no physical screen or projection but a 2D image projected into thin air along the side wall.

She made a quick hand motions on her desk. "5:22 and 30 seconds please."

The whole room was fixated on the images. In it the Professor could be seen leaning against the bars on the vault door.

They all looked at each other in amazement.

"Sorry Ma'm that was live."

"My Heathen we've locked the Professor in there. Open the vault door and get the Professor out of there, in the meantime get me that data I requested."

"Yes Ma'm, will do. I'm patching in the feed now."

The group watch hypnotised, they can clearly see the two stones in the security cabinet. The drone is seen circling the room and passes in front of the camera and obscuring the view for a second as he approaches the door. Once the cabinet is back in view they are gone.

The scene is replayed again and again in super slow motion and the clock runs down.

"Freeze, go backwards."

The scene rewinds and the clock goes backwards. The stones reappear inside the case. They sit in thought and look at each other.

"I'm going to have to get this drone examined to see if it's possible he could have any part in this." She then looked around the room and focused on Maxtor.

She knew it just wasn't possible without the drones cooperation, she'd been there when those stones were tested and locked away.

Now it was the drones turn to be offended. "Ma'm. I am designed and programmed by Syntex Cybernetics who are endorsed by the Saviour Machine itself."

"I don't care who programmed you, those stones disappeared right in front of our eyes, I want you to run a full diagnostic check. Then I want you to upload your security data to my servers and send a copy to Syntex for analysis."

He turned to leave. "Before you go, run me through your security deactivation programming."

"I'm programmed to be on 24 hour guard and intervene or report anything of suspicion regarding the items in my charge. I will deactivate from security mode once the mission is complete. This is deemed to be the point you access the vault."

"Once we request the vault be opened?"

"Yes."

"Any problems with DNA ident, speech rec?"

"No Ma'm."

"So what is the purpose of the indicator light, is that to tell you we had arrived?"

"I provide no physical indication of mission termination," said the drone.

She sighed. "Rewind the tape and play at full speed please."

The tape is replayed at full speed and there's a very brief flash inside the room.

"Did everyone see that?"

Nods of heads from everyone to acknowledge the very brief single flash of red light. "What is that?"

"It's a visible power changeover indicator, to indicate the vault's power source has changed," replied the drone.

"Why would it not set off an alarm?"

"It's designed to avoid alarm conditions when alarm power sources are switched from local generation, to mains or any other portable source. It has no effect on security status."

"But we only have one power source," she said quizzically.

"On the Lazarus this may be the case but the system is designed for numerous applications Ma'm."

Voodoo tapped her comm again. "Victor."

"Yes Ma'm?"

"Run some power diagnostics for the Lazarus from 5:22 to 5:25 and see what you get."

"Spooky, could the 'Black-Star' have just gone home?" said Seiren in a vain attempt to lighten the mood in the room.

Voodoo simply glared at her. "Let's not go down that road with fanciful ideas, they are aboard this ship."

Whilst they waited they studied the film as it played back and forth and could see the stones disappear and reappear in front of their eyes. Every time the drone walked past they were gone.

At last Victor came back across the comms. "Ma'm, our system shows a power failure to arc 44, this includes the vault."

"Time?"

"Around 6:23."

"How long was the power off for?"

"0.004 of a second, undetectable to humans but its recorded on the ships log." Voodoo paced up and down again, thinking aloud.

"No one went in, no one came out and yet?"

"Victor."

"Ma'm?"

"Do we have three dimensional simulation on the camera in the vault?"

"Yes Ma'm," he said. "The drone visual camera is usually deemed reliable as this is purely back up."

"I understand," said the Captain and then addressed the group in the room.

"Surely there is no proviso for something happening this quickly."

She turned back to the screen, addressing Victor again. "I need a simulation from a different angle, so the drone doesn't obscure our view."

"I'll set that up now."

"How long?"

"Maybe 5 minutes?"

"3."

She stared up at the screen and then at the drone. "Do you have the stones, maybe increased security protocol, a possible threat?"

"No."

"This whole thing is impossible," she whispered then she looked up noticing someone was missing.

"Where's Leroy?"

"He's er sick, in his cabin," said Maxtor.

"Get him here."

"Yes Ma'm," Seiren set off.

"Have you ever come across anything like this Maxtor?"

"Never."

"Ma'm, I have the three dimensional simulation, it's on your drive." came the voice of Victor at last.

Voodoo tapped the back of her neck and it came up on the screen. The camera they'd used had a facility to simulate an environment by moving to a new angle or wiping out obstacles. It could mash up digital data from the drone camera and the wall camera to provide a 3D simulation. It could effectively remove an obstacle or move to a different angle. Now they were looking at the same scene but from in front of the drone. The shot zoomed in and in the background they could see themselves at the barred door. The drone walked past the cabinet and as he did so the stones disappeared right in front of their eyes.

"Look at that?"

Seiren burst back into the office breathless. "Ma'm he isn't in his cabin."

Voodoo tapped her comm. "Victor, Leroy Payne is still aboard this ship, find him please."

She walked around the room looking at the drop crew and the drone one by one. "No one and no thing entered the vault and we had detection and security online for 40 days and still we see the 'Black-Star' disappear before our eyes."

"39 days 18 hours 28 minutes and 32.009 seconds," said the drone.

"Shut up," she rubbed her chin as Victor's voice broke the silence.

"Ma'm we have a shuttle preparing to leave at dock 4."

"I told you nothing was leaving this ship, switch it down," said Voodoo.

"I can't Ma'm it's out of service."

"Out of service, how?" she replied.

Victor sounded a little embarrassed. "There was a fault with the shuttle when we left. You suggested we decommission it until we returned."

Voodoo waved at the air. "So recommission it then!"
"Yes Ma'm. I'll need some time. I'll get on it straight away."

TWENTY SEVEN

"Where the hell is he?" Juliette was running up and down the shuttle stairs for the tenth time. He rushed back down and into the cockpit once more. "No sign."

Leroy sat cross legged inside the door of the electronics panel inside the cockpit. He was now busy trying to undo the sabotage he had committed over 2 months ago. A small screen illuminated his face as he simultaneously touched both it and a series of pins in a board. As he probed a series of lights began to switch from red to green and back again. He noted and tested until he had a complete set of four and pulled a pin from the board and shifted it along. The grey screen burst into colour and the text became discernible.

"I think we are done Mr Juliette," he said calmly.

"Don't ever call me that again," sneered Juliette, "there's still no sign of him."

Leroy stood up. "I'm going to have to start booting up before he gets here, we won't have long before the Lazarus work out what's going on."

"Can't we wait till he's aboard?"

"No, we have to start the sync sequence right now, if we go without syncing we will be catapulted into who knows which direction."

Juliette went through the cockpit door into the main cabin and was standing at the base of the stairwell up into the roof into the main ship. He gazed upwards hoping to see Touchreik behind him, between the empty seats into the cockpit. The door stood open and Antoine was now strapping into the pilot's seat. The main dash was lighting up and screens were going through initiation and the synchronisation sequence. The Lazarus was a huge spinning tin can and just as they had done when they landed they would need to catch her up under their own power. This meant when the shuttle detached from the Lazarus she could pull away.

"We have started sync, we need to start locking down Mr," shouted Antoine

"Where the hell is he?" Jak was staring up from the bottom of the stairs, nothing.

228

Antoine's voice came over the passenger tannoy. "Will the final remaining passenger please make his way." Antoine stopped speaking. "Oh Shit."

"What?" shouted Jak down the cabin. "There's still no sign of him."

"The Lazarus have initiated the artificial intelligence sequence, they are going to recommission the shuttle," shouted Antoine over his shoulder.

"Meaning," asked Jak.

"Meaning we have to detach, we are hard wired to the Lazarus. If we are going to get away we go now. Once we detach it will be harder for them to get us back."

"What can we do?"

"We have no choice, we have to get ready to leave."

"What about Touchreik?"

Antoine jumped from his seat and ran down the shuttle. "Now Jak," he said using his real name. "We're hard wired to the Lazarus, we have to start the release or we are done for."

"Touchreik has the Black-Star."

"If he doesn't make it here in the next 60 seconds we go," he grabbed Juliette by the collar and began dragging him back towards the cockpit.

"If we wait they can lock us in here and we are done for. If we go, then we live to fight another day. We fucked up man, that element is indestructible, it will always be there. We won't." They were both frozen in place as Antoine looked at Jak. His eyes were wet as he shook his head slowly. Jak screamed as he hit the airlock button. There was a hollow thud from above. They both ran forward between the rows of empty seats and into the illuminated cockpit. The lights had dimmed and the coloured displays were flashing up with detailed information.

The shuttle was still attached by its roof to the rotating craft and under normal circumstances pulling away meant accelerating and then decelerate slowly. There wasn't time for normal circumstances.

"Hold on," said Antoine and the pair pulled their seatbelts tight and Antoine set manual and prepared for release. The A.I. initiation sequence continued to roll out data regardless. Once Antoine began initiating the preparation to unlock from the Lazarus alarms immediately started screaming at them, they could hear safety announcements in the cabin. Warning the non-existent passengers to assume crash positions and brace, brace.

Inside the cockpit a calm voice gave a warning. "Relative speed too low, caution; relative speed too low."

A red light flashed on the ceiling and across the bottom of the windscreen. Long lists were coming up on the display in red and Antoine tapped over and over again - override, override, override.

"Try and stay conscious," shouted Antoine. "We haven't got time to sync with the ship, one or both of us might pass out."

Jak took a deep breath, looked across at his companion as he hit the launch button.

There was a hiss of compressed gas as the ship released itself and was fired into space, proportionally it was an insurmountable increase in speed and trajectory. They were jolted back into their seats with an incredible force. The shuttle was thrown from the spinning Lazarus like water droplets from a dogs back. Antoine allowed it to follow its own trajectory for a short time until it stabilised. He knew he couldn't leave it too long. The fuel they had on board was precious but they had to gather some data about where they were now heading. The ship shuddered violently as Antoine tried to decrease speed in relation to the Lazarus as quickly as possible by running short conventional engine bursts. Just pushing his arms forwards to the controls was an immense effort. He summoned all the strength he had to push the stick forward and bring the craft under some control. The seat belts had held them physically in place and the ship left the Lazarus behind in the distance. Now the shuttle stopped shuddering and through the windscreen they could see the Earth. There was no time to stop and enjoy one of the numerous sunsets they were about to witness in the coming hours. Beautiful as it was they had other major concerns, such as where they were in space, were they able to set some coordinates to get them home. They would have to apply maximum power and manage their trajectory as soon as possible. Being thrown off the Lazarus they had no time to plan an economical trajectory. If they were a long way out then they might be shot into space without the fuel to get back, or fired at the Earth to burn up like a shooting star. If they were anywhere in between those two extreme scenarios then they might have a chance.

Struggling to stay conscious Antoine wrestled with the navigation system to determine their trajectory. They'd been lucky and managed to attain a relative 60 degree angle to earth. Bad but not entirely unsalvageable. Now it would be a case of balancing fuel with the requirements to get the shuttle under control. After a few minutes the craft stabilised and Jak started checking the instruments for damage. After twenty minutes of consistent work from them both the shuttle settled into its orbit, things were looking better.

"The Lazarus will keep trying to get A.I. control, we are going to have to take the express route home," said Antoine. "Strap in friend."

Jak flicked through the hologram views above the dash and was able to see the shuttle in relation to Earth. The craft was floating at right angles to its orbit, after some manoeuvring it was brought into a direct reverse. He flicked a switch and fired up the booster rockets and they were pushed backwards into their seats. He was using fuel sparingly but had to slow the shuttle down enough that it would begin to fall from space. According to the instruments they were on a collision course with Earth, exactly what they wanted. Their next job was going to be managing that collision and turning it into a landing. He rolled the shuttle over, pulled the nose up to allow the underbelly to absorb heat and maintain a normal speed. They would have to use the tilt and angle of the ship to dissipate energy and save on conventional fuel. The Lazarus was now far behind them yet there was nothing they could do about the attempt to regain control of the shuttle.

"Not the most conventional route but it's as hard as I dare go," Antoine chirped as he pinged another override. "Any faster and we will burn up like a shooting star. Hold on."

The cockpit smelled of burning plastic and fuel but the craft had performed way outside its normal parameters, for now they were still alive at least.

ห

Inside the vault, the Professor was resigned to his fate. Like so many ventures he'd heard about over the years, it looked like they had been undone by the tiniest of details. Through all the years of planning they had never considered that he might be inadvertently locked in the vault. He leant on the wall with his arms folded and stared at his feet. Surprisingly his biggest shame would be with the Humanists, especially Antoine who's tireless work had got them this far. They had all thought he was crazy when he decided to upgrade the cabinet security system. Adding Chameleon IAR (Invisibility Augmented Reality) had given it the ability to make its contents invisible to the naked eye. This was a little known option they had added to the standard set up. After all, the sales literature had proclaimed 'it would be harder to steal something that you couldn't see'. This was by no means the only feature Antoine had shown interest in, another was its standard power failure option. Whenever changes to the power supply occurred, the system would not go into alarm condition provided it happened almost instantaneously. This would avoid false alarms when transferring between vehicles or battery power etc. Antoine's genius had been his ability to combine these two strengths, into a weakness. If they could switch on the Chameleon IAR then it would appear the stones were missing causing enough confusion to provide them a window of opportunity. One problem remained, settings could never be changed whilst the unit was in service without an alarm condition. That is unless the software was on hold, or technically asleep. This almost never happens whilst in service except of course, during a power changeover. If that was going to happen then the whole thing would have to happen simultaneously within 0.02 seconds to go undetected. This task was impossible for a human to carry out of course, not without some technical assistance. The genius of Antoine's device was to instigate a power failure and at the same time switch on the Chameleon IAR feature. His device was rigged to the electronic coil that operates the vault door, it didn't need to intervene, but simply detect it opening. In the following 0.001 seconds it would then, shut the power off, switched on IAR and reboot the power. All completely undetected by the security system. All that had come together perfectly in a textbook scenario only for him to find himself trapped like a bee in a bottle.

At that moment the doors to the vault slid open silently, had he not seen them out of the corner of his eye he might never have noticed. The Professor pushed himself off the wall with his shoulders and looked around. Cautiously he approached the gap, expecting a welcoming party of security personal, surprisingly there was no one there. Straightening his long coat he pushed his chin out and began walking along the passageway. As he calmly made his way to the shuttle dock he mentally tipped his hat to the genius of Leroy Aka Antoine Feng. If he could make it to the shuttle then the failure of the scheme wouldn't fall on his shoulders after all.

The Professor didn't push his luck by breaking into a run but it took all his will to hold back. Along the walkways where there seemed to be no one around he might burst into a bracing stride. He was already late for the rendezvous but they would undoubtedly hold back until he was there.

After what seemed an age he was meters away and pushed on into the dock corridor. He went under the overhead sign that clearly indicated this dock was closed until further notice and to make your way to docks 5 or 7. At last he could see the stairway that led down into the roof of the shuttle where his accomplices would be waiting for him. Breathing heavily he stopped at the top of the short stairwell and looked down. His worst fears had come true, the airlock was sealed and the shuttle had clearly left without him. What to do now was the question?

The theft had been carried out with such precision it was possible he wasn't a suspect. Maybe he could leave the ship in the normal way by smuggling the stones back with him? If there was any chance of this happening he wouldn't want to have to answer questions about why he had been seen hanging around dock 4. The first thing to do was get away from here and back to his cabin. Turning quickly he headed back up the corridor and was soon back in the public areas. He felt a little safer here and would arouse less suspicion. He was sure he'd be on security footage around dock 4 but only be if he gave them a reason to check. Being in the public area was less likely to arouse suspicion if he was seen by any of the others. By now they will be busy working out what happened to their precious stones, his job was to get back to his cabin.

Just then, as if in reply an announcement came over the tannoy.

"Ladies and gentlemen we apologise for the delay in departure, we expect to start disembarkation shortly, thank you for your patience."

Touchreik made haste through the frustrated groups of travellers who were now strewn around the departure areas, finally he entered his cabin and closed the door. It was possibly just a matter of time, perhaps a few minutes to examine the spoils before they were returned to their rightful owners. Pulling the two stones from his pocket he pushed them around his palm with his fingertips. They felt colder than ice to the touch, the texture was smooth and faultless. The deepest black and yet so smooth a surface as to reflect his face. He noticed how when they each made contact the sensation was more what one might expect from rubber yet with an audible clink. He could appreciate now how the rightful owner may simply be a collector, one who wished to admire their beauty. Not necessarily one who wished to travel in time or in the least prevent someone else's attempt to do so.

As he dropped the stones back into his pocket he heard the first of the voices outside his cabin. They were muffled at first followed by a loud urgent banging. He tapped his comm and deadlocked the door to give himself time to think. On the display he could see that there were security outside, this answered his question. There would be no smuggling of stones or proclaimed innocence. He had muted the sound outside but could see they were now joined by the Captain herself. It was only a matter of time before they were able to override the cabin security doors. On the bed were his sunglasses and bag, exactly where he left them earlier. He felt an urge to fight on but he was cornered. Thinking back to the memory he had seen so many times before in Nova's trace was quite likely something that might have happened, could have happened. Knowing what he knew about time travel perhaps it actually did happen? There would be plenty of time to think about that in his own future, not now. He didn't know what to do next but hide, pointless but still it might delay the inevitable. He picked up his things and looked around the tiny room.

ん

Inside the shuttle the atmosphere was calmer. The air smelled cleaner once the filtration system had kicked in. The stomach churning lurches had stopped as the A.I. system had taken over control. The craft was entering the Earth's atmosphere and was searching for a re-entry pathway that took into consideration the battering the ship had been through. Whilst the A.I. system took over the actual flying, Antoine was busy running through the diagnostic systems. There was an endless stream on red error warnings on the screens. Using his own augmented reality he was able to read through the process of clearing them. The tiny adrenalin rush of turning each red error to green was satisfying in itself. There was nothing too threatening so far, most were the ships request to check various systems after the shock it had been through. The unconventional launch from the Lazarus and current re-entry sequence had pushed the shuttle to its design limits resulting in damage to the ships dark underbelly. The sensors were indicating that large patches of heat absorbing coating were way above the expected temperature range. Had Antoine been given the luxury of an exterior inspection he might not feel so confident. The outer edges of the sweeping wingtips, the under nose and tail fins were scarred. The curvature of planet Earth could be seen clearly and the cloud layer was a long way below them but gaps revealed the comforting sight of Earth itself. Her sweeping blue oceans and green landmass offered a feeling of security. There was no real sense of scale from up here and time passed with no real signs of progress towards the ground.

"We're gonna make it," said Antoine as they stretched to see over the nose cone.

"We might not have a great deal of choice on location," said Jak as he scanned the holographic map.

"I'll take anything, right now," said Antoine.

"Do we have any choice?"

"Not entirely, I'll try for the North of the city, where we will have a chance of getting home."

The shuttle felt stable and secure at last and their demeanour changed. They didn't have the stones they came for but at least they'd fight another day. Jak longed to be home now, to see Louey and Vanilla. Also a long rest and recuperation to think about their next move.

"It's going to be a rough landing; a service highway would be our best option. The A.I. on the drone service vehicles should pick us up. That means provided they detect us in time they will take avoidance measures."

Jak pulled up a holographic map and scanned the options for landing. There were none. He typed some instructions in thin air and changed the search from landing locations to a highway map, this looked different. It showed the mass of arteries that fed out from Heathen proper. Most were highlighted in red, these were either too small or were underground. There were a couple in green. "I think I have two options," he said tapping and illuminating his choices.

"Looking good, I think we can walk home from there," joked Antoine.

At that moment all the colour displays flashed red and the interior lights dimmed and brightened.

"What did I do?" said Jak.

"That wasn't you," said Antoine. "I think we might have a problem?"

"Problem," repeated Jak.

"The controls have stopped responding." Antoine held his hands up as the lights and displays switched to a paused information only mode.

"We are re-logged in to Lazarus."

"What does that mean.?"

"It means they can take the ship back."

"What now!" said Jak.

"I don't think there's anything we can do; the Lazarus has our controls."

"Can we bail out?"

"Now that's definitely not an option," said Antoine.

Jak looked concerned. "Look at our conventional fuel, is there enough to even get us back? We might just fall out of the sky before we get there."

The holographic image of the shuttle over the control panel tilted slightly and all the panels flashed red. A warning sign lit up and a voice said, "Attention trajectory angle +6 degrees manual adjustment override required." There was a pause. "Access denied."

Jak looked over at Antoine for an explanation.

"How clever they are," said Antoine to himself.

"What's going on Ant?" said Jak.

"They have manually lifted the nose 6 degrees, not a big change but with the engines off we are going to start getting lift."

"Meaning?"

"Meaning we will effectively skim back into orbit, then they can simply catch us up and bring the shuttle back in using A.I."

TWENTY EIGHT

Captain Voodoo was pacing like a caged beast with her hands behind her back. She was furious at what they'd all witnessed. She still had no explanation for what had happened but she had an idea who did.

"Victor, who's aboard that shuttle?"

"I won't know until we recommission her Ma'm."

"Do it, bring that shuttle back here." Voodoo looked up at Maxtor.

"Commander we need to talk." Maxtor shifted his shoulders and nodded.

"Privately please," she said turing to Seiren and Sinus. They both nodded and left the room. She sat back in her chair and indicated for Maxtor to sit on the opposite side. On the side wall the screen was frozen, on it were the frozen faces of her and Maxtor's crew waiting for the drone to let them through the bars.

"I have information that may have some bearing on the situation," she looked up to the heavens as if in prayer. "There may have been a plot to remove the 'Black-Star'."

Maxtor leaned forward and clasped his hands leaning on his knees. "Remove?" he said cynically.

Voodoo looked up. "I'm serious."

"I wasn't informed?" said Maxtor.

"It wasn't defined or seen as a threat to the mission, there was little or no chance of them making a move until we were back in orbit. We certainly never considered that anyone might be able to access the vault."

"Unless it was me?" said Maxtor.

"I do my job Commander."

"So I might be a suspect?"

"Those decisions are not mine. I just follow orders."

"Captain Voodoo," he stood up and leant on his knuckles over her. "You're not the only one with orders, do you realise you may have jeopardised this entire mission?"

He was right and Voodoo knew it. "It wasn't considered a possibility that anyone could penetrate the vault."

"It appears someone did."

"Yes, and it appears they are all aboard that shuttle. We can contain this."

"Who do you suspect?"

"Right now we can't account for Leroy or the pilot of that shuttle, this Juliette Tiding. They are known to each other, it's too obvious."

"Do we have clear public communication with Earth," said Maxtor standing. He towered over her, not just in physical stature but in moral stature.

"Yes."

"May I make a private communication, I need to check something?"

"Be my guest."

"I'll be right back." The Commander left and walked briskly back to his cabin and opened his comms screen. He clicked and a female came up on the image in front of him. Some children were heard playing in the background.

"Hi Margery," he said smiling.

The woman looked excited. "Theodore, your back! How are you. Amazing, we didn't expect to hear from you for a few days."

"I'm fine Margery, real fine."

"We can't wait to hear.," He cut her short.

"Well, I can't wait to tell you, but this is just a quick comm, is Nathaniel around?"

"He is, yes," she turned and shouted. "Nathanial, its Theodore," there was no response so she went out of sight and was heard shouting again.

"Quickly, you won't believe who is on the comms," he heard her say. Nathaniel appeared and stared into the screen.

"My word, Theodore how great to hear from you, surely you're not back yet? The media said you might be in orbit for a day or so."

Maxtor shook his head irritated but smiling all the same.

"I'm coming straight over to see you but I just wanted to quickly thank you for something."

"Really."

"Leroy, Leroy Payne the guy you recommended for the mission, the guy who you say worked with you."

"Payne?" Nathaniel appeared puzzled. "I don't recall," he looked mystified as if trying to remember the name. "No I don't know that name. I recommended him you say?"

"Yes, I thought you had said he was highly recommended?"

"No, Theodore, not me. You must be mistaken."

The Commander laughed. "Hey, it's of no matter anyway. I was only going to say that he did a hell of a job for us up here."

"That's great, really great but I'm afraid I can't take credit for that one," said Nathaniel slightly confused.

"No problem, but the crew are loading up now, tell Margery I can't wait to see you both. Perhaps in a day or two."

"You do that, we can't wait to see you and hear all about it."

"Bye."

There was a click and the screen went blank. Maxtor paused for a moment, shaping his beard with his fist. He slammed his fist down hard to cut off the comms and threw a cup against the wall. He tried to regain his composure by gently shutting the door of his cabin and briskly walking back to the Captain's cabin. Along the way he overheard frustrated passengers venting their anger at crew members. Official announcements were greeted by groans and jeers across the ship.

"Ladies and gentlemen we apologise for the delay in disembarking. We are waiting for our orbit to align. We thank you for your patience."

He burst back into the Captain's cabin where Voodoo, Seiren and Sinus were watching the 2D screen indicating the position of the rogue shuttle. It was plummeting towards Earth.

"How's it going?" he said.

"They're heading down fast, we might not get it in time," said Captain Voodoo with hands on hips analysing the data running down the side of the screen.

"And if you do?"

"If we do, then we can bring them back here," she stopped to hit the comm. "Victor, have you got that shuttle yet?"

"Shouldn't be long, it can't handover without getting a full course diagnostic from the computers, there's no way round that."

"Good, stay on it and keep me informed."

Maxtor scanned the faces before him. "I have something to tell you all," he said glumly.

"We have them Ma'm the ship is back in control and we have set coordinates to bring it back to the Lazarus. It's going to take some time."

Voodoo looked at the team around her and then at the drone.

"Have you finished the self-diagnostic session?"

"I have no faults and have operated at 100% efficiency throughout my mission."

"Get out," she snapped.

The drone turned and left the room.

The Commander held his hands up and took a deep breath. "It looks like I've been duped. It's very unlikely Leroy is who he claimed to be."

"And your other crew members?" said Voodoo looking at the other two.

"I get that," said Maxtor. "I'll deep check every one of them, in the meantime I think the fact they're here tells us we can be fairly sure they're on side for now."

Seiren shrugged. "Thanks."

"So," Voodoo paused, "we have two suspects. In all likelihood Leroy and one of the shuttle crew but it still doesn't explain how those stones disappeared in front of our eyes."

She hit comms again. "Victor, get some security to access the cabin of Leroy and Juliette and see what you can find."

She swung back in her chair and stared up at the 2D images on the screen. It was the same frozen image they had stared at for an age. The glass cabinet in the vault was empty and in the background she could see their faces. All of them waiting to get into the vault as they waited for the drone to open up. Then she noticed another face, behind in the darkness almost indiscernible. She sat upright and pointed into the air and opened her thumb and forefinger. The still image zoomed in even closer to the blurred shape. She could just make out the face of the Professor. The others watched on as the cogs in her head whirred and connected what she knew with what she didn't.

She stood bolt upright. "Victor."

"Ma'm."

"Do you still have the camera data for a little later, after we left the vault?"

"Yes."

"Put it up please."

The footage appeared on the screen almost instantly. Swiping forward she moved to the point where Voodoo had been called into the room to examine the empty cases. Then they all left the vault and the Professor stood still for a moment.

Maxtor interrupted. "Captain?"

"Wait." Without taking her eyes off the screen she raised a hand. The Professor watched them leave and then he walked across where the camera was and glanced up for a second.

"Zoom in," she said. The Professor had placed his right hand onto the cabinet and opened the glass. As the glass opened he seemed to pick something up and drop it into his pocket. He then closed the lid and began checking his samples.

"They were there all the time," she whispered.

Maxtor rubbed his forehead with his thumb and finger. Sinus and Seiren looked at each other in dismay.

"Victor," Voodoo fumed. "Do you have access to the shuttle data?"

"Yes Ma'm."

"How many occupants?"

"Two Ma'm."

"Are you sure there's just two?"

"Two occupants on board."

She thought for a moment. "Who are they?"

"We can't say Ma'm we don't have full control of all the systems since the shuttle was decommissioned."

"What do you think?" Maxtor pursed his lips thoughtfully.

"It looks like the Professor is in on this so he is likely to be on that shuttle with the pilot, Juliette. So where the hell is Leroy and is he involved? One of them is still aboard." She hit her comms again but it was open already.

"Ma'm, security here. Both cabins are unoccupied."

"Get over to Professor Touchreik's cabin. We'll meet you there."

Voodoo headed out of the door followed by Maxtor, Seiren and Sinus.

On a separate arc of the ship two large security personnel were pushing their way through groups of increasingly excited passengers, stepping over piles of luggage and down crowded corridors. Some had given up on getting home and had luggage drones returning them to their cabins to call friends or simply to wait it out.

TWENTY NINE

Antoine and Jak sat helplessly in the cockpit and could only watch as events unfolded. Neither one knew of the Professor's fate or that of the stones. The shuttle shook now and then, as they sat motionless and silent. One of the ships paper manuals floated across their field of view, through the holographic image of the shuttle and crashed into the windscreen. Jak swiped it with the back of his hand and it span off crashing into a side wall. A few moments later a small hammer drifted into Antoine's view and he plucked it from the air, rolling the handle in his palm. He watched it thoughtfully as it span in the palm of his hand, then he caught it and span it the other way.

"I don't know which is worse," said Jak, crashing to our deaths or being dragged back to the Lazarus."

Antoine let go of the hammer and let it float in space whilst he undid his seatbelt. He pushed himself upwards in a sitting position and grabbed the hammer once more. Then he pushed himself backwards, grabbing a ceiling rail above him with one hand. Jak spun his chair and faced his friend and locked his fingers across his chest, curious to watch whatever foolishness Antoine might be readying.

Antoine stared back. "There might be a way?"

"What do you mean?" said Jak.

"What you said about us running out of fuel and crashing back to Earth," he said glancing to the left where the book was still spinning in mid-air.

"I don't understand," said Jak.

Antoine held on with his left hand, floating in free space. "This shuttle has all the cat7 standard safety features and more. Let's suppose we did run out of fuel or became damaged in some way, what would happen?"

Jak rubbed his chin. "The A.I. safety procedure kick in and try an emergency landing."

"Exactly!" Antoine cast an eye at the hammer spinning in his palm.

"What are you saying?" said Jak nervously.

"What I'm saying is we scuttle the ship, it goes into emergency mode and takes us back down to Earth."

"Jak looked up at his comrade in surprise. "Antoine, we would have no way of knowing our survival chances, what damage we could do. It would be suicide."

Antoine pushed himself backwards, closer to the control cabinet. Jak shook his head in disbelief. "No Antoine, no!"

He froze for a moment at the sheer horror of what Antoine was contemplating. He knew his colleague well and he had no doubts he would consider this lunatic idea. In those seconds of doubt he saw his friend turn and punch the glass door on the control cabinet. Tiny blood red droplets burst from the cuts in is hands, hanging in the air like cherries. This seemed to wake Jak from his trance and he thumped his seat belt buckle with the side of his fist. By now Antoine had delivered his first blow with the hammer, forcing the head into the array of electronics inside. Jak rolled and pushed himself full force across the room towards Antoine. The momentum carried him at such speed he crashed through a cloud of blood and shards of glass, straight into his friends middle. The pair span towards the back wall and Jak ended up taking the full force as Antoine careered into him. One of the levers went full force into his kidneys, winding him and his limp body hung in the air for a moment. Gasping for breath he tried to right himself but in weightlessness there was no up or down. He saw his friend as if sideways on ready to take a second swing at the panel. Sparks and smoke could be seen inside the cabinet but they just hung in the air. Connecting with the cocktail of blood and glass. The cockpit lights flickered and the smoke was acrid, like burning plastic, even more shrapnel was now floating around in the space. Jak propelled himself once more at Antoine but this time he misjudged it completely. A shift from Antoine was enough to send Jak tumbling in the opposite direction to ram against the windscreen. Jak felt his eyes burn from the tiny specs of dust and burning smoke as he passed by.

The interior lights went out for a second and were replaced by red flashing beacons. They could hear the A.I. announcer offering calm instructions to the non-existent passengers.

"Ladies and gentlemen, please do not be concerned. The shuttle has developed a slight technical fault. We will be forced to make an emergency landing. Please return to your seats and ensure your seat belts are securely fastened."

Jak was coughing but had accepted defeat as he pulled himself into his seat and attached his seat belt. He looked up to see the face of Antoine framed in the floating droplets of blood and shrapnel. The lights flashed red, white, red, white. Amongst the smoke and the flashing he was smiling like the devil himself. Not for the first time but possibly the last, he genuinely thought Antoine to be insane. The argument was all over now, Antoine had decided for both of them that they would fall back to Earth rather than face the music on the Lazarus. How hard or how far they fell was up to the machine technological brain. The only thing that could save them now was the artificial intelligence of the shuttle itself. He recognised the irony of a situation he found himself in, his life was now in the hands of the thing he had fought against all his life.

THIRTY

The Captain and drop crew arrived at the Professor's cabin to find the security personnel outside.

"There's organic life detected inside Ma'm, the door is set to security level 1," he said, knocking with the side of his fist. "No answer Ma'm."

"No answer," she tipped her head sarcastically. "Get it open."

"Just a moment Ma'm." The security guard nervously tapped a series of codes into a pad on his arm and then offered it to her. She placed a finger on the small pad and the door slid open. The Captain pushed him out of the way and barged inside before the others. The cabin was silent and still except for the low unconscious hum of the Lazarus. The cabin felt cramped with so many bodies inside, the two security guards as well as Maxtor, Seiren and Sinus had followed her in. Conspicuously the bed radiation shutter had been lowered on the side and end that weren't outer walls. The holo display was on and displayed the empty hallway they had just left. The holographic image projected across the mystified faces of the drop crew as they looked around the room.

Voodoo stood by the bed with her arms folded. "Professor, open the shutters and come out please," she shouted.

There was no response, she glanced around at the others. "Professor we will use force, there's nowhere else to go."

Still there was silence. Voodoo turned to the security guard and shouted at the same volume, "Get some equipment and get this open."

Her words clearly intended as a threat to the bed's occupant.

"Ma'm," said the guard, clicking his fingers at a colleague. The younger man nodded at the Captain to step back and crouched down near the control panel. He popped open a small hinged door and began to peer inside quizzically. Taking some tools from one of his arm pockets he set to work, guided by a light fixed on his headgear. He pushed some buttons on his arm pad copying some codes from the inside the door. A page of text then appeared in front of the guard's eyes and he bit his lower lip as he absorbed its contents. The guard was becoming self-conscious as the rest of the room waited and watched. There was some relief when Victor's voice came over the comm.

"Ma'm?" he said.

"Yes," the Captain responded.

"Are you on a common channel?"

"Yes, that's fine what is it?"

"It's the shuttle Ma'm, we have a problem."

"Which is?" as she spoke she pushed Maxtor and the others towards the door to give security more room to work.

"The shuttle has been scuttled and it's going down, probably deliberately."

"So what exactly does that mean?"

"It will go into cat7 safe mode and make an emergency landing on Earth. It's programmed to make a swift safe route to the nearest point of alignment. I'm afraid we've lost it for now."

"Can you track it?"

"At the moment yes, if the damage includes communication then we may lose them on their descent. I have our systems currently making predictions for the various landing scenarios just in case."

"Keep me posted and inform authorities on the ground to be aware."

"Ma'm."

Voodoo looked down at the security guard fiddling with the bed panel and then at his colleague. "Don't just stand there man, search this cabin and find those stones."

He immediately went to work rummaging around the bedside draws and bathroom.

The Professor could hear everything from his hiding place but knew from the cold feeling on his thigh that the stones were safely in his possession. After a couple of minutes there was little progress and the Captain was becoming irritated.

"Nearly there," said the security man.

Just then Victor came on to the comms once more.

"Ma'm there's been a development with the shuttle."

"Report."

"We lost contact with it. Our predictions indicate it has most likely burned up on re-entry with total loss of life."

"You're sure?"

"The computer predictions indicate this to be a 90% probability considering their trajectory, speed and altitude."

From his hiding place Touchreik had heard every word, his blood turned to ice. His eyes stung with the tears, running down his face but he daren't move to wipe them for fear of being heard.

The Captain looked physically shocked as did the others. Regardless of what had happened Maxtor and the crew still had some affection for Leroy. Maxtor gripped his temples to compose himself. Voodoo took a second and then snapped back into the task at hand. Seiren's eyes filled with tears and she stepped outside into the corridor.

"Excuse me," she said.

"Get this open," ordered Voodoo.

"Almost there," he said and indicated for his colleague to join him. They scrutinised some code and nodded in agreement. The security engineer hit a button and the radiation shutters around the bed slowly slid upwards. The guards stood poised and ready to apprehend their man, Maxtor protected the door as Seiren looked over his shoulder.

As the shutter raised everyone moved forward into the room, there was no one inside.

Voodoo turned to the security guard in amazement. "You said you'd detected organic life in the cabin?"

He looked down at the instrument on his arm. "That's correct Ma'm."

She turned to look at the stunned faces behind her and then shifted her focus over their shoulders. Behind them, built discretely into the back wall was the wardrobe, the door was ajar just a few millimetres.

Everyone span in unison to see what she was looking at but she was first to react. Voodoo lunged forwards between the group, pushing them sideways and grabbed at the door. As her fingertips touched the handle it slammed shut and there was an audible click as the lock bolted.

Security joined in banging and pulling on the wardrobe door but it was no use.

The Captain was becoming even more frustrated now and leant in to speak to whoever was inside.

She spoke calmly, "Professor, please open the door. We are going to go through the same scenario again." As she spoke she waved at the security guys to get to work.

She waited with her ear to the door but there was no response.

Inside, Touchreik switched on the small light and fell back onto the seat. The thick walls of the radiation shelter muffled most of the noise from outside. He could hear the muffled voice of the Captain and he knew she was right. It would be a matter of minutes before they were able to release him. Through the fabric of his clothing he could feel the chill from the two 'Black-Star' stones against his thigh. He wiped tears across his sobbing face with his sleeve and in the dim light his eyes started to become accustomed. Looking up he noticed a square panel in the door which was surrounded by yellow and black stripes. The text was blurred through his water stained eyes but he could read it regardless.

'Caution - Emergency only'

He could hear the group outside mumbling and pushing against the door. Slowly and with a shaking hand he reached out and gripped the lever which had been flush with the door and pulled it towards him. It popped out from the panel and protruded into the wardrobe a couple of centimetres.

Then he heard a calm voice speak inside the wardrobe. "You are about to initiate the emergency lifeboat system. This cannot be undone; do you wish to proceed?"

The Professor gripped the handle tighter and took a deep breath. He'd later remember that what he did next took no thought or consideration, as if he'd been a spectator in his own actions. His state of mind being that of a man making a suicidal leap off a bridge with no regard for consequences, only the result.

He took another huge inward breath, gripped the lever firmly and twisted hard to the right. Instantaneously a system of alarms went off across the ship. The Captain and the others looked at each other in horror outside the wardrobe as the seriousness of the situation sunk in. Inside a large display showed a countdown timer and a voice inside spoke to the Professor.

"Caution - Emergency lifeboat system initiated. Please fasten your belt." The Professor was jolted back into his own consciousness, grabbing the belt he fell backwards onto the belt and strapped himself in firmly.

Pandemonium broke out across the ship as alarms were being sounded everywhere. Passengers who were already nervous because of the delays were now pushing and running in all directions, oblivious to the reassurances from crew or safety drones. On the bridge the crew were desperately trying to work out what the emergency might be and where. They set up diagnostics and began following procedure but the computer systems could only find one possible scenario. An event had occurred in or around the Professor's cabin, this was a fact the Captain was now fully aware of.

The voice emanated from every room aboard the ship.

"Caution - You may be asked to abandon the Lazarus for a short time. We apologise for the inconvenience. The lifeboat system is designed to return you to the ship at the earliest opportunity."

After all the delays in disembarking the passengers were in no doubt that this was a genuine emergency, this only added to the sense of panic. Those that had queued for shuttles seemed to be heading for their cabins whilst others did the opposite. People were pushing and tripping over each other in the corridors.

Voodoo hit her comms and was screaming at her crew on the bridge, "Victor, silence the alarm, do you hear me, it's a false alarm."

"I don't have clearance Ma'm, I need you up here," he shouted back above the din.

Some passengers went to local muster points whilst others charged down corridors, pushing and screaming as they went. As the timer counted down the Professor calmly put his thumbs in the strap around him and held on, he heard the hiss as it pressurised.

"Three, two, one, zero, brace, brace, brace."

With dizzying whoosh he was fired from the ship and into the blackness of space above the Earth. His guts were in his trousers as the tiny life craft settled into space and began its descent, one very familiar to him after his problem on Mars.

As the tiny pod stabilised he was soon far enough away to see the Lazarus in the distance as he rolled towards Earth. The porthole in this craft was much smaller than his pod on Mars but as it slowly span in the weightlessness of space he lost sight of the ship and Earth came into view. He was rotating slowly in space and as the Earth passed, once more saw the Lazarus in the distance.

Then he saw what looked like a tiny spark coming from the side of the ship. A moment later another one, then tens, followed by many more, maybe a hundred. Each one spinning away from the Lazarus like tiny drops of dust. Like a dog flicking off water the Lazarus was distributing its passengers across space. The Professor smiled, sniggered and then began laughing out loud, partly through fear and partly through joy. The panic he'd inadvertently caused amongst the fleeing passengers would serve as cover for his escape should he reach Earth alive. Something he'd never considered when he pulled the lever. His stomach churned and his head span as he started the long and uncontrolled trip back to his home planet. He had no way of knowing how or where this lifeboat would get him down but he hoped it would. After that he'd be on his own until he was rescued but at least he'd have a chance. Judging by what he'd just witnessed the rescue drones would be particularly busy. It took over an hour to fall but as he did so he was occasionally reassured by intermittent bursts of jet propulsion.

Eventually the blanket of white and grey clouds appeared a long way below and rose slowly to meet him. When he reached them the blanket wasn't as soft and yielding as it had appeared and he was buffeted violently as he went through. Exploding through the other side he hit clear sky and saw a vast green space below.

At one point as he span he was treated to a beautiful sight as the city of Heathen came into view. He found himself smiling as he span relentlessly downwards and the city went further away from him. In time the Earth's features became distinct and a pillow of green became a line of tall trees, rocks and cliffs rushing towards him at a frightening pace. Heathen had long disappeared over the horizon, the rocky mountains and deep forestation loomed. He braced himself as the craft showed no sign of slowing down and prepared to be shattered amongst the trees and rocks below. At last there was a whoosh and a thump and as a chute opened above him. Everything fell silent and the air became still. He couldn't see down as the tiny craft drifted and slowed towards the barren landscape. As it hit Earth a shock wave ran up his spine and everything went dark as the chute draped itself across the window.

After a moment to compose himself the Professor sprang into action hitting the button to open the door that had once been his cabin wardrobe. The cooler air hit him straight away and the aroma was of the reserve, of nature. It was only now he knew how long it had been since he enjoyed fresh clean Earth air. The pod lay on its side and he crawled out onto the rocky surface, elated to be alive. He stood up and looked around. The pod was much more rounded than he'd imagined and the outer skin was strewn with tubes, wires and sensors. He'd landed a long way from Heathen there was no doubt. The pod had come to rest on a high cliff edge. Once safely outside of the Pod he was able to admire the fortunate view of the surrounding wasteland. Standing on the edge he could see a river running along the deep gully below and into the distance. The landscape was a beautiful array of greens and greys that stretched as far as the eye could see.

After all the time he'd spent with the humanists on the outside he felt so at home here. That night he hadn't strayed far from the pod and sat by the fire he'd made, enjoying its warmth when a thought struck him. Why was he waiting here to be rescued, in all likelihood his comrades were dead? He stood up and walked back to the rescue pod and searched around the interior. He found a pack of basic tools, a navigator and some basic food and water supplies. He placed them by his fire and returned to the unit.

Looking it over he wondered if he could move it?

He pushed hard against it and the metal rocked and creaked against the rocks. It didn't take him long to salvage a long stick from the woods to use as a lever. He prised it under the pod and it rolled a quarter turn towards the edge of the precipice. Two more shoves and it was ready for the push that would take it over the edge. With an almighty heave he pushed the pod over and strolled to the cliff side to see it disappear into the darkness. He could hear it crashing downwards as it bounced off rocks and trees until there was a final distant splash.

He walked back to his fire and settled down to a night's sleep, starting tomorrow he had a lot to do and a lot to learn out here. He was a very long way from Heathen but he had to go back there and finish this crusade. Not just for the sake of his two friends but for the sake of humanity itself.

EPILOGUE

The weather had been kinder this year, hardly as cruel as the Winter's he'd remembered from his days in Greenwich. Touchreik crawled from his makeshift shelter as he had done many hundreds of times before. Smelling the wisp of smoke from the dying embers of the previous night's fire.

Standing lazily he stretched and pulled his ragged overcoat close to him and walked to the precipice. The years spent out here had toughened him as a man and as a human being too. With no one and nothing to depend on, he'd learned to love this life on the outside. Far from the fears he held as a young man, there were no virus's or deadly creatures. There were smells that ignited the senses as well as food and shelter all around. After all these years he'd spent on the outside he felt native now. Healthy and well he stood strong, no viruses, germs or rampaging animals. Of course there were sniffles and there were dangerous creatures but he had learned and improved on his ancient skills. He had physically changed too, and despite his age he'd gained muscle and felt more nimble. He was ready to set off again as he had done hundreds of times before, to walk with a single goal in mind. Before he'd rested last night he'd seen her for the first time in years, his beloved Heathen, glowing like a crown on the horizon.

Heathen was less than two days walk now and he could soon reach the outer perimeter. From there he would be able to make his way up to Greenwich.

He felt a shiver, perhaps the Spring wasn't quite here yet but he placed a hand into his pocket and felt them once more. The ice cold chill of the two elements known as 'Black-Star'. It always felt like having two ice cubes in his pocket but that feeling had become reassuring. It was a feeling of hope.

ꑄ

Three nights later a boy rolled over in his half-sleep, unaware of what might have caused him to stir. It might just be his father again, appearing in his dreams as he often did. He would enter the room and stand in the darkness, watching over him. Lou dare not open his eyes on these occasions and sometimes felt his father stroke his forehead. If Lou wasn't disciplined, if he couldn't hold back then he would open his eyes and his father would always be gone. As if just a dream or figment of his imagination. This time it felt different, more physical and he didn't know why. He'd later recall that it was the sound that made it different than all the other times. The tiniest clink as if two glasses may have touched. Still in a daze he peered through the tiniest slit in his eyelids. He dare not fully open them, but he was there alright, a dark shadow against the shelves where he kept the mementoes of his father. After all these years he'd had the courage to peak in the hope this time might be different, the next day he knew it had been. In the coming years when he told the story he'd be frustrated that he did nothing, hadn't recognised the sign.

The next day the two belts he'd been given by his father were gone. Lou would forever feel bitter at his father for failing to keep his promise to say goodbye before he left for good, but perhaps in a strange unfathomable way he did? Growing up he'd realise that maybe there was closure, because once the belts known as Black-star were gone then his Father was finally gone too.

ABOUT THE AUTHOR

Michael Mendoza is the name given to an Award winning author for film, stage and page. Unique concepts, tireless research and fact based writing are his hallmarks. Behind Michael Mendoza there's a vegetarian athlete and technology geek from Cheshire in the UK. Shortlisted in two National Channel Four writing competitions as well as a number of regional accolades.

www.blackstar-redplanet.com

www.michaelmendozabooks.com

35505797R00155

Printed in Poland
by Amazon Fulfillment
Poland Sp. z o.o., Wrocław